THE MOON & HER SUN

S. MARIE

Printed in the United States of America

Second Edition

First Edition Published November 2021

Published by:
Between Friends Publishing, LLC
1114 Highway 96,
Suite C-1, #340
Kathleen, Georgia 31047

Cover Art by S. Marie

ISBN: 978-1-956544-57-2

To my husband, the light of my life, my inspiration, and my rock. To my parents, who fostered my creativity and always supported me, and to everyone who encouraged me along the way. Thank you.

Part 1

The torture was nearly unbearable.

Her insatiable love of the blinding sun.

Standing deep in the woods looking up, watching as beams of light danced along the rim of the trees, bouncing from the waxy leaves to the early morning dew.

Her eyes squinted.

The rays burned her retinas, yet she could hardly look away.

Like a moth to the flame, the darkness longed to be in the light.

Chapter One

"The air today is thick," a fiery-eyed woman addressed her brother.

"I agree. I can hardly smell anything," he replied.

The raven-haired pair turned toward a barely visible pathway.

"I suppose that's it for today then. We've been walking since dawn and have found nothing," the male companion sighed. He was the taller of the hunting pair and had hair that was coarse and black as night. His voice was deep and low like a snarl.

His sister lowered her head, shaking her midnight locks in frustration. "We haven't eaten in days. Why can't we go to the Realm and buy some food, or take it? It wouldn't be difficult. I would settle for a single rabbit, or even bread, at this point," she scoffed.

"You know what Mother says. It is forbidden. We're nothing but a legend to those people. If they ever found out about us, it could be catastrophic for our way of life," he countered.

"Ahh," she huffed violently. With a long sigh, she dropped her shoulders and looked to the sky. "I suppose you're right. Why don't you return to Dorchas and tell them why we were unsuccessful? I'm going to keep looking for just a bit longer. Besides, I do have a better nose than you," she winked as she nudged her brother.

He rolled his eyes and replied, "Yes, you waste your energy. I'm going back to take a nap."

As she turned to head deeper into the woods, her brother called after her, "Shaerico, if you find something to eat, you better save me some!"

Shaerico sighed and barked back, "Of course, brother."

The faint smell of fresh fruits and succulent meat drew her ever closer to the edge of the forest Collitte. She knew that she shouldn't wander so close to the lake villages, but the potential of food was too great a temptation. Shaerico wandered on, stepping over the fallen trees and weaving her way effortlessly through the thick brush.

"Forbidden," she scoffed aloud to the forest creatures. "Those people could not harm me."

She followed the frail scent until she came to a clearing. It was serene and eerily quiet. The birds stopped their song, the wind barely seemed to whisper, and suddenly her acute senses returned. The fog had lifted.

Driven by curiosity, she stepped forward into the clearing. She was enthralled with what she saw. Evergreens encased the swath of emerald grass and lilac wildflowers, seeming to guard their secrets. Great willow trees dipped their stretched and finger-like branches into the clearest body of water she had ever seen. Rocks hid behind a slow trickling waterfall. Unruly rose bushes encircled the small body of water and the turquoise pond reflected it all, like a sheet of the purest glass, or the surface of a frozen lake. Small lavender flowers lined the edge of the pool, and everything seemed at peace.

Shaerico sat there a while longer, basking in this mysterious place and wondering how no one had discovered it before.

"We have been in these woods for as long as I can remember. I can't believe I've never seen or even heard of this place," she said to herself as she dipped her index finger in the clear pool.

Lost in the wonder of her discovery, she barely noticed an unfamiliar scent drift into her nostrils. She quietly left the water's edge and knelt behind one of the rose bushes that was adjacent to the clearing. Facing the direction that the stranger approached from, she positioned herself so that she could see through the web of rosebuds, thorns and leaves. A black nose soon appeared from between the brush, followed by a gray head and a pink and black marbled tongue. Shaerico's head cocked and she stayed motionless until the beast leapt toward her. The canine's thick tail knocked the leaves from the bushes that surrounded her.

"Oh, what a lovely creature!" Shaerico exclaimed as the canine ran to her arms. She clasped her hands around the wolf's curious face and stared into her amber eyes. "You have a kind soul," Shaerico smiled, patting her head.

Twilight soon came upon them. Moments of bliss had gone by as the two sat there, enjoying one another's company, until Shaerico caught yet another unfamiliar scent. This time she was deeply intrigued. She looked down at her new friend, "I have not smelled this in Collitte for many years. Is he yours, I wonder?"

Not long after, a young man appeared. He was handsome, well-built, and possessed the kindest, most curious eyes. Shaerico backed away just slightly, releasing her grip on the gray fur beneath her. His voice was smooth. She listened as he called out in obvious frustration.

"Tavi! Tavi! Come on, I'm about to just leave you out here!" he sighed.

"That must be your name," Shaerico whispered to her newly found friend, as she gently pushed her away.

Tavi gave one last wag of her tail, then headed back to the man's side. Shaerico took another look at the man, peering between the thorns of the rose bush. She was certain that she remained unseen, but then he gasped and fell backwards over an exposed root. Crashing to the ground, he landed on the forest floor with a thud.

It was nearly dark now. Shaerico was incredibly hungry. Her stomach roared and churned. She stood slowly and with hesitation walked to where the man had fallen. She put a hand on Tavi, who had been releasing a steady low whimper since his fall.

"Well, I can't leave him here," she sighed. "That's for certain."

She knelt down to reach him better. Lying her head lightly on his chest, she felt his steady breath. He was alive. Her nostrils filled with his scent. It was a sweet smell, like a mountain breeze hovering over wet river rocks on a warm day; like the ending of the life of a fire on wood that had burned all night, leaving the aroma of security of the morning.

"Oh," she said aloud. "And you're a baker." The smell was faint but it was undoubtedly the scent of bread.

Shaerico couldn't help but imagine where he was from. She pictured him basking in the sun, arms full of delicious morsels. Surely, he had the whole lake and surrounding villages as his playground. How nice that must be to run freely in the sun.

A deep sorrowful howl ripped through her daydreams. The piercing chorus thrust her back into reality. "I have to get you two out of these woods," she murmured.

Shaerico slid her slender moonlit fingers under the young man's head, running them through his rich brown hair. He was scarred and dirty, but still she found herself struck by his beauty. His skin was warm and smooth. She traced her fingers along the line of his copper-brown beard, wondering what he would be like if he were awake.

Chapter Two

The warm sun shone brightly, sending rays bouncing over the dew-laden fields. A young man lay sprawled in the sunrise, not in the least bit aware of his surroundings. Slowly, the sound of the awakened town bustling around him woke him from his slumber. In a stupor, he lifted himself from his bed of grass and rubbed his eyes. Stretching out his hand, he grazed something soft. Turning abruptly to face this mysterious contact, he found his loving companion, Tavi. Tavi was a creature of incredible beauty and agility. She was his pride and joy. Her soft, silvery gray coat glistened in the morning sun, bringing a smile to her confused companion's face.

"Ghrian! What are you doing out here?" The peaceful moment was broken as a man approached.

"Um," Ghrian's smile faded as he ran his fingers through his long amber-brown hair, trying to answer that question for himself.

"Well?" the familiar voice barked. "Did you even deliver the bread I asked you to yesterday?"

In a moment, it all came flooding back to him like a dream that had been forgotten and found again. He looked into the face of his father as he stood.

"Yes. Yes, I believe I did," he replied.

"Good," his father huffed.

Ghrian's father was a large man. His shoulders alone were nearly as big as his son's chest. He lowered his head and stroked his red peppered beard. He continued, "I have some more deliveries for you today in Vael, if you think you can handle that."

Ghrian exhaled dramatically and nodded. With Tavi at his side, he eyed his father as he walked. He could not help but run the events of the day before through his mind. After he had delivered the order of bread to the village nearest his own, something had come over his canine companion. He had sat at the Ailceimic, the town's local pub, as was his usual habit after a delivery. He remembered Tavi's ears perking up and her bolting into the busy street, which was a very unusual occurrence. This was completely out of character for her, as she was often praised as being the most well-trained beast in his own town of Yoaruq. She may have been the best trained animal in all the Realm of the Lake. Ghrian had shouted for her to return, but she ignored his calls without hesitation. He had downed the contents of his drink and run after her.

After running through the fields that bridged Vael and Yoaruq, he reached her at the mouth of Collitte, the Forbidden Forest. Though he often explored the woods behind his own village, he had never before ventured into those parts. Tavi had taken a moment to turn back and look at him, but then, tail wagging, leapt into the thicket. Ghrian inhaled sharply, trying to catch his breath. As much as he did not want to keep up the chase, he felt he had no choice but to continue his pursuit. He did not want to lose his closest companion. However, as the brush thickened and the forest darkened, he began to regret running after Tavi.

"Stupid creature is not worth my getting lost," he had mumbled under his breath.

He searched for hours until his nose caught a faint whiff of what seemed to be water.

As far as Ghrian knew, there was no body of water this deep in the woods. The lake and its river were the only water source for miles until the sea. He kept walking, calling Tavi's name slower and quieter. The sun was barely visible. He could not tell if it was the time of day or the density of the trees, but he began to get uneasy. Soon after, he spotted her white-tipped tail, wagging waves of twilight in between the green brush that surrounded her. Ghrian let out a sigh of relief and called sharply to his disobedient companion. Tavi had never behaved like this. Ghrian took great pride in the skillfulness of his training of Tavi. Beginning to get angry, as she was still ignoring him, he called louder.

Tavi jumped and spun around to face him. She seemed to have been

in some sort of trance. As her slender body pushed the bushes aside, Ghrian caught a glimpse of something in the fleeting light. There was a faint sparkle of blue.

There must be water in the woods after all. As the light and his astonishment faded, he noticed something else in the thicket of green. There was a flash of orange. Was it fire?

He steadied himself, as Tavi returned to his side. He leaned forward and peered into the bush to get a closer look. There were no flames in sight. No, those were eyes. Ghrian stumbled back and tripped over a root. He tumbled to the forest floor in a heap.

"I remember now," Ghrian said with amazement to his traveling companion. "I can hardly believe what I saw," he paused. "And you! You could've killed us both! How on earth did we get out of the forest last night?"

Tavi looked up at him, her tail swayed slowly, and her pink and black marbled tongue hung jovially out of the right side of her mouth. She didn't seem concerned in the slightest.

Chapter Three

"Good morning, Ghrian," a silky voice chimed upon his approach.

"Good morning, Ginger," Ghrian replied as he reached the neighboring town of Vael for yet another delivery of bread.

Ginger was the daughter of the town's High Priest. She was innocent and beautiful, with long ringlet curls. She bounded over to Ghrian, dropping to the ground as soon as she reached him to wrap her freckled arms around Tavi.

"How are you today, milady?" Ghrian said, raising her hand to his lips as he helped her up. Ginger blushed a deep red.

"I'm wonderful now," she smiled. "And I see you've brought our bread!"

"Yes ma'am! Unfortunately, only rye this time. We had a fire at the bakery last month and are still recovering from the loss."

Ginger's face fell, "I'm so sorry."

Ghrian smiled and lifted her chin, "Don't worry. We'll have plenty of bread by this time next week. We've been working like mad on repairs to the oven and we've nearly replaced the grain that was lost. Things will be back to normal in no time."

Ghrian was well-known in the villages surrounding the lake. His family owned the bakery in Yoaruq and supplied most of the area with the finest bread. He was a known charmer and was always incredibly kind to everyone. Not only did this help the sales of his shop, but it also gave him remarkable leverage with the ladies.

Ginger's hazel eyes glistened as the pair stood at the edge of town. When the conversation came to an end, Ghrian went on to make the rest of his deliveries. After he finished at his final stop, he headed to the Ailceimic and seated himself on a bench closest to the bar. He looked down at Tavi, wondering if she would try to run off again. She looked back up at him as he placed a hand on her soft, warm head.

"You're not going anywhere today are you?" Ghrian asked. Tavi wagged her cream-tipped tail across the stone bar floor. "I'm going to pay a visit to the tanner in Lochta tomorrow. A nice leash may be just what you need."

The next morning Ghrian awoke, wrapped in a black bear pelt on his kitchen floor. He heard the bear-like grumble of his father behind him.

"When are you going to finally marry one of those girls and move out?" he sighed.

He stepped over his son and walked out of the front of the house and into the bakery.

Ghrian shrugged and laid back on the floor. "I think I may have had more than usual at the Ailceimic yesterday," he chuckled to himself. He really had no care in the world for what others thought of him, except Tavi. She began to lick his face impatiently, begging to go outside. "Alright, alright. I guess I've had enough sleep."

Ghrian sauntered into the bakery, leaving the crimson wood door swinging on its hinges. Grabbing the bag of deliveries for the day, he looked at his father and with a smirk said, "But Pops, who would deliver your bread if I ever left?"

His father looked up from kneading a large amount of rich brown dough and replied with a smile, "I think I'd manage."

The air was thick. Dust had already formed plumes on the road. Ghrian was elated still, for today he was going to Lochta, the largest town in the Realm. His father had worked long hours to get enough bread baked for these deliveries. Ghrian couldn't help but wish that he had a donkey or horse to ease his travels and help with his burden. Unfortunately, nearly all of the excess funds that he had managed to save were used to pay for supplies to repair the damage from the fire. What little he had left for this week would be going toward a leash for his little escape artist.

He walked on with the incredibly large and over-stuffed burlap bag slung over his shoulder. Lochta was the furthest town from his village. It was at the opposite end of the lake, complete with a castle and a small moat. It was quite a sight to behold. Ghrian relished every moment in Lochta. His deliveries were less frequent there, as there were a few other bakers in town. Fortunately, the bread of Ghrian's family had a great reputation and was seen in Lochta as somewhat of a specialty.

One could be anything one wanted to be in Lochta, from a blacksmith to a breeder of the finest horses. It was also the closest town to the lake and was home to Ghrian's favorite pub, the Adharc. Lochta was the original settlement in the Realm. It was said to have been established in the third age by a people who had long since passed into legend. It was a very different place then. Now it was full of noise and assaulting smells. The Royal's castle rose high above the market streets that wove their way through the rectangular maze of roads. The cobblestone beneath Ghrian's feet was worn and marred with scars given by horse hooves and carriage wheels. As he entered the city, he walked beneath the marble arch and was met with the enormous stone walls that surrounded the inner city, the Temple and the castle. Three more rows of homes and shops stood on the exterior of one side of this massive square wall of stone, the lake and open fields as far as the eye could see flanked the others. Ghrian followed the cobblestone thoroughfare. He had always marveled at the seemingly unnecessary and excessive structure of Lochta's confines. To his knowledge, there had never been a war in the Realm. He was unsure when or why the outer walls had been erected. At any rate, they were a wondrous sight to behold, draped in moss yet still shimmering in the sunlight.

He and Tavi spent the entirety of the day delivering their delicacies. As the sun began to set, he made his way back to the edge of town that was closest to the lake. He was going to visit his favorite person in Lochta.

Approaching the door to the tannery, he spotted the familiar golden hair. Oir was his oldest friend. They had grown up together since childhood, playing in the surrounding fields and spending their days swimming in the lake, causing chaos everywhere they went. Excited to surprise her, Ghrian tapped his knuckle on the side of the thick birch doorway.

"Sorry, we're closing up. You'll come back tomorrow," Oir said without turning from her work.

"Well then," Ghrian huffed with dramatic sarcasm, "I see my services are not wanted."

Oir spun around at the sound of his voice. "Ghrian!" she exclaimed. She ran toward him and leapt into his arms, nearly knocking him backwards into the street. "I feel like I haven't seen you in ages!"

Ghrian smiled and set her back on the cobblestone shop floor.

"It has been a few months," he said as he grabbed the last loaf of bread from his sack.

"Oooh!" Oir squealed at the sight of it. "You do love me! Pumpkin bread is my favorite!"

"Of course, I do!" Ghrian replied with a sheepish smile. "But I also have a favor to ask."

Oir raised an eyebrow and placed her free hand on her hip. "Uh huh?"

"Well, you see," he began. "The other day, Tavi and I were making our usual rounds to Vael, and all of the sudden she just bolted. It was so strange. She's never done that before, let alone run as far as Collitte."

Oir's face shifted from interest to concern, "Well, I mean she is a wolf. But you know they say those woods are haunted. Not to mention forbidden."

Ghrian scoffed, "Yeah, yeah, I'm sure it's for our own good, too."

"No, I'm serious. There have been stories," Oir countered.

"Oir, you worry too much," Ghrian winked.

She shrugged and returned to her work bench. "Ah, whatever. What did you want from me anyhow?"

"Right! I really need a leash for Tavi. Just something to tether her to me when we're out. I don't want her running off like that again," he explained. He looked down at his little companion, still discouraged by her actions.

Oir looked over her shoulder at her longtime friend and smiled. "I think I *may* have something for you," she said, brushing his shoulder as she walked past him to a small storage space on the other side of the room. She opened a tan drawer that was hidden under a mound of raw hides. Ghrian watched as she rummaged around, dropping loose strings and strips of forgotten fabric to the floor. Finally, she pulled out a single band of turquoise dyed leather. She held it up to him, "Will this do?"

It was an astonishingly rich and unique color, and yet somehow seemed familiar to him. Most of the fabrics and leathers in the surrounding areas were raw or dyed with oranges and reds that were made from berries and flowers that were readily available. Purples were rarely seen, and usually reserved for royalty, as they were made from shells found by the seashore.

Blues, however, were the most precious of all. They were made from stones found in the mountains beyond the kingdom of man.

"It's incredible," Ghrian said with an exhale. "How did you get this dye?"

"Well," Oir beamed with pride. "I was commissioned to do the Lord's bridle for his new stallion. Naturally, his majesty wanted royal blue. This little band was the test piece for the reins. As you can see, it came out far too light. I had to buy this specific purple shell from a tradesman all the way in Cladach to mix with the blue in order to get the desired color. The blue stone was even harder to acquire. I couldn't help but keep this piece though. It is a rather mystic color," she said, running the band through her fingers. "Anyway, I think it suits Tavi's lovely gray coat."

Ghrian looked at her and then at the band. He smiled and thanked her, then leaned to tie it around Tavi's neck. She seemed content with her new accessory.

"Perfect. You were right, it does compliment her. Thanks, Oir," Ghrian hugged his generous friend and continued. "I'm headed to the Adharc. Care to join?"

Oir smiled, "I have to close up shop first, but then I think I could use a quick pint."

The pair caught up as Oir closed her shop for the night. After all was done, they headed to the pub.

"I haven't been out causing trouble with you in a while," Oir commented, playfully punching Ghrian's shoulder.

"Yeah, I know. I miss those days," he grinned.

They walked in silence down the main thoroughfare of Lochta, looking out toward the lake. The moon was very near and nearly full. She had just begun to take her place in the sky, casting her light over the water, creating cascades of yellow illumination over everything beneath her. The lake glistened and morphed as the fishermen returned from their days work, pushing the water from the sides of their vessels, creating undulations of light.

Ghrian looked down at his canine companion, intending to admire the turquoise cord. Seeing it under the moonlight made him realize why the color looked so familiar. The body of water in the woods was the same mysterious blue. He looked at Oir, wondering whether or not he should share his discovery. She would probably think he was crazy or have some tale of caution for him, which made him scoff inwardly.

When they entered the Adharc, they were greeted with a smile from a barmaid. They sat facing the lake and ordered their pints. Oir had kept some of her pumpkin loaf with her and tore off a piece. She offered it to her absent-minded friend.

"You're usually far more talkative than this," she noted.

"I know, I'm sorry. I have had a lot on my mind lately," he replied, still debating whether or not he wanted to tell her of his discovery. He opted to change the subject. "Actually, I had another intention for coming to Lochta as well."

"Oh?" Oir replied, her curiosity piqued.

"I would really love to purchase an animal to ease my delivery travels. Tavi here is wonderful for companionship and protection, but the more deliveries I have to carry, the harder it is to transport. Before the fire in the bakery, I was saving for a mule," he explained.

"Right," Oir sighed quietly, "I was sorry to hear about that."

Then she took a swig of her beer, returned it to the table, and leaned forward to face Ghrian. "Well, what if I told you that I knew of a draft horse that is in need of a home?"

A draft horse would be perfect. They weren't as surefooted as a mule, but they were much more capable of carrying large loads. However, Ghrian knew not to get his hopes up. Horses were notably more expensive than mules, and Oir was notoriously overly optimistic. She sensed his lack of excitement.

"His name is March. He's a feisty young stallion that was supposed to be the steed for Lord Valdin. Unfortunately, he was untrainable, or at any rate, he refused to be broken within their time frame," she shrugged.

"Well thanks, Oir. A horse that I am unable to ride is just what I need!" Ghrian said, his words dripping with sarcasm.

"Listen here, Ghrian, I'm saying that he would be a great pack horse. Even if you have to walk, at least he could carry the bread. And besides, he may be tamable yet. Look at the way you trained Tavi, a pup that was said to be feral. You were the only one that could train that wolf. If anyone has the capability, it's you." Oir took another sip of beer. "At the very least, he will be far cheaper since he cannot yet be ridden."

She did have a point. An unbreakable horse often became nothing more than an expense after a time. They were simply killed or released into the woods if not trained well enough to be sold. Oir did have a good mind for business and sniffing out a deal after all. It may be worth a look.

"Alright. I can see your point. Thank you for the information. Do you think you'd be able to take me to the stable tomorrow? Looks like I'm staying the night in Lochta anyhow," he chuckled, empty beer stein in hand.

Oir laughed and agreed. The sun had long disappeared, and it would have been far too dangerous to travel back to Yoaruq at such a time. Besides, it was good to be together again. They sat for a while longer discussing business and how well her tannery had been doing. She seemed to have made a success of herself, working with people from all the surrounding villages and even some outside of the Realm of the Lake. Ghrian was intrigued by her tales. She had even done business with a man who mined in the mountain range beyond the woods. He had provided her the blue stone she had needed to grind for the dye for Lord Valdin's tack. This tradesman had told her stories of a great demon that guarded the mountain caves near the place where the stones could be found. It was a rather perilous journey.

Ghrian smiled and said "Oir, please tell me you don't believe in those insane tales. He was just trying to get you to pay a higher price for his goods since there was so much peril surrounding their acquisition," he said as he mimicked the gesture that he imagined the peddler making.

Oir smiled and replied, "I know belief has not been a part of our society for many years, but you cannot discount the possibility that some magic still exists."

Ghrian rolled his eyes and motioned to the barmaid for another beer. "Well believe what you want," he said. "I believe in facts, not legends."

The next morning, Ghrian awoke to Oir standing over him, her hands planted firmly on her hips. "I had kind of hoped you'd grown up a bit," she huffed playfully.

Ghrian rubbed his tired eyes, trying to wake himself. "What do you mean?"

"I have been trying to wake you for the past hour! I tried loud noises. I tried kind persuasion. I even wasted my best coffee hoping the smell would wake you! I swear, you haven't matured one bit," she sighed.

It was true. Ghrian had always had issues waking up. He never really knew why. It was known that he often stayed up far past the hour everyone else had fallen asleep, but it wasn't for lack of trying. He was simply a night owl. Ghrian stood up and wrapped the fiery girl in a bear hug. Oir's anger melted a bit.

"Don't try to make me less upset by manipulating me with affection," she barked, hiding a smile behind his shoulder. She gently pushed him away, and holding his shoulders, looked into his handsome, hungover face.

"How much money do you have?" she asked.

Ghrian pulled a small leather pouch from under his deerskin cloak. He poured the contents into his hand.

"Okay, so two silver pieces and a single gold coin? Is that what you were going to use if I had charged you for the tether?" Oir blushed.

Ghrian smiled, "Well, you are an incredible tanner."

The blushing blonde pulled herself back to business and shook her head. "I'm still not sure we can pull this off with just that amount."

Her companion replied with a smile. "We shall see." He loved a good negotiation.

The stable was stationed on the farthest side of Lochta from the lake. It would be a half a day's trip. Although this placement was an inconvenience for those living in the Realm of the Lake, it was the perfect setting for travelers and provided ample room for many horses. Though there were few visitors to the Realm, aside from those hoping to make it rich during the annual and widely known festivals, the path to get to the Realm was so treacherous and far from the next cluster of towns, that many travelers required a new horse upon entry. The famed breeder, Capall, knew this and positioned himself accordingly.

The old friends and Tavi made the trek through town. It was a beautiful day. The sun shone brightly, bouncing rays of light through the streams of people going about their business. Man and animal shared the road. There were innumerable booths in the marketplace. People negotiated the price of goods at every turn. As they reached the center of town, Lord Valdin's castle became visible, towering above the busy streets, with a shallow moat encircling it. Granite gargoyles guarded the tower, looking down upon the Temple that sat at its base.

"I do love visiting this place," Ghrian confessed, as he stretched his arms and lifted his head to the sky.

Oir glanced over at him and giggled. "Yes, the wonderful aroma of meat and manure is quite breathtaking," she replied.

They both laughed.

"I will admit, the smells in this town are far more assaulting to the nose than in the surrounding villages. But still, there is much more possibility here," Ghrian noted. He was often filled with wanderlust and though there was not much unknown in the Realm of the Lake, Lochta held the most opportunity for adventure.

After walking for a while longer, they stopped for a quick bite and a beer. When they were full, they walked farther to the edge of town.

"It's funny to think that I've never been further than this," Ghrian contemplated.

Oir replied apathetically, "There is really no need to leave the Realm of the Lake."

Ghrian looked out into the green fields. He could just barely see the line of trees and the single opening in them that led on to endless adventures, and potential profit for he and his father. As they continued to walk, Capall's stables took shape. The white barn towered over the green landscape, standing out like a swan on a murky lake. The faint smell of hay and horses drifted to their noses. Oir inhaled deeply. She came here often, getting measurements for commissioned tack. Tavi began to wag her tail and release short, sweet yips.

"Hush, girl. You certainly have to behave today," Ghrian fussed.

"Capall!" Oir called.

"Oir! How wonderful to see you!" Capall yelled in return.

He was a giant of a man. He made his way to the gate where Ghrian and Oir waited. Ghrian could hardly believe that this man could ride at all, let alone fail to break a horse. He began to wonder just how unruly this creature truly was. Capall opened the gate for them and clasped a massive hand around both of Oir's.

"It is a surprise to see you today. How did Lord Valdin like his saddlery? They fit remarkably well on his new stallion," he said.

"He was indeed pleased with both his horse and his tack," Oir nodded with a beaming smile.

"Did he send you to make another bridle for one of his steeds?" Capall asked.

"No. Actually, I may have a buyer for March," Oir responded proudly.

Capall's face fell as he turned to Ghrian. Looking him up and down, he noted his thick arms and broad shoulders. "Well stranger, you do seem to have some strength," he reached out his hand. "I'm Capall."

"It's a pleasure," Ghrian responded.

"Let me take you to him. He's out to pasture currently, as he refuses to stay in the stables. He even demolished one of my doors yesterday," Capall grumbled.

Ghrian glared at Oir, wondering if this horse would even be worth his coin and all the trouble. She giggled and hid her mouth behind her fingers.

They approached the stable that was filled with incredible beasts. There were sunburnt black stallions with glossy flaxen manes and beautiful bay mares with chestnut foals. There were drafts and warmbloods alike. Every stall was encased in a rich, dark wood marked by a different color. The color purple was for the steeds of the royal family and shades of yellow for those horses who were being boarded there or recently sold. Green for those who were ready for purchase, already trained to their purpose and awaiting a new home. Finally, there were the stalls marked red, for those unruly and untamable horses. Luckily for Capall, these were few. There were only two to be exact. One stall stood empty, presumably March's, and the other belonged to a massive draft stallion. Ghrian had never seen a horse so large. He gazed in awe as they came to his stall. The giant, nearly solid black beast, towered over his stall door. His eyes were equally unearthly. They were not a color that could be easily described. The only thing Ghrian could relate them to was ice and fire, swirling like a marvelous storm, surrounded by a strange mask of white. The stallion's face was badly scarred. A grotesque gash ran from his forelock to the tip of his muzzle. His pure white mane cascaded down the front of his face, covering what seemed to be the worst of the scar. Capall noticed the attention this horse was receiving.

"Ah. That's Fiáin," he said, knocking the door with his fist. The horse did not flinch, but stood steady in the corner of his stall, his wild eyes locked on Capall. "This beast was untamable from the start. I found him badly wounded on the trail entering the Realm. I nursed him back to health as best I could, but as he healed, he became increasingly unruly. I even set him free after a few years since he'd become nothing more than a waste of resources. But no matter how many times I released him, he would return, as if he'd chosen to reside here. I keep him now in hopes that a passing knight or mercenary may take him on as their own problem."

"He would indeed be an astonishing war horse," Ghrian agreed.

As they passed the great animal's stall, the far fields came into full view through the open barn doors. There were no trees in these pastures, just grassy expanse. The sunlight played with the wind in the grass, causing the eye to question if the grass itself were shifting shades of green. There were few horses out in the heat of the day, but off in the distance, a gray flash could be seen.

Capall looked at Ghrian and pointed, "There's your horse."

The nervous young man released a short, breathy laugh.

"I'll call him over," Capall said, patting Ghrian's shoulder, nearly knocking the wind from his lungs. "I'll be glad to have him off my hands."

The whistle was loud and piercing, and it nearly sent Tavi into a frenzy. "I'm thankful for this leash right about now," Ghrian whispered to Oir.

She giggled, "Give her to me so you can introduce yourself properly."

As the stallion galloped toward the noise, Ghrian couldn't help but notice his small stature. He was indeed a draft, with thick, sturdy limbs and long white feathers, but he was much smaller than his buyer had anticipated. Capall threw a lead rope around the horse's neck as soon as he came close enough, and with a little effort, tied him to the fence.

"Uh, he's a little," Ghrian began apprehensively.

"Ah, yes. He is sired from a stallion whose line was from an ancient village nearest the base of the mountain, Beinn. They are horses of the mountain. They're small, but stocky, and extremely agile." Capall turned to Ghrian. "What are your intentions behind purchasing this fine animal?"

Ghrian puffed out his chest, ready to negotiate and state his case.

"Well," he cleared his throat. "You see, I often travel for work and need a horse that can aid in carrying my goods. However, I was looking to purchase one that could ease my travels as well. Since he is unable to be ridden, I may not be inclined to make this purchase."

Capall slowly lifted his hands to his large round face, caressing his chin between his thumb and index finger. He was silent for a long moment. Ghrian knew this game well. He stepped toward the stallion in question. The horse tossed his head to the sky, shaking his snowy white mane. His eyes were full of fire, a deep and rich brown, that shimmered like gold in the sunlight.

"Oh!" Oir exclaimed. "He has your eyes."

Man and beast stared at one another, neither breaking their gaze. Ghrian stepped forward slowly, holding out his hand. The stallion took a step back and pawed the ground with his large hooves, but curiosity soon won over apprehension, and he stretched out his neck to inspect the extended hand.

He was indeed a beautiful horse. His coat was a deep gray, flecked with dapples like snowflakes resting on his withers and flanks. His white mane glistened in the sun, and he had two solid black ears. As the stallion's muzzle neared Ghrian's hand, he noticed a small white snip on the tip of his soft pink nose. Finally, they met. Ghrian sensed that the stallion may attempt a bite, but he held firm. He lifted the horse's nose to his own and slowly exhaled. The horse's nostrils flared and he jerked his head away, neighing loudly.

Ghrian smiled. He admired the spunk in this stocky stallion. He may indeed make a great traveling companion after all. Ghrian turned to Capall, "I don't know, Capall. It seems that he will certainly be a handful," he said, trying to mask his mounting interest in March.

"Perhaps, but he has such personality. He would make a marvelous packhorse for certain. He is strong in body and in spirit. I imagine he could even defend you against wolves!" Capall stated.

Now it was Ghrian's turn to be silent. He weighed the benefits against the obvious obstacles, being careful to hide his true emotions.

"Perhaps. How much are you looking to get for him?" he asked softly.

Capall clapped his hands together in excitement, "There's a smart lad! I'm sure he will make a fine pack animal for you. I was asking five Airgead for this fine horse, but for you I will accept four."

Ghrian looked at Oir. "Hmm, Oir. How much do you think it would cost me to commission the necessary bridle, lead rope, and saddlebags for this rambunctious stallion? I may eventually need a saddle as well. They would need to be of the finest quality and very firm. I am confident you could create these for me, but at what cost? Would this horse be worth the labor?" he asked.

Oir smiled, sensing what he was doing and replied, "Ghrian, my friend, I had thought that March would be a wonderful fit for you, but you make a good point. It would be rather costly for me to find the highest quality leather to create all that you would need to hold him. I'm afraid that he would break free from anything less than my finest material."

Capall was getting agitated. This horse had already cost him a great deal. At this point, March was nearly five. He should have been sold or released to fate long ago and would have been if not for his fine breeding.

"Fine, son. Since you will also need to commission the tanner, how about three Airgead?" Capall said, holding out his hand.

Ghrian clasped it firmly, "Two Airgead and your choice of the finest bread from Yoaruq's famous bakery."

Capall's jaw clenched as he reluctantly agreed, realizing that he had been outwitted. Composing himself, he placed his other hand on Ghrian's shoulder and sighed, "I prefer pumpernickel."

He was truthfully just glad to see the horse go. Ghrian gave his last two silver coins to the breeder. He then turned to his new horse, pulled the lead rope down a bit, and placed his hand on March's forelock.

"I'm sure we will have many adventures," he whispered.

The horse, the wolf, and the two dear friends made their way back to Oir's tannery.

"I honestly cannot believe you got him down to such a low price," Oir said with excitement. "I am so happy that you purchased him! He's so beautiful!" Oir's eyes gleamed. She was thrilled with herself that she facilitated his procurement.

"It was all thanks to you," Ghrian replied with a wink. "I would have had no idea which horse to pursue otherwise. Although, I can already tell that he may a bit to handle, even if he's been eerily easy thus far," he said, looking over at the curious stallion.

March had indeed been surprisingly docile since they left the stables. They were armed with nothing more than a single lead rope, yet he had not fought them once.

"I'm going to need that bridle and reins fairly soon. How quickly can you get them done?" Ghrian asked, turning toward Oir.

She smiled and rubbed her rough hands along the stallion's flanks. "The bridle, reins, and lead rope shouldn't take more than a few days, but the saddlebags will take me longer."

"Here," Ghrian dropped his final coin into his friend's free hand. "I will wait for the saddlebags. I can make do for a while."

Oir grinned and nodded, her icy blue eyes and the single gold coin sparkled in the twilight.

Finally, the tannery was in sight. Upon their approach, Ghrian was struck with the realization that he had nowhere to store his new stallion.

"Uh, Oir?" he said sheepishly. "I have no place to put March until I return to Yoaruq in the morning."

"Huh," Oir huffed. "I can't believe we hadn't thought of that."

Tavi barked as March came close to her. They were still unsure about one another. Her teeth bared as the massive creature thrust his head in her face, playfully pulling her half-folded right ear with his lips. Tavi yelped in fright and, tail tucked, hid behind Ghrian.

"I may not have fully thought this through," Ghrian admitted as he scratched his head and let out a nervous laugh.

"Perhaps not, but don't worry," Oir agreed with a giggle. "We can try and fit him behind the shop. There's a small alley where I hang my dyed leathers to dry. I'll go and make space for him."

As Oir went to prepare a makeshift stable for March, Ghrian looked out over the town. Night had fallen, and it was a particularly quiet evening. The usual bustle was softer than the night before and there were less lights. He looked over at his new pack animal, wondering how on earth he would train this beast. March looked at him, golden eyes reflecting the moonlight. He took a step toward his new owner, raised his massive gray head, and snorted loudly in his face. Ghrian sighed as he placed his hand on March's muzzle. Perhaps he was too impulsive with this purchase.

After a while, Oir returned from behind the building. "I think I've created a suitable place for him. Now, let's get him back there and go to sleep," she said wiping her brow. "I'm beat."

Chapter Four

The beautiful, raven-haired maiden wandered slowly back into her decaying village. Dark green ivy crawled its way up the sides of the ancient stone buildings. Upon her approach, a stunning snow-haired woman came out to meet her in the road.

"Where were you last night?" the woman said in a cold, smooth voice.

"Sorry, Mother," Shaerico replied, quickly contemplating whether or not to ask her about the mysterious body of water. She wasn't sure if she even knew about it. Shaerico decided not to bring it up, since it was quite near the forbidden edge of the forest. She knew that Mother would get upset. "I couldn't resist continuing the hunt."

The woman laughed. It was a frozen, ringing laugh. She wrapped her arm around her daughter. "My lovely loner," she chimed, brushing her long pale fingers against Shaerico's cheek. "Were you at least successful?"

Shaerico's eyes flitted from the tall, white creature to the leaf strewn road. "Unfortunately, no," she admitted.

The woman sighed, her eyes traveling to the occupants of the village that had come to the street.

"See, my loves," she spoke to all present. "This is why we hunt together. We have a much greater chance of finding something to eat. Poor Shaerico here has to go yet another week without a decent full meal," she said, lightly squeezing her disobedient daughter's cheek. It was no light matter to stay out past nightfall.

Shaerico pulled her face away and left the crowd. She headed toward her home, a small cottage at the back of the village. It was a cold, circular stone building with nothing more than two hay beds, a small kitchen, and a wood burning stove. Shaerico poured dark frothy beer into an antler mug and fell back onto her bed. She let out a loud sigh and took a drink.

"So, what happened last night?" a dark figure appeared from the other side of the room.

Shaerico rolled her eyes, not ready to defend herself against her brother. "I got lost," she said, hoping that he would drop it.

"Hmmm. Somehow, I don't believe that," he snarled.

She looked up at him, her eyes ablaze, and responded, "I simply wanted a night of peace."

"Right," her brother laughed, his muscular shoulders nearly tearing through his tattered and worn white cloak.

"You don't survive here by being alone, Shaerico. You know that much," he said with a quiet hint of concern. "Besides, you missed an incredible meal. Cain and the other hunting party managed to take down a deer." He headed out of the front door with a smirk.

Shaerico released another heavy sigh. Truthfully, she had no real family. She was alone. The white-haired woman, whom all called Mother, was the head of the village. She had found and raised all those who lived in Dorchas. Shaerico had little memory of her true parents at all. Her brother, Bruid, had been found alongside her when they were children. Therefore, they were considered to be siblings, abandoned by their parents. It was strange. All who resided in the Forbidden Forest had similar stories of parents that either passed away or abandoned them. Alphaline graciously took them in, sacrificing her freedom to care for so many. The residents of Dorchas were a strange breed. All had experienced so much, and for many years had been isolated to one town, one wood. Alphaline told her people that the outside world was cruel and unworthy of exploration. Shaerico had always questioned this, but had never gone so far as to disobey her mother, until now. She could not ignore what she had seen.

Why travel to the base of Beinn for the mountain stream, when there is a deep and beautiful pool so much closer? That boy and his wolf were no threat to her, so why were the people of Dorchas not allowed in the Realm of the Lake? The questions burned in her chest. They tumbled through her mind as she wrung dry every drop of possibility.

Her thoughts were interrupted as thunder began to rumble in the distance. She could hear the rain tumbling to the forest floor less than a mile away. This would be the perfect time to go back to that pond. There would certainly be no hunt tonight.

Shaerico was indeed a loner. She enjoyed spending time with herself. It was much less trouble that way. Besides, the town was overwhelmingly male. Venturing into the heart of Dorchas often meant being berated with false compliments. Shaerico had the uncanny ability to see through people, and coupled with her abrasive personality, she kept most men at bay. The downfall of this trait was that she had very few close friends. No one really knew her.

The one friend she did have was Beanrua. Beanrua was a lively girl with a fiery temper. They complimented one another well. Shaerico cooled her hot head, and often finished the fights that she could not. In return, Beanrua gave Shaerico company. As the rain began to fall closer, Shaerico decided to curl up for a nap. After all, she had been up the entire night.

Hours passed as the rain fell. It drenched the forgotten town. The crumbling stone buildings groaned, aching for a time lost. The once grand Dorchas now lay in rubble. For over two thousand years it had been home to a populous people. Layers upon layers of history coated every moss laden stone. Ruin upon ruin, the once ancient city of grandeur was now home to a mere thirty. A lost people with no history, no knowledge of their own past. It had once been a hub of trade. Before the Realm of the Lake had been established, Dorchas had been the main thoroughfare of goods passing from beyond the mountains to the east. It was a place of knowledge and prosperity. The forest Collitte, was still a dangerous place during that age, but the people were braver then. They hungered for profit, peace, and survival. Now, the town was quiet and lazy. The primary activities of its inhabitants consisted of drinking, eating, hunting, and occasionally, fighting.

Shaerico awoke from her nap in a daze. In the distance, she could hear voices barking angrily. She sat up and stretched. As she listened closer, she began to make out the distinct voice of her hot-headed friend.

Shaerico sighed and arose from her bed.

"Well, at least I had a decent nap," she said aloud to herself as she sauntered to town.

Upon her approach, she saw Beanrua, her red hair splashed crimson with blood. She was pinned to the ground by a rather large man, still shouting insults in his face.

"Beanrua, enough!" Shaerico called to her as she approached the scene.

The burly man stood straight as she approached, "The little lone wolf. What do you think you're doing?"

"Let her go, Cain. You know how she can be," Shaerico said, looking down at Beanrua.

"Whatever, Shaerico! This thief was trying to steal from the pub!" Beanrua defended herself.

"Shut up! You wouldn't serve me!" he snarled, cupping his hand around her thin lips. Beanrua quickly broke free and sunk her teeth into his palm. Cain screamed and pressed her harder to the worn cobblestone below.

"You're going to pay for that!" he yelled, holding his bloodied hand. Beanrua sat up and wiped the blood from her forehead.

"Listen here, asshole," she continued. "Just because you're a big guy doesn't mean you get to cut in line, drink all the beer, and get any female you want!"

They steadied themselves to run at each other again.

Shaerico assessed the situation. Cain was easily twice, maybe even three times, the size of Beanrua and equally as hard-headed. Beanrua was spritely and quick, but no match for him in the end. Shaerico knew she had to put an end to it before either party went too far. As they ran toward one another, Shaerico stepped forward between them. She was accustomed to breaking Beanrua from these fights. Her small fist lifted to Cain's chin as he lunged for Beanrua. Pulling the fiery girl from her trajectory with one arm, Shaerico's other fist met Cain's throat. In one motion, she had removed Beanrua and downed the giant man. It did not take long for Cain to regain his composure and catch his breath. He began to get up, a croaking exhale escaping his lips.

"Come on," Shaerico said, continuing to pull her friend away from the scene. Beanrua protested, but eventually gave in.

They walked past the pub and up the main path that divided the center of the ancient town. After a few minutes, a tall stone building with dozens of mostly shattered windows came into view. The giant cylindrical structure had been turned into housing for Dorchas' residents. There were no longer many people living in the town and so much of the village was in ruin. And though there were miles of buried ancient ruins, the current residents of Dorchas used only what had been the main thoroughfare and the surrounding buildings. The townspeople made do with whatever still stood in decent condition. Although this building was covered in ivy, it stood strong. Some speculated that it had been an inn for travelers and tradesmen, while others said that it was a storehouse. Either way, it was a suitable home for multiple individuals. Upon reaching the thick wooden door, Shaerico turned to her friend and released her arm.

"Seriously, I can't keep bailing you out of these things," Shaerico scolded.

"Oh, you know you love it. Besides, I had it covered," Beanrua said proudly, brushing her fiery red locks from her bloodied face.

Shaerico chuckled, "Sure you did."

"Listen here, honey, I got a few good licks in. At least now he may think twice before he demands an insane amount of drinks before anyone else has had a drop and tries to steal a kiss again," she huffed. Turning to face her even-tempered friend, Beanrua placed one hand on Shaerico's shoulder. "Thanks for your help though. Sometimes I wish I had a cool temper like you. It seems so hard to get you riled up."

"Yeah, in this form," Shaerico mumbled.

Beanrua wished her friend good day and went inside. The slow trickle of rain that had continued throughout this ordeal began to grow heavier. Shaerico watched as the water ran down the leaves of the nearby trees, creating oblong puddles of reflection on the cobblestone. She looked down at her bare feet and watched as the droplets of rain distorted her mirrored face in the water. Her thick, wet hair clung to her pale face. As the rain grew steadily heavier, she decided to see if she could find that pond again. A longing ache had set upon her heart, festering since she had found and left that mysterious place. No one had followed her and Beanrua earlier. If anyone had watched their departure from the fight, they would naturally assume that she went inside with her friend. Besides, it was beginning to get dark. Since one hunt was successful last night, there would be no need for another tonight.

Slowly, Shaerico made her way to the edge of the cobblestone road. The path turned to dirt and soon disappeared into the brush. She remembered the way as best as she could. Weaving her way through trees and thick foliage, she tried to catch the scent. Unfortunately, the rain was too strong, overpowering her ability to smell the small body of water. With no luck finding her destination, she decided to change her course. Now that she had a glimpse of what beings lay beyond Collitte, she wanted to see for herself how their existence was different from her own.

Night began to fall, and the rain continued, as she pushed on through the forest. The woods were her true home. She craved solitude, as she distrusted most everyone in the village, including her brother. On the outside, she was ruthless and cold, but on the inside, all she desired was to be known. The woods understood her. The trees and the animals here asked nothing of her. She could simply exist with no explanations, no forced conversations, and just be.

As she continued on, Shaerico noticed something. The small path that lead out of Dorchas was still visible. It was thin, covered in fallen trees and partially overgrown, but visible to the trained eye. If she followed that path, she was sure to reach the edge of the woods. Shaerico walked on into the night, enjoying her solitude. Eventually, she came to the edge of Collitte. Streams of moonlight poured into the woods from above. The foliage was lighter and more maneuverable here. She had never intentionally ventured this far to the edge of the forest. She had traveled to the mountain's base, as far west as she could manage, but never before had she dared head east. Mother forbade it.

Tentatively, she stepped to the last line of trees. Placing her hands on two thin pines, she leaned her head out just beyond the cover of the woods. What she saw was breathtaking. How long had she dreamed of open fields and running without confinement? Her bright eyes wandered as she took it all in. A lattice of rain laden clouds drifted above the vast openness with thin rays of moonlight piercing them through. In the distance, she saw the gleam of the lake; the nearly full moon releasing ribbons of light that danced upon the water's surface. The open field in front of her looked like an ocean of green, as the wind brushed over the grass. The rain fell like drops of silver onto the plain. Beyond the lake, she could see the great castle of Lochta. A river wove its way out of the lake to the south, splitting two of the small towns. She smiled as she noticed the three small villages that accompanied Lochta and made up the Realm of the Lake.

"How beautiful," she whispered to herself. It was truly a view to behold.

After moments of taking it all in, a faint and familiar smell drifted into Shaerico's nostrils. Her ears perked, and her attention changed in an instant. She smelled food. Her head turned back to the forest and the peaceful moment evaporated into the thick and humid wood air. She had not eaten in days, and it was wearing on her. Since the people of Dorchas

no longer traded with any of the neighboring villages, they lived solely upon what they could grow or the gifts of the forest, which mostly consisted of berries and game.

The smell became stronger. Shaerico turned back down the faded path and ran toward the scent. It was a rabbit. Not her favorite food, but it would do nicely. Weaving her way through the brush, she spotted the perky white tail. She crouched down and began inching toward her unsuspecting prey. The hare's ears stood tall, moving slightly as they scanned for danger. Shaerico froze, hovering above the unsuspecting creature. As soon as the rabbit turned back to its foraging, Shaerico lunged. In one motion, she snatched the rabbit and crushed its fragile neck.

Certainly, she would not be sharing with Bruid. "He doesn't deserve you anyhow," she said to the hare, as she sank her teeth into its side.

The people of Dorchas were a strange breed indeed.

Chapter Five

Ghrian set out to return home the next morning, leaving his last coin with Oir. She promised that she would get his bridle, reins, and lead rope made swiftly. As he and his traveling companions made their way back home, he hoped her words held true.

March was truly an unruly creature, nothing like the docile beast he'd been the day before. He continuously tugged at the cheap rope Capall had given Ghrian to restrain him. It was as if he longed to be free. As if he longed for the very fate that Ghrian believed he had rescued him from.

March would walk calmly for a while, his head low, ears perked, just listening. Ghrian would take a deep breath and begin to relax. At that very moment, March would rear or pull away. This happened for miles. The tired rope was beginning to wear thin. Finally, they neared the northern tip of the lake and Yoaruq came into view.

"You best be settled this time horse," Ghrian panted as he tied the frayed end of March's lead rope to his equally worn leather belt. March had settled himself for the moment. "I can't afford to have you running through town like some wild beast."

Tavi grew restless as they neared home. Her plush white-tipped tail wagged more and more rapidly. The fur that lined her back stood on end. She looked up at Ghrian with excited eyes. He thought back to when he had rescued Tavi. She was a wolf, so naturally, when she had wandered into the village, people tried to run her off or kill her. The feeble pup had wanted nothing more than food. The sweet smell of freshly baked bread had brought her to the bakery. Ghrian's father had spotted her first. His initial instinct was to run her off to keep her away from the food and protect his family from potential danger, but Ghrian had stopped him. After all, she was alone and only a pup.

He wondered if he could train March the way that he had trained Tavi. Providing her shelter, food, and affection seemed to be all it took to build her trust. She had been scared of her freedom. She had longed for a home. March was different. He seemed to long for his freedom above all else.

"Son," Ghrian's father stood at the bakery doorway, arms crossed and awaiting his approach. "I was about to ask what took you so long, but I'd better change my question. What did you do?"

Ghrian smiled and stood tall, ready to defend a decision he wasn't even fully sure of himself.

"Father, it takes Tavi and I far too long to reach our delivery destinations these days. The bakery is doing so well that I can hardly carry the orders. I've told you how I'd hoped to get a pack animal, and well."

"A pack animal!" his father interrupted. "That is a stallion! He is short and certainly sturdy enough, I'll give you that, but a pack animal is a donkey! A sure footed, predictable, little donkey. This beast looks wild as the woods!"

"I understand your concern," Ghrian replied calmly. "But I got him for a better price than I could have gotten a donkey or a mule. I believe he was an excellent purchase."

Before he could finish his explanation, he felt the cold cobblestone against his cheek. It took him a moment to regain his bearings, but when he did, all he could see was Tavi's figure in the distance and the village drifting out of view. Ghrian tried to turn his head, but was only able to look down the length of his leg.

The beating of March's hooves rang in his ears. He reached for his belt, feeling around for the copper clasp. Finally, he felt the cold metal against his fingertips and tugged. He was suddenly flung into the grass. His body flailed and tumbled until he finally came to his landing place. The grass was soft and covered in a thin blanket of dew. Ghrian took a moment to comprehend what had just occurred. He envisioned his father laughing at the sight of his son's helpless body being drug by the very being he had been defending. He groaned as he rose to his feet and ran his hands over his body to make sure that he was alright.

Remarkably, the only injuries he sustained were a large lump to the side of his head and a substantial blow to his pride. Looking further into the direction that he had been taken, Ghrian spotted the stocky gray body. March was grazing as peacefully as ever. It was as if he hadn't just run for his life through town with Ghrian in tow. His silky coat and long white mane caught the sunlight and bounced beams across the dew strewn grass. Perhaps he was hungry, Ghrian thought, trying to excuse his new horse's rash behavior.

"No matter," he said to Tavi, as she made it to his side, lapping his hand with her soft tongue. "At least I have one loyal beast." He reached over to pet her head. "I suppose that now is as good a time as any to start his training."

Tavi whined in response.

Slowly, he eased his way to his unruly horse. The nearly useless rope hung loosely around March's thick neck, swaying lightly in the wind. The horse perked his ears as Ghrian drew closer. He let out a breathy snort and continued grazing. Tavi sat back, her head cocked, as Ghrian approached the stallion. Ghrian held out his hand and placed it gently on March's side. The horse's fur was soft and plush, nearly engulfing Ghrian's fingers. For a moment, there was peace. Man and beast stood at rest together until Ghrian reached for the rope. March immediately reared, towering above the man and his canine, his great hooves packed with dirt. He had a wild look in his eyes. Ghrian stumbled back and released the rope as March returned to the ground and headed further into the field, bucking jovially as he went. Once he was a few hundred feet away, he thrust his head in the air and neighed loudly before prancing in circles on the grass.

A smile crept across Ghrian's face. He was not easily angered. Though brashly passionate at times, Ghrian possessed the uncanny ability to maintain composure in a myriad of stressful situations.

"How can I be mad at that?" he said, smiling down at Tavi. Her plumed tail brushed across the grass beneath her in agreement. "Now, what to do about him?" Ghrian continued. "You were born in the wild and came to town searching for a home, but he was born in the stables and yet seems to want nothing but the wild. What a strange trio we are."

Ghrian pondered his situation for a moment longer. He knew that if he approached March again, chances were the same thing would happen. If the horse did manage to escape Ghrian's grip again, he would most likely return to this field or cause trouble in the town. Ghrian could hear his father's sarcasm ringing in his ears.

"I guess I have no choice but to leave you then!" he called to his horse. He motioned to Tavi and they headed back toward Yoaruq. March didn't flinch. The only indication that he heard anything was a slight swivel of one silky black ear.

Upon returning home, Ghrian received what he had anticipated. His father was ruthless in his berating, but also completely amused by the situation his son had found himself in. Ghrian had three days before his next delivery. It seemed that he was out of money and a pack animal. A day passed, and he spent it helping his father with the bakery. He kneaded the dough as his father stoked the flames of the newly revived stoves. All of the necessary repairs had now been made and deliveries were about to increase, as the summer was ending. A hint of fall lingered for a moment in the air around the village before being overtaken by the heat. The winds danced and battled, but Ghrian knew that autumn would win, and that winter would soon be upon them.

The next morning, Ghrian awoke in a sweat. He had two days until the next delivery. He shook the sleep from his body and leapt up. Grabbing an apple from the bakery countertop, he ran out the front door. He had yet to check on March since his escape, and half expected him to be gone. As he remembered how he had won Tavi's trust, he figured that he may as well try one last time. If shelter and affection weren't what the horse wanted, perhaps an apple would sway him.

Tossing the apple in the air as he walked, Ghrian headed off the road and into the grass to the place he had remembered falling. Tavi sat at the edge of the road, head cocked, as she watched her companion survey the field. There was nothing in sight. Ghrian huffed, as defeat began to settle on his heart.

"I'd half hoped he would be here," he said to Tavi. "Alas, I suppose I can't tame every wild animal." Ghrian continued, patting his loyal companion's head as he made it back to the dirt pathway. He knelt down, coming face to face with the beautiful creature. Her amber eyes sparkled. She leapt to meet him, lapping her wet tongue across his cheek.

"Ahhckk," Ghrian wiped his face. He let out a hearty laugh and picked up the turquoise leash. "While we're halfway out here, we may as well go pay Ginger a visit," Ghrian smiled.

Tavi let out a shrill yip of agreement in response.

As the pair headed further down the path, the day grew hotter. Fall was upon them, but the summer would not go lightly. The sun shone brightly above the Realm of the Lake. With little shade, it was easy to get overheated. Tavi was tiring but Ginger's town was not far. Thankfully, it could be seen in the distance now, but the clouds had rolled back over the forest and the sun blazed. Ghrian noticed his companion was slowing. Her pace had waned and she was panting heavily. The turquoise tether made him much more aware of Tavi's movements. He decided to sit down and give her a rest, still holding the apple in his hand.

"I suppose I shouldn't let this go to waste. No use in saving it for a lost horse," he said to the gray wolf as they sat. He took a large bite from the juicy red apple as he looked out over the field. The midday sun sent rays dancing across the green plain. Aside from a few lone trees strewn sparsely across the field, there was nothing to be seen but green from the path all the way to the woods of Collitte.

Ghrian and Tavi sat taking in the beauty of the day and munching on the apple. After a few peaceful moments, a low rumble became audible in the distance. It grew steadily louder. Suddenly, a giant gray form had shoved itself in between the young man and his companion. Ghrian could hardly believe his eyes, or his luck.

March stood above them, crunching the leftovers of the fruit he had just stolen and devoured. "Well," Ghrian sighed, "I suppose I was right in my assumption."

He laid his hand on March's chest, feeling his breath as the horse occupied himself with the final chews of his apple. March was covered in mud from head to hoof. Twigs and leaves sprouted from his once pure white mane.

"You didn't actually go into the Forbidden Forest, did you?" Ghrian asked.

March tossed his mane and lifted his head. Ghrian stood and pulled a few twigs from his horse's coat.

"Crazy beast. If I am ever able to ride you, I imagine we could go anywhere," he sighed.

Ghrian had a few decisions to make. Should he continue on to see

Ginger or should he attempt to bring March home again? After some time standing with the stallion, he decided that it would be best to leave the horse to avoid further destruction to his body or the nearby towns. Besides, March seemed to be doing just fine. Ghrian gave a slight tug to Tavi's leash and they continued on down the road.

After walking away and nearly reaching Ginger's town of Vael, Ghrian turned around, and to his astonishment, March was following. He was pleasantly surprised, but because he didn't want to scare the beast off, he simply ignored him, smiling to himself. Approaching the bar at the edge of town, he could see Ginger serving drinks to the regulars of the Ailceimic in the mid-afternoon. She waved as she saw him approach.

"Ghrian!" she called. "Just the man I wanted to see."

Ghrian smiled and sat at the bar, wrapping the turquoise leash around his wrist.

"Oh, I like Tavi's new accessory," Ginger chimed. "I was wondering if you got our order for bread? The usual?" she said, tipping the antler mug toward Ghrian's beer of choice.

He nodded. "I should have your bread to you in a few days," he smiled to her as she handed him his brew.

"Wonderful," she smiled back. "That means I'll get to see you twice this week!"

They smiled at each other for a moment until Ginger's face fell then quickly turned to panic. She backed away from the bar and rested her hands firmly on the stone counter behind her. Ghrian had just enough time to turn his head before the object of Ginger's surprise was upon him. There was an uproar on the bar patio as the gray stallion came galloping into the seating area, knocking over benches and tables as men were thrown from their seats. Freshly poured beer splattered to the ground.

"MARCH!" Ghrian yelled.

"This animal is yours?" Ginger shrieked.

Without answering, Ghrian got up and ran to calm the beast, not knowing if he would even be able to do so. As he walked toward March, the horse ran straight toward him, burying his soft nose is Ghrian's hands, his tail twitching as he nibbled on Ghrian's palm.

"Oh, I see. Ginger, do you have any apples by chance?" Ghrian asked.

"Apples? You think I am going to give this creature a treat after he has decimated my bar!" she shouted.

Ghrian smiled sheepishly as the attendants of the pub groaned and

began voicing their discontent.

"Just throw me one and I'll get him out of your hair," he smiled.

"Fine," she said, throwing him a partially browned apple as she stepped out from behind the bar and began cleaning the mess. "You best have my bread to me soon," she said, unamused.

Ghrian nodded and turned, partially hiding his face from the other customers with March's head. He was amazed by this animal. "Your love of apples is truly astounding," he said to March as he led him out of the bar by his silver mane.

Tavi trotted at his side, seemingly oblivious to all that just occurred. She was surprisingly calm for a wild beast.

Ghrian headed back down the path toward his home with the wolf and wild horse on either side of him. He considered leaving March in the field again, but after his display this afternoon, he was concerned that March would wreak havoc in the town in search of apples. Reluctantly, he removed Tavi's leash.

"For years you never needed this. Prove to me that you no longer need it now," he instructed.

The gray wolf gazed at Ghrian and slowly wagged her bushy tail as he freed her. She circled his legs excitedly, but did not leave his side. Now for the fun part. Ghrian still had a firm grasp on the stallion's mane but had no idea how March would react to something new around his neck. Ghrian could not afford a repeat of last time. Slowly, he reached his right arm around March's neck, firmly holding his mane in the left. The horse tossed his head a little, but kept his pace, seemingly unfazed. Soon, the ends of the turquoise tether met, leaving a decent amount of line to direct the horse. Ghrian was skeptical of the success of this endeavor, but March seemed to be responding well.

That evening, Ghrian spent his time making a place for March. He laid hay and a few apples at the base of the post he tied his steed to by the side of the house. The stallion responded surprisingly well to the turquoise cord. It was much softer and stronger than his original lead rope.

The man, the wolf, and the horse spent the evening together, learning to be comfortable with one another. By dusk the moon was already bright. The swollen yellow ball hovered just above the horizon, casting its lustrous light over Lochta and the lake.

"It's going to be a full moon tonight," Ghrian commented as he bit into a warm, fresh piece of bread. The air was still. The noise of the town lulled in the distance. He fed Tavi her usual bones and scraps of meat from that week's big meal. March munched on an apple. All was calm and all were content.

"Ghrian," his father called. "Come inside so we can discuss tomorrow's delivery. That beast is hardly fit for work."

Ghrian sighed and went inside, leaving his companions to their meals. The young man and his father talked for hours about the delivery route, about the coming winter, about Ginger and Oir, and about his plans for March, until the moon was high and fuller than any before. As the hours passed, the men grew weary. Shortly after the door was locked, Ghrian fell fast asleep. March stood tied tightly to the post and Tavi lay curled next to him. This was the first night that Ghrian had ever left Tavi outside. She rarely left his side, let alone stayed out all night and under a full moon.

As the night drew on, a chilling wind swept through the town. The biting cold rustled the trees and awoke the sleeping stallion. March tossed his head about to shake the chill and tugged hard on the tether. As he became aware of his immobility, he grew agitated. His anxiety became so great that he began neighing loudly. Ghrian awoke in a sweat. It was now the early hours of morning and the darkest time of night. The full moon drenched Ghrian's window in a cold, yellow light. As he came to, he could hear March's neighs. He scrambled awake, throwing a bearskin robe over his bare broad shoulders. He straightened his worn, dark gray trousers as he ran through the bakery and out the front door.

"Hush! You'll wake the whole town!" he hissed.

Ghrian found his way to March by the light of the moon. The stars shone like candles in the night. The wind whipped and tugged at his robe as he stroked the stallion's neck, trying to calm him.

"Shhh, boy," Ghrian said softly. "You really don't like to be restrained, do you?"

He slid the cord from the post and wrapped it around his wrist. The stallion released a low snort and pawed the ground. Ghrian's eyes followed his horse's hooves. It was at that moment that he realized they were alone.

"Where's Tavi?" Ghrian said aloud with panic mounting in his voice.

March snorted again and turned his ears toward the forest as a piercing howl ripped through the night.

"Alright, now I need you," Ghrian said, pulling the stallion's head to face his own. "You have to let me ride you. If Tavi is out there alone with wild wolves," his voice trailed as he dared not complete the thought.

March freed his head from Ghrian's grip and lunged toward the open field. Without thinking, Ghrian kicked off the ground and wrapped his arms tightly around March's neck, not that he would have had much of a choice since his wrist was still tethered to the stallion. Ghrian held on for his life as the pair raced through the night across the dark blanket of grass. Sky and land became one vast darkness, sprinkled with light by the moon, dew and stars. The stallion raced on, fearless and free, while Ghrian worried for Tavi's safety, barely realizing the fact that he was riding his horse. Once Ghrian settled himself on March's back, with his fingers dug deep in the horse's mane, he began calling out for Tavi.

"I should have never untied her. I should have never left her outside!" he moaned. He paused and took a deep breath before shouting again, "Tavi!"

There was no response aside from the rustling leaves. The pair neared the Forbidden Forest. Ghrian sighed with distress as he remembered where he had found Tavi the last time she ran away. A short-lived sense of relief washed over him as he recalled that mysterious pond, but it soon faded as he realized that he would have to enter Collitte yet again, and now under cover of darkness.

Slowly, he began to pull back on March's mane. March was not amused. He went from full gallop to immediate mid-air buck. Ghrian was thrown over his steed and onto the ground faster than he could blink. He sighed as he watched March and the remaining pieces of the turquoise cord disappear into the night. The part that he had wound tightly around his wrist was now dug deep into his skin. Ghrian groaned as he sat up, rubbing his lower back, on which he had fallen. A sharp pain immediately sprung to his attention as he tried to stand. He opened his robe, which had cushioned his fall a bit, and saw a dark stain beginning to form on the fur of his cloak. Placing his hand gently on the left side of his lower back, he searched for the source.

The pain grew worse as his fingers brushed over a deep puncture in his side. He clenched his jaw as he leaned down to pull some grass to stop the bleeding and inspect what could have caused the wound. A small stone was glistening in the moonlight, like a brush tip dipped in red paint.

Now, not only was he without Tavi, but his horse had also run off yet again. He was far from home in the middle of the night, and now bleeding. Ghrian stood and pushed the grass further into his open wound. He refused to leave Tavi out all night. He pulled himself upright and pushed on through the moonlit field.

Ghrian was a man with a strong will. Though some may have counted his courage as sheer stubbornness, he was not one to give in under any circumstance. Dawn was still a few hours away and the darkness of Collitte was more ominous than ever, but Ghrian pressed on. He could not leave his best friend alone in the wood for a second time.

He walked for what seemed like an eternity, his path lit only by the glimpses of moonlight that broke their way through the thick blanket of trees above. The ground beneath his bare feet was moist and uncertain. One moment he walked over a bed of leaves and the next he tripped over a ball of roots or fallen branches. He began to tire as his wound continued to bleed. His robe dragged the fallen leaves behind him. He needed to rest. He had been calling for Tavi endlessly, but was answered by nothing aside from the occasional screech of an owl.

After trekking through the dying woods for hours, Ghrian was nearly ready to give in and succumb to his fate in the wilderness. As he fell to his knees, exhausted by all that he had just endured, a faint and familiar scent tempted his nose. It was water. He pulled himself back to his feet and stumbled toward the scent. As he reached the clearing, the memories came flooding back to him. The last time Tavi had left him, this is where he had found her. A new hope dawned in his heart. Maybe he would have some luck yet. He looked over toward the rose bushes. The memory of those eerie eyes rushed back to him, and for a moment, he froze as he stared between the thorns, but his vision was poor in the dark and blurred by pain. Seeing nothing, he turned back toward the water which was completely visible in the light of the full moon. Even in the darkness Ghrian could see its pure and unique color. It was still, like a sheet of the purest glass. He almost felt guilty for disturbing the serene water, but he knew that he needed to clean and examine his wound.

The air was thick and humid but held a biting chill. An eerie stillness hung in the atmosphere above him. The owl had been quieted, and no sound broke the deafening silence. It was as though the water was drawing him in, calling to him, offering him sanctuary. For a moment, the fear of drowning stayed him, but this pool of water was incredibly enticing. Ghrian removed his robe, laying it onto the grass. He lowered himself into the clear water, bracing his arms along the shore for its depths were dark and unknown. His body broke the surface and sent smooth ripples throughout the blanket of turquoise. It was as if the water had captured the light of the moon and sent it undulating to the opposite shoreline. For a moment,

Ghrian could not feel his pain. He did not fear the woods, nor the loss of his companions. For a moment, he was frozen in peace.

Then, from the darkness, something approached. He was pulled from his heavenly lull and turned in time to see the piercing orange eyes from his memory. The early morning black was no match for the darkness of this beast's fur. The only visible breaks in the cavernous black were the eyes of fire and the glistening white teeth. Ghrian knew the legend of the wolves in these woods. They were said to be the largest and fiercest of all creatures, ruthless and unafraid. The namesake of the Forbidden Forest.

Ghrian held tight to the shoreline, frozen in the water, and stared into the face of his worst nightmare. The great black wolf eyed the man and lowered its muzzle. The beast's sheer size was enough to intimidate even the bravest of men. Its eyes were like gold in a forge, blazing hues of orange and yellow, surrounded by a ring of smoky blue. For a moment, Ghrian was not afraid; he was simply in awe of the creature's eyes. That soon faded, as the wolf bared its teeth and prepared for attack.

As the beast lunged, Ghrian reached around with his left hand and pulled his right arm in front of his face. First, all he felt was the cold, then the crushing pressure of the great wolf's teeth. The beast's canines tore through his right wrist and ripped a chunk of muscle and skin from his arm. In terror, he screamed, gazing at the wolf in front of him, teeth still bared, flesh and the last cord of turquoise leather dripping from its powerful jaws.

Adrenaline coursed through Ghrian's veins as his left hand met its mark. He pulled with all the might he had left and as he dug his fingers into the thick fur of the beast, pulled it with him into the water.

There was a struggle as fur and flesh tore at one another. Blood and water swirled together, until there was only flesh. The water rushed around the entangled pair and both came up for breath.

A great storm had rushed in as the early morning light pierced the water's surface. Rain came down upon the pair and the stillness of the water returned. Thunder roared and lightning crashed in the surrounding woods.

Ghrian began to lose consciousness as the rain pounded against his bloodied and broken body. As his eyes began to close and he began to slip away, he thought he saw a body lift itself from the water and disappear into the forest.

Then all went black.

Chapter Six

A thick fog hung heavy and low over the forest. As the events of the night before flooded his mind, Ghrian awoke in a panic. He ran his hands frantically over his body. His wet clothes clung to him, slowing his movements. Gasping for breath, he felt for the wound that prompted his entry into the water, but there was nothing there.

As he continued to check for the wounds that he was certain he had sustained, he realized that his hand was intact. The wrist that had been torn to shreds and the deep gash that had opened his arm to the bone were completely gone.

"How? I was mauled by that creature! Was it all just a dream? A trick of the night in the Forbidden Forest?" he whispered to himself.

His heart pounded as the events replayed over in his mind. He laid back on the cool grass adjacent to the mysterious pond and looked up toward the sky. The crushing weight of the overcast glare from above bore down upon him as he thought to himself. Surely he had been dreaming. He must have fallen into the water and passed out. Somehow, he had pulled himself to the water's edge during the night and dreamed these awful things. As he played the events again in his head, he knew that his excuses made no sense.

He lifted his hand to his head and ran it slowly through his thick brown hair. There was no one else around. He must have been dreaming, but deep down he knew how ridiculous that sounded.

The yellow leaves above him swayed in the wind as it blew. Fall was certainly upon the Realm of the Lake. As Ghrian laid there, hoping to himself that it would all make sense in time, he watched the leaves sway. They were beautiful, delicate things controlled by the changing seasons. They were slaves to the weather, to any circumstance thrust upon them. Yet there they stay, succumbing to their fate each season. They encompassed every moment of beauty, death, and rebirth in an inescapable cycle. They were imprisoned by their home in a constant state of surrendering to providence. Their only choice was to exist. A lone leaf fell to the forest floor and Ghrian watched it land gracefully onto the grass next to him. He lifted his arm to pick it up and realized then that the turquoise cord was gone.

All the hope that the nightmare had existed solely in his mind evaporated. The missing leather was proof. Something had indeed attacked him, and he had, miraculously, lifted himself from the water fully healed. He contemplated heading deeper into the woods, continuing his search for Tavi, but how could he? He was shaken, terrified even. Besides, he had deliveries to make. He tried to push the events of the night from his mind.

"I have to focus on getting out of these accursed woods," he scowled aloud to the creatures of the forest. "I have to get home."

This time Ghrian's confidence had been severely shaken. He had lost Tavi and March. He had been attacked by one of Collitte's infamous wolves and was lost, again, deep in the wood. The fog was so thick that he could barely see his feet beneath him. He focused on taking one step at a time.

He whispered to himself over and over, "Just don't think about what happened. It was a dream or a, no, miracles don't exist."

The Realm of the Lake had long forgotten the ages of old. Its people had all but abandoned the ways of their ancestors and their beliefs. Long ago a people lived alongside the lake in a single united village. After years of peace and acceptance, some of its people grew skeptical of magic and miracles. They began to distrust what they could not explain. There was a split in the lake villages and nearly half of its people fled to the woods to reside with the neighboring people of Dorchas. Lochta grew to become the hub of trade and science for miles. The residents of the wood clung to their tradition and were also a prosperous trade post, though of a much different kind. People from all across Domhaen would come to visit the great library and purchase goods that were forbidden in Lochta. Over time, science became god, ruling in the minds of all. Only things that could be seen and understood were accepted as reality. Those who questioned the authority of the Order of the Temple in the Realm were persecuted. Those

who still believed the ancient ways were quieted. Thus, the ancient people of Dorchas passed into legend, and as the Realm of the Lake grew, the people forgot their history, for it was riddled with the magic of old.

Ghrian's mother had been an outspoken believer. He remembered when he was a young boy the stories of mystery and unexplainable occurrences she would tell. She told him stories of magic and belief, and stories of their supposed true history. He had always felt that there was something more to the world than what could be seen, but he dared not question it now. He toiled to push the thoughts of her from his mind. He never truly got to know his mother, never got to delve deeper into her knowledge of forbidden things. She disappeared when he was four and his belief left with her. His father rarely spoke of her, and when he did, the light in his eyes would dim and his voice would become so low that it was nearly inaudible.

Ghrian continued on, crunching the leaves below him as he tried to make his way out of the maze of green and brown. His mind became lost in his thoughts as he wandered deeper into the woods. He couldn't shake the memories of his mother, of where she had gone, of if she was even still living. She was said to have been lost to this very forest. He shuddered at the thought, but still, a quiet hope began to prick at the back of his mind, maybe he would find her out here.

The day drew on and the gray sky grew angry. The clouds darkened into a deep blue, full of water, ready to spill their contents to the world below. Ghrian had nearly given up. He was exhausted and confused. He was upset with himself for not thinking clearly and not marking his trail. Now he was lost, just like his beloved Tavi.

After another hour or so, as his pace slowed, he heard a rustle in the woods beside him. The back of his neck ran cold with an icy sweat. Fear pricked the hairs below his scalp and the chill ran down his arms. The first thing that came to his mind was the great black wolf he had encountered the night before. He froze in his tracks. Following a few breathless minutes, the culprit of his panic revealed itself. A beautiful white doe placed one foot onto the menagerie of red and orange fallen leaves in front of Ghrian. It was as if she was blocking his path. He settled himself and stood tall. Her inquisitive and kind eyes stared back at him. They were the deepest brown he had ever seen. They were nearly black, but with a gentle sparkle, like the midnight sky or still burning embers of coal. This deer did not seem afraid of him. She stood tall and walked gracefully toward Ghrian. He could hardly believe that such a gentle creature survived without fear in these terrible woods. The deer came closer, and lowering its head to Ghrian's chest, gave him a slight nudge.

His astonishment froze him for a moment. Hesitantly, he placed his coarse hand on the doe's soft, white head. The pair stood silent in the forest. A light rain began to fall through the lattice openings in the trees where the leaves had left their post. Time passed and Ghrian felt as if he somehow knew this creature. Perhaps he was just happy to see an animal that was not trying to devour him. As the rain grew stronger, the deer turned and began weaving her way through the brush. She turned after walking away and looked back at her new acquaintance. It seemed as if she wanted him to follow her.

"I suppose I have nothing better to do," he huffed to himself.

Ghrian was beginning to relax. He had been in the Forbidden Forest more often within the past few days than in his entire life. Now he understood why people were forbidden from entering. The stories of the massive wolves were all too real for him. He rubbed his forearm as he continued to follow the white deer. He could still feel the wolf's canines sinking into his flesh, ripping into his skin as easily as if it were a freshly buttered loaf. He shuddered at the memory that was still so fresh.

He grappled with the impossible in order to ease the strain on his beating heart. The missing cord must have just gotten hung in the woods or lost in the water.

Suddenly, as if it had never existed, the white deer disappeared. Ghrian stopped and surveyed both sides of the forest adjacent to him. The doe had truly vanished. He walked forward slowly, puzzled, until miraculously he reached the edge of Collitte.

"She must have led me out." He realized how ridiculous it sounded as the words left his lips, but it was not the strangest occurrence of his time in the woods, so he let the thought slide. "What a day. I think I'd be fine if I never entered these woods again," he sighed.

Relieved, he stepped into the field and made his way home. Every so often he would peer over his shoulder, hoping that Tavi would emerge from the thicket of trees, bounding obediently after him. He had given up on his packhorse.

The tattered wood siding of his home slowly came into view. The rain had passed, and a strange row of clouds covered the red setting sun. A pink glow was cast over the green grass turning it to a murky violet. Silver lined

the plush cluster of clouds. For a moment, the weary young man stopped to gaze at the beauty. As he drew closer to home, his mind was consumed with the words he could only imagine spewing from his father now. He was in no mood to hear it. Besides, he had far too many deliveries to prepare for to stop and chat. After all, he was now a day late and his customers would be none too happy.

To his surprise, his father was nowhere to be found. Ghrian sighed as he entered the bakery and began filling his burlap bag with the most recent orders.

He searched his mind for things to look forward to. At least he would get to see Ginger. His bridle and lead rope would also be ready soon. Maybe they would prove necessary someday when he found a reliable steed.

The smell of freshly baked bread rose to his nose. He realized that he had not eaten anything aside from a mere apple in nearly two days. Leaning over the counter, he snatched a loaf and began to eat. As he chewed and packed, he went over the following day's route in his mind. He would visit Ginger first, work through his deliveries in Vael, then hit Baile, and end his travels in Lochta. It would be a troublesome and lonely walk without the horse or Tavi, but he had no other choice.

Once he finished packing the loaves, Ghrian retired to his room. He removed his dirtied robe that was now torn and covered in branches, leaves, and blood. He slumped onto his worn mattress and turned toward the small wooden table that sat nestled between the bed and the wall below the lone window. Ghrian removed a stout blade from its single drawer. Its handle was formed from an antler, the blade visible all the way down to its base. At the tip of its hilt sat a small marble griffin. Ghrian spun the glistening blade between his fingers, sending silver splinters of moonlight dancing around the cracked plaster walls of his narrow bedroom.

"I suppose you're my traveling companion now," he mused.

The following morning, Ghrian set out alone. He slung the massive bag over his shoulders and set off toward Vael, Ginger's hometown. There was a part of him that missed exploring Yoaruq like he had as a child. Since his father made the local deliveries and ran the bakery, it had been years since Ghrian spent any great length of time in his own village. He had grown up well and had a good childhood, aside from the disappearance of his mother. Oir's mother, Vaeke, had essentially stepped in to fill that role. The two children had spent nearly all of their time playing in Yoaruq before Oir's father moved his family to Lochta to become a tanner there. It was only then that Ghrian and his father even began to have a relationship. Ghrian's father, Mòr, was a stoic man. He rarely spoke, especially after the disappearance of his wife. Oir's mother used to tell Ghrian of a time when his father was boisterous and loud, even witty. Unfortunately, Mòr's son rarely saw that side of him. His heart had fallen so deep within him that it was nigh unreachable. He was kind, but it was a distant and cold kindness. He had built a fortress of gentleness and passiveness around his heart, keeping it safe from both anger and passion. Ghrian remembered how the Order had come to their home late at night on the evening of his mother's disappearance. They appeared out of darkness, formed out of the formless black of night, cloaked in shadow. Instead of bringing comfort and peace, as they were expected to bring in times of sorrow, they brought stinging inquisitions and biting accusations. Ghrian had expected his father to rise in anger and fight for the honor of his mother, but he had instead simply nodded as the High Priest explained how it was better this way. The Priest conjectured that she would have poisoned young Ghrian's mind with fantasy had she been allowed to raise him. They said that she was now at peace and that her misguided belief in magic and mystery had driven her into the woods in a maddening quest for knowledge outside the Temple. This, they said, had led to her demise. They told Mòr how they'd located her mauled remains in the Forbidden Forest. Ghrian was young when all this occurred, yet still, he remembered the cold patronizing gaze of the Priests.

Following that night, Mòr no longer spoke of his wife to his friends, fellow villagers, or even to his own son. It was as if it had never happened, as if she'd never existed. Over the years that followed Oir's move, Ghrian built a cordial relationship with his father, but essentially, the boy had raised himself. Although Mòr had softened over the years, Tavi was and had always been Ghrian's truest confidant and now she too was gone.

Ghrian's heart was heavy. He hoped that Ginger would be a consoling presence. As he walked, he passed the fields that divided their towns. This was the last place where he had seen March. The stallion was nowhere to be found.

The sounds of Vael grew louder as he approached. He saw Ginger standing behind the bar of the Ailceimic and smiled. She looked at him, her eyes wide with excitement.

"Ghrian!" she called from afar. "I am happy to see that crazy horse wasn't the death of you!"

Ghrian forced himself to keep the artificial smile on his face as he reached the bar. He set the giant bag of bread on the bench below him and rested his knee next to it.

"Hello, lovely," he smiled.

Ginger's face looked sad upon his approach. "What's wrong?" she asked.

Ghrian looked up from removing her orders from the sack. "You know that crazy horse you met the other day?"

"Yes," she said, as she received her loaves.

"Well, he ran off," Ghrian sighed.

"I can't say that I'm surprised," she said, smiling as she brushed the baker's hand. "He was certainly a challenging beast."

Ghrian let out a gruff laugh and replied, "I did manage to ride him once though."

Ginger clapped her hands together with pride and was about to congratulate him before he continued, "Right before he threw me and ran off."

She could not help but giggle at the image. "I'm truly sorry. I can imagine that was a great loss."

"It's alright. I have deliveries, so the money will be replenished in no time," he smiled and lifted the bag back to his shoulders. "I'll be back to tell you that story once these deliveries are done."

Ginger nodded and told him she looked forward to it. She promised to pay him in coins or beer when he returned. Ghrian and Ginger had an intriguing relationship. They had always fancied one another, but with Ginger's father being the High Priest of the Temple of Vael, who had acute knowledge of Ghrian's mother's disappearance and belief, not much had come of their mutual interest. Every time the two had tried to spend time together outside of the Ailceimic, Chuis had intervened.

Ghrian continued on through Vael making deliveries and debating just how much he should tell Ginger about the strange occurrences of the night he lost Tavi and was thrown from March. Her father was, after all, the High Priest in this town and would not take lightly the talk of miracles or wandering into forbidden forests. How could he even explain what had happened? He hardly knew himself.

Vael was the second largest town in the Realm of the Lake. It held the Realm's only other Temple, the first and greatest of the two, the Order's Head Temple was in Lochta. The people here were quiet compared to the other villages in the area. These townsmen were well mannered, soft spoken, and orderly, for the most part. Truthfully, Ghrian felt uncomfortable in this sterile place, but being the neighboring town to Yoaruq, most of his orders came from Vael.

"Good afternoon, Ghrian," a slow voice sounded from behind him. He turned to face the Priest.

"Good afternoon, Sir Chuis," Ghrian replied.

"I assume you have already paid a visit to my daughter?"

"Of course." Ghrian nodded. "I gave her your bread. I plan to stop by again on the way back to Yoaruq."

The pompous man nodded and moved on. He distrusted Ghrian. He knew of Ghrian's mother, her belief, and her disappearance. He thought it unnatural that a boy should be raised in any manner of believing in anything other than what can be seen, even if it had only been in his early childhood. He also had a distaste for the way his daughter pined after him. The Priest was a suspicious man. He was hardly anything like his trusting and innocent Ginger. He desired knowledge above all else. The Temple of Vael was more of a library than a sanctuary, as it was full of books on science and order. Oddly enough, there were hardly any parchments concerning history. Of course, people could come and seek answers to life's pressing questions from one of the men of the Order, but it was not a compassionate place. Vael's Temple was a place of reason. Problems were met with practical answers, and if the issue was one of emotion, it was discarded.

Alchemy and science ruled this age of the Realm.

Upon Ghrian's return to Ginger's bar, he noticed that a beer was already set out for him. He smiled as he approached. "Thank you, Ginger."

She smiled back at him. "It's your favorite, Black Ale."

Many of the drinks made at the Ailceimic were created and accelerated by feats of science. Ginger's Black Ale was a sort of potion: a mixture of hops, barley, caramel, coffee, chocolate, salts, and other substances unknown to its consumers. It, as well as the other drinks, were created in large wooden barrels behind the bar itself. Ghrian had watched Ginger mix the substances that would have taken months to prepare under normal brewing circumstances. It was a fascinating process. The Ailceimic was the only place he knew of that created beverages this way. He could only imagine that this was because of her father's station and insatiable love of science.

Ghrian brought the brew to his lips and downed nearly half of its contents in one gulp. He wiped the froth from his mustache and called to Ginger, who had been tending other customers.

Once she finished, she came to him. "More beer already?" she smiled.

Ghrian nodded and continued to drink.

"Weren't you going to tell me what happened to that stallion of yours? And where is Tavi? I noticed she wasn't with you earlier today," Ginger said with concern in her voice.

Ghrian let out a heavy sigh as he slouched over the bar. "They're both gone."

Ginger laid her slender hand on Ghrian's head and lifted his face to hers. Gazing into his golden-brown eyes, she said, "I can't speak for the horse, but I know Tavi will find her way home."

He smiled and took her hand in his. "I surely hope so. I had never left her outside all night before. She was lying next to March and they both seemed so content that I just," he paused. "I forgot and fell asleep. Next thing I know, March is making a racket, and by the time I got outside, Tavi was gone."

Ginger refilled his beer and returned to listen as he continued.

"Good thing is, I did finally ride the beast, so I know it's possible, not that it matters much now," he took a swig and sat up straight. "I set out immediately to find Tavi once I realized she was gone. It was not long after that when he bucked me off and I landed," Ghrian paused, wondering how to continue. Should he tell Ginger of his encounter in the woods? He quickly decided against it. He knew that she would not understand, and worse, she could tell Chuis.

Yoaruq and Baile were such small settlements that they did not have their own Temples. The Order thought it best to focus their efforts on the larger towns. Therefore, the High Priests in Lochta and Vael were seen as ruling bodies for all in the Realm. Even the Royals of Lochta bent to their will. Word of their disapproval would travel fast and could pose a threat to the bakery's business.

"Then, the next thing I know, I'm waking up in the middle of a field covered in grass with a ruined robe," he let out a hearty laugh, masking the truth and his pain.

"Well, I'm glad you didn't get more hurt! A fall from a horse like that can cause some real damage. I'm sure Tavi just got a wild hair. She is a wolf after all. She's never strayed far from you. I know she'll return," Ginger replied with a warm smile.

"Mhmm. Well, I have more deliveries to make," he said as he surveyed the warm glow that now covered the fields. The sun was making its trek across the horizon all too quickly. "I will see you in a few days," Ghrian said as he stood to leave.

"Oh wait!" Ginger chimed. She ruffled through her belongings behind the bar. She brought out a small velvet pouch. "Your pay for the bread. The beer is on the house," she smiled.

Ghrian took the pouch with a wink, then headed back to Yoaruq to gather the orders for Lochta.

Upon his return home, he met his father. Mòr was not the bearer of brutal reality that Ghrian had anticipated. He reassured his son that the wolf would return. Of course, he could not say as much about the horse, but Mòr was a kind man, in his own, distant way. He may be stern and abrasive at times, but he was also compassionate. He helped Ghrian gather the rest of the orders for Lochta and bid him farewell as he watched his son saunter off alone.

By evening, Ghrian had reached the great entrance of Lochta. The fields that spanned toward the woods and hills and on to the mountain range were behind him, the lake shining in the evening sun before him. Ghrian entered under the large stone archway. He walked through the bustling town. Lochta was busy nearly all hours of the night. The sun was beginning to set and still the streets were filled. Rows of lamps lined the wide cobblestone road, each lit by a chemical fire that never faltered. As he walked, he passed children playing. He watched as they kicked a mesh ball and laughed as it knocked the nearby metalsmith into his tools. Ghrian enjoyed visiting the neighboring towns. He loved people. He never failed to see the good in every being he met.

A little while later, he made it to the familiar door. Now he could finally get the nightmare off his chest. He was full of nervous energy as he approached the stone entry way. He knocked and Oir's kind face appeared from around the shop door.

"Ghrian! Just in time. I completed your tack yesterday!" Oir smiled.

She paused for a moment and looked at her friend's side, then behind him. "Honestly, I was half expecting you to come in riding that new horse of yours," she laughed half-heartedly, visibly disappointed. "And where's the lovely Tavi?"

Ghrian ignored her and stepped inside, closing the door behind him.

Oir protested, "Excuse me, sir, but I am not closed yet!"

"I have something to tell you," Ghrian said, again ignoring her. He was all too anxious to share what he had experienced. He needed someone else to assure him that it must have been a dream or delusion induced by stress. Maybe he'd hit his head.

Oir settled herself, sighed, and locked the door behind her somber friend. He was rarely this serious.

"I am assuming you're about to tell me where Tavi and March are?" she mused.

Ghrian sat on Oir's work bench and looked up at her. "Actually, their disappearance isn't the strangest part of this story."

Ghrian knew that Oir would scold him for entering the woods, but he also knew that she would be intrigued. She was one of the few people he knew, maybe the only, that still had the desire to believe.

"A few nights ago," Ghrian began. "I had had a fantastic evening with March. We were just starting to bond over apples. I had successfully secured him to the post next to the house and he seemed rather content. Tavi had curled up and fallen asleep next to him. I know I never leave her out all night, but I was so exhausted that I fell asleep inside before I realized."

Oir pulled a stool from across the room over to her workbench. Facing Ghrian, she settled herself against her desk.

Ghrian continued, "I awoke sometime in the night to March neighing loudly. I got up to quiet him and found Tavi was missing. Immediately, I released March and tied that lovely tether you gave me around my wrist. To my surprise, he actually let me ride him."

"I knew it!" Oir chimed excitedly. She took a quick breath, as if she meant to continue, but Ghrian put a finger to her lips. "That was before he threw me," he interrupted.

She slumped back against the desk. "Well, at least you *did* ride him. I told you that you would." Ghrian smiled as she continued. "I do have your bridle, reins and lead rope for you. And you already paid for them."

"If he returns, I will try again. I'm not wasting my money if I can help it," he smiled.

"Oh stop. It's not about the money. I know you won't give up on him," Oir stated with confidence.

"Anyway, as I was saying," he continued with a smirk. "For a moment, all was right. I was so focused on Tavi that I hardly realized I was riding him, but then he threw me. I don't remember why. But I fell onto a stone and it put a nasty gash in my side."

"Please tell me you got up and went home after that," Oir said, knowing full well he did the opposite.

"How could I? Tavi was still out there!" he argued.

"Ghrian, she's a wolf, for goodness sake. I'm sure that she can handle herself in the wilderness better than an injured man-child," she smirked.

"I resent that." Ghrian eyed Oir, then turning serious, he crossed his arms and leaned back against the desk. "Listen, I have not been without that creature since the day I found her. As long as I could still look, I was determined to find her."

"Let me guess," Oir said with disapproval. "You went into the woods."

"Yes. I went into the woods."

"You know Collitte is forbidden! Not to mention dangerous, and even more so without your wolf and with an injury!" Oir bickered.

"Do you want to hear the story or not?" Ghrian exhaled.

Oir composed herself and planted her chin on her arm. As upset as she was, she was equally interested. "Continue."

"So, there I was wounded and calling for Tavi in the darkness. I continued walking for hours, bleeding as I went. Then, I found a clearing and a pond as turquoise as the cord you had given me."

Slowly, Oir lifted her head and leaned forward. "I thought the Lake and its river were the only sources of water 'til the Sea?"

"That's what I thought, too. But there it was, clear as day," he recollected. At this point, Ghrian had determined that he would tell his old friend the entire tale of events. He had to talk to someone about it. "Being in the state I was, I became exhausted. I figured that this pond was as good a place as any to rest and clean the wound. So, I got in the water."

"Rather risky move, you have no idea what could have been lurking in those waters!" Oir scolded.

"Would you hush and let me finish," Ghrian said. "I'm trying to get to the craziest part."

"Oooh," Oir crooned, pulling her knees to her chest, balancing on the stool in anticipation.

Ghrian's eyebrow raised as he chuckled at his friend's excitement. Then he got serious. The tension rose and Oir held her legs tighter, barely breathing as she waited.

"So, there I was, washing my wound in this beautiful pond, when all of the sudden I heard something behind me."

Oir's eyes widened.

"As I turned to look, the biggest, blackest wolf appeared from the shadows. Its eyes were like glowing coals fresh from the forge, and it had the sharpest and largest teeth I had ever seen."

Oir was barely in her seat now. She had thrown her legs down and was trying to swallow the "I told you so" statements every few seconds until Ghrian finished.

"Next thing I know, the wolf is in the water on top of me. It sinks its teeth into my forearm. I can still feel the cold and the staggering pain." He shuddered as he continued. "It tore a chunk out of me and took the last of the cord." He held up his wrist to show Oir.

Visibly confused, she took his arm and searched for the wound that should be present, but there was nothing. No bite marks, no puncture wounds. She looked up at Ghrian for an explanation.

"The giant wolf and I battled in the water, then all went dark," Ghrian continued.

He contemplated telling her about the body that he thought he had seen emerging from the water, but the story was already strange and inexplicable enough. Besides, he was not even certain he had seen a human. He wasn't certain he had experienced any of it. He sat, still trying to convince himself that it was all just delirium, hoping that Oir would say the same. Perhaps she would tell him that he must have hit his head and possibly had a concussion. She'd tell him to get it looked at and check into the Temple of Lochta.

Instead, Oir looked dumbfounded and skeptical, but incredibly curious. "So, what happened then? Where did the wolf go? What happened to your wounds? Why..."

Ghrian interrupted, "I have no idea. I was in the water, then I was on the bank. When I awoke, I thought that it had been a dream. But then," he held up his wrist again. "I was healed. I can't imagine a dream feeling that real. And even my side was healed!" He stood and turned to show Oir where he had fallen, where the wound had been. "And even beyond that, the cord is gone. It had been wound so tightly around my wrist from my fall from March that I couldn't remove it. I tried to convince myself that it was all a dream, a fantasy, but how could that have come off on its own? How could I have been healed of all my wounds? There is only one explanation," he leaned in close to Oir, fully convinced now that it had truly happened.

Something began to burn somewhere deep inside his heart. It was a small flicker of hope, an unquenchable desire to know. Perhaps his mother had been right. That thought hurt, so he pushed it from his mind and whispered. "Magic; I believe it may be real."

Oir was the last person to judge, but she had known Ghrian's mother. Oir was a few years older than Ghrian and remembered spending time with her. She was a remarkably enchanting woman, but she openly talked about magic and miracles. It had gotten her into trouble. The people of Yoaruq were skeptical, but were not confrontational. The people of Vael, however, were unhappy with her outspoken belief. She was ridiculed endlessly and told often by the Priests of the Temple to keep quiet. "There was no use for belief, science is all that is necessary," they would say.

Oir was there the night that Ghrian's mother had fled. The threats had turned to violence, and she feared her son's life would be put in danger if she stayed. At least, that's what Oir and her parents had come to believe. Oir was seven when Ghrian's mother fled into the woods. She remembered that horrid night like it was yesterday. She remembered Mòr's protests, then his resignation. His promise to keep their son safe. Oir's parents had tried to pull their daughter from the situation. They tried to take her home before it got worse or the Order made an appearance to check the disturbance. Word traveled fast in the Realm. As they left the house, Oir had heard one last phrase that haunted and confused her to this day.

"I should have never left in the first place," Ghrian's mother had whispered. "I should have never left my post."

Fíor's words rang in Oir's ears as she looked into the sparkling eyes of her dearest friend. Ghrian had known so little of his mother, and yet was so much like her. They were both strong and valiant to a fault. Word in the Realm had been that Fíor was killed not long after she fled into the woods. It is unknown whether this was the truth because no one ventured into the Forbidden Forest. And if they did, they never returned. That is, except for Ghrian.

The last thing Oir wanted was to quell his belief in something more, but she equally longed for his safety. She did not want to see him meet the same fate as his mother. She chose her next words carefully. "Ghrian, I

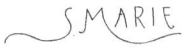

can't say what happened in those woods, but promise me you won't bring this up to anyone else."

Ghrian was a little taken aback by her words. He had expected her to be skeptical, but not concerned. He thought she would have been excited by the intriguing mystery surrounding the events in Collitte.

"I told you it was a dangerous place!" Oir said. She lightened the mood, playfully scolding and punching him on the shoulder.

Ghrian moved with the blow but did not respond. He simply stared at her, trying to decipher what was truly bothering her.

Oir continued, "Anyway, there could be a number of reasonable explanations, as well as unreasonable ones. The important thing is that you are alright." She got up and put her hand on Ghrian's shoulder. "And don't worry, that cord was a scrap anyhow. Would you like some tea? I think I need some tea."

Before waiting for his answer, Oir disappeared to the back of her shop. Ghrian sat alone contemplating the events. The more he tried to convince himself that it had been a dream, the more details he remembered. The memory of the feelings, the sounds, and the pain would not leave him in peace.

"There's truly no way that could have been a dream or the result of head injury," he whispered to himself.

It was then that the obviously insane idea crept its way into his thoughts. "I have to find out for myself, I have to go back." There was no doubt in him now. "What if Tavi had also been attacked by that creature?" he whispered. He stopped himself at that thought, not willing to consider her harm. He needed a distraction.

"Oir, I think I'd prefer a beer," he called to her in the kitchen. "I promise we don't have to discuss this anymore."

"Thank the stars," Oir said as she rounded the corner and returned to the shop. "Let's go get drunk."

The night was beautiful and calm. The moon was still massive, waning on the other side of full. The pair walked in the moonlight to their usual destination. Once they were seated, beers in hand, Ghrian asked Oir how business had been. She admitted that it had been slow.

"I'm not worried. The Winter Solstice Festival is approaching. I almost always sell out of cloaks, bridles, boots and trinkets before winter sets in," she said.

The Winter Solstice Festival was known far and wide. It was one of the Realm's greatest annual attractions. The Winter and Summer Solstice festivals were the primary reason that anyone from the Kingdom came all the way to the Realm of the Lake. Since Lochta was historically a grand hub of trade and commerce, people came from miles around, making the trek down Cossan Crossing. Most would stay through the entirety of the festival, and some would remain there all winter. The Realm's location was ideal in the warmer seasons, but once winter set in, there were hardly any visitors. The people of the lake relied heavily on the trade and funds from the festival to make it through the winter months. Lochta and the other three villages surrounding the great lake were nestled deep in the woods, far from any other civilization. Once the ground froze and the single trail that led in and out of the Realm became laden with snow, there would be no more tradesmen until the thaw.

"I'm rather famished Ghrian, we should eat," Oir said.

"I could really go for some jerky," he agreed.

"Mmm, great choice!" Oir exclaimed, as she summoned the barmaid.

"Ghrian," she said, once she ordered a plate a jerky. "Are you going to bake the Hearty Loaf this winter for the Festival?"

Ghrian laughed. The Hearty Loaf had to be his least favorite to make, but one of Oir's favorite to eat. It was created by his father one year when food was scarce in Yoaruq. He combined all sorts of grains, wheat, barley, and whatever he could find, and baked it into one giant, lumpy loaf. It sold fairly well in the winter, perhaps because it was so filling, though no one truly seemed to enjoy the taste, that is, except for Oir.

"I think you are the only person who actually enjoys that bread," he laughed. "But yes, I will make a few batches."

"Marvelous," Oir said before sipping her beer. "I'm trying to think of what I will need for the winter."

"I definitely need a new robe," Ghrian huffed.

"Oh, I know!" Oir exclaimed, a sudden gleam in her eye. "Go find that blasted wolf and I'll make you a leather lining from its pelt!"

Ghrian rolled his eyes at her jest.

The two friends sat eating, drinking, and talking until the bar emptied. When they stumbled back to the tannery, Oir disappeared to her room and Ghrian slumped over the work bench.

They both slept well.

The next morning, Oir awoke to the sound of birds chirping and wind whistling. She sauntered into her tiny kitchen behind the shop to make herself some coffee. As it brewed, she peered into her studio. To her surprise, the work bench was empty. She shrugged her shoulders and returned to her brew. The dark emerald paint on the wooden cabinet door was beginning to peel. She reached inside, searching for a spoon to stir in her cream. Oir grumbled at the inconvenience as a few green flakes fell into her mug. She was usually rather cheerful in the mornings, but today, she was not. The previous night had proven to be a bit too much for her.

"I can't believe he's awake. I thought for certain I'd find him half dead and drooling on the floor," she mumbled to herself, amused by the thought. She noted that the bridle, reins and lead rope were still there. Oir sipped her coffee and promptly returned to bed.

Outside, just a few feet away, Ghrian had begun his delivery route. By this time, it was nearly ten o'clock, which was quite early for him. The night had been a particularly restless one. A few hours after he had passed out on the bench, he had fallen to the ground, which promptly woke him. He had then spent the rest of the night contemplating Oir's strange response to the events that he endured, as well as the events themselves. As he wandered through Lochta delivering his bread and receiving the coveted coins, he started to wonder about March. What if he had returned to Capall's stables? It seemed unlikely, but since Ghrian was in Lochta and owed him a loaf anyhow, he decided that he may as well pay the stables a visit.

Ghrian made his way through the bustling town. His deliveries were relatively spread out in Lochta. There were many bakeries in the area, but Mòr and Ghrian had made a name for theirs, as it was the only bakery in Yoaruq. This week the pumpkin and rye loaves were the favorites, but Ghrian knew, as winter drew near, the Hearty Loaf would prevail.

The day drew on as the sun crawled across the murky gray sky. Ghrian's bag grew light. Finally, all of the necessary stops had been made. The small velvet pouch that Ginger had given him hung heavy and full at his side. It chimed as he walked. The wide cobblestone roads were filled with people and animals alike. Horses pulled carriages laden with hay and produce, bound for the market at the center of Lochta. Women sat in the windows of shops, going about their daily duties as men went about selling whatever goods to whoever would listen. Ghrian very much enjoyed his trips to Lochta. He had always craved adventure, and within the Realm of the Lake, aside from the deadly woods of Collitte, adventure was found only in Lochta.

By this time, Ghrian had reached the town's edge. He looked out over the fields to the single road that lead out of the Realm. He had half hoped that he would spot the little dot of gray somewhere in the green before he went to Capall.

He walked the path to the stable, the final pumpernickel loaf in his hand. As he entered, he heard Capall's voice. "Come to buy another horse, lad?"

Ghrian ignored him and peered around the stalls searching for March to no avail. He noticed the great black stallion from his last visit. "I see Fiáin still has yet to find a home."

"Indeed," Capall responded. "You here to buy him?"

Ghrian sighed, unamused. "No, Capall. I am here to deliver your bread. As per our prior agreement."

Capall stepped out from behind one of the stalls. Setting his rake to the side and brushing hay from his hair, he stepped toward his visitor. Smiling down at Ghrian, he took the bread from his hands and immediately took a bite.

"Mhmmm," he sighed with content. "This is really good!"

"Thank you, sir," Ghrian replied.

"Now, if you don't mind me asking, where is March?" Capall inquired.

Ghrian had hoped to avoid an explanation, but truthfully, he knew it was inevitable. "Well," he began, thinking carefully through his words. "He has been a difficult horse, as was expected."

Capall nodded slowly, waiting for him to continue.

"And we were finally beginning to bond. I rode him, but," Ghrian paused.

The surprise on Capall's face was unmistakable. He had failed at even getting close to riding March. "Wow. I have to admit. I am a little impressed. I wasn't sure you had it in ya," he said in jest. "But if you rode him once, why haven't you continued?" This time Capall's words were sincere.

Ghrian's ego deflated and he responded, "Well, after riding him for a way, he threw me. I haven't seen him since."

"Oh," Capall seemed genuinely disappointed. "Son," he said as he clapped his arm around Ghrian's shoulders. "I'm willing to offer you a discount on another horse for your troubles. Maybe a mare this time?"

Ghrian thanked him for his offer. "I think I will wait a while."

"I understand. But hey! While you're here, why don't you just take a look at our new arrivals?"

"I suppose there's no harm in looking," the young man conceded.

The two men walked through the stables to a large stall that housed a beautiful palomino mare. She had a silky cream mane and a thin white blaze. Laying beneath her on a bed of hay were two snow white foals. They were so small and seemed so frail. Ghrian could not imagine how they would survive the coming winter, though their coats were quite fitting for their untimely birth.

"They won't be ready for three years or so, but they are going to be stunners," Capall said proudly.

"They are certainly beautiful," Ghrian agreed.

"I'm hoping the daughter of the Royals will want one of these fillies. The other may be available for sale," Capall nudged.

It was a well-known fact that Lord Valdin's daughter was his favorite child. Every year on her birthday in late June, he threw a party so large that the entire Realm was invited. He always doted her with flowers and a menagerie of luxurious gifts, but her birthday celebration was all extravagance. A golden-white filly would make the perfect centerpiece for the event. Ghrian couldn't help but admire the horseman's audacity.

"Yes, Capall, I'm sure they will make fine horses. Perhaps, I'll return in three years." Ghrian shook Capall's hand and began the trek back to Oir's shop.

The stars had long taken dominion over the sky by the time Ghrian made it back to the tannery. Oir was hard at work when he entered the shop.

"You must have had a busy day," Oir said, without even looking up from her work bench.

Ghrian melted into a small wooden chair that sat in the corner of the room. "It was. I made all my deliveries and went all the way to Capall's stables."

"Wow. That *is* a busy day. I've just been completing some orders before I start preparations for the Winter Solstice Festival," Oir said, turning to Ghrian with a gleam in her eye.

Everyone enjoyed the Winter Solstice Festival, but no one as much as Oir. It was her favorite week of the year. Every year she tried to outdo herself with trinkets and sales. She always created one show stopping project in the hopes that it would bring more attention to her shop. Each year she successfully outdid herself, but the time and resource consuming product almost never paid off.

"Please tell me you aren't trying to top yourself this year," Ghrian said as he leaned his head back and closed his eyes.

"Do you know me at all?" Oir replied with a chirp.

Ghrian laughed. "Oir, you have so many show stopping products from past years. Why not just bring them out and save some work for yourself?"

"No! My idea for this year is the grandest yet!" she asserted.

"What tops a saddlebag with gold inlay?" Ghrian argued, remembering how much she had spent on last year's project.

"A saddle lined with precious stones," she smiled.

This time Ghrian opened his eyes to respond, "Oir you can't be serious. That will be more expensive than the gold!"

"But it is almost sure to sell! Nearly a third of the people in this town own a horse, and every person who travels into Lochta for the Festival has to get here somehow! Every merchant, every visitor, they all need saddles."

"Yes," Ghrian agreed. "But if they are making the journey here, chances are they already have one."

"But they'll want a better one," Oir argued stubbornly.

"There's really no reasoning with you," Ghrian huffed as he rested his eyes again.

Oir smiled and turned back to her desk. "Now I just have to wait to see what Dearthair brings me."

The name piqued Ghrian's interest. He hadn't thought of his other childhood friend in years. "Dearthair is coming to the Realm?"

"A few weeks before the Festival begins," Oir blushed.

"Huh, I haven't seen him since he left when we were children," Ghrian sat up and looked at Oir. Her blue eyes sparkled in the candlelight. "How do you know he's coming?"

"I may have received a few letters," Oir glowed as she spoke about him.

This was no surprise to Ghrian. Dearthair was often part of their childhood adventures. For most of their childhood, the three of them roamed the Realm of the Lake. They'd been like family. Dearthair was shy and aloof, but Oir had always fancied him. His father had been killed in Collitte one tragic night. No one knew what had happened, but everyone guessed it was the wolves, as was the common conclusion when someone vanished into the Forbidden Forest. Dearthair and his mother left Yoaruq not long after. His uncle, his mother's brother, was a mason in a town far east outside the Realm. His mother had been pregnant at the time and had no choice but to leave their home and move in with her brother and his wife. Ghrian recalled the day that they had left. Oir was heartbroken. The boys were twelve at the time, and it was a bittersweet goodbye.

"So, in these letters, he told you he was bringing you precious stones?" Ghrian asked.

Oir responded proudly, "Dearthair is now an apprentice to his uncle and has traveled to the mountains to mine. He may have mentioned a few stones that he would sell me for a reasonable price."

"It will be good to see him. It has been many years," Ghrian said, smiling at Oir's excitement.

"Would you like to see the plans?! We have a little over a month until the Festival so I'm going to get started soon."

Ghrian smiled, "Sure. I would love to see them."

Oir pulled the plans from her desk. Ghrian admired her handiwork. It was very detailed and elaborate. "I expected nothing less from you," he laughed.

The drawings were beautifully done. The saddle had a thick horn and intricate sides. Three spots for large stones rested just below the saddles horn. Oir had written to the side the colors that she wanted for each stone. Black onyx for the sides, and the precious blue stone, usually reserved for royalty, for the center.

Oir saw what he was focused on and commented, "I want that center stone to be the same color as the one used for the dye on that cord I gave you. Dearthair said that they are very hard to come by. They are found in the most dangerous part of the mountain range and have been guarded by some sort of demon, so he says. But he managed to get me one," Oir swooned.

"Oh yes, I'm sure he didn't exaggerate that at all," Ghrian smirked and rolled his eyes.

Oir snatched back her drawings. "It's going to be perfect. You're just jealous that you're not off on adventures in a perilous job like he is."

Ghrian sighed and gathered his things. "Well, my dearest Oir, I really should be heading back."

"Oh, don't be that way. Come, it's already dark. Eat and stay another night. I'll wake you early in the morning," she countered.

Ghrian reluctantly agreed, acting as if he had really meant to make the trek home in the dark. He was fast asleep before Oir had even straightened her desk.

The next morning, Ghrian awoke to the smell of freshly brewed coffee wafting through the air. Oir was already hard at work next to him. Ghrian arose and went to the kitchen for coffee. The morning air was fresh as it mixed with the sweet aroma of the brew. He inhaled deeply and returned to Oir's side.

"Thank you for the coffee and the hospitality, as usual my friend." He gulped down the coffee and set the ceramic mug on the wooden bench.

Oir looked up from her work and stood to hug Ghrian goodbye. He wrapped his arms around her and lifted her from the ground. She laughed as he set her back down.

"Anytime, Ghrian. You know you are always welcome," she smiled as she handed him his bridle, reins, and lead rope. "Hopefully March will return so you can let me know how well these work," she winked. "I know Tavi will come home soon, as well."

Ghrian stepped out into the morning light. The rising sun banished the encroaching darkness, shooting beams of light from the heavens, casting pink hues across the clouds, turning them from gray to a brilliant red. Oir watched as Ghrian headed down the already bustling cobblestone road in the early morning light. He had slung the leather tack over one shoulder and held the empty delivery bag in the opposite hand. She smiled as her handsome friend began the trek back to Yoaruq. She admired how often he traveled and how positive he managed to stay. In the face of all adversity, with every reason to be upset, he stayed optimistic.

The morning was pleasant. Ghrian traveled alone down the road that bridged the large city and his own village. As cobblestone turned to gravel, and gravel turned to dirt, the weight of the bridle bore down on him. It was not the physical weight of the leather, but rather the weight of disappointment with himself. He still wrestled with the fact that he had failed March and lost Tavi. He had truly believed that he alone would tame

March, and though he had made progress to that end, he feared that he may never know what could have been.

The day drew on and the sun rose high, but as hard as it tried, it could not drive the chill from the air. This had been the first clear day in weeks, and it was cold. The wind was blistering. Ghrian began to regret not bringing more loaves for himself. He had made the journey many times, but this trip seemed particularly lonely. For now, he was not only thinking of Tavi and March, but also of Dearthair. He had not spoken to his old friend for many years. Although he was excited to be reunited, he could not help but wonder how different things would be. Dearthair had left the Realm of the Lake, he had seen the cities beyond the forest. He had traveled. Ghrian longed to do the same, to see more of Domhaen. He yearned for freedom, to travel without destination and task. He wanted to traverse the mountain trail and wander to the end of the mountain range and beyond. Few knew what lay beyond the mountain range Beinn. Some said that it was all wasteland, desolate and cold. His mother had said that the West held great forests of red wood, the oldest trees to still live from the ancient days. The East, beyond the Kingdom of Miath, she had said, was indeed a wasteland, but it was not cold. Seas of sand stretched as far as the eye could see. To the South, was an entire nation on another continent. That knowledge had been hardly fathomable to Ghrian at such a young age, but he longed to learn more about the people beneath the sea. His mother had never spoken of the North and she never said if anyone lived beyond the mountains, no matter how many times he and Oir had asked.

As Ghrian daydreamed, he neared the humble entrance to Yoaruq. He strode through the quiet town, saying hello to those who greeted him. Upon reaching his home on the other side of Yoaruq, he saw his father. Mòr was in their small front yard, standing tall above the woven willow fence.

"Ah, my son," he said outstretching his arms. "How did the deliveries go?"

"They went well," Ghrian answered as he laid the burlap sack in his father's hands. "Oir has informed me that Dearthair is returning for the Festival."

"Oh, how wonderful," Mòr said. "I haven't seen that boy in many years."

"Neither have I," Ghrian replied, still lost in thought, looking out into the fields that spanned between Yoaruq and Vael.

As he absentmindedly scanned the carpet of green, something unexpected caught his eye. A spot of gray stuck out in his vision. Staring intently, Ghrian left his father, and headed further down the dirt road. Mòr shook his head and took the burlap sack inside with him. Ghrian walked slowly, trying to determine if his eyes were betraying him. As he drew closer, he was certain of what he saw.

It was March.

A wave of relief washed over him and he rushed toward the horse. Fortunately, the bridle, reins and lead rope still clung to his shoulder. Now he could keep March by his side for certain. He slowed as he neared the back of the gray stallion. He was surprised and excited to see that the horse seemed to be in good health and standing still. But as he drew closer, he noticed that something was holding March steady.

Calmly, Ghrian approached. From behind March's flanks, he could see only a pale white hand and raven black hair. He rounded the side of his horse and came face to face with a woman he had never before seen.

She had black hair richer than the deepest well of ink. It cascaded down her slender shoulders and nearly shone blue in the light of the afternoon sun. One small, pale hand rested on March's neck. It was badly scarred and brandished sharp, black nails. A strange deep green cloak covered her frame, and Ghrian could see that she was barefoot. He had never seen anything like her before. It was apparent by her skin tone that this woman did not often see the sun. Her complexion was pale and remarkably smooth. She had full pink lips and a peculiar line of freckles dotted her nose and cheeks. Her cheek bones were high and framed the most enchanting eyes the young man had ever seen. He was captivated by their strange orange hue. It was as if he were gazing into a blazing fire.

The woman turned to him, her straight, black hair rolling in waves over her shoulders. Ghrian was speechless. The two strangers stood there, eyes locked, both trying to determine what to say.

Part 2

Chapter Seven

Shaerico returned to her town, having been unsuccessful in her search for the pond. The rain had slowed by the time she reached Dorchas and evening was upon the forest. As habit for the majority of residents in the quiet village, Shaerico headed to the pub. The tattered roof lay heavy with rain. Its woven canopy dripped a monotonous song that broke the silence on the streets, but as she passed through the courtyard to the interior of the bar, the roar of voices grew loud.

Beanrua sat atop a stool with a pint in hand. Her time behind the bar had ended and she had immediately turned around and began drinking. She sat behind the massive wooden bar top. It was a section from a tree that had been felled by Mother for exactly this purpose. Its edges were rough and knotted. It was uneven and gnarly, but its surface had been glossed smooth. Beanrua turned and threw her arms wide as she saw Shaerico approach. Reluctantly, Shaerico walked into her friend's embrace, lightly patting her back. She was not a fan of physical touch. To her, it was the opposite of comforting, or inviting. Touch felt suffocating and unnecessary.

"You cleaned up nice," Shaerico commented.

"Yeah, yeah. It wasn't that bad of a brawl," Beanrua responded with an eye roll. "Hopefully, he'll think twice before getting handsy and demanding again."

Shaerico laughed and turned to the man behind the bar, "Beoir, an ale please."

"Absolutely," the giant man responded. His long brown beard glided along the glossy bar top as he turned to pour the ale.

Beoir was the other barkeep at the Dorchas pub, alongside Beanrua, and he certainly took his duty more seriously than his partner. He was easily the largest man in the village. Surprisingly, he was also the most well-mannered. The people of Dorchas were generally far from mild-tempered. Fights arose often, with little to no reason. Shaerico rather liked Beoir. He never uttered an unkind word and rarely lifted a fist.

The only issue with him was that he would also never stop a fight. Of all men, he was certainly the most capable of ending a brawl, but he never wanted to be involved in any controversy. He avoided all avoidable confrontation.

"So, Shaerico," Beanrua began "Where did you go off to today? Please tell me you found food. You must be starving after missing the last meal."

"I just went for a walk," Shaerico replied, surprised by her own sudden secrecy.

"In the rain?" Beanrua asked suspiciously.

"Yes, I rather enjoy the rain." At least that was not a lie.

"Uh huh. You're so strange," Beanrua giggled into her beer as she took a swig. "Well, our next meal isn't for another few days, so, want to go for a midnight hunt?" Beanrua nudged her friend excitedly.

"Sure, sure. It may be nice to have some company," Shaerico smiled.

"Perfect! I want to know your best spots for finding hares," Beanrua replied.

Shaerico smiled and for a moment, she envisioned the green swath of grass that rolled like an invitation to the Realm of the Lake.

"Maybe we could head to the base of the mountain? I haven't been there in a while," Shaerico said. She had this strange desire to guard the mysterious pond. She wanted to tell Beanrua, but she knew that her boisterous friend was incapable of keeping secrets. Besides, the creek that trickled from the mountain was surely better water. The trail to the Western side of the woods was also the best spot in the forest to hunt for Shaerico's favorite meal, deer.

The two women sat, drank, and talked until night fell.

"I'll come by your house on the way out, it's closest to the mountain trail anyhow," Beanrua said as the pair walked into the twilight. "See you then."

As the sun faded and darkness fell, the village grew quiet and cold.

Alphaline forbade her children from leaving Dorchas past nightfall, aside from those who were chosen for the organized hunting party. No one stayed out late. No one went out at night without reason and express permission. As soon as the sun set, all in the village closed, including the pub, the single eatery, the only seamstress, and everything else. Alphaline would prowl the streets to make sure her nearly thirty children were safe from harm. Beanrua knew this. She crept from her home and circled back behind the buildings where the ancient ruins provided welcome cover. She raced to Shaerico's abode on the outskirts of Dorchas. The black-haired beauty was already waiting outside. Beanrua caught the glint of her eyes in the moonlight and the pair made their way down the mountain trail in silence.

The moonlight split the trees, bathing the path in a soft silver glow. The dark mass of foliage became a black blur as they raced down the overgrown pathway. A few hours passed and the two slowed as the mountain came into view. The calming trickle of the nearby creek drew them off the path and deeper into the woods. The sweet smell of fresh water tickled their noses upon approach. They drank their fill in the moonlight and then turned to the forest, ready for the hunt. After a few moments of silence, there was a rustle to the left of the creek, back closer to the trail. The two looked at one another. Shaerico motioned for Beanrua to head the hunt. They spoke with their eyes and their bodies, in order to not disturb their prey. Beanrua moved in, circling the unsuspecting deer. The young doe was munching on a small patch of grass at the very edge of the trail. Her white tail twitched as she continued to graze without a care. Beanrua stepped out slowly from behind her. She went for the kill, but just missed the doe as it leapt further into the woods. Unfortunately for the deer, she was leaping to her death. Shaerico waited in the shadows. As the doe bounded forward, anticipating her freedom, Shaerico matched her movements. Soon she was cornered against the base of the mountain. One final leap and her fate was sealed. Moments later, the pair enjoyed their feast.

The next day the sleepy town awoke as usual. Nearly everyone headed to the single eatery for coffee and pastries. No one bothered to name any of the few shops that existed in Dorchas and no one paid. The community was so tight, primarily out of necessity, that money was hardly ever used. Little of it existed still in the town, and what remained from the days of old had little value to a people who never ventured into society. All was shared and all had responsibilities, a unique role to play. Lili ran the eatery, but nearly everyone contributed to its contents in one way or another. When Lili finished baking or cooking, whatever it was that she felt like creating, someone else would serve. After the meal, someone else would clean up. Even in spite of the frequent fights, Dorchas residents knew their places well.

After the previous night, neither Beanrua nor Shaerico wanted breakfast. The two friends made their way into the large building that housed the eatery. The counter itself was to the far left, in front of a large window that spanned nearly the entire face of the building's first floor. At one point in Dorchas' history, this space had been a great hall and gathering area.

"Good morning, Lili," Shaerico addressed the spritely blonde behind the stone counter.

"Good morning, Shaerico!" Lili chimed. "What are you in the mood for this morning?"

"Oh, just coffee," Shaerico responded with a smile.

Lili was unique in Dorchas. She was odd in that she did not match the usual countenance of her siblings who remained cloaked in boredom, despair, angst, or anger. Lili was always happy. One could assume that her job was part of the reason she always smiled. She ran the great hall not because she had to, but because she wanted to. She thoroughly enjoying cooking and the community her establishment created. It gave her purpose, something that few people in Dorchas felt that they had.

Lili handed Shaerico a clay mug full of the black liquid she often craved. Coffee in hand, Shaerico sat at a table closest to the window. She looked down at the brew that swirled like the dark clouds outside.

"How about you, Beanrua?" Lili asked.

"Got any beer over here?" Beanrua said jokingly.

"You know good and well I don't serve any of that," Lili huffed.

"I know, I know. I'm just messing with you, Lil'. I'll just have a coffee and um, what are those?" Beanrua pointed to a flaky yellow pastry on the shelf behind the counter.

Lili responded with a smile, "Oh! Those are lemon tarts. I just made them this morning!"

"Lord Lil', how early do you get up?!" the red head responded in shock. The sun had risen only an hour prior.

"I like my mornings. There's a certain joyful energy about them," Lili said as she handed Beanrua her order. "Let me know how you like it!"

Beanrua joined Shaerico at the table. She watched as her friend sipped the warm, bitter drink slowly. Shaerico was lost deep in thought, questions swirled through her mind like the specs of ground coffee in her mug.

Why did she feel such an intense need to protect the knowledge of that pool? She was certain that Alphaline must know of it. Mother had been in the woods longer than any of them. What was she hiding? Maybe she knew of something else that the residents of Dorchas should fear, and that's why she didn't allow travel at night? Maybe something lurked beneath the crystal water.

"What are you thinking about so intensely over there?" Beanrua whispered as she shoved the remainder of her lemon tart into her mouth.

Shaerico was preparing to answer when Beanrua interrupted her by yelling out to Lili, "That was delicious, Lil'! You should definitely make them again."

Shaerico looked at her friend, watching as the crumbs tumbled from her pursed lips.

"Sorry, she told me to tell her what I thought."

Shaerico simply laughed and lightly shook her head. Beanrua may have been a bit moody, but she was equally entertaining.

"So, what were you thinking about?" Beanrua continued.

Shaerico leaned over the table and began with a whisper, "Have you ever thought about why we aren't allowed out at night?"

"I always assumed that it was for our safety," Beanrua shrugged as she sipped her drink.

"But what if there's more to it? What if Mother is hiding something from us?" Shaerico asked.

Beanrua knew well the skepticism that made its home in Shaerico's jaded heart, but it was never acceptable to question Alphaline. "Hush, someone may hear you," she spewed as she leaned across the table as well.

Shaerico continued, "I'm not necessarily saying that she is, but don't we have the right to openly explore the woods for ourselves?"

It was at that moment that the elegant white-haired woman joined her children for breakfast. Beanrua eyed Shaerico, urging her to keep quiet.

"Good morning, my darlings," the silky voice crooned. Her golden-brown cape flowed behind her as she made her way to Lili's counter.

"Lili, dear, I'd love some tea this fine morning," she crooned.

"Of course, Mother," Lili replied.

The place had gone silent upon her entry. Every resident of the Forbidden Forest adored Alphaline, but her children had as much fear for her as admiration. She had strict rules for her people, and when she was disappointed, she made it known. Her usually warm demeanor would harden to icy words. Shaerico recalled a time when she and Bruid had tried to enter into the Realm of the Lake. The two children wanted nothing more than to explore outside the forest, to test their boundaries, as all children do. The siblings had spotted some villagers playing in the fields. Bruid had taken the first step. The moment his feet had left the forest, Alphaline was upon them. She had lifted Bruid by his arm and thrown him back into the forest. Then she turned to Shaerico and breathed some icy threats. Bruid had run home, bloodied and angry, but Shaerico had stayed. She stood there, at the edge of Collitte with Alphaline, looking out into the world she longed to be a part of, imagining a world of more than thirty people. Shaerico had been very young at the time. She and the other children had been under Alphaline's care for almost three years. That moment had been the moment that sealed Shaerico's place in Dorchas. She was rebellious and unafraid, and Mother did not like that.

Shaerico watched as Alphaline sipped her tea. The others resumed their conversations and soon the eatery returned to its normal pace. Shaerico couldn't help but think how lonely it must be for Alphaline. She had been the only adult for many years and had spent her life in darkness compared to what she had once known. She had witnessed the downfall of the great city of Dorchas. Though no one knew how long ago that had been, nor how old Alphaline was, it seemed that the pale woman had been alone for decades. Shaerico longed to ask her questions, but was afraid of Alphaline's response. She remembered brief excerpts of her childhood, and knew they were not memories one would want to recall.

"I've lost you again," Beanrua said as she watched her friend stare a hole into Alphaline. "You really shouldn't glare at her like that."

Shaerico shook herself from her thoughts and looked to her concerned friend. Her furrowed red brows made Shaerico laugh.

"Beanrua, stop. She already dislikes me, there's no more harm to be done." Shaerico stood and returned her mug to the counter. "What shall we do today?"

That question was one of continuous thought. There was very little to do in Dorchas that had not already been done time and time again.

"Hmm," Beanrua contemplated. "Well, naturally, we will end up at the pub. I do need to work the afternoon shift for Beoir, but we could return to the creek?" She stood and followed Shaerico to the door, whispering in her ear. "We had so much luck there last night."

Shaerico smiled and nodded. It was a long trip and would take up most of the day. "I think that's a fine idea."

The path looked much different in the daylight. The brush was still thick, but the visibility through the woods was quite far. Beanrua and Shaerico chatted as they walked, a stark contrast to the night before. They discussed the recent brawls that had occurred, what they were over, and who won. Although the daily responsibilities of the villagers rarely changed, the authority shifted every few months between the largest males as they continued to grow and age. Apparently, Cain was working his way up and Beanrua did not approve.

"You took him down, really. I don't understand why you don't rank higher," Beanrua said.

"I don't want to," Shaerico replied. "Besides, Alphaline would never give me any major responsibility aside from hunting duty. And she certainly does not want me in a place of authority."

Beanrua grumbled in disagreement and responded, "Maybe she wouldn't want to, but she would have to if you proved yourself worthy."

"I know what you're doing, Bean', and it's not going to work. I'm not starting any worthless fights for meaningless titles that accompany more work," Shaerico interrupted.

"But please," Beanrua whined, clasping her hands together. "You're so brutal! I bet you could take Cain down again with ease."

"I said no. Not unless it's absolutely necessary, and because you hate him does not count as necessary," she smiled at her heated friend.

They continued to walk in silence as the redhead fumed. The day was overcast, but a few rays of sunlight found their way to the forest floor. The woods were deep in the throes of fall. Vibrant burgundy, yellow, and orange leaves swirled along the pathway in front of them. One of Shaerico's favorite attributes of the season was the transition of temperature. She craved the cold. The sharp sting in her lungs made her feel alive. She enjoyed the biting wind on her face that replaced the awful sweat of summer and the peaceful silence that fell over the forest when the cold set in. These were the things that made Shaerico's soul content.

A few hours passed, and the mountain came into view. It was much grander in the daylight. Through the half-barren trees, its summit became visible. Towering in the distance, it looked down upon the forest.

Shaerico had always wondered how it would feel to stand on that precipice, but as one could imagine, the people of Dorchas were not permitted to travel the mountain trail. It had remained untouched for decades and its entry point was hardly visible amongst the brush.

"There are too many dangers. I don't wish the wrath of the mountain upon my children." Alphaline's words rang in Shaerico's ears. What was she hiding?

The creek's soft rush filled their ears. They made their way through the thicket and sat at its bank. Cupping their hands, they drank the sweet mountain water. They talked and laughed and drank until they grew tired. Shaerico braced her arms behind her and rested as Beanrua collapsed in a dramatic heap onto the lush bed of fallen leaves below her. Shaerico watched as her friend drifted off to sleep, envious of her uncanny ability to sleep anywhere. Shaerico laid back and tried to do the same. Instead, she ended up staring at the sky above, tracing the deep blue-gray clouds with her eyes, wondering what it would be like to join them in their freedom.

Some time passed and Shaerico was just beginning to succumb to sleep when a foreign scent drifted in on the air overhead. Beanrua caught the scent shortly after and sprung awake. It was not a pleasant aroma.

"What is that?" Beanrua said, rubbing the sleep from her eyes.

Shaerico inhaled deeper, "I'm not sure."

Both women stood and began searching for the source of the smell. Following her keen nose, Shaerico came to the base of the mountain. The source became evident before it was seen. Dark red stains dotted the sparkling gray and white slope. Flies had already gathered over a once white bed of flowers, now red with blood. Beanrua came up behind Shaerico, peeking curiously over her shoulder. The stench was nearly unbearable, but intrigue drew them forward. It had been many years since most Dorchas residents had seen an outsider, alive or dead.

It was unclear if the mangled man had been killed before his fall from the mountain or if the fall itself had killed him. Beanrua stepped back at the sight, but Shaerico approached, driven by curiosity. What or who did this man encounter on that mountain that brought upon his demise? Was Alphaline right to forbid its ascent?

Shaerico lifted her eyes to the mountain's peak, straining against the glare of the gray blanket above, attempting to spot the culprit through the dying leaves. She couldn't see much of anything. She knelt down next to the corpse, studying his dark features and clothing. They were very different from the cloaks and robes that adorned the people of Dorchas. The man wore a linen shirt tucked into plumed pants, held together with two strange straps of leather. A small black leather pouch stuck out from under his matching belt. Shaerico pulled the pouch from the man's lifeless body. She emptied the contents into her hand and felt the cold of coin on her palm. Shaerico had never seen gold coins. She returned them to the pouch and tied the pouch to the cord that held her green cloak tight.

Shaerico was interested in all of this, but what attracted her attention the most was a single stone in the man's left hand. He had obviously been gripping it tightly, as his knuckles were white, but his grip had been loosened by the impact of his fall. The gray stone sparkled in the afternoon light, glistening a beautiful, mysterious, and yet somehow familiar blue. Shaerico studied the hand that held it. Scorch marks marred his left palm. It was as if the stone had burst into flame. Was this the cause of the man's death or did this cause his fall?

Beanrua inched closer, seeing that something had caught her brave friend's attention. Shaerico hesitated as she debated taking the stone. She was curious. What was it about this rock that had burned this man? So many questions raced through her mind.

"What happened?" Beanrua said, as confused and intrigued as Shaerico.

"Best I can tell, this man fell from the mountain. It's hard to say the cause, but look at this," she pointed down to the stone. "It left burn marks."

"Woah. That's a pretty little pebble," Beanrua commented, ignoring the fact that it most likely had something to do with the man's death. She leaned down and reached for the stone, but Shaerico grabbed her hand.

"Wait," she demanded. "Use something other than your hands to pick it up. Just in case."

Beanrua looked at her and nodded, "What should I use?"

"I don't know," Shaerico admitted.

They both scoured the ground for anything that would work. Beanrua picked up a leaf, "Maybe this?"

Shaerico looked at her friend, "Seriously? This stone potentially scorched a man's hand and you want to pick it up with a wet leaf?"

They both laughed.

"Oh! I have an idea," Beanrua exclaimed, as she brought the corner of her thick blue cloak to her lips. In one swift motion, she tore off a piece with her canines.

"Well, that's one way to do it," Shaerico sighed.

"What?" Beanrua said to her condescending friend. "I can get Cló to mend it later."

Shaerico shrugged her shoulders and took the fabric in her hands. Leaning forward, she wrapped the stone in the corner of the cloak. The stone was still hot.

"This would have been far too hot to touch," she said. She stood and dropped the stone into Beanrua's pocket. "Make sure Mother doesn't see this. We still don't know what it is or what happened here."

"Shouldn't we report him though?" Beanrua asked.

Shaerico contemplated this for a moment, weighing her options. If Alphaline discovered that they knew about this and did not report it, she would be suspicious, not to mention furious.

"I think it would be best."

The friends agreed to tell Alphaline of their discovery upon their return, but promised to keep the stone a secret. Beanrua was excited to have something sparkly of her own. Aside from a small iron donkey that she and Shaerico had found amongst the ruins as children, this was her only nonessential possession.

Upon their return to Dorchas, Beanrua went immediately to her home. She had to prepare for her shift. They both knew that this meant she was hiding her precious new trinket. Unfortunately for Shaerico, that left her in charge of explaining their find to Alphaline.

Shaerico entered the pub, knowing good and well she would not find Mother there.

"Beoir, a drink please?" she addressed the burly man upon entry. She knew that she needed a drink before any one-on-one conversation could be had with Alphaline.

Beoir brought her a beer and returned to his other customers. In one gulp, she downed the contents and set the mug back behind the bar. She sighed as she stood and wiped her cloak to free the dirt and leaves that clung to it.

"Have you seen Mother this afternoon?" she asked Beoir.

"I believe I saw her in the fields earlier," he said. "I'd start there."

Shaerico thanked him and headed to the fields. Since the residents of Dorchas were not allowed to leave the forest, Alphaline made sure to grow all of the necessities for her people. Although there was not much variety, the clearing behind the pub held all of Dorchas' crops. It was sufficient for the small clan of people, as their diet consisted primarily upon meat. There was wheat and barley, garlic, squash, potatoes, and an assortment of other vegetables that were encased by a few spindly fruit trees.

Alphaline's white hair was visible from the road. Her slender figure swayed in the fields like a tree in the wind as she gathered potatoes from the dirt. She heard Shaerico approach and stood. "Yes, my child?"

Shaerico rarely approached Alphaline of her own accord. "I have something to report," she stated.

Alphaline cocked her head. There was hardly much to report in Collitte anymore, aside from the results of the hunting party.

"Beanrua and I went down to the creek today," she began, trying to gauge Alphaline's response. The icy blue-eyed woman simply stared, waiting to hear more.

"We drank and rested by the creek until a foul scent disrupted us. When we went to discover its source, we found a man."

Shaerico could see Alphaline's jaw clench. It was obvious that she did not like where this was going. Still, she reacted calmly. "Go on," she said.

"At first, we were hesitant to approach, but eventually we went to check it out. He appeared to have fallen from the mountain."

Alphaline went silent, her lips drawing a thin taught line. Shaerico could see the light behind her eyes grow dim. She could sense the mix of fear and anger that welled up inside her Mother. By this, Shaerico's suspicions were confirmed: Alphaline was indeed hiding something.

"What would you like us to do," Shaerico said, her curiosity piqued.

"Nothing," Alphaline barked. "I will take care of this myself. Tell the others we are only using the well for the next few weeks. No one goes near that mountain."

Shaerico started to protest, but was promptly hushed. She began to regret telling Alphaline of their find.

"Mother, we have to find food. That creek is the best source. All animals for miles go there to drink," she continued, pushing her luck. "That is the only natural source of water the animals of the forest have. Where else will they go?"

Alphaline had not been suspicious of her daughter until this comment.

She drew close to Shaerico, standing over her and replied, "We have the well. Prey will be drawn to us."

Shaerico backed away and nodded, now more convinced than ever that she knew of the pool in the woods.

"So be it. I will alert the others."

When Shaerico returned to the pub, Beanrua was already behind the counter. Shaerico motioned for a beer. Beanrua approached, immediately noticing her friend's cold demeanor.

"I'm assuming you told Mother."

"Yes," Shaerico replied.

"And?"

"And we are not allowed near the mountain, nor the stream," Shaerico turned to her friend and took the mug of beer from her outstretched hand.

Beanrua's expression turned from playful, to troubled. "Not allowed near the creek? But where will we get water from? And those are the best hunting grounds, where will we feed?"

"Don't ask me, Beanrua. I brought all this up to Alphaline and she stood firm in her decision. We are to use the well," Shaerico sighed.

"But the well hasn't been used in ages! Who knows if that water's even any good?" Beanrua scowled.

Shaerico sighed and looked at her friend, "Hush, I know. This is all suspicious to me as well. Something has her spooked."

"Then I guess we all should be," Beanrua said quietly.

Alphaline was an attentive leader and may have even seemed timid or quiet to those outside Dorchas, but she was never frightened. One night, when the children were still young, the village had been attacked by armed men, claiming that one of their friends had been slain in the woods. Without hesitation, or further questioning, Alphaline had taken care of them in minutes. She was swift and accurate in her attacks. So, if she was on edge, everyone in Dorchas should be.

Shaerico leaned back on her barstool, contemplating her next move. She wanted to follow Alphaline to see her reaction to the fallen man. If she was so scared, why was she adamant about heading alone into the woods? It made no sense. Something was amiss.

The following afternoon, the scene was similar to the night before. Shaerico had told her siblings of the command to repair and drink only from the well. The repairs had been made, but no questions had been answered. Alphaline had yet to return from her trip to the stream and everyone was tense. The pub was quieter than it had ever been. Shaerico spared the details of what they saw, but people had guessed someone had been found dead. Some were simply unhappy at the missed opportunity to see an outsider from beyond the forest.

Finally, after nearly a full day, Alphaline returned. Many of her children rushed to her side as she entered the village. Some asked questions, a few brought her food and drink. She answered their questions vaguely, but consumed nothing. The white woman looked even more pale. Her face betrayed her and for the first time in their lives, the remaining people of Dorchas could see their Mother's fear. She tried to tell the others that everything was alright. Shaerico had never seen her like this before. She was weak and she was angry. Something was coming.

"Where is Shaerico?" she said, nearly a growl under her breath. Lili pointed to the doorway of the pub, where Shaerico stood. "Come, my child. I must talk with you," Alphaline motioned.

Shaerico headed toward her reluctantly but was driven by curiosity. Alphaline dismissed the others. She told them to have a final round of drinks, then to head home. It was a full moon tonight, and no one was permitted to be outside for any reason.

The two women walked down the road until they came to the edge of the village. Beanrua's building was on their left, the fields to their right. Alphaline confronted Shaerico until her back lay flat against the stone wall of the old storehouse.

"I have a few questions for you, my curious daughter," she hissed. She was no longer trying to hide her emotions. Her icy gaze seemed as if it were trying to pierce through Shaerico's flesh to uncover the truth.

"Yes?" Shaerico replied, stiffly.

"I'm assuming that you searched the man?" she demanded.

"I did, I found a few coins," Shaerico replied starkly.

"Anything else?"

Shaerico was a bit surprised that Alphaline glossed over the coins.

She began to realize that stone may become more of an issue than she or Beanrua had originally thought.

"I was surprised by his clothing. The people outside the forest wear such strange attire," Shaerico shared.

At this stall, Alphaline lost her patience entirely. She wrapped her long white fingers around Shaerico's neck and lifted her from the ground. "I asked if you found anything else?"

Shaerico had momentarily considered giving Alphaline the stone after explaining Mother's panic to Beanrua, but that ship had now sailed. Glaring at Alphaline from above, she managed to growl through the crushing grip, "There was nothing else."

Frustrated, Alphaline let her daughter drop to the ground. Shaerico rubbed her neck as she caught her breath.

"You didn't see anything in that man's scorched hand?" Alphaline continued.

"Only dust," Shaerico said firmly. "I thought it strange that he had obviously been wounded by something and then thrown from the mountain, but I know nothing of the people outside Dorchas. I don't know what sort of magic entangles them."

Alphaline looked into the woods back toward the Realm. "The people no longer deal in magic."

Shaerico studied Alphaline's face. This time she saw confusion and pain. What was really going on here?

"Go back to your home, daughter. The moon is nearly risen. And tonight, it is full. You should not be out." With that, Alphaline disappeared into the faded light of the rising moon. The ominous silver-blue glow cast suspicion over the raven-haired daughter of Dorchas. Why was Mother so concerned with a single stone? There was something critical she was not telling her family.

Shaerico did not heed her mother's command. She did not return home that night. She needed answers, and she had a feeling she knew where she may find them.

Shaerico set out to find the forbidden pool. She was even more motivated now than before. She would not fail. Fueled by both rage and inquisition, she pressed on through the woods. The warmth of sunlight had faded, and the full moon was beginning to rise above the trees.

As Shaerico walked, she came across a spider, clad in elegant yellow and black stripes. She stopped and gazed at its incredible web. The moonlit rays pierced through the branches, illuminating the intricacies and immense detail of its craft. Not long after, a small moth trapped itself in the spider's web. But the spider was patient. It waited as the moth drew deeper and deeper into its deathbed. After a moment, the spider pounced. In a motion too quick for the eye to see, the spider began encasing the moth with its silky thread. Every time the predator would pause the moth would break free of some strands, decimating part of the spider's home. Shaerico leaned back, wondering to herself who would be the victor as the battle raged on. The spider driven by hunger or the moth with a will to live, driven by the possibility of freedom. She continued on, leaving the battle of life or death.

The moon was now full. The crisp fall air ripped leaves from their perch and thrust them in a whimsical whirlwind to the forest floor. A bed of grass and fallen debris blanketed the ground. Collitte was quiet. The birds did not sing their evening song. The bugs of the woods made no noise. The only sounds that could be heard were the soft thud of a predator's paws and that of a beating heart.

Thump-thump. Thump. Thump-thump. Thump.

The moon hung high over the turquoise water. It shone on a lone black wolf and an unsuspecting man below. It watched with the stars as a battle raged on beneath them. The chilling chorus of a fight for life and death filled the air. Blood and water. Flesh and fur.

Then all went silent and two bodies emerged from the crystal blue pool.

The disoriented woman awoke from a daze, gasping for breath. She was freezing cold and covered in icy droplets of water, sitting outside of her home. The night was a blur. Had she found the peculiar pond? Had Alphaline followed her and punished her somehow, trying to give her frostbite for her disobedience?

Shaerico stood and wrapped her frigid arms around her cold, naked body. She opened the door to her home. Bruid was sleeping soundly in a heap under two or three blankets. The confused and exhausted woman walked to the kitchen and downed a glass of water. She tried to recall the events of the night, but it was all too cloudy. As she was drinking, she felt something strange nestled in her back teeth. She set down the glass and reached her slender hand down her throat. Astonished, she pulled a small turquoise band from between her teeth. It was a beautiful, rich blue. She twisted the cord in her fingers, feeling the soft leather, and wondering where it had come from.

She tied the beautiful cord around her slender wrist, hoping she could use it to track down some answers. She wrapped herself in a large black blanket and laid down on her bed. "Why am I like this? It's a full moon," she wondered to herself.

Her mind raced as she tried to determine what had happened. She waged war on her clouded memory until she drifted off to sleep.

The next morning, Shaerico awoke to birds chirping and an empty house. She wondered where Bruid was, as he was not usually an early riser. When she stood up, she realized that she was naked. Slowly, the events of the night returned to her, rushing through her mind in a blur. She looked down at her wrist. Her new bracelet shone in the morning light and concern returned to her. She had to find out what happened.

Per usual, she met Beanrua at the Great Hall after finding an old cloak of Bruid's to wear until she located her own. The two sat in silence over coffee. Her friend could sense something was troubling her. Beanrua asked Shaerico what happened the night before and why her cloak was gone.

Shaerico answered honestly, "I do not know."

After breakfast, Shaerico headed back out into the woods. She needed her cloak and was even more in need of an explanation. She had not found the answers she was looking for the night before, and only hoped that the mysterious place could shed light on questions both old and new. The sky above was like a blazing fire. The sunrise had dispersed rays of red across the horizon. The brilliant display of pink was a backdrop to the deep evergreens and golden-edged leaves of the dying trees. She walked on, crunching debris below her. She was achingly cold, as Bruid's old cloak was far too large for her.

By mid-afternoon, she made it to the ring of lilac rose bushes. Pushing through the thorns, she saw the brilliant pond. Hung on the furthest rose bush, caught between the peculiar violet flowers, she found her cloak. Throwing off Bruid's, she draped the familiar fabric around her shoulders and looked back at the pond. It was glistening under the midday sun, reflecting the rays, sending ripples of light to the canopy of trees above. Shaerico drew closer. A familiar scent caught her attention as she circled the pond. She was almost to the rock face that encased the far side of the water and housed the slow trickling falls, when she found the source. A deep reddish-brown liquid stained a large area of grass adjacent to the crystal blue water. Shaerico knelt beside the pool and put her nose to the stain. It was blood.

What was worse, she recognized the smell. The man she had met and the turquoise band she now wore on her wrist both held the same scent. She began to panic. Never before had she not been able to remember a hunt. Shaerico had received answers, but not at all what she had expected or wanted.

She sat at the water's edge mortified, hoping that there was another explanation. Suddenly, something broke her concentration. A rustle came from the trees behind her. She turned and stood, half expecting Alphaline ready to attack. To her surprise, it was a stunning white deer. Its rich brown eyes stared at Shaerico as its soft ears twitched in the breeze. It was completely unafraid. Shaerico slowly stepped toward the doe, but the calm creature turned and bounded back into the woods.

As strange as the sight was, Shaerico needed to focus on the task at hand. She had to have answers, not just vague suspicions. She needed to know if the man was still alive. If he was, she had to find him.

Shaerico knew that Alphaline would be furious if she found out that her daughter had been outside the woods, but she no longer cared. Alphaline had obviously been keeping secrets from her people. Shaerico needed answers, and perhaps this man had them. She knew so little of the people outside of Dorchas. It was time she learned the truth of the outside world for herself.

Hours passed as more and more questions spun in Shaerico's mind. Her thoughts had twisted into a column of confusion that she could not settle. Eventually, the fading afternoon light pierced through the thicket of underbrush. She could see the blanket of green between the trees indicating open fields. Excited and nervous, she followed the scent further along the line of trees that stood as a barrier between the Realm and the cursed woods of Collitte. As she walked, she looked out over the fields. In the distance, she could see a village. Its quaint buildings lined a dirt and cobblestone road. She couldn't help but wonder what life must be like there out in the sun.

Soon the scent became strong. Her stomach churned and her heart lurched with excitement. Her keen sense of smell led her to something entangled in a thicket of aspens. She was surprised to find not a man, but a giant gray beast. Shaerico had never seen a creature like it before. To her, it resembled a great, fat deer. It had thick hooves and velvety black ears, but it was much larger than any deer she had ever seen, and it was loud. The mysterious creature made a noise like a falling tree. It bellowed as it thrashed in the underbrush. As she neared, she saw that one of its hind hooves was caught in a twisted bed of vines and thorns. Shaerico slowly made her way to the beast. He was stocky, yet graceful in his movements, even in his obvious distress. She drew closer until she could see his hot breath billowing from his flared nostrils. As she neared the animal, his wild eyes turned to gaze at her. Flowing white locks fell from his neck and lined his hooves. Shaerico was mesmerized. This creature smelled so strongly of the man she had met in the clearing. She inhaled deeply as she laid her hand on the soft dappled hide of the thrashing animal.

"Maybe you will lead me to him," she whispered to the beast. She stroked his side, trying to determine the best way to free him without causing harm. He settled at her touch.

"It will be alright. I will free you, just hold still," she said to him.

She kept her hand on his soft coat as she walked down his body. He had stopped fighting and Shaerico could see the vine of thorns dug deep into his hind leg. The thorns had torn the skin and were wrapped in his white feathers, now stained red with blood. She used her sharp nails to slice through the vines and remove the thorns that ensnared him. As soon as he was free, the great creature lunged from the thicket out into the open field. Shaerico watched as he pranced in the tall grass, elated by his freedom.

"Now it's your turn to help me," she said as he circled back to her. "Perhaps you can help me find the man I am looking for."

The great beast trotted toward her until his soft muzzle pressed against her arm. Shaerico smiled and stroked his velvety black ears. She could still smell the man's scent, so she knew he must not be far. The woman could sense that this creature was not like any she had met before. He was not fearful like a deer, nor was he aggressive like a bear. He had a depth to him that she had never experienced. She sensed that he was eager for freedom, but also for companionship. Shaerico wondered how he had come to be separated from the man.

The two spent the afternoon together, exploring the fields that lined the woods. Shaerico was still far too apprehensive to enter any villages, so she remained at a safe distance. She had all but forgotten her purpose for

entering the Realm as she relished her quiet moments in the open sun. The horse had grown rather comfortable with the foreign woman. She seemed to have no interest in taming or riding him.

The day drew on. It was late afternoon. Shaerico knew that she could not stay with this wonderful new creature. As she began to say her goodbye, a strong and familiar scent wafted between them. She was taken by surprise and froze, trying to determine her next move. Sure, she had planned to find him, but not now, and certainly not at nightfall. She had become distracted. She heard the slow fall of footsteps and held the horse steady. He had begun to get uneasy, as he felt her nerves. Shaerico had dreamed of this moment in secrecy for her entire life. For years she longed to know of the outside world, of life in the Realm. The usually steady beat of her heart fluttered and as the young man rounded the horse, she got a glimpse of him for the first time in daylight.

Although Dorchas was predominately male, she was rarely attracted to anyone, but this man struck her as remarkably handsome. His deep golden eyes were framed by red-brown locks that fell wildly around his face. His mustache sat poised beneath his nose and full lips lay nestled amongst a short, lush beard. His features were strong, but also held a soft kindness. He was much taller than her, though not nearly as tall as some of the men in Dorchas. His clothes were strange, like the man she had found in the woods, but she could see beneath them that he was quite fit. She scanned his body for the wounds that she expected, but somehow, he seemed completely unharmed.

He looked as surprised to see her as she was to see him, maybe even more so. She stared back at him, wondering what to say.

A hailstorm of thoughts brewed in her mind. Should she ask him what happened? How was he completely healed? She was certain that she saw the stain of his blood this morning. Would he even remember her?

The two strangers stood, their eyes locked and minds racing. They had no idea that the questions were just beginning. They had no idea of the adventure on which they were about to embark.

Chapter Eight

The black-haired woman and the red-bearded man had just met and were already at a loss for words. Not only was Ghrian struck by her beauty, but he was also plagued with questions.

Why was she here? Where did she come from?

Shaerico had numerous inquisitions of a different kind. She was frozen by the possibility that he did remember her. Although, it certainly seemed that he did not. She lowered her hand from the horse's withers and turned to face the young man. Ghrian decided to break the silence that had seemed an eternity, and spoke first with the only thing that he could think to say, "Where did you find my horse?" It was a burning question, though not the one he truly wished to ask.

Shaerico's bright eyes flitted back to March. "Horse. So, that's what you are."

Ghrian gazed at her, confused. Has she really never seen a horse? He lowered the bridle, reins and lead rope to the ground. March shifted his weight away from Ghrian. The man watched as this mysterious woman settled his horse.

"How did you?" he began, but changed his question midthought. "Where did you find him?"

Shaerico pointed to the edge of the woods. "He was caught in a bed of thorns."

Ghrian's eyes followed her slender arm. The sleeve of her cloak fell away as she lifted her fingers. A glimpse of turquoise stuck out between her pale skin and the deep green of the rich fabric. He was struck speechless again, as his eyes landed on the leather cord.

He looked to March, assuming that she had just stolen it from around his neck, but the rest of the tether was in its place, wrapped loosely around him, strung in and out of his snowy white mane. Ghrian struggled to wrap his mind around where she could have found it. After all, it had been ripped from his body by a giant wolf. He settled with the fact that she too must have discovered the pool and found it there, or elsewhere in the woods. That meant she had also explored Collitte.

"Thank you," Ghrian continued. "I was getting worried about him."

Shaerico looked at the horse and then back to the man. "You did not know where he was?"

"No," Ghrian said in a low voice.

"He's rather hard to misplace, I would imagine," Shaerico retorted.

"Well," Ghrian began, a bit embarrassed. "You would be surprised. He has a knack for escaping. He was doing well for a time though. I even rode him before he bucked me off and apparently got himself stuck at the mouth of the forest," Ghrian huffed.

"Rode him?" Shaerico was confused. Why would anyone need to ride another creature when they themselves have the capability of motion?

"Yes, rode him. What other use would I have for a horse? I am a baker. I purchased March hoping that having him would make my delivery journeys easier." Ghrian could see the confusion on her face. "Where are you from?" he asked, thinking of how difficult life and travel would be without the use of such creatures.

Shaerico was unsure how to respond. Alphaline had warned her children of the brutality of the outside world. She had forbidden them from ever leaving Collitte, let alone speak to someone outside the village. She wondered if this stranger even knew of Dorchas.

"From outside the Realm," she answered. It was not a lie.

"Well, I figured as much," Ghrian laughed. "Do your people not ride horses?"

She was still confused by this concept. "Why would we?" she asked.

"It makes travel much quicker. I would offer that you could learn on March, if I wasn't sure he would immediately throw you," Ghrian smiled.

All Shaerico heard was travel.

That illusive word that had always evaded her. "I've never traveled," she admitted with disappointment.

Ghrian could see the soft sorrow on her face. "It's not that great, to be honest it gets kind of lonely. Especially since I lost this guy," he said as he motioned to March. "And my Tavi."

"Tavi?" Shaerico said inquisitively, already aware of the answer from their first encounter in the woods.

Now it was Ghrian's face that showed sorrow. "She was a wolf that found her way into my life many years ago. She's been my traveling companion and rarely left my side."

Although Shaerico had met the beautiful creature, she was interested to hear this story. "Where did she come from, and why did she travel with you?"

Ghrian looked into her enchanting eyes as she held his gaze. She seemed genuinely interested. Ghrian sighed and looked toward his home. "As a pup, she had wandered into Yoaruq. The townspeople were shooing her from their homes and businesses, some even tried to kill her, but she was swift. I never understood why she was so determined to stay in the town. Eventually, she made her way to the edge of the village where my home is. My father saw her first. He was just trying to protect his family. Tavi had entered into our bakery looking for food, I'm certain. I had seen my father try to kill her. He threw a knife at her, luckily missing his target. I had never seen such a lonely creature. Her creamy gray and white fur was matted and dirty. I felt so sorry for her. She must have been no more than a few months old. As I watched her dodge my father's blows, I decided to intervene. I stood between he and Tavi. Of course, he was surprised, but eventually he agreed to let me keep her, provided I train her. It was strange, she was a wild animal by nature, but seemed to want nothing more than shelter and companionship."

Shaerico could not help but wonder at this. A wolf with no pack and so young, going willingly into a human village. How very strange.

Ghrian continued, "So, I raised and trained her, as best I could. She's been with me ever since." His voice trailed a little as he added, "Well, until now."

"Where do you travel?" Shaerico shifted the conversation, as she could see the pain the current topic brought Ghrian.

"Oh, just throughout the Realm. I do all the deliveries for the bakery, so I am on the road every other week or so. I hope to one day travel outside the Realm."

Shaerico smiled, as her thoughts wandered to distant lands. "That does sound wonderful," she agreed.

The two strangers stood with the horse for a few moments in silence, both minds still racing. Ghrian was trying to determine why he recognized those seducing eyes. Shaerico was wondering about Tavi, Ghrian's people, and life outside the woods. Ghrian was eager to learn more, to get to know this beautiful and mysterious woman. Shaerico was not so eager. She certainly wanted to ask him questions, but she was skeptical of his intentions. Who rides another animal? Why would a wild wolf choose to stay with a human? She looked down at the heap of leather and metal that lay in the grass between Ghrian and March. Pointing at it, she asked, "What is that?"

Ghrian suddenly remembered March and resumed his excitement. "Ah! Yes. The finest tanner in Lochta made these for me." He lifted the beautiful dark stained leather with silver buckles to show her. "These are the bridle and reins." He pulled the lead rope from the ground. "And this is a lead rope," he explained.

Shaerico stared at the peculiar attire. She lifted her slender hands to the leather and ran her fingers along the metal cinches. The sweet aroma of fresh leather and the stinging scent of metal wafted to her nostrils as she inhaled. "What is their purpose?" she asked, looking at Ghrian.

"They're for March. They go over his muzzle to help me direct him as I ride. Maybe if I'd had them during the last ride, I could have avoided being bucked off and never would have lost him," he said.

Shaerico looked at the stallion who was happily grazing next to them. "He would not have accepted these."

Ghrian was a little taken aback by her words. How would she know what the horse would or wouldn't do? She didn't even know what he was just a few moments ago.

"How can you be so sure?" he inquired.

She looked at March and walked toward him. Slowly, she ran her hands down his soft dapple-gray neck. March lifted his head and looked at her. Shaerico smiled and rested her hand over his nostrils. She felt his warm breath on her palms and responded, "He wants freedom. He's not meant to be kept." She looked at Ghrian, "Trust is earned, not forced or bought."

He was astonished by her brazen words. She was bold. It was apparent that she spent little time in conversation. He watched as Shaerico took the bridle and reins from his hands.

"You have to ask him, not tell him," she said.

She lifted the leather to the horse's muzzle, allowing him to smell and explore them. March pawed the ground with his massive hooves, his mud clad feathers swaying in the wind. Shaerico looked back at Ghrian.

"If he does allow you to ride him, or use whatever these are, it will be because he is your partner on your journey, not your possession," she explained.

She returned the bridle and reins to Ghrian's hands.

"Now, you ask him. If you really do need him to make your job easier, tell him," she went on.

Ghrian was apprehensive and a little mesmerized by this woman's abrasive nature, but he was also curious. After all, March was still standing next to them. He took the bridle and stepped toward his horse. He felt ridiculous asking an animal for its compliance, but at the same time, he had such a strong bond with Tavi, he figured it was worth a try. The gray stallion tossed his head as Ghrian approached and allowed the man to put one hand on his muzzle.

"So, what should I do now?" he asked Shaerico.

Shaerico smiled back at him. She found it peculiar that these people could not communicate with their own animals. She stepped forward and placed her hand just under March's left eye. Ghrian felt the horse lean into her hand. He could hardly believe how tame March had become around this foreign woman.

Shaerico continued, "Just ask him." She removed her hand and motioned to Ghrian.

He held the bridle and reins to March's nostrils, as he had seen the woman do. "Please, let me put these on you?" he stuttered, a bit embarrassed.

March immediately grabbed the bridle in his mouth and tossed it high into the sky. Rearing, he turned and ran through the high grass toward Yoaruq. Ghrian yelled after him, "Fine then! Arrogant animal, you have no respect! Let's see you find apples on your own!"

Shaerico could not help but laugh. She tried to hide her amusement as the fuming man turned back to her.

"Well, I asked him. Looks like you don't know horses as well as you thought."

She smiled. "It will take time. Be patient."

Ghrian calmed himself and sighed, "I'm not too good at that," he admitted. "I want results. He is supposed to be an asset, not a liability."

Shaerico looked at the frustrated stranger. Even in his childish anger, he was still rather charming. As Ghrian gathered the bridle and reins, the lead rope slung around his neck, she realized that night drew near. She knew that she could not be in the open as night fell. She turned to head back into the woods, when Ghrian called out to her.

"Wait! You can't go in there. It's dangerous and full of ravenous wolves!"

Shaerico looked at the concerned stranger and replied, "It would be much more dangerous for me to stay here."

Ghrian watched as she began to head to the Forbidden Forest. His confused mind raced as he tried to think of a way to get her to stay. He still had so many unanswered questions, and he was beyond intrigued.

"I need your help. Please," he called.

Shaerico stopped again, now at the edge of Collitte.

"It seems I may need your help training my horse, please, stay," he begged.

Shaerico looked toward the sky, then to the woods. "Fine. Tomorrow. Early."

"What is your name?" he called, as she faded into the forest.

She hesitated as the sun began to disappear behind the mountains in the distance. As she lunged into the darkness she called out, "Shaerico."

Ghrian stood in the fading light. The sun slid behind the mountain range, allowing the shadows of the woods to creep into the field where he stood paralyzed by what he had just experienced. He tried to process what had just occurred. He tried to make sense of the beautiful stranger's relationship with his wild horse and the turquoise cord wrapped around her wrist. Most of all, he wondered why she went into the woods. The doubt that he would ever see her again crept into his thoughts. Who in their right mind would go to the Forbidden Forest at night?

He knew there were tales of a people that had lived in those woods many years ago. Before Ghrian was born, there were stories of a great town that dominated trade from the mountains and beyond. He knew his father would have some knowledge of this, so Ghrian headed home to find answers.

On his way, he saw March frolicking in the high grass taunting him. He couldn't help but laugh at the ridiculous animal. Even though he had become a huge pain, he was an enjoyable and spirited creature.

Once Ghrian made it to the house, he saw his father hard at work

kneading the next batch of bread. As his son entered, Mòr looked up from his task.

"Any luck?" he said, seeing the bridle, reins, and lead rope in his son's hands.

Ghrian let out a sigh as he set them on the floor next to the crimson door. He wasn't even sure how to begin to tell his father the story. The mysterious woman's striking face was etched in his mind, permeating his thoughts. He looked at his father and began, "Father, do you remember the town that used to be in Collitte? Do you remember the tales of those people?"

Mòr immediately stopped kneading the dough. It was apparent that he did. He looked up at his son, who still stood in the doorway. "Why do you ask?"

"I'm just curious, really," Ghrian said apathetically, trying to hide his interest. His father did not buy it.

"When I was young, people still talked of Dorchas. The town was once a great hub of trade. The people there traded goods that came from the mountains and lands beyond, places that have since passed into legend. It was said that the people of the woods once sold magic goods to the people of the Realm. As you can imagine, the Order and its followers were none too happy about their thriving business in belief. After a while, the Order forbid anyone from entering the woods and trading with Dorchas. Those people held tight to their ways and beliefs, and it was their downfall." Mòr gazed through the window that looked out upon the fields that led to the Forbidden Forest. "We shouldn't talk of the town in Collitte. Besides, it has long been abandoned," Mòr said definitively. Ghrian nodded and thanked his father for the information. Mòr eyed his son as he went through the bakery to his room, and then returned to his own work.

Ghrian laid down on his bed and removed the knife from his pocket. He studied the antler handle and unique hilt. The marble griffin carved at the end of the knife was hunched into a ball over the tip of the handle. Its eyes were a deep black stone, flecked with gold. Ghrian gazed into the griffin's lifeless eyes and remembered the night that he had received the knife. It was the night his mother had left. He was four when she disappeared from his life. And though he'd been young, he remembered the night well. She had come into his room late in the evening and sat at the edge of his bed, until he awoke, surprised to see her there. His fair mother had taken the knife from her hands and placed it on Ghrian's chest.

"Never let this leave your side," she had said in her soothing voice.

Ghrian remembered how he had thought this strange, but he was so young. The knife had more or less stayed in the table next to his bed from then until a few days prior. It was only now that he kept it with him, that he truly needed it, that he realized how precious this gift was. He missed his mother dearly. He wished that he had been able to hear more of her stories. Ghrian knew so little of his mother's disappearance, or of who she really was. As he thought of her, he drifted off to sleep, forgetting his early morning meeting.

It was noon and the sun was high. The biting cold crept its way into the sleeping man's room. Ghrian rolled over, knocking the knife from its resting place on his chest, sending it crashing to the ground. In a sweat, he awoke. He jumped from his bed, realizing that he was supposed to have been in the field hours ago. He wanted to make a good impression on the mysterious woman he'd met the day prior, and he feared that he had already made a bad one. Shaking the sleep from his head, he grabbed March's tack and rushed to the field.

Shaerico had been at the edge of the forest since daylight. She'd had her morning coffee with Beanrua, then headed stealthily out of Collitte. In truth, she was more excited about seeing the strange beast called March than the human, as she was still rather skeptical of the man of the Realm. However, she was surprised by her excitement as his flailing form came barreling through the grass.

"I am so sorry I'm late!" Ghrian huffed as he approached and slowed his pace. He stood in front of Shaerico, hands on his knees, as he tried to catch his breath.

"You are indeed very late," she said dryly.

He looked up at her and was again struck by her beauty. Shaerico kept a sour expression on her face as she stepped toward him, but in truth, she was amused.

"Let's go find your March," she said, holding out her hand to help Ghrian upright.

Ghrian smiled and took it softly, "I'm sorry I forgot to introduce myself

yesterday," he said, keeping her hand in his. "I'm Ghrian."

They stood hand in hand for a moment until March neighed in the distance. Shaerico turned immediately toward the sound and headed through the grass, as Ghrian gathered the bridle, reins and lead rope. The two strangers and the horse spent all afternoon together. The boy from the bakery and the girl from the forest talked for hours. Shaerico soaked in every word he said, getting a clearer picture of life in the Realm. She responded with awe, curiosity, and sometimes disgust at their way of life, but she never spoke of Dorchas or her own people. As evening approached, they hardly remembered the reason for their meeting. March had finally become accustomed to the bridle, but he would only allow Shaerico to put it on. Ghrian decided to leave the bridle on overnight slinging the reins loosely over March's neck. This was mostly because March would not allow him close enough to remove it. Evening came upon them fast.

"I'm glad you seem to be making progress with your horse," Shaerico laughed as Ghrian had given up trying to retrieve his bridle.

"Yes, thank you for your help," Ghrian said, sitting on the soft grass next to Shaerico. "But I have to ask, how do you know so much about this animal when just yesterday you had never seen a horse?"

Shaerico looked to the ground and replied, "Animals are predictable. They desire and care for few things."

"And those are?" Ghrian asked.

"Primarily food, companionship, and freedom," she expounded.

Ghrian looked into the woman's peculiar orange eyes as she looked up at him to answer. "And how do you know what animals desire?"

Shaerico kept his gaze and replied, "I have lived among them all my life."

For most of the afternoon, both of them had forgotten their more pressing questions entirely, but in this moment, they came flooding back. Questions and concerns about the blue leather strand being worn as a bracelet, the blood, the miraculous healing, a home in the Forbidden Forest, all raced through their thoughts. The familiarity that they had formed faded away, as the realization of how little they knew of each other returned to the forefront of their minds.

Shaerico sensed the coming questions and stood to leave. She brushed the grass from her cloak and turned toward Collitte.

Ghrian grabbed her hand, "Wait, please. We don't have to talk about where you're from." He could sense that she was uneasy about this topic.

"I promise I won't bring it up again."

Though the questions still burned in his mind, he found her company more important than answers. He reassured himself, hoping that those answers would come in time. Shaerico looked down at him and smiled. She was relieved that he would no longer bring up what she could not explain, but still she could not stay out as night fell.

"I really must head back," she said. "But I promise, I will return tomorrow."

Ghrian released her hand and stood. "I look forward to it," he smiled.

"Don't be late this time, okay?" she winked at him as she jogged toward the woods.

Ghrian called after her, "I will be here before the sun rises!"

And he was. The next day, he arrived in the field before the sun rose. He was eager to learn more about this woman, desperate to spend time with her. In the coming days, the two strangers became fast friends. They spent nearly every moment that Ghrian wasn't working together, slowly becoming more. He would often ask if she had spotted Tavi in the woods. Admittedly, Shaerico had searched for her, as she too was fond of the gray wolf, but she was nowhere to be found. Ghrian and Shaerico spent most of their days together talking and training March. On occasion, Ghrian would bring Shaerico items from the Realm that she had never seen, predominantly food. He also brought her beer. Though Dorchas had their pub, all the beer was essentially the same. There were hardly choices: dark beer or light. But in the Realm, the choices were endless. Every pub had an assortment of brews and on one occasion Ghrian came to their meeting place in the meadow with two large mugs of beer and a small bushel of apples.

Shaerico's eyes widened with excitement. "What is that?" she inquired upon his approach.

"This is Black Ale," he said lifting the mugs in his right hand, releasing a few droplets of the brew to the grass below.

"And those?" Shaerico said as she gazed at the tantalizing red fruit.

"These are apples," Ghrian beamed, thrilled that he had assessed correctly that she'd never had an apple before.

The pair sat in the grass and enjoyed their delicacies. Shaerico downed the contents of her mug within minutes, hardly noticing the myriad of flavors, though she did manage to note that it was far superior to the beer in Dorchas. Ghrian watched with adoration as Shaerico took her first bite

of the delectable fruit. She seemed to thoroughly enjoy it.

"Can I have another?" she said with her mouth still full of the first.

Ghrian smiled and nodded. As he handed her the second apple, their hands brushed. Shaerico's luminous gaze flitted to Ghrian's charming face. Their eyes met. She wasn't sure how she truly felt about him, as she'd never felt anything remotely similar to this for anyone. But as they touched, her heart began to beat harder. A part of her felt like jumping up and running back to the comfort of her woods, but another part of her, somewhere deep, had the sudden urge to grab his hand and bring him closer. They sat in the moment for a few breaths. Ghrian's thoughts were much the same as hers, but he dared not make a move. This hesitance was unusual for him, but he had come to care deeply for the lady from the woods, and he did not want to act rashly. Shaerico was the first to break the tension. She grabbed the apple suddenly and took a large bite. Ghrian sighed and sat back, taking another swig of his brew. Much of their time together was spent in this way: suspended in the unknown.

After some time and continuous help from Shaerico, March allowed Ghrian to use the bridle, reins, and lead rope. Eventually, March even came to Ghrian's call, and he never had to tether the stallion again. This growth brought Ghrian hope, not only that March would become a useful companion, but that his dear Tavi would return. He also relished the fact that he was getting to spend so much time with Shaerico.

Shaerico was growing equally as fond of the man from the Realm, though she was much slower to show it. She was not open with her feelings like Ghrian. It was apparent when he was happy or upset. He would tell her all of his frustrations. Shaerico would listen, soaking up all that she could about the world outside her woods. Life in the Realm was so fascinating to her. She noted the daily tasks and chores and the fact that every being had a purpose and a job in such a large community of people. She was filled with confusion and laughter at his tales. She loved hearing of Oir and her feisty spirit. She especially admired her work on March's tack. Shaerico longed to meet her, but was afraid to ask if it were possible, let alone venture the thought of going into town. What if Ghrian was the only kind man? What if the people of the Realm were as evil as Alphaline had always warned? There was only one way to find out.

The primary issue was that Alphaline had become increasingly suspicious of Shaerico. Ever since the discovery of the man from the mountain, the leader of Dorchas had been on high alert. Shaerico still attended her hunting parties. She rarely missed a breakfast, and although the rest of the villagers expected her to spend most of her time alone, the fact that her bitterness was fading made those who took notice uneasy. The icy glare she wore on her cream-white skin had begun to thaw. Shaerico had stopped snapping at her peers. She no longer fought to eat first. She became less picky with what she would hunt. Her focus was faltering, and she spent less and less time at the pub. Beanrua had become aware of the growing suspicion. One morning following breakfast, as Shaerico was preparing to head to meet Ghrian, Beanrua confronted her.

"Sister," she called after Shaerico as she headed down the winding path into the cold. "I know you prefer to be alone, especially of late, but I have to warn you, people are becoming suspicious."

Shaerico stopped and turned to face Beanrua. She had not once considered that her actions would raise suspicions. Her attention had been so far from Dorchas that she had not realized how much she had indeed changed. Her icy demeanor was melting, and it was painfully apparent.

"My dear friend," she sighed. "Will you walk with me?"

Beanrua was excited to be asked to accompany her friend again. Admittedly, she too had grown curious. She ran to Shaerico's side and whispered, "What is going on?"

Shaerico knew that Beanrua was trustworthy, but she had lived half her life in secret for weeks now. She was unsure how much to share or how to start. Shaerico looked at her lively friend who was eagerly awaiting to hear what had been keeping Shaerico's focus.

"Do you remember the night we found that man?" she began.

Beanrua looked puzzled. This was not at all how she anticipated this conversation beginning. "Yes," she said.

"Do you remember the stone you took from his hand?" Shaerico reminded her.

Beanrua stopped walking. "Yes," she said slowly.

Shaerico gently pushed her shoulder to keep her moving into the woods, further from town, further from listening ears.

"Well, that following night, after Mother had gone to inspect the situation, she came to me infuriated. She didn't seem too concerned with the man's death, though she was frightened, but she was far more concerned with that stone. She thought I had taken it. I told her it was nothing but lumps of ash by the time we found the body, but it seemed like she did not believe me," Shaerico explained.

Beanrua looked confused. "Why would she care about a single stone? There are so many in the woods." Though neither woman had ever seen a stone with such a vibrant turquoise hue.

The obsession and fear in Alphaline's voice had been real.

Shaerico shrugged her shoulders, "I have no clue. But I was suspicious of her fear and her anger. She is hiding something. I can feel it. So, I decided to search for answers."

Beanrua looked even more confused. "What do you mean search for answers? Where?"

They were deep in the woods now. The morning sun was high and Ghrian had long been waiting for Shaerico to exit Collitte and join him in the fields, but she knew that she could not allow Beanrua to see him. Instead, she took her friend to the pond. It was strange, winter was fast approaching, and the trees of the forest were rapidly losing their leaves, but the evergreens and weeping willows that stretched their branches to the mirror-like surface were still a vibrant green. The violet flowers of the rose bushes that hid the crystal water from view were also still in full bloom. The grass surrounding the clear blue pool was as lush as the day she had first discovered them.

"What is this place?" Beanrua whispered.

"I'm not yet sure, but I feel that it holds answers of some kind," Shaerico said.

Beanrua knelt beside the pond. She leaned over the edge and gazed into the turquoise water. The reflection shook her wavy red hair.

"Why are we not drinking from this while we are banned from the mountain stream? The well took days for us to clean and I'm still uncertain of the water's quality," she huffed.

"I know. Alphaline is hiding this place from us and I aim to find out why," Shaerico snarled.

"So, is this where you've been spending your days?" Beanrua asked.

Shaerico faltered before she answered, "Well, some of the time," she admitted. "But one night when I was here, something strange happened."

She knelt beside the water, the blood-stained grass had turned a rich brown, but had not died. Shaerico looked at the turquoise band around her wrist and wondered how much she should tell Beanrua. She also wondered when she should bring up that night to Ghrian. The question that had burned so ravenously in their minds when they'd met had calmed and hardened, stored cool, and nearly forgotten in the back of their memories.

Beanrua had settled herself along the bank of the pond. She was laying in the grass, waiting for Shaerico to continue, running her fingers through the icy water.

"What happened?" she said, as Shaerico kept silent.

"I met someone," she stated abruptly, not sure how much she should say. She had a sudden urge to tell Beanrua everything about the charming man from the Realm.

At this revelation, Beanrua shot up from her peaceful position. "Met someone?" she gasped. She rested her weight on her hands as she leaned closer to her friend. "You don't just meet someone out in the woods. There are only thirty of us in all of Dorchas! Do you mean to tell me that some poor soul from the Realm wandered their way into Collitte? Do you know what Mother would do if she knew?"

"Yes, I know Beanrua," Shaerico interrupted. "I was out hunting and found this place. He was here. I don't know why," she trailed off as she thought about the first night she met Ghrian. "He had fallen in the woods and I drug him to safety."

"Shaerico, tell me you have not been outside this forest!" Beanrua gasped again.

Shaerico smiled at her friend, but didn't answer.

"Please, Shaerico! Why are doing this? Alphaline already has it out for you, she always has. You can't be bringing this much attention to yourself!" Beanrua pleaded.

"Beanrua, you just answered your own question. Alphaline has always had it out for me. She's never cared for me because I question her. And now I know for certain that she is hiding things from us. If I have to find answers outside of Collitte, I will," Shaerico explained.

Beanrua sighed heavily and returned to the grass, "You're impossible."

"Think about it," Shaerico continued. "What could really hurt us outside these woods? The only men we've met from outside Dorchas were dead or unconscious."

Beanrua laughed. "I suppose you have a point. Just please be more careful," she began to stand. "Actually, we should return to Dorchas now."

Shaerico looked further into the woods toward the Realm. She knew that Ghrian would be waiting, but Beanrua was right. If they were caught, he would be killed on the spot. She had become careless. As they returned to town, Ghrian and March continued to wait patiently near the edge of Collitte.

The horse and his man had certainly created a bond. March was rather proud to wear the bridle now, as he realized that he was free to roam the fields adjacent to Yoaruq. He trotted in circles around Ghrian as the anxious man awaited Shaerico's arrival. It was unlike her to be late. In all their planned meetings, Shaerico had always shown on time. He wasn't sure whether or not to be concerned, as she was so private about her life outside of their meetings. As morning waned to afternoon, and afternoon to evening, his anxiety grew, as did his sadness. He could not understand why she wouldn't show. They were beginning to prep March to be ridden and Ghrian was especially excited to see that through.

"Well," Ghrian sighed to March as the sun began to set. "I suppose we should return home. I have officially wasted a day," he said with both frustration and disappointment.

The pair headed back through the unruly grass toward Yoaruq. Ghrian could not help but run he and Shaerico's last conversation through his mind. She was rather elusive, but she seemed to tolerate him at the very least, perhaps she'd even become fond of him. Maybe she was just busy and didn't have a way to let him know. They had been spending a substantial amount of time together.

Though Ghrian had continued completing the bakery's orders and deliveries, he had all but stopped visiting Ginger. And he hardly even noticed. He and Ginger had always fancied one another, but deep down Ghrian knew that with her father in the picture they would never work out. Besides, there was a depth and mystery to the daughter of the Forbidden Forest that consumed his thoughts. She had begun to steal his heart. He had not seen Oir in weeks either. All of his spare time had been spent with Shaerico.

The gray stallion trotted happily at his side. Ghrian was astonished by how far his horse had come in the time he'd spent with Shaerico. She was truly a remarkable individual who had a unique understanding of animals.

The dark leather bridle and reins were removed easily from March upon their arrival home. Ghrian watched as his horse ran back out into the fields for the night. Ghrian had learned that in turn for his freedom, and the occasional apple, March was indeed capable of reaching his potential. Just a few more days of training, and he would be comfortable enough with Ghrian to be ridden, or at least carry the deliveries through town. Ghrian would finally have his packhorse.

As Ghrian entered his home, he found a fire lit in the fireplace. The days were growing colder, and the biting frost was becoming too much for their coats and blankets alone. Mòr sat quietly in his chair. He was hunched over something, staring deep into the fire. Ghrian approached him.

"Father, are you alright?"

Mòr looked up at his son. The blazing fire cast an orange glow across his burly face. The light and shadows danced on the wall behind him.

"This was the night," he said as he kept his son's gaze.

Ghrian joined him and sat on the hearth. The warmth of the fire blazed behind him, but it could not thaw the chill in the air.

Mòr continued, "Fifteen years ago. It's hard to believe I've lived that long without her."

Ghrian and his father rarely spoke about that night or his mother. He knew that his mother had disappeared into Collitte, but he never knew why. Tentatively, he asked his father, "What happened the night she left?"

Mòr leaned back in his chair and sighed. "It was a cold night, much like this. Your mother had been acting strange for months. The Templemen thought it was fever. They tried treating her, but nothing worked. She insisted that it was guilt. Guilt from what, I will never know. She went on and on about duty and truth. Then she left. I can't imagine what duty is more important than the commitment you have to your family."

Ghrian was speechless. This was the most his father had spoken of that fateful night.

Mòr stood, spilling the contents of his lap onto the floor. "No more questions. I'm going to bed. We have to begin baking for the Festival, so I need you here tomorrow."

Ghrian nodded, waiting for his father to disappear down the hall. He wanted to see what his father had been pining over. He knelt down on the floor in front of the worn leather chair and lifted broken pieces of stone

from the dirt clod floor. It was a gargoyle, similar to the griffin on the hilt of his own knife. Ghrian removed his knife from its sheath beneath his robe and held it and the broken pieces of the gargoyle in the firelight. The griffin's eyes glinted as the gold flecks shone in the spray of sparks. In contrast, the gargoyle's eyes were lifeless, though they too were flecked with gold. Ghrian studied the cracked stone and roughened edges. The gargoyle's face was frozen in anguish, not at all like the watchful expression of his griffin. A few moments passed and Ghrian became uneasy by the sight of the stone creature. He returned his knife to its sheath and placed the broken stone sculpture on the wooden mantle. He could not help but wonder about his mother. He had a nagging sense that she was not lost to them.

Chapter Nine

Days passed and Ghrian spent his time preparing for the Winter Solstice Festival with his father. Dearthair had made it to Lochta and Oir had brought him to Yoaruq. It was apparent that she had not lost her feelings for him. Dearthair still had his boyish charm, but he was also successful. His uncle had taught him many skills. He was not only skilled in masonry, but he had also become a renowned silversmith in the town of Miotal, where he lived. Oir flaunted her new silver braided bracelet that their old friend had made specially for her. Dearthair had come to see Oir and Ghrian, but he had also come to sell his work at the Festival in order to make a name for himself in the Realm as well.

"Look what he made me, Ghrian! Isn't it marvelous?!" Oir said, lifting her wrist and twirling upon her entry into the bakery. Her golden hair nearly blocked Dearthair from getting through the crimson door. Ghrian agreed that it was a beautiful piece, hoping that it would cease her gloating. It did not.

"I just can't believe how successful you are Dearthair," she continued. "And after such a short time!"

Dearthair smiled, but Ghrian commented, "Oir, it's been nearly ten years."

Oir gave Ghrian a sharp look. She liked Dearthair, but she liked irritating Ghrian even more. "It has been nearly ten years, hasn't it! And how's business coming along for you? Have you mastered some new skill I am unaware of?"

Mòr let out a hearty chuckle and lowered a batch of bread into the oven.

"My business, dear Oir, is actually going rather well," Ghrian retorted.

"Oh? And your horse is finally of use to you?" Oir released a beaming grin.

Everyone laughed at Ghrian's expense. He softened and rolled his eyes. He was easy to fluster, but not easy to offend. As the friends spent the afternoon catching up, Ghrian could not help but wish Shaerico were there to meet them. It had been some time since he had seen her last. The Winter Solstice Festival was fast approaching and Ghrian wished she would join him in Lochta. Especially since Oir now had Dearthair. Usually, he spent the entirety of the Festival in Lochta at the tannery, but he was a bit concerned with the dynamic of the old friends now. Oir and Dearthair had obvious rekindled chemistry and Ghrian did not want to impose.

Afternoon turned to evening and evening to night, as the friends talked of their everyday lives. Oir spoke proudly of her tannery and how excited she was about her new project. Dearthair asked Ghrian about life in Yoaruq, about what had changed since they were boys. Truthfully, not much had changed, except for his mysterious new friend. Ghrian elected to keep that relationship a secret until the time was appropriate. Dearthair told him of his new home, Miotal, a fair-sized town outside the Realm, not far from the Castle Nicíl, home of the King. He talked of the stones that they had found on the mountains that towered above the great castle, far west along the mountain's ridge. He had gone there once with his uncle when he had just begun his apprenticeship. It was apparent that Dearthair was proud of his journey to the mountains, but Ghrian could also sense a deep fear in him. Soon, he discovered why. A few weeks prior, his uncle and a few other masons and smithies from the towns surrounding Lake Muina had journeyed to the far western side of the mountain range beyond Collitte to mine the valuable stones. These unique stones, like the one ground to create the cord Oir had gifted Ghrian, were sought after for their immense beauty. Dearthair's uncle was supposed to meet him in Lochta days prior with a fresh batch. The turquoise stones seemed to be a favorite among the Priests and royalty. Dearthair had waited for his uncle, but he had not made it to their meeting place. Dearthair had one single stone from his uncle's last trip years prior. He had gifted it to Oir for her saddle's center jewel. He assured her that his uncle would make it in time with enough stones for him to create some pieces for the Festival, but there was worry in his

eyes. Ghrian knew what those woods held. If Dearthair's uncle had tried to reach the Realm by way of the forest, hope was lost for him.

As night fell in Collitte, the people of Dorchas prepared to hunt. Shaerico and Bruid were placed in a hunting team with three other members. Cain led another hunting party toward the mountains.

Alphaline had lifted the ban to the stream just in time for the hunt. The two parties leapt into the night as darkness fell. Driven by hunger, they ventured deep into the woods. Immediately, Shaerico caught scent of a deer. The five hunters turned in unison as she led them further and further south. After racing through the forest for miles, a single white doe became visible. She gleamed in the moonlight. It was the same deer Shaerico had seen before. She came to a halt as the other four surrounded the tender animal. The deer stood motionless, staring into Shaerico's fiery eyes. Shaerico stood from her crouch and tilted her head. She could not imagine why this deer was not trying to flee. She was obviously aware of the danger surrounding her. Bruid closed in on her right, but Shaerico could not pull away from the doe's gaze. Why was she standing still? Why was she unafraid?

The three other members awaited Shaerico's cue, inching closer and closer to their prey. Bruid, however, did not wait for his sister. He lunged for the white deer. There was no struggle. No noise. No blood.

Shaerico held the creature's gaze as it transformed into a solid white hawk. Her eyes remained locked on its large golden irises. She watched as the bird of prey gracefully slid from Bruid's grasp. The great hawk screeched loudly as it tore through the branches above and disappeared into the starlit sky. Shaerico said nothing. She could hardly process what she had just seen, but somehow, she felt that this creature had some tie to the crystal waters.

Bruid howled in anger and turned in rage to Shaerico. "What was that! And why did you not give the cue?"

"What does is matter anyway, brother? You're the one who lost the creature, whatever it was," Shaerico said, eyes still locked on the starlit sky.

The other members of the party glanced at one another, unsure of what they had just witnessed. Bruid ignored the mysterious occurrence and snarled as he brushed passed his sister into the darkness. "We follow my nose tonight," he growled.

The other three turned reluctantly to follow Bruid as Shaerico did not protest. Usually when Bruid stepped out of rank, she would have put him in his place, but instead, Shaerico followed in a daze. She was too busy trying to come to terms with the strange occurrences that had been happening around her since she found the mysterious pool. She could not make sense of any of it.

The following morning, Shaerico met Beanrua as usual. She had fallen back into her old routine from before she'd met Ghrian. She spent most of her days with Beanrua at the pub or wandering around Collitte. After the events of the night before, she was even more determined to find answers, but she had to be cautious. She suspected that the shapeshifter had something to do with the turquoise water and she aimed to find out more.

After spending time with Beanrua, Shaerico set out into the woods. Her friend could sense that she was up to something as she exited the hall with clear purpose. Beanrua walked out behind her. Hands on her hips, she called to Shaerico, "Where are you going?"

Shaerico slowly turned and walked back toward her. "I'm going into the woods, Bean', what else?"

Beanrua raised a fiery red brow and continued, "This is not your usual wander into the woods. You are walking with purpose again. Tell me you are not leaving Collitte."

"I am not," Shaerico sighed. "When are you going to stop being suspicious?"

"When you return to your lonesome, pensive self," Beanrua laughed.

"This is getting rather irritating," Shaerico mumbled under her breath.

Beanrua had been keeping a sharp eye on her friend of late. She was still not convinced. "You're going back to that place with the strange water, aren't you?" she whispered.

"Perhaps, but it is in the woods," Shaerico smiled as her concerned friend shook her head.

"I suppose that's better than you leaving Collitte," she admitted.

"Just be on guard, if Alphaline is trying to hide the existence of that place, you should be wary."

Shaerico nodded and headed down the dusty cobblestone. She was becoming familiar with the path to the pond.

The days were growing colder as winter approached. Nearly all the leaves had fallen from the trees and many animals were preparing for the coming frostbitten months. Shaerico favored the cold. The chill in her lungs made her feel alive. She inhaled an icy breath, the crisp air nipping at the back of her throat, as she ran through the forest, dodging trees and fallen branches, until finally she made it to the clearing. The trees here still held most of their leaves. The evergreens and rose bushes were as vibrant as ever, but the deep violet flowers now had a mixture of blue amidst the lavender. Shaerico walked to them, confused. She had never seen anything like them in all her years in the forest. The roses' petals were thick and soft and displayed a swirl of rich turquoise within the vibrant purple. Every time she visited this place it became more and more peculiar.

As Shaerico inspected the strange flowers, she felt eyes upon her. She scanned the crystal water, the surrounding grass, and finally, the trees. High in an evergreen, a single white hawk gazed down upon her. She froze as she recalled what she had seen before. Could this be the same creature? She stepped through the bushes, ignoring the thorns as they sliced her arms. The elegant bird spread its massive wings and slowly glided to the grass below. When it neared the ground, it transformed back into a doe of the same hue. Now Shaerico was certain.

A gust of wind rustled the surrounding foliage and rippled the clear water. Shaerico was speechless. She watched as the deer walked to the pool and stooped to take a drink. The water shone like molten silver in the glare of the setting sun overhead. For a moment, Shaerico did nothing but stare at the incredible creature. By this time, evening was upon them and Shaerico knew that she had to return to Dorchas, but she was mesmerized by this being. She had never known of a creature who could change form at will.

Not long after, the deer lifted her head and took one last look at Shaerico, then disappeared into the forest. Shaerico exhaled deeply and was turning to leave the clearing when she heard footsteps. She feared it was Alphaline. She knelt behind a rosebush and stared in the direction of the noise. Whomever this creature was, it was not light of foot. Soon, a man appeared. He was tall and handsome and had a knife at his side.

Shaerico stood with anger, "What are you doing here?"

Ghrian looked at her, surprised. "I was looking for you to be honest. I thought you would be happy to see me," he said, a bit disappointed by her reaction "Wait, how do you know of this place?"

"How do you know of this place?" Shaerico replied. She feared now more than ever that he would remember their meetings by the pond. "You should leave, it is not safe for you here."

"Listen," Ghrian said. "I came to find you. It's been weeks. I had to make sure you were okay. Besides, if it isn't safe for me, it certainly can't be safe for you. I've been patient. I haven't asked once about where you are from or where you go at night, but I would like to know now."

"Ghrian, I am begging you, get out of these woods," Shaerico pleaded, panic mounting in her voice. With that, another rustle came from the surrounding underbrush, this time from the opposite side of the clearing.

"What is this?" A voice boomed from the forest behind Shaerico. She closed her eyes and inhaled deeply before turning to face her brother.

"Bruid, let me explain," she began.

The sunlight was fading and Shaerico feared that Ghrian would get his answers before she had the time to explain. She needed to tell him that he had begun to change her, to open her eyes to hope. That she thought of him every day and ached to see him again. But none of that mattered now. Besides, it could have only ever been a beautiful and fleeting dream. She turned and looked at him over her shoulder as the moon took its place in the sky.

"Run," she said, as the blue light bathed her body in the clearing.

Ghrian watched as the emerald robe slid from her slender form. Her gleaming white complexion turned black, and her smooth skin turned to coarse fur. The turquoise cord was still tied tightly around her arm as massive paws beneath the once fragile wrists hit the ground with a thud. Her orange eyes gazed at Ghrian as they turned to a fiery gold.

"It was you," Ghrian stuttered, heart skipping a beat and lodging itself in his throat. He fell back into the thicket of trees, unable to move any further.

The beast from the shadows leapt into the clearing. He was after Ghrian. His eyes were wild as he tried to pass by Shaerico, but she did not allow it. Ghrian watched as the two massive black wolves fought, silhouettes against the sky. Howls filled the air and blood spilled to the ground. Shaerico was much smaller than this other wolf, but she was quicker and more agile.

Ghrian noticed small tufts of white fur between her eyes, creating a thin diamond that he had not noticed before, a single distinguishing feature amongst the beasts as they fought on.

He tried to make sense of what his eyes were seeing. The wolves battled on as Ghrian tried to determine what he should do. He had found the illusive woman. He had found answers to some of his questions. However, he could not help but feel more confused and saddened by the reality of who Shaerico really was, or rather, what she was. The somber realization that she had been the one who attacked him that night in this very place sank in his stomach. He should have listened to her. He should have run.

After gazing once more upon the battle that raged in the clearing, Ghrian came to his senses and fled Collitte. He wished that Dearthair and Oir had not returned to Lochta. He longed to tell Oir what he had experienced on this trip to the Forbidden Forest. He felt foolish for thinking that he and Shaerico could have shared a life in the Realm, yet even after his return to safety, he still felt himself drawn to her.

When he finally made it out of Collitte, breathless and panicked, March was there waiting for him. Ghrian ran to the gray stallion and tore the last of the turquoise cord from around his neck. He left the leather on the ground at the edge of the forest and rode March back to his home. He did not wish to the keep the item which reminded him not only of the loss of his beloved Tavi, but that was now also a reminder of the true nature of the woman he had come to love.

It was a love that had almost killed him.

In the days that followed, Ghrian was quiet. He prepared the bread for the Winter Solstice Festival in a somber silence. The festival would begin in the morning and he had to be ready. March and Ghrian's relationship had grown considerably, even in Shaerico's absence. March accepted the bags of bread that Ghrian piled upon his back. He shifted his weight uneasily, but did not run. He could feel Ghrian's sadness and his need for his compliance. The bridle and reins no longer startled the stallion. He wore them proudly and allowed Ghrian to lead him down the cobblestone pathway toward Lochta.

Mòr walked with them to the edge of Yoaruq.

"Sell well my son," he said, placing a heavy hand on Ghrian's shoulder. "I must stay back so we do not get behind on our deliveries."

Ghrian nodded and replied, "We have plenty of Hearty Loaf. I doubt I'll return with anything but the sacks."

Mòr smiled and turned back toward their home. Ghrian could not quiet his mind as he and the horse journeyed to Lochta. The streets were filled with people and distractions, but all he could think of was the black wolf. His black wolf. The mysterious woman he had fallen for who had suddenly become all the more a mystery. He wasn't sure what to think. He had mulled over it for days with no resolution. Why did the other wolf attack her? Who was it? Is she even still alive? Guilt pulsed through him as he considered how he had left her.

As he continued on, lost in his thoughts, he paid little attention to his surroundings. Amidst the families and merchants traveling to Lochta for the festival, a pair of unsavory men took notice of his goods. The two men began to follow closely behind Ghrian. March noticed and nickered, pawing the cobblestone in warning. The men backed away and walked off the road into the grass away from the aggressive stallion. For some time they walked in the fields adjacent to the road, but their eyes never left Ghrian or his packhorse. Unfortunately, the baker was so consumed by his daydreams that he failed to notice them. March grew more restless as the men drew closer again. Ghrian placed a hand on March's flanks, trying to calm him. Suddenly, the men rushed the pair, but before they could attack, he heard a whispering voice forewarn him, "Behind you!"

Ghrian turned just in time for one of the men to release a punch just below his chin. March bucked and knocked the second man to the ground. The first came back around trying an under cut this time. Ghrian dodged the blow and landed his fist in the thief's face. He pulled his knife from its sheath and held it to the man's throat. The second thief, who had risen from his fall, fled the streets leaving his partner to fend for himself.

The captured man looked at Ghrian and begged, "Please, sir. We are just hungry."

Ghrian held the knife still. "Well, then you can attend the Festival tomorrow and purchase all the bread you desire like every other man."

The thief looked to the ground and then back to Ghrian. "Fine," he said, as he lifted his hands.

"Be on your way then," Ghrian said as he kicked the man backwards.

He went to sheath his knife and heard another whisper, "Foolish men, always thinking with their stomachs."

Ghrian turned and saw no one but March, tossing his neck and awaiting Ghrian's instructions.

"Maybe I am losing my mind," Ghrian said to March as he took the rope in his hands and continued his journey toward Lochta. "Horses can't talk.

Back in the town of Dorchas there was much unrest. Bruid and Shaerico had fought until Ghrian was safely home. Bruid had refused to listen to reason. He was hungry and could not comprehend why his usually merciless sister had not slain the human intruder. Shaerico had not known what to say. She was doomed no matter her explanation. How could she explain her relationship with the man when she herself was unsure?

Bruid had returned to town fuming. Alphaline could see his anger and asked him what was troubling him. In his rage, Bruid betrayed his sister. He told Alphaline of her defense of a human. Fortunately, in his blind rage, he had not noticed the crystal pool and said nothing of it.

Alphaline watched as Shaerico entered Dorchas. The morning sun was rising and she shed her wolf form as she approached Alphaline.

"What do you have to say for yourself?" Alphaline snarled.

"It is true," Shaerico replied. "The man meant no harm. We had eaten the night before, so there was no reason for senseless bloodshed."

Beanrua and a few other residents of the town walked into the street. Beanrua wore her worry plainly on her face as she witnessed her greatest fear.

"So, you chose a stranger over your own brother?" Alphaline inquired, disappointment dripping from her condescending words. "Shaerico, I have never known you to be merciful. Why the sudden change of heart?"

Shaerico recognized this as a trap. She could not tell Alphaline of her trips outside the woods, nor her time spent at the curious pond, nor her attack on the man she had come to adore. She looked at Beanrua and then down. "It was a moment of weakness."

Alphaline approached Shaerico and lifted her chin with a single finger.

All the members of Dorchas who had come to watch stood breathless, awaiting the inevitable.

"You are no longer a member of this pack. You have chosen the safety of a stranger over your own family. You have chosen your side. Now you have the freedom you've always craved, little lone wolf," Alphaline said as she turned away.

"Alphaline, please!" Beanrua pleaded, stepping close to the confrontation.

"You will be silent, child!" Alphaline barked as she removed her hand from under Shaerico's chin, leaving a thin gash that released a single drop of crimson blood where her nail had been. "Which one of you wants a sister who betrays her own for a stranger from outside the forest? How can she be trusted to protect her people now? You have no idea what will become of us should those monsters out there discover Dorchas. I have made my choice. There can be no place for someone who does not value the safety of Collitte and its people over all else." She turned to the crowd that had formed. "She chose to protect a foreign man above her own people. The same men that condemned our ancestors to roam these woods alone, separated from all other society and trade of the world. They made their choice when they isolated us. They hunted us for our belief." Alphaline snarled, "This woman has aligned herself with them. She is banished to roam the woods alone or to join the Realm and be slaughtered, as is their way."

Shaerico was silent.

"And children," Alphaline continued. "If you see a man in these woods, kill him."

The people were split. Some howled in agreement and others stood motionless. Shaerico was known to be the greatest huntress in Dorchas. Her banishment would surely take a toll on their hunting success. Beanrua was enraged, not only at Alphaline, but also at Bruid and Shaerico.

She stepped forward and took Shaerico by the arm, as Alphaline walked away. "This is why I warned you. How could you let this happen?"

Shaerico laid a hand on her friend's shoulder. "You know where to find me. I must seek answers. Have you ever considered why Alphaline keeps us hidden in the forest? She claims it is the doing of the men of the Realm, but I believe that there is more to it. She wants me gone for more reasons than last night."

Beanrua wanted to ask her about the man she had saved. Was he the same one she had left the woods to meet? She dared not speak of it in front of the entire clan. They both watched as the proud white-haired woman walked into the forest on the other side of Dorchas.

Beanrua turned back to Shaerico and sighed. "Sister, my dearest friend, I cannot bear the thought of you alone for eternity."

"I do not fear loneliness, Beanrua. I will find answers and return, for all of us," she said looking over the crumbling, antique town. "We deserve to be a great people again."

Beanrua nodded. She knew that if anyone could find answers it was Shaerico. "I will bring you what I can as soon as I am able to get away."

"Thank you," Shaerico said as she removed her hand from Beanrua's shoulder and turned toward the woods. Now all she had was the forest.

Weaving her way amongst the stark trees immediately felt different. Knowing that Collitte, the place she had escaped to her entire life, was no longer the only place that she could go made her feel both confined and free. Now she could go to the mountains. She could go to the Realm, or beyond. That thought struck her like lightning. If she was banned from Dorchas, if she was no longer under the control and protection of Alphaline, she could go wherever in the world that she pleased. She could travel. Shaerico inhaled the frosty forest air, no longer feeling the sadness of her banishment. She instead chose to focus on her first moment of true freedom. She headed for the pond.

As the crystal blue water came into view, Shaerico felt a sense of relief. It was not that she feared she would not find it, but rather she feared that it would have been discovered and disturbed. Luckily, her brother had little interest in exploration or natural wonders. When he was hunting, he saw and smelled nothing but flesh and prey. Every blade of grass, every rose petal, was securely in its place. She sat at the water's edge wondering what to do with her newfound freedom. She thought of Ghrian. She wondered what he was doing and what he must now think of her. The thoughts weighed heavily on her heart.

Shaerico looked to the sky, half hoping to see the mysterious white hawk. Somehow, she felt that it may hold answers. The events of the evening before played over in her mind. Her ruthless brother had attacked her without a second thought. Bruid had always lived to please Alphaline. Ever since his first moment of discipline, he had become obsessed with pleasing her. It was this way with many of the men of Dorchas. They longed to be her right hand, but Alphaline had always preferred to be and to lead alone.

Shaerico could not help but wonder about her story. How long had she lived in Dorchas before she found all of her children? Shaerico laid back on the grass and allowed her thoughts to fade. She fell deep into a much-needed sleep.

Shaerico had never stayed overnight at the pond before. She must have slept for nearly an entire day. Luckily, her cloak that had fallen off in the previous night's transformation had not been disturbed. It lay in its spot and when Shaerico awoke, she wrapped it around her now furless and frigid body. She was hungry and missing her morning coffee with Beanrua. She missed her friend dearly already. Beanrua had not been able to escape from under the watchful eye of Alphaline in order to bring Shaerico any goods or companionship to ease her exile.

Shaerico sat up and looked around her. The clearing was truly breathtaking. It brought her solace. The serene setting helped calm her wandering mind. She inhaled deeply and worked her way over to the water's edge. Dipping her toes in the frigid pool, she felt the shock of cold pulse through her body. She smiled and slid all the way into the icy water. The rush of turquoise liquid encased her. Shaerico felt weightless in its arms, as if she were floating on the clouds above. She laid on her back and stared up into the sky. The early morning light darted from tree to tree, leaf to leaf, dancing over the water and across her pale skin. She breathed in her freedom and for a moment, forgot about her questions, her concerns, and her loneliness. Every fiber of her being, every worry, became nothing in light of the water in which she rested. This moment was all that mattered, submerged in the purest water, every atom one. For a moment, she was at peace, whole.

As she floated, she neared the edge of the pond that she had never gone near. The rock face that lined the furthest edge of the pool was jagged. It was not a mountain, but it looked as if it were the same stone as the mountain Beinn. Moss grew up each side of the dome-like rock face. Shaerico drifted near it and her peace was disturbed. She turned herself upright in the water and tread as she faced the stone. She ran her fingers across the jagged edge, feeling the cold stone and wet moss on her fingertips. The lush, mint green moss housed small sprouts of iridescent brown mushrooms. The closer Shaerico looked, the more she noticed that every pebble, every fungus, every patch of moss shone with a deep turquoise sheen. As the morning sun drifted its way higher into the sky, it illuminated the strange glisten on the entire face of the rock. The curious

intruder continued to run her fingers across the surface, fascinated and mesmerized by what she witnessed. As she ran her hand down the stone and into the water, breaking the surface tension and sending ripples around her, she realized that this rock face was not solid. She slid her hand under the water's surface and felt an indentation. The moss ran under the water and continued.

Drawn by curiosity, Shaerico carefully lifted one leg and explored the opening with her foot. It was a cave. Her mind raced as she realized that what she had thought had been just a pond was actually an underwater spring, a well of life. Eager to explore, she took a deep breath and plunged into the depths. As she sank, she opened her eyes. Though they were filled with water, they did not burn, nor were they clouded. She could see that the spring went deeper and further than she could have imagined. The water was as clear as air, but the bottom of the spring looked black, like an endless gaping mouth. Shaerico steadied herself and swam in small circles, taking it all in. There were no fish, nothing living but strange plants that were unlike anything she'd seen before. Tall fingerlike weeds swayed in the water and a few turquoise pebbles dotted the sides of the spring, stuck securely in the rich red mud. Shaerico thought it strange. These were the same peculiar color of the leather strand around her wrist. She looked down at the cord. The water caused the loose leather to undulate in the movement of the ripples caused by her swimming. She stared for a moment more before returning to the reason she had submerged herself. As she turned, she came face to face with the open mouth of a cave. It had only taken a few minutes to soak up all that was around her, but her lungs were beginning to burn. She had to emerge. Shaerico came up for a breath as she weighed her options.

She was taking a huge risk by entering. She had no idea how deep the cave was, if there were any places to come up for air, or what may reside in the cave itself. But somehow, she felt certain there were answers in this cave. She could feel an inescapable tug to delve deeper.

Shaerico inhaled deeply and returned underwater as she propelled herself into the darkness. She swam as the pulsing blue-green light faded behind her. The cave mouth narrowed, and she began to fear that she may be trapped. Her hands were her guide as she pressed on. The moss had disappeared and all she could feel was rock, smoothed to velvet by constant contact with water. She was soon unable to move. She started to gasp for air. Now she was in total darkness. The light that once followed her from the mouth of the spring had been swallowed by black. Totally blind and immobile, her mind struggled to find a solution. As she attempted to turn herself around, she felt a small string of bubbles burst between her fingers. Frantically, she swam in the direction of the bubbles, trying her best not to panic as her lungs began to burn. She continued to swim and search the rock face with her hands until finally she felt an opening in the smooth stone. She pushed her hands through and then her head. Gasping for breath and coughing up the water that had made its way into her lungs, she pulled herself into an open cavern. There was a faint glow in the distance, through what seemed to be another tunnel. Shaerico feared that she had entered a labyrinth she would not escape.

Catching her breath, she sat and determined her next move. After a few moments passed, and she had recovered from her near-death experience, she began to assess her surroundings. The cavern was small, but she could stand. Shaerico lifted herself to her feet and slowly walked toward the faint light. As she walked, she could feel the thick, still air dissipate and turn to a chilling breeze. Her vision adjusted in the dim light and she noticed that the smooth rock face had again turned jagged. As her fingers ran across the stone, guiding her way, she realized that the cave walls were not just jagged, they were carved. She stopped in her tracks and leaned closer to the markings, trying to determine their origin. They were like nothing she had ever seen, or rather, felt. The markings resembled letters, but of no language Shaerico recognized. They were not cleanly carved, but rather engraved in the stone with rudimentary uneven edges, almost as if they were carved with blades. As she inspected the foreign text, she did not notice the flicker of light in the distance begin to fade. Soon, she was blinded by darkness again and thrust back into reality. A cold sweat dripped from the nape of her neck, but curiosity drew her on. She had come this far.

Eventually the distant light became visible again, seeming to toy with her. She followed the light through the maze of stone tunnels. Shaerico was amazed by the depth and craft of the carvings as she continued, her fingers lightly tracing them as she walked. The walls began to grow smooth after a while and eventually her soaked feet were free of water. Shaerico continued on. She was not one to let fear rule her, but as she drew deeper and deeper into the ground, she could feel the claustrophobia closing in, and she began to feel her freedom slip away.

Suddenly, the light stopped its playful motion. She was close enough now to see its reflection in the once again smooth gray stone walls of the cavern. Now she could clearly see the color of the light. It was as if this fire was made of water. Blue flames cast a strange glow upon the face of the stone, allowing Shaerico to see veins of pure turquoise and white that divided the rock. She stood still, gazing at its eerie reflection. Then all went black.

Shaerico rubbed her eyes, hoping that they would adjust in time. An uneasy feeling crept its way into her stomach. She sensed that she was not alone. A warm breath pricked over her left shoulder. She could hear the weight of the creature hovering behind her as it exhaled. Shaerico leapt to the other side of the cavern tunnel and slowly slid further into the darkness. A great rumble sounded from where she had been. Her heart was beating hard. She wished more than anything that it were night, or that she had the ability to choose her form. Surely, she would be able to take on this beast then. Unfortunately, she had no choice but to face this creature of the dark as a human. Although they only took the form of a wolf by night, the people of Dorchas had keener senses than the rest of humanity. Shaerico stopped for a moment and listened for the sound of breath. Her eyes were beginning to adjust now, but still all she could see was stone. Every so often, a glimpse of blue would catch her eye and divert her attention. The fierce woman held herself upright, ready to attack whatever emerged from the shadows. The oddest and most concerning aspect of this being was that she could smell nothing of it. Whatever this creature was, it had no scent. Shaerico was getting frustrated by her blindness. She became impatient.

"Whoever you are, show yourself!" Shaerico demanded. "I saw your flames. You mask yourself in darkness on purpose. If it is to strike fear, you will not succeed. Show yourself, or are you too afraid to face me in the light?"

Slowly the blue flame was revived, but this time it was directly in front of her. The strange fire was completely visible to her now. Deep unearthly blues swirled and raged with vivid greens, dancing between streaks of the turquoise that seemed to exist only in this place. Little was visible aside from this mesmerizing flame. Shaerico looked into the raging fire as it grew. Then she noticed something even more peculiar. What she expected to have been some sort of torch was encased in a row of pointed, glistening diamonds. She barely noticed them in front of the blue flames. It took a moment longer before she realized, this was no torch and those that encased the flame were no mere diamonds, they were teeth.

A bellowing laugh came from between the sharp teeth that guarded the flame, "I am not afraid of you."

Shaerico watched as the flames burst forth with the beast's words. She flattened herself against the cavern wall as her surroundings became clearly visible in the glowing light of fire. The great creature towered over her, blue flames spilling from its mouth like water onto the ground below, illuminating all. Shaerico quickly realized why she was unable to smell this creature. It was reared on its hind legs, displaying an underbelly of solid stone.

"What are you doing here, Shaerico Langhealach?" it roared.

Hearing her name startled her. Langhealach? The word was buried so deep in her memory that it felt foreign to hear it spoken aloud. She had not heard her birth name since the death of her parents. What was this giant of stone that knew such things?

Shaerico was unable to speak or move. She had certainly found answers, but much like Ghrian, they were unexpected, deadly, and produced more questions. Without a word, Shaerico lifted her eyes to the creature. Its jaws were long and lined with massive rows of diamond teeth. Its emerald eyes were flecked with white and gold. They were encased by a brow of black stone that shone blue and extended behind its head into curved horns. A ridge of the same black ran down its spine and tapered to the tip of its pointed tail. It had talons of emerald green and a stance familiar to Shaerico.

The beast resembled an elongated, giant wolf in its anatomy. The hind legs bent backward in a crouching position, but what struck her most was not its similarities, but its differences. This beast was entirely stone. The white marble shone regally and gave off a terrifying glow.

"What, what are you?" Shaerico stammered.

The creature leaned back on its hind legs and curled its long tail around the front of its body, covering its large sharp talons. "I am Marmair. King of the Living Stone."

Shaerico couldn't help but let the words slip, "There are more of you?"

Her eyes darted around her, bouncing along the cavern walls. She saw nothing living, but as the blue flames continued to pour from Marmair's jaws, she began to make out shapes in the stone. Giant beasts that resembled the one in front of her were carved in rows high above her head in the open cave. She counted six, but there were three empty holes and one partially crumbled. Shaerico could feel that something earth altering had occurred here.

Marmair followed her gaze with a turn of his massive, slender horned head. He turned back to her and ended the flow of flames. "These are my kin."

Shaerico looked into his intoxicating green eyes that swirled with gold and white like galaxies in a night sky. Her words escaped her as she tried to think of what to say next. Should she devise a plan to escape? Or should she use this opportunity to perhaps gain some clarity? Was there even hope of her getting out of this cave?

Marmair watched as she wrestled with herself.

"If it helps you, young one, I am not going to eat you." Marmair said calmly. His voice was like a rushing river, smooth and powerful. "You have asked what I am, and I have told you. Now it is my turn. What are you and why have you come?"

Shaerico noted the odd question. He had known her full name, which she had buried deep in her memory. She looked back toward the direction from which she had entered the cavern. Shaerico removed herself from the cold wall and stepped toward the great beast. Her head came to just below his shoulder. She couldn't help but think to herself that if she were in her wolf form, she would be nearly eye to eye with him as he sat. Marmair looked down at her and lowered his head to her height. For a moment, she forgot every question she wanted to ask and was simply lost in the creature's eyes. They held the destruction of a raging ocean and the renewing growth of spring all in one.

He blinked slowly and lifted his head again. "You came here because you were curious. You have questions."

Shaerico straightened herself and looked up at him. "How did you know my name?"

"Hmm," Marmair began. "That is not the first question I would have thought you would ask." He smiled and huffed. "I know everyone in this place."

Somehow Shaerico could tell that his knowledge was deeper than what he could see, still she replied, "But I have never seen nor heard of you. Surely, you would have been spotted if you came above ground."

"It is my duty to know of every creature in the Forest of Collitte, and even all of Domhaen," he said, ignoring her comment.

Shaerico was puzzled. How could a beast who lived underground know of every being in the world?

Marmair continued. "The question you should be asking, is not who am I, or how I know you, but rather, who you are."

Shaerico was taken aback by this unexpected comment, "I know who I am," she barked. "I am Shaerico of Dorchas."

"But what is Dorchas?" Marmair replied.

Shaerico was perplexed and at this point getting frustrated by the beast's riddles. "It's the town in Collitte," she began. "It was forgotten by humans, abandoned, but strong. Surely you know this since you know everything concerning the forest." She couldn't hide her sarcasm.

"But you don't know what Dorchas was, you don't even know the history of Collitte, or your people here. How can you know yourself?" Marmair breathed.

Shaerico calmed herself and began to think. She had come here searching for answers. She had discovered that Alphaline was indeed hiding something, though she was unsure of how much the White Wolf knew. She could not understand why her people had not been forbidden from coming here, yet they were forbidden from the Realm. These creatures of stone were certainly far more deadly than mere man.

"Enlighten me then, please," Shaerico sighed, sitting on the cold stone in front of Marmair. "Teach me what I do not know."

Marmair grinned, his teeth glistened in the light of the still burning fire that lined the ground around him.

"Teach you?" he purred. "Let us start with what you do know. What do you remember of your earliest years?"

Shaerico did not remember much of her childhood. Her earliest memories were not pleasant and she loathed revisiting them.

"Not much, truly," she said. "Alphaline found Bruid and I when we were young. Like she found everyone else. I'm assuming you already know this?"

Marmair looked at her, nodded, and pressed deeper. "But why were you rescued by Alphaline?"

It was as if Shaerico had no control over her thoughts. The horrid night came rushing back to her.

"There was a fire," she started slowly, staring into the blue blaze not far from her. "A vast, red raging fire. I remember houses and people burning. I remember the screams and the panic. I remember the fear." Shaerico continued to stare into the blaze. Marmair waited, allowing her to continue. "I remember the white-haired woman that saved us. I remember the first night in the Great Hall with all of the children huddled together. It was the first night that I," Shaerico looked down at her hands and watched as she moved her fingers. "It was the first night we changed."

"Do you know why that was? Did the White Wolf never tell you the story of your people?" Marmair inquired.

Shaerico looked up from her hands. She had never considered there to be a story of her people. The story that had always been told was that Alphaline had found the children and raised them as her own in the once glorious town. That was it. No one dared ask more. No one cared, as they had never known, or at least never remembered, anything different.

"I know that Dorchas was once a great city, but Alphaline said nothing of where she rescued us from, nor why," Shaerico said.

Marmair shifted his weight and let out a heavy sigh.

"You are Shaerico of Dorchas, though your parents were not native to this land. The city was no longer as great as it had once been, but it was still full of people when your parents arrived here," Marmair explained.

Shaerico listened as his words sank in. If her first flashes of memory were of her home burning, then that had been Dorchas. Questions flooded her mind. Who were her parents? Why had they not rescued her if they were in the same town? How did Alphaline survive the destruction if no one else did? Who caused the final destruction of Dorchas? For years, Shaerico had buried thoughts of her birth family. She had never known them. She had always assumed that she was from another land, so she never bothered to waste thoughts. But now these questions burned in her like the fire in her memory. No matter how hard she tried, she could not recall the faces of her parents. She held Marmair's gaze. He looked back at her calmly; she could see a gentleness in his eyes.

"You are a cursed people," Marmair said. "That night, the night of Dorchas' true and final destruction, the night of your rescue, was the night your life ended and your story began. It was the night that you became part of something greater than yourself."

"What do you mean? Who destroyed my home and my family?" Shaerico demanded. Rage began to boil inside of her. For the first time, she felt a need for vengeance.

"Your birth family was destroyed by the flames. You will know more about them in time. And though you still hold their name, you have found a new family," Marmair continued.

He was right, she had found a family in the strange pack of cursed children. She thought of Beanrua and Bruid. "Who cursed us then? The

125

same one who destroyed Dorchas, I assume?"

Marmair nodded. "You were not always a shapeshifter."

Shaerico had never questioned this either. Everyone around her had always changed to their wolf form at night. It was how she grew up, how all the children of Dorchas had. Truthfully, she had never considered that it was abnormal.

"You cannot control your form after night fall, which I am sure you have realized. The full moons are far worse, as your animal instincts take over and your humanity disappears entirely. You are a being torn between two worlds, two bodies," he said.

This made complete sense. This is why she had no memory of attacking Ghrian. Why Alphaline forbade her children from going out at night aside from hunting duty, why punishment was even more severe if they went out during a full moon.

"So, our wolf form is a curse then?" Shaerico asked. She had never disliked her wolf form. In truth, she rather preferred it, except for the night that she had almost killed Ghrian.

"Yes," Marmair said. "You were cursed by a jealous sorcerer of no fault of your own." The Living Stone stood and motioned for Shaerico to follow. "Come."

Her head ached with this new knowledge. Adrenaline pulsed through her veins as waves of truth cascaded over all that she had known, crashing in white bursts of light over the darkest questions that she had long ago pushed to the depths of her mind. She had a family. A true family somewhere out there, beyond the forest. She stood and walked beside the beast as they drew deeper into the cave. After walking in silence for some time, they came to another large opening. This one was much grander than the resting place of the Living Stone. The cavern opened and its walls sparkled in the moonlight. Shaerico looked toward the ceiling and noticed a long slit that ran through the solid stone, revealing the night sky above and illuminating the contents on which they stood. Lining the walls, glistening in the soft blue light were hundreds of turquoise stones. Shaerico looked at her feet and realized that she was standing in a thin layer of crystal-clear water. It reflected not only the moonlight, but also the glimmer of the stones. The whole place seemed alive with the movement of light.

Shaerico stood in awe for a moment before realizing that it was indeed night. She turned to face Marmair and declared, "It is night. Why am I still a human?"

Marmair smiled and entered the cavern, splashing the water behind him with his massive tail. "Curses have no power here," he bellowed.

Shaerico looked at her bare feet and knelt down to let the water run through her fingers. It was soft, almost weighted, like molten silver without the heat. "The water frees me from my curse?" she asked.

"The water is the conduit of the Creator's power. It is not the water itself that heals, but the Creator through which all life flows."

Shaerico thought back to the night that she had attacked Ghrian. Though her memories were vague, she recalled how she had awoken outside her home, naked, human and covered in droplets of water. She must have entered the spring. Now she had a new set of questions.

"Who is the Creator?" she asked.

Marmair smiled. "He Who Is," was all the explanation the beast gave. "He placed the one who made me here to guard this gift to all He created," Marmair said as he raised his emerald talons and motioned to the stones around him. "The very sorcerer that cursed you was also made to protect this place, but he became consumed by greed." Marmair's talons returned to the ground and dug deep into the stone below. "He betrayed us and turned instead to lust and power."

Shaerico returned upright. Her head swam with this new truth. Her entire existence had changed in one moment. Was Alphaline trying to hide the truth of her children's existence? Was she hiding the fact that they are all cursed?

Shaerico walked to one face of the cavern and ran her fingers along the smooth facade. As she came to a turquoise stone, she pulled it from the wall. She held it in her hands and felt its soft surface. It was similar in shape to the one Beanrua had taken from the dead man, yet was much brighter. It was not a gray stone that possessed the mesmerizing blue sheen, instead it was solid in its turquoise shimmer. She turned to Marmair and asked, "What is the purpose of these stones?"

The beast stepped toward her and gently removed the stone from her hand with his emerald talons, returning it to its place in the rock.

"They hold great power, the Iómhara. Like the Living Water, they are conduits," he spoke as he stood on his hind legs. "Their power is tied to the water, and the water to He Who Is. They were formed to be used as tools for healing and growth, but in the wrong hands, these stones can be used for great evil. The sorcerer that was charged with guarding these stones from those who may be tempted, fell himself into temptation. He made the choice to remove the stones and choose for himself their use. Instead of guarding their power, instead of fulfilling the purpose for which he was created, he decided to remove the stones and use them for his own will." The blue flames again began to bubble from Marmair's throat as he spoke. The memory of the sorcerer's betrayal enraged him.

Shaerico interrupted him, "But there are many stones still here. So, he did not succeed?"

Marmair calmed himself and the blue fire receded back down his throat. "No, he did not succeed in obtaining them all," he breathed. "However, he took many and a few more precious things than Iómhara."

Shaerico remembered the empty places carved into the rock in the first cavern. "He took some of your family?"

Marmair looked at Shaerico and replied, "One. But what is worse, two followed him."

The great beast returned to all fours and continued, "He spoke lies to them. Twisting the truth, he convinced them to follow in his rebellion. My second left with him, abandoning his duty like it was nothing in the face of the illusion of freedom and power. But now, he is a slave. I have no knowledge of what became of the other, Yuko."

Shaerico was silent.

Marmair sighed and circled around her. "I was awoken in the disturbance and mutiny. All because a poisoned mind grew selfish. Now I will ask you again," he stopped in front of her, lowering his horned head until his blazing eyes were in line with hers. "Why are you here?"

Shaerico feared that he would not believe her answer. She did not know what to say, nor how to explain how she had found the spring or why she felt so drawn to it. She began slowly, choosing her words with caution. "I found this place on accident. The water, I mean. Ever since I first laid eyes on the spring, I have been drawn to it, felt a need to protect it. I've been in the water only twice, and had I known it was sacred and living, I would not have disturbed it." She lowered her eyes and continued, "I was banished from Dorchas." She paused, afraid to continue, not knowing what his response would be at her affection and protection of a human. "I was banished for saving the life of a man of the Realm."

A grin crept slowly across Marmair's slender jaws, the deer-like ears below his great horns twitched and rested against his stone head. Shaerico looked up, surprised to see his smile. Alphaline had banished her for saving a man, yet this guardian beast of the forest seemed pleased.

"You risked your life for a being you did not know? That is the greatest act of love," he mused.

Shaerico blushed, embarrassed to admit that she had left Collitte and spent time with this being. He was certainly no stranger.

"So, what you are telling me now, Shaerico Langhealach, is that you have no home?"

"Well," she looked into the night sky through the sliver of an opening above. "I suppose not."

Marmair lifted his head and looking around at the glistening cavern asked, "This man that you saved, does he have a name?"

Shaerico stammered for a moment. She hardly expected him to harp on that detail. "His name is Ghrian," she replied after a pause.

The stone beast continued his search for something in the cavern walls. "Fine name," he said. "Do you suppose this man would want to see you again?"

"I," she began. "I'm not sure. To be honest, I think he's afraid of me and probably with good reason."

"Aha," Marmair chuckled. "Well, wouldn't you want to find out? Especially if you could keep from scaring him again?"

Shaerico was unsure what to say, or what he meant. "How would that be possible? You said yourself that I am cursed."

"Indeed, you are cursed. Yet, you stand here now in the light of the moon and remain human." Shaerico looked to her hands and back to Marmair. "I told you, curses have no power in the wake of the Living Water."

Shaerico sighed, "Well, I cannot live in a cave. Besides, I doubt he will ever return to this place. He has almost lost his life here twice because of me."

"I am not saying that you should, or could, stay here. Did you listen to nothing I said earlier?" Marmair reared again on his hind legs and stretched himself, reaching for something nestled in the ceiling of stone closest to the opening that allowed thin rays of moonlight to soak the crystal-strewn cavern walls.

"The stones have power," he said, returning to the ground with something between his marble talons.

"I am saying that you need to keep the Living Water with you. You need a stone that cannot be turned. One that cannot be used for evil. The purest crystal full of the Living Water's immeasurable power," he smiled, eyes glinting in the ribbons of light.

He unfurled his talons and displayed a stone of immense beauty. A single white stone smoothed by water and flecked with three black crystals that glistened like stars. It winked the familiar sheen of turquoise in the moonlight. Marmair placed the Iómhara in Shaerico's right hand. The oval stone fit perfectly in the center of her palm. It felt like velvet against her skin. She could feel the weight of the stone, not just in physicality, but in its power. For a moment, she was afraid. She had just been faced with a new reality entirely. Now she was not only free to walk the forest and mountains alike, but she was free to roam the Realm of the Lake and beyond. The weight of her fulfilled dreams hung heavy with responsibility. Somehow, she could feel that this gift was intertwined with the fate of her future.

"Keep this with you at all times," Marmair spoke as Shaerico continued to gaze at the stone. "It will help you control your curse. In time, you may find that it does even more. Its name is Solas."

"A stone with a name?" Shaerico inquired, holding the stone to the moonlight that escaped through the small opening in the cave.

"It is a stone of immeasurable power. One of few that exist. It should not leave your side."

Shaerico nodded. "Not to leave my side, I understand."

"Good, then your journey begins."

Chapter Ten

A few miles away, in the quiet town of Dorchas, the air was still. The early morning light was beginning to creep over the treetops. Beanrua awoke in a sweat. She had nightmares of Shaerico's banishment. The loyal friend could not help but worry for the woman alone in the woods. She had tried to visit her the day before but had been followed by Alphaline. Beanrua planned to try again, but she knew that she had to move in cover of shadow.

Waking early, the determined friend stretched her slender body as the sunlight made its way through the single, small high window in her room. The rays of light illuminated her red fur as she returned to her human form. She yawned and continued her stretch. Beanrua knew that at this hour only Lili would be awake. She grabbed a piece of bread and her stone, which she rarely removed from her body after Shaerico had warned her of Alphaline's interest in it, and headed to Lili's for coffee. As Beanrua stepped outside, a foreign scent irritated her nose. It smelt of something burning. Rounding the corner heading into town, she saw a strange man entering Dorchas from the mountain trail.

His figure was tall and strong. Beanrua could hardly fathom who this man was or why he had come to Dorchas. No one ever came to the village, let alone from the mountain side. As the people of Dorchas awoke, they flocked to the streets, completely intrigued by their first visitor in remembrance. Oddly enough, Alphaline was nowhere to be found.

Beanrua sighed, realizing that she had missed her chance yet again to see Shaerico. The stranger was an alluringly handsome man. His hair was as black as night, a few silver strands strung above his ears. He wore a large black cloak, but it did not hide his obvious physique. A long and twisted wooden staff rested firmly in his right hand. It seemed he had traveled far. Beanrua wandered closer. He had eyes like the ocean, as blue and as deep as the waters, but they had a darkness to them. They resembled the depths of the sea, where not a spark of life could be found.

The stranger began to address the crowd as he approached. He explained that he was a passing tradesman here for the Winter Solstice Festival, and that he wished to sell his fine jewels to those in the Realm of the Lake. It was a strange scene. Beanrua became suspicious. There was still no sign of Alphaline and this man seemed oddly familiar with the relic of a town.

As the children of Dorchas gathered, the words of their mother rang in their ears: "If you see a man in these woods, kill him."

Bruid was the first to attack. He did not know if this man were the same that Shaerico had defended, but he did not care. The burly man approached the stranger, ready to defend his home and avenge his sister. The cloaked man did not seem frightened. As Bruid rushed the intruder, he lifted his staff to the sky. With one swift motion he knocked Bruid from his course with the blow of his twisted staff. The enraged man regained his footing and charged again. This time, the intruder was on the offensive. With another swing of his staff, this time with more force, he launched Bruid into the side of the Great Hall. With a loud thud, Bruid fell to the cobblestone, unconscious.

After a few moments of stunned silence, the children of Dorchas inched closer to the stranger. Some went to tend to Bruid, some readied themselves to continue the fight on his behalf. But before an attack could be mounted, the dark man reached into his cloak and offered a single stone to the nearest villager. It was a deep gray stone, that shone with hints of brilliant blue.

"I did not come to fight, good people. I am here to bring prosperity. This is an Iómhara, a precious stone found in only one place in all of Domhaen. Coupled with a few more ingredients, it creates the finest dyes for royalty and the like," he smiled as he turned to address everyone present.

His voice was like a crack of thunder, vibrating through the trees. "Where is the Lady of Dorchas?"

There was a wave of murmuring throughout the crowd. No one had seen her since the previous evening. Beanrua started to take this distraction as a chance to head into Collitte and find Shaerico, but she did not trust this visitor. Instead, she went to Lili.

"Good morning, Beanrua!" Lili called out.

"Lili, don't you ever leave this place?" Beanrua said pulling the attentive Lili to the window.

"Oh," Lili said. "How peculiar. I don't think I've ever seen a stranger." Her eyes filled with innocent curiosity.

"He says he's here for some festival in the Realm. I don't trust him," Beanrua said.

Lili laughed and brought Beanrua a hot cup of coffee. "You are too suspicious. I suppose you took Shaerico's place as the skeptical one in her absence."

"Seriously?" Beanrua said. "When have you ever known someone to come to Dorchas? He came from the mountain pass and he already knocked Bruid unconscious with ease. Though he claims he's no threat."

Lili looked back at the stranger. "I admit, that is odd. Why would anyone be on the mountain and at this time of year?"

"I'm telling you, whoever he is, he's up to no good, no matter what he claims," Beanrua said.

Cain had come forward to speak with the mysterious man in Alphaline's absence. Beanrua watched as the dark man gave Cain a single stone.

"Kiss ass," Beanrua growled, "Bruid had the right idea. We should be defending Dorchas like Mother said, not taking gifts from intruders."

She absentmindedly felt the similar gray stone in her own pocket. She could not help but feel that this tradesman had something to do with the death of the man she and Shaerico had discovered near the mountain stream. It was a shame she had to keep that information to herself.

The crowd continued to gather in the streets until everyone, aside from Beanrua, Lili, Beoir, and Alphaline, surrounded the stranger. The man continued to talk about his business in the Realm and his need of a place to stay. Finally, he was ushered into Lili's hall. The people of Dorchas were far too interested in him for Beanrua's taste. In Alphaline's absence, curiosity won over apprehension. She was infuriated that they could not smell the stench of deceit on him. She eyed the man as he sat at a table not far from her. Lili, being the kind soul she was, offered him a drink. He accepted a tea and turned to Cain. Beanrua could just barely hear their words.

"So, are you in charge in Alphaline's absence?"

Beanrua rolled her eyes as Cain puffed out his chest. "Well, she has never appointed me as such, but I am certainly the most qualified."

A low murmur ran through the hall as many listened to the conversation. Some agreed with his bold proclamation, while others argued against it.

"What sort of idiot would follow a senseless beast like Cain?" said one. "Alphaline would never appoint him second in command. Where is she?" replied another. "I think he would do a fine job. He certainly has the brawn," a third remarked.

Cain's eyes darted from table to table. He hoped that this traveler would hear only the positives. Cain was a vain being, but his most dangerous trait was his blind ambition.

The tradesman set down his beverage and again addressed the entire room. "My good people, I have been to Dorchas once before and remember a town of plenty. Where have the rest of you gone? You can't be more than thirty now."

The townspeople had little knowledge of the days of old. Their knowledge ended with their savior. All they knew was that Alphaline had rescued them and given them a home and a purpose.

One person replied, "None of us remember the time of which you speak. We were but children when Alphaline rescued us from destruction."

"Then why have you not joined the Realm of the Lake? Surely, you would have been welcomed by your neighbors."

Another responded, "The lady forbade it. She assured us that those people would not accept us, that we were safer here."

"Safer in the darkness of the woods? My dear children, I have heard the tales. I know of what you are. The men outside the walls of this forest are nothing to fear!"

Beanrua's suspicions turned quickly to mistrust. How could this man know what they were? Who was he really?

The cloaked man stood. "I believe that you deserve better. Why should you have to hide in the woods simply because you are different? There is a world to explore and to enjoy!" He beat his staff against the stone floor. "I ask you, come with me to the Festival, see for yourselves the dangers of man. You are a people of power, embrace it."

The whole place erupted. No one had thought to disobey Alphaline, especially publicly. It had never been openly discussed. She was their leader, their protector, their mother.

"Why should we trust you and not Mother?" one man called. "How do you know of what we are?" said another.

The dark man cleared his throat. "I apologize, I have failed to properly introduce myself." He bowed as he continued, "My name is Feir. I am an ancient being of magic and knowledge. It may surprise you, but I too was born from within these woods, not far from here. I know the form you take at night. I know that you are prisoners of Collitte. I promise you it is not you who should fear. Come," he said, holding out a handful of stones. "Take one for yourself. They are good for more than the making of expensive dye. They will help you control your gift. Come and explore the world with me."

Beanrua watched as many stood and received a stone from the stranger. Lili looked at Beanrua with understanding, as she too was now suspicious. Only three refused the gift of the stones: Lili, Beoir, and Beanrua.

Day turned to evening and the gathering moved to the pub. Beanrua filled Beoir in about the events of the day. He watched Feir as he continued to speak with Cain and the others. They seemed entranced by him. Listening to his stories of travel and trade, the people of Dorchas became more and more uneasy about their simple and sedentary lives.

"Where is Alphaline?" Beanrua whispered to Beoir, as she downed a beer.

"I don't know. It's not like her to be away this long. And I don't trust this man," he said softly.

"Nor I. This talk of leaving Collitte is absurd! Why would we leave our home? Just days ago, our people looked with pity upon Shaerico as she was banished, yet now they would willingly abandon the forest?" Beanrua rued.

Beoir shrugged and returned to serving his guests. Beanrua sat, wishing more than anything that Shaerico was with her.

Night came, and it was exceptionally cold. A chill filled the air that cut through even Beanrua's thick red fur. She awoke in the middle of the night and listened. Some were still awake. Following the voices, she slunk to the inn above Lili's place. It had long been abandoned and was primarily used for food storage. Cain had put Feir there as a guest of Dorchas. Beanrua crept up the stairs. Her soft, agile paws moved quietly as to not disturb the old wooden beams. She could hear Feir's voice and another she did not recognize. Her soft ears swiveled as she listened.

"Have you gathered them yet?" a voice hissed.

"Patience, friend. Nearly all have received their gift," Feir said with pleasure.

Beanrua stepped closer, nearing the door. With one eye, she peered through the opening in the doorway. She saw the sorcerer's back and a red light illuminated his head. There was no one else in the room. She slowed her breath and drew closer still. A single claw scraped across an uneven beam. Feir's head turned quickly toward her, his eyes glowing red. Beanrua jumped backwards and swiftly retreated down the stairs. She raced back to her room and curled in a breathless heap on her bed. She prayed that the man had not seen her.

When morning came, Beanrua slipped her cloak over her pale skin. She wandered down to see Lili. Feir and Cain were already discussing Dorchas' future over tea. Bruid sat to the right of Cain, hunched over the table like a wounded dog. Lili quickly walked to Beanrua as she sat in her usual spot by the window.

"Here's your coffee, Bean'," Lili whispered. She was on edge this morning. Beanrua grabbed her wrist, "What's the matter Lil'?"

Lili leaned down to whisper in Beanrua's ear, "Cain is talking of turning Dorchas into a trade post once more. Feir has convinced him that we should reclaim our part in the Realm. I don't like it. This sorcerer has more motives than our success."

Beanrua looked around. The people were attentive to Feir's words and even more enamored with their new treasures. She could not blame them though, as she too had desired the beautiful stone. The people of Dorchas had no possessions, aside from their cloaks and whatever trinkets they had accumulated over years of fumbling through the neighboring ruins. Still, the captivating affect that these stones had over her siblings troubled Beanrua greatly. She had all but forgotten that her own stone lay securely in the pocket of her cloak.

That afternoon, as the townspeople returned to their business, Beanrua and Beoir were alone in the pub, preparing for the usual afternoon rush. As Beoir went to the back to prepare the brews, Feir stepped through the door, knocking lightly on the wooden frame.

"Are we open for business yet?" he inquired cordially.

Beanrua looked up, startled. "I am surprised to see Cain is not with you," she snarled.

"Mmm, such a warm barmaid you are," the sorcerer said as he leaned his staff against the bar top and took a seat.

"Sorry, we receive few strangers here. Didn't you say you had somewhere to be?" Beanrua asked as she placed a warm beer in front of him.

Feir laughed and took a sip. "That I do, but I have some business to attend to here first."

"I cannot imagine what business you could have in Dorchas. We have no money with which to buy your trinkets," Beanrua said, as she continued to clean.

Feir laid one hand on his staff. "Well, firstly I need to ask you a question."

Beanrua gulped, trying to hide her concern as she turned and faced him. "And what might that be?" she huffed.

Feir could sense her fear. She knew now that she had been spotted the previous night. The handsome man leaned across the bar one hand placed firmly on his staff. "I quite like Cain, but I prefer the company of someone with a bit more stealth," he said as a sinister smile crept across his face.

Beanrua swallowed, attempting to keep her brashly beating heart at its place in her chest. "You wouldn't want my company, sir. I have no intention of leaving my home."

"But my dear, you don't have a choice," he countered.

The stone that was nestled in Beanrua's pocket began to quiver. It grew hot like a burning coal. The heat spread from her thigh to her entire body. She watched as Feir's eyes turned a fiery red. The black stone in his staff blazed the same hue and she began to lose control of her body.

"What are you doing to me?" she stammered as she fell to the ground.

"You will be the inspiration for your people, my love. You will be their freedom," Feir crooned as he stood above the red-haired woman writhing in pain on the floor. Her mind fought the power of the stone as her body began to transform. Her once beautiful eyes drained into a lifeless gray and her body shifted into her canine form. The giant red wolf heaved in labored breaths as the sorcerer knelt beside her. He stroked her thick fur.

"Are you ready to fulfill your purpose, my pet?" Feir said as he helped the wolf rise.

The ruby wolf shook her head and with dead eyes returned the sorcerer's gaze. "I am ready to lead my people to glory."

"Good," Feir smiled. "Then let us gather them."

The black sorcerer and scarlet wolf walked into the streets. Everyone present stopped in astonishment. Never had anyone in Dorchas turned to their canine form in daylight. No one knew it was possible. No one could control their transformation. Beanrua stood strong, her back as high as the tip of Feir's twisted and towering staff. The sorcerer laid one hand on her fur as Beanrua this time began to address her people.

"Brothers, sisters! We have hidden long enough! We have hungered and suffered boredom long enough! Where is our Mother? Where is our savior? She must have grown tired of tending to her children. It is time we restore Dorchas to its former glory!"

Her pack gathered, confused, but united as she spoke. Cain walked out into the street. He was surprised to see Beanrua's speech and her physicality.

"How is this possible? How are you in this form?" Cain stammered.

It was well-known that Cain preferred his wolf form, as he preferred anything that made him more powerful. He stood in front of Feir and Beanrua. In this moment, he was rather jealous of the red wolf.

"You already have the power." Feir stepped toward Cain. "You can all have the freedom and independence that you desire. No longer will a single being direct your steps. Follow me into the Realm and experience all that you have been missing."

Every being but Beoir and Lili seemed in agreement with the sorcerer. Lili watched from the window of the hall as Feir lifted his twisted staff. He released his grip and as it struck the ground, she watched in horror as the gray-blue stones turned to blazing coals and became one with the flesh of her people. Every human fell to the cobblestone and turned to their wolf form. They were one pack united under the deceit of a sorcerer.

Where was Alphaline? Certainly, she would never allow this. Something was terribly wrong.

As the pack of massive wolves began to leave their home, Beoir ran out of the pub. "Beanrua!" he called. "What is this? Where are you going?"

The red wolf stopped and turned to Beoir. He stepped back when her lifeless eyes locked with his. He knew she was no longer herself. She was now governed by the sorcerer's power. She had become a prisoner in her own body. They all had, under the gilded guise of freedom.

Beanrua turned back to Feir and followed as he led his new army into the darkness of Collitte. The last members of Dorchas met in the street, completely in awe of what they had just witnessed.

"What do we do?" Lili said, leaning against Beoir with clouded eyes.

The giant man wrapped his arms around her as they watched their family vanish into the forest. "We have to find Alphaline."

It was late afternoon and Shaerico had spent a few days at the spring. She emerged from the cave a new being, no longer burdened by gnawing questions. Her time with Marmair had given her a new sense of life, a new purpose. Shaerico knew that she could not turn back to her forest and she was at peace with this knowledge. She knew that Dorchas was no longer her home. Now she had no choice but to venture into the Realm, to accept the change and growth that was thrust upon her. She now knew the truth of her people. As she walked into the woods, the spring at her back, she held tightly to the white stone.

Afternoon waned into evening. Shaerico continued to walk slowly, taking in every moment with her forest. She felt the pulse of life of Collitte as she touched the trees and crunched the dying leaves beneath her feet. She would miss this place, but the lure of open fields and new worlds beckoned her on.

Eventually, she came to the edge of the trees. As she had done many times during her meetings with Ghrian and March, she stepped out into the still lush grass, feeling the soft blanket beneath her toes. She savored the moment as she walked into the field, no longer feeling the strain of worry that she may be caught. No one cared now. She was truly free.

She was walking down the line of trees, trying to determine where she could find Ghrian, when she smelled his scent. Her pace quickened as she discovered the source. The turquoise cord that had once been wrapped around March's neck, part of the same tether that Shaerico wore around her wrist, lay hidden in the grass. She leaned down and pulled the leather lead from the dirt.

She smiled at the cord and whispered, "You will certainly aid me in finding my Ghrian."

Shaerico took the cord and inhaled deeply, then wrapped the leather around her oval white stone and tied it securely around her neck. She had Ghrian's scent and she had time on her journey to think of what to say.

The raven-haired beauty walked further into the fields and closer to the Realm than she ever had before. As she walked, she began to hear a rumble in the distance. It sounded like thunder over the mountains, but it came from Collitte. Shaerico stopped and turned toward her forest. The ground began to shake as the sun began to fade behind the clouds. A piercing chorus filled the darkening sky. She could hardly believe her eyes as she watched as her most cherished friend came barreling out of the woods. Atop the red wolf's back sat a dark man with a twisted staff. He held the staff out in front of him, a black stone blazing red lead the pack, a deadly wave of destruction leading her family into the Realm of the Lake. She knew she had to find Ghrian fast. Whatever this was, whatever had occurred in her absence, was something of terror.

Shaerico looked to the sky. The sun was low, but it had not yet given its place to the moon. How had they changed?

She took a deep breath and removed her thumb from the back of the white stone. Marmair had not told her how to control her curse, only that she could. Shaerico looked to the rising moon and began to run, matching the pace of the pack that was large enough to decimate anything in its path. Soon her feet turned to massive paws, the dark hair that flowed in the wind against her back turned to silky black fur. The pads of her paws tore the grass from the ground as the giant black wolf raced along the edge of the forest, following the scent of the man of the Realm. Shaerico had always been the swiftest hunter with the keenest sense of smell, but coupled with the power of the stone, her speed was amplified. She ran along the edge of Yoaruq, like a shadow unseen and unheard in the night. Her journey was exhausting, but driven by concern for Ghrian, she made it to the great entrance of Lochta. The black wolf stepped onto the cobblestone path. In the light of the lake, she could see him, sitting by a fire with a beautiful golden-haired girl and another man. They were laughing and drinking, completely unaware of the desolation headed their way.

Shaerico inhaled deeply as she stopped for a moment, "So, our journey begins."

Part 3

Chapter Eleven

Ghrian laughed heartily. He was truly happy to be back with his oldest and dearest friends. Oir tore her glistening eyes from the crystal Dearthair had gifted her. She and Dearthair lifted their antler mugs and proposed a toast.

"To my dear Ghrian, you have created some fine bread this year," Oir giggled.

"Indeed, sir, and you have grown into a fine man!" Dearthair said.

Ghrian laughed, thanked them, and downed his beer. "I don't know about you two, but I need another drink."

"Certainly! We have much to celebrate," Dearthair said, tightening his arm around Oir's waist.

Ghrian rose from his seat by the blazing fire and made his way to the bar. The fire pits were nestled between the Adharc and the great lake, a perfect setting for an evening of celebration. The moon danced slowly across the lake's waters, a still contrast to the festivities upon the shore. The first day of the Winter Solstice Festival had been a monumental success. Ghrian had sold much of his bread already, primarily the Hearty Loaf, as expected. This winter was going to be a remarkably cold one. The people knew this and were preparing accordingly.

Ghrian ordered his usual and tossed a coin to the barmaid. Without a care, he turned from the bar, beer in hand. As he turned, he was met with a pair of brilliant orange eyes. He gazed into the eyes of the unexpected beauty.

"Ah!" he called out, startled, spilling the contents of his freshly poured brew all over himself and the feet of the raven-haired woman before him.

"Where the! Where did you come from?" Ghrian stammered, trying to dry himself.

Shaerico stood in front of him, her right hand tightly clutching the white stone wrapped in the turquoise cord around her neck. She could hardly believe where she was, let alone the fact that she was in her human form, and it was night. She smiled at Ghrian awkwardly, unsure how to begin. Ghrian cleaned himself and brushed the droplets of beer from the wavy hair that cascaded around his shoulders.

"Uh," he began, trying to recover from his embarrassment. "Would you like a drink?"

Shaerico smiled, "Sure."

The world seemed to slow, and time stood still as the two sat at the bar and sipped their beers. Much had happened since they had last seen one another. Ghrian watched in amazement as Shaerico downed beer after beer. It was apparent that she was on edge.

"Is everything okay?" he said.

He still was unsure about how to bring up what had happened the last time they were together. He could not help but be a little afraid of her. Tension hung heavy in the air.

"You must be here for the Festival!" Ghrian said, trying desperately to ease the strain.

Shaerico stared blankly at him, her mind searching for a way to get him to safety. She did not honestly know where safety was, what was happening, or if Ghrian would even follow her. She had no idea what was truly going on, or why her people were leaving Collitte. She only knew that the wolves of Dorchas would soon be upon Lochta. She hoped that he would remember her fierce defense of him and not just the horrifying truth of what she was.

Downing a third beer, she gently grabbed Ghrian's wrist, "Can I speak with you in private?" Her sudden sense of urgency was alarming.

Ghrian was doing his best to hide his concern. He was wary, but still so enamored with this alluring woman. Shaerico pulled him outside, away from the mass of people drinking in celebration. Shrouded in darkness, she leaned in close. He backed himself into the cold outer stone wall of the pub.

"Listen, I am not going to hurt you," she assured him, seeing his obvious tension.

"If you aren't here for the Festival, then how did you find me?" Ghrian asked. "Were you looking for me?" He remarked shyly, hoping this was true. For though part of him was still afraid of her true identity, he had a nagging desire to be near her.

"I am trying to warn you. There is something coming," she revealed.

Ghrian lifted an eyebrow and smiled. "You mean something more than a wolf woman stalking me?"

"Listen here," Shaerico growled. Ghrian froze at the sound. "I am trying to tell you that you are not safe here."

Ghrian sighed and stepped toward her. "Shaerico, I know you come from a, uh, different world. If I lived in Collitte, I would probably believe there was danger around every turn as well, but this is Lochta. It is the Winter Solstice Festival and there are many royal guards wandering about. Nothing will hurt you, I promise."

Shaerico whined at his insolence, "Do you remember what you saw last time we were together?" She had hoped to avoid bringing it up, but in this moment, she felt that it was necessary.

Ghrian sighed and nodded, "I do."

"You know what I am. I am not the only one. My people are the same. We are cursed," she winced as the word escaped her lips.

Ghrian looked at her with concern in his eyes.

"From the beginning, we were lied to by our Mother. We were taught that the Realm was the dangerous place. Leaving the forest was forbidden. We were taught that *your* people were the monsters, but as it turns out we were the dangerous ones." Her bright eyes looked up at Ghrian. "I can't explain it all now, we don't have the time. Ghrian, they are coming to the Realm."

Visions of the two giant black wolves battling by the spring flashed into Ghrian's mind: their enormous teeth, their black claws, the fur, the blood.

He looked at Shaerico. "Why?" he asked.

"I'm not sure, but there's no time for speculation," she replied.

"No, why?" he said bringing his hand to her face, he rested his finger just under her chin, lifting it up. "Why did you save me that night? Why did you leave your people to come for me now?"

The pair locked eyes and as Shaerico opened her mouth to speak, a cacophony of howls ripped through the joyful noise of the bustling town.

Every being stopped in their tracks. Not a single breath could be heard.

Shaerico lowered her eyes and offered Ghrian her hand. "You have to trust me."

He was unsure what she meant, but he had his suspicions. Shaerico removed her fingers from the stone. Ghrian watched in astonishment as there in the shadow of the tavern the woman from the woods again took the form of a wolf before Ghrian's eyes. Seeing her now in the light of the fire, he was struck again by her canine form. He stood motionless, frozen in awe.

"Get on," the beast demanded as she threw her emerald cloak over her back. Her voice was a bellowing snarl and her wild orange eyes blazed with fervor. Reluctantly, Ghrian laid one hand on her thick black fur. He felt her warm body heave with each long breath. Another chorus of howls pierced the night and people began to scatter. The royal guards ran in their shining armor toward Lochta's entrance. They were getting closer. Shaerico tossed her head impatiently, knocking Ghrian's legs from under him and throwing him to her back. The black wolf leapt away from the pub, heading through the city. Ghrian clung tightly to her neck, holding the turquoise leather. He smiled for a moment when he saw it. Then he heard a loud cry. It was a familiar voice.

"Oir! Shaerico, we have to get to the fire pits, please!" he cried.

Shaerico was overwhelmed by the chaos around her. Never had she seen so many people. Never had she heard so many cries. Flashes of her first memories burst through her thoughts. She shook her head, trying to focus on her reason for being there. She whirled around and turned back toward the running crowds. The fires of the pits were raging as beer and wood caught flame. Ghrian spotted Dearthair trying to remove Oir's mangled foot from between two rocks.

Shaerico leapt over the debris. Just as they made it to the couple, Feir and Beanrua entered the city. Enormous wolves of every size and color descended upon Lochta. Nearly the entire town of Dorchas had fallen to Feir's deceit. Almost thirty strong, the deadly pack laid waste to the great city. Booths that had been set up along the wide cobblestone street were crushed under the weight of the beasts. Goods and coins sprinkled the air along with a steady hail of fire. Feir drew the chemical flame from the large street lanterns of Lochta and rained fire upon the city, leaving all else in darkness. The citizens scrambled, trying to find their way out of the chaotic mass of debris and people. The royal knights, unprepared and mostly drunk from their night of celebration, were no match for the sorcerer and his wolves. They had not experienced anything like this within their lifetime. Attacks from beasts like these were stuff of legend. Fires blazed, livelihoods were destroyed, and people were torn apart. It was complete devastation. Shaerico gazed on, stunned, as her people decimated the city. Children were torn from escaping parents, blood and bodies littered the ground within minutes of their arrival. Like a wave of ruin they fell upon the grand city. Her own people. Alphaline had not kept them hidden for fear of what outsiders may do to them, but for fear of the great havoc they would surely reap on the outside world.

Feir smiled and yelled to his pack, "Every stone, every jewel, every piece of silver, bring them all to me!"

Shaerico could guess now who this man must be, a being of lust and greed. Ghrian leapt from her back to help Dearthair.

"Ghrian, what is happening? What is that?" Oir said, pointing to the black wolf, fear gripping her breath.

Ghrian stopped and turned back toward Shaerico. "A friend," he replied.

Oir wanted to question why one of these monstrous beings would be a friend to him, but she had not the energy. Dearthair and Ghrian tried to remove Oir's wedged foot. In the chaos, she had stepped too close to the fire pit and her foot and been twisted between two large stones.

"Leave her!" Shaerico barked. "You must run!"

Not long after the words left her lips, Cain appeared from the other side of the fire. His wild eyes locked on Shaerico. "My my, what have we here?" he growled, as his low tail twitched across the pit. Oir could hardly comprehend what she was caught between. Ghrian and Dearthair continued to work on freeing her.

"The banished wolf. You certainly are alone now, aren't you?" he laughed. "Was this the being you destroyed your future over?" Cain said, pointing his muzzle toward Ghrian. Ghrian looked at Shaerico, confused. "I would hate for you to lose every semblance of family all in the same day, but it's the price you must pay for your weakness."

Shaerico could take it no longer. She leapt over the fire and landed on Cain's back, sinking her claws deep into his tender flesh.

"I would rather be alone than a puppet," she said as she sunk her teeth into the soft flesh behind his ear.

Cain howled in pain as he threw Shaerico from his back. He lunged at her, but she dodged his blow, her black claws scraping against the cobblestone road. Finally, the men freed Oir. The three rose and tried to escape unnoticed behind the fighting wolves.

"So sorry, sister," Cain growled. "But I can't let that woman go. She has something he wants."

He lunged at Oir. Ghrian unsheathed his knife, but before it could taste action, Cain swept Ghrian and Dearthair from their feet. Dearthair screamed in opposition as the villainous wolf wrapped his jaws around Oir. The old friends watched in horror as her unconscious body was thrown upon Cain's back.

Shaerico considered going after Cain as she saw the terror on Ghrian's face, but the woman was lost. She had to get those that still had hope out of Lochta. Without further thought, she wrapped her jaws around the stunned Dearthair, throwing him onto to her back. Ghrian came to and leapt behind his friend, holding him steady.

Shaerico raced through the night. Through fire and blood shed, through screams of terror, and down the cobblestone road that led out of the city, she ran. Though her heart hung heavy and she longed to know the fate of her family; she had fulfilled her purpose. She had saved Ghrian.

When they finally came to a stop, Dearthair fell in a heap to the grass. Shaerico tried to catch her breath, but the man was quickly at her throat.

"How dare you!" he screamed. "Who are you to choose who lives and dies! You are one of them!"

Ghrian stepped between them and tried to settle Dearthair.

"I am heartbroken too, do not forget that I have been with Oir longer than you," he said. "But this wolf saved us. She chose to save us!"

Shaerico laid down in the grass, resting her head on her crossed paws, watching the two men as they argued. She truly did not understand these people. That woman was clearly the only interest to Cain. She was lost. Why needlessly sacrifice more lives?

She began to understand as Dearthair continued to wail and weep at his lost love. For a moment, she thought of what Cain had said. She had chosen Ghrian over her own family. She watched as he continued defending her. A warmth grew inside of her. Even in the chaos and destruction, the loss of her home, her family, this man whom she'd only known a short while in comparison, gave her hope. Hope that there was life beyond fear.

As he and Dearthair continued to roar in anguish and frustration, Shaerico's hopeful thoughts turned to horror. In the adrenalin of their escape Ghrian had not noticed a shard of flying debris. Stuck deep in his left calf was a spike of wood, drenched red with blood. Shaerico rose quickly as she noticed it. The sudden movement startled the men from their conversation.

"What is it?" Ghrian asked. As the words left his lips, his eyes followed Shaerico's gaze to his calf. A pool of blood lay beneath his foot and his dark leather boots were soaked through. Suddenly, he became aware of the pain and exhaustion overcame him. Shaerico braced him against her body as he began to fall to the bed of dewy grass below.

"I'm fine, it's nothing," Ghrian commented, trying to believe his words as he felt the heavy thud of his heart throb in his leg.

Dearthair looked on, unsure what to do. Shaerico barked a few orders at him and he sprang into action, tearing a piece of his shirt and wrapping Ghrian's wound tightly to stop the blood flow. As his friend continued to mend his calf, Ghrian drifted in and out of consciousness.

Shaerico felt hopeless. She was no help in this form. The least she could do was allow Ghrian to rest against the plush fur on her side. She looked down at her massive paws, they were gray with ash and crusted crimson. She leaned down and pulled splinters of wood from between the pads of her charred paws. It had been a long day.

Ghrian was completely asleep now. At least he seemed at peace. She watched him as he slept. He was so beautiful. It amazed her how calm he looked while he slept, even in the wake of such a horrific day. His red-brown hair fell softly around his handsome face. His full lips nestled between his curled mustache and auburn beard. Even in the depth of sleep, after a more stressful day than she had ever had, his resting face brought Shaerico peace.

Dearthair broke her gaze. "What are you doing, wolf? You can't eat him. I won't allow it."

Shaerico snarled, "Careful boy."

She turned her head toward the forest behind her. She was hungry. It had been days since her last meal. Shaerico stood, lowering Ghrian gently to the grass, and looked beyond Dearthair. Her body towered high above the men as they lay. Lochta was burning behind them in the distance. Rage began to build in her again. Not only for the loss that she bore, but for Ghrian's loss as well.

Slowly, she walked toward Dearthair, who rushed to rest one arm defiantly over Ghrian.

"I am actually a bit hungry," she teased, bringing her muzzle close to Dearthair's face. She curled her lips, exposing fangs the size of Dearthair's fingers. The proud man stared back into her fiery eyes.

Shaerico released a low growl, "Keep him safe and stay here. I will be back by morning."

Dearthair watched as the black wolf disappeared into the night. He looked back toward Lochta. The great city was still in flames. People were rushing to and fro, carrying water from the lake to try and stop the fires from spreading. He thought again of Oir and fought away the nagging despair as his dream of a future with her faded to ash.

"We should be doing something," he said to himself. "We should not be resting while the Realm burns."

In defiance, Dearthair headed back toward the chaos, leaving the sleeping Ghrian unaware and alone.

"Damn that beast. Savior or not, it abandoned Oir," he said as he headed to the flames.

Deep in the foreign woods that surrounded the Realm of the Lake, a lone black wolf searched for food. In truth, though she was indeed hungry, Shaerico had desired comfort. Images of what she now knew had been Dorchas burning in her childhood tormented her mind. What was worse was that she knew that the sorcerer had been the cause of both the destruction of her home and Ghrian's. Her blood boiled as she raced through the forest. She had no idea where she was going. She simply ran. Feeling the biting chill of the crisp night air in her lungs helped to momentarily cool the fires of rage that burned in her heart. She made a vow to herself then, under the moon and the smoke that rose from the destruction behind her, that she would find her family and make the sorcerer pay.

Chapter Twelve

The next morning, Ghrian awoke alone in the fields beyond Lochta. Smoke billowed into the gray winter sky. He had nearly forgotten the horrors of the night before. They seemed but a nightmare as he lay in the dew heavy grass staring up at the endless blanket of gray. He lifted his hand to his head; it throbbed with regret. Realizing that he was alone, he tried to rise to his feet. A sharp pain shot up his leg as he attempted to stand. He fell back to the grass, a throbbing ache rising in his calf. He had forgotten this too. The stake in his leg stuck out like an oversize thorn. Hesitantly, he gave the wood a light tug. Another stab of pain tore through his body. This did not bode well for him. He began to panic until he spotted a figure coming out from the woods. The black-haired beauty emerged from the forest and stopped in front of Ghrian. Blood stained the pale white skin around her soft pink lips.

Ghrian swallowed. "You're a messy eater I see," he chuckled in an attempt to mask his rising fear and pulsating pain.

Shaerico looked embarrassed for a moment, then wiped her mouth with her green sleeve. "Your friend thought I was going to eat you last night," she chuckled lightly. "Where is he?"

Ghrian had almost forgotten that Dearthair was with them. He looked toward Lochta. "He must have gone back. We should go find him." He said as the dread of the night they had survived returned to the forefront of his mind. His limbs felt heavy, and a weight settled into his chest.

"No, they could still be out there, and you're injured," Shaerico protested, eyeing their surroundings and his calf. As she knelt down in front of him, she removed a few plants from her cloak.

"Hold still," she said softly, "this may hurt."

Back in Dorchas, injuries were a common occurrence. Whether from carelessness as children or full on brawls as adults, the residents of the Forbidden Forest all wore scars. Alphaline had taught them all which plants had the ability to heal.

"Bite onto this," she demanded as she handed Ghrian a stick. He was reluctant but accepted with little persuasion. "I have to remove the thorn." She said with pity in her eyes. Ghrian gave her a slight smile and leaned back against the grass, the stick between his teeth. Shaerico inhaled deeply and with all her might, she tore the stake from his calf. Ghrian's jaw clenched and sweat dripped from his forehead. In the moments that followed, Shaerico chewed and pressed the leaves into his wound, then she tore a piece of her cloak and tied it securely over the mess of flower and flesh.

Ghrian exhaled. The pain was still present, but he was grateful that the stake was removed. "Thank you," he said, his brown eyes locked on hers. She met his gaze and smiled. But her smile soon turned to frown as he continued.

"Shaerico, I am not leaving another friend behind," he stated without hesitation. "We have to go back. We cannot leave Dearthair. You said yourself that they could still be out there."

Shaerico looked toward the fallen city, then to the far fields, then to the forests beyond the Realm. She could not smell her family, or the sorcerer.

Shaerico had not thought this far. She had considered that she would save him, but not the events following. She had no idea what life was like in the villages of man. All her life she had been taught to fear them. Now she was thrust into the middle of a great shift in the Realm of the Lake. She had no home to return to, especially now that her family was also gone. Memories of the days that followed the fire of her childhood came in cascading waves over her mind. The smell of decaying bodies, the lingering ash and smoke, the feeling of utter hopelessness that hung heavy in the air. She did not want to experience that again, but she had no real choice. She had nowhere to go but with the man she had come to rescue. Reluctantly, she lifted Ghrian to his feet and they walked together back to Lochta.

The cobblestone roads were caked with ash and blood. The massacre of the previous night enraged and devastated Shaerico. Her people were the monsters, not the people of the Realm. Reality sank heavy on her heart. She watched as residents of Lochta removed broken bodies and goods from the streets. The fires were out now, but the stone buildings were scorched, their bases turned to a charcoal gray. Stepping over debris, Shaerico followed Ghrian's directions to Oir's tannery. They found Dearthair there crumpled in a heap on the floor.

Ghrian ran to him, stumbling as he went, and turned him onto his back. He patted Dearthair's face lightly until his smoky eyes opened. They were bloodshot, and a look of horror stained his face. He looked up at Ghrian and began to speak, "Ghrian, those horrid wolves, those cursed creatures, they took Oir! She was alive I saw her." Dearthair coughed as Ghrian sat him upright.

Dearthair looked up at Shaerico's face. "Who is this?" he said, stunned by her beauty.

"My name is Shaerico," she responded before Ghrian could answer.

"Where did she come from?" Dearthair said, looking toward his friend. Ghrian was unsure how to respond.

"That is none of your concern," the woman answered, sensing Ghrian's anxiety at his friend discovering her true nature. "I am here to help."

Dearthair was suspicious, but too preoccupied to press any further. He had been away from the Realm for years and there were many unfamiliar faces. He watched her walk around Oir's shop. Shaerico inhaled deeply, drawing the girl's scent to her nostrils.

"You said they took her?" Shaerico asked, looking to Dearthair.

"Yes, last night. I thought she was gone, but I ran back here and," he paused, as fear glazed over his eyes. "There was a man. A giant man cloaked in black and accompanied by an enormous red wolf. They were looking for something." He recollected, "Then the big one appeared again with Oir and once they'd searched the place, they took her."

Shaerico knew that Beanrua would never do something like this of her own will. She knew that she had to follow them, she had to find out what was going on. She had to know for certain what that man had done to her family and why.

"We should go after her," she stated suddenly.

"Are you crazy?" Ghrian said. "A moment ago, you didn't want to come back to Lochta because you thought they may still be here! Now you want to leave the Realm and follow them?"

Shaerico walked to Ghrian's side, looking at him as he sat with Dearthair.

"I know you don't want to lose your friend." She turned to Dearthair. "If she was still alive when you saw her, then she is not lost as I had previously thought," she said.

Dearthair looked at Ghrian, confused. "Do we know her?" He turned to Shaerico. "Why would you help us?"

Her orange eyes met Dearthair's, "They took my friend as well and I will not abandon her."

Many people of the Realm had gathered at the Temple of Lochta seeking both answers and aid. The Priests there tried to explain away what had occurred. It was simply a pack of wolves from the forest. They were hungry, preparing for winter, according to the men of the Order. Some cried out that they should alert those beyond the Realm. Surely, the wolves would head down Cossan Crossing and enter into the Kingdom. The towns of Lake Muina needed to be warned. The Priests had dismissed this idea, claiming that mere wolves would simply return to their forest after they had their fill. But what of the fires? They had spread accidentally amidst the people's panic. Fires were nothing out of the ordinary for this time of year. They had seen this before. They reminded the people of the notorious wolves of the Forbidden Forest and why Collitte had been given that name, but still, they assured the people, they were ordinary wolves. All in Lochta had assumed that they were simply regular wolves, not the monstrous beasts of legend that had laid waste to the city.

"But the fire!" one man protested.

"And those were no common wolves!" another called. "Those were the demon wolves of Collitte! It's true! We have all heard of the legends."

"Those are nothing more than fairy tales! They have never been seen outside the forest!" one argued.

The bickering and denial continued as Ghrian, Dearthair and Shaerico walked into the courtyard. High walls surrounded the large white tiles that coated the courtyard floor. The pristine tiles were a stark contrast to the wave of ash that the people brought with them as they entered. Shaerico had no knowledge of the Realm's disbelief. She had no knowledge of their loss of faith. Back in Dorchas, she had read in the old decaying library of the history of these places. From her understanding, Lochta had rich roots in belief. People would travel from far east to get a glimpse of something precious that resided in the Realm, but it seemed that Lochta had turned from that path long ago.

Ghrian and Dearthair discussed amongst themselves how to go about asking for aid to ensure the return of Oir. Shaerico watched the spectacle, as people argued and turned on one another in despair. She saw marred faces, blistering burns, and one man near them had lost his sight. She saw a woman trying to comfort a child as it held a disfigured and torn doll. Men shouted. Horses and animals wandered aimlessly through the streets, some badly injured. How could these people not see that something was afoot? Had they not seen the wolves and the cloaked man? Or had they chosen to abandon their own senses for the sake of a reasonable explanation?

After some time and much discussion, Ghrian stepped forth to the marble steps of the Temple. He began to address the men of the Order. "Wise Priests, we come with a request."

The men had heard requests all day, from peasants asking for aid and shelter, to the royal princess herself desiring comfort of knowledge and peace of mind. They grew tired of the people's questions, to which they had no real answers.

One man, tall and lean with a long and twisted beard, stepped forward to meet Ghrian. His hands were knotted and his skin wrinkled, but his eyes were lively and full of youth. "What is it, my son? State your request."

Ghrian bowed and looked again to the man. "Our friend has been taken. You may know her, sire. She is a wonderful tanner here in Lochta, she owns Lilted Leather. We ask for aid in returning her home."

The old man stroked his matted gray beard. This was the first time he had heard such a request. All others who had encountered the wolves did not live to tell their story.

"You wish to go after a pack of ravenous wolves in search of a single tanner?" he asked.

Ghrian could tell his cause was not being taken seriously. "Sire, my friend saw her alive. He watched as she was taken by one of them."

The Priest raised his hand. "Silence young man, you know not of what you speak! Wolves do not steal away with their prey, they devour them."

He turned to the crowd. "Tell me, any of you, have you found survivors? Were your kin taken? Or were they destroyed?"

No one spoke. The bickering ceased and the crowds were hushed. None that had been attacked survived the night.

"See," the Priest said. "Wolves do not take prisoners."

Ghrian lowered his head, seeing that his fear was realized. They were on their own.

Shaerico then stepped forward, enraged by these people's lack of faith. "Those were no ordinary wolves. A curse is upon them and we must rescue those that were taken!" she shouted.

The Priest glared at Shaerico, his eyes wild. "Who is this foreign woman who dares to defy me?"

Ghrian stepped behind Shaerico, who had gone to the steps and had one bare foot on the cracked marble.

"Come," he whispered in her ear. "It is not worth it. He abandoned belief for the sake of reason long ago. He does not see clearly. He will believe nothing you say."

Dearthair intervened and bowed to the old man. "Gracious sire, she is not from this land and knows not of what she speaks. Forgive her, we will be on our way."

The Priest nodded and turned back to the black doors of the Temple of Lochta. Shaerico stood still in her place as Ghrian tried to pull her away. She could sense evil in this Priest.

"His heart is as twisted as his beard," she growled as Ghrian pulled her from the steps.

The townspeople watched as the trio left the courtyard. Murmurs floated behind them. "A curse?" one woman cried, startled.

"I suppose that would explain it," a man retorted.

"We should consult the library," another replied.

"What do we do now?" Dearthair said, as the voices of confused citizens droned on behind them. "How can we fight a hoard of gigantic wolves alone, and ones that are supposedly cursed at that?" He turned to Shaerico and said, "I saw a wolf take Oir. Although my better judgment says you're simply insane for believing they are cursed, as such things do not exist, I am more concerned with how you know this."

Dearthair's suspicion of this strange raven-haired woman was ever increasing.

Ghrian's face fell as he shot a nervous glance in Shaerico's direction.

She remained calm and did not appear concerned in the slightest. "Did you not see the cloaked man riding the red wolf?"

Dearthair nodded.

"Whether you believe in curses or not, no wolf would choose to be ridden. He must have cursed them. It is the only logical explanation," she stated.

Ghrian released a breathy chuckle. Her explanation may have been odd, but her reasoning was sound enough. Dearthair had no retort. After all, he had been rescued by a talking black wolf the night before. He dared not pry further.

Ghrian interrupted, "I'm not sure how, but we have to do something."

They had walked too far to hear or see the events that followed their departure from the courtyard. A few of the townspeople had demanded answers from the Priests of the Order, determined to consult the ancient texts that were kept hidden in the Temple. As the Order refused, some tried to enter. Thus, dawned an age of great unrest in the Realm of the Lake.

"We have no idea where they are going! We have no idea if Oir is even still alive," Dearthair moaned.

Shaerico interjected, "She is still alive."

"And how do you know? Who are you again? I don't think you ever even told me where you are from," Dearthair said.

Shaerico lifted her head to face Dearthair. Annoyed, she answered, "I am not from this land."

Dearthair looked at the stubborn woman and then to Ghrian. "Where did you find her?"

Ghrian laughed and looked at Shaerico, before replying, "Actually, she found me."

Shaerico blushed a deep red, then averted her eyes from Ghrian's gaze and continued, "So, how should we begin?"

Ghrian smiled and answered, "Well, we should first gather supplies. I'm not entirely sure how to approach this. I usually just grab the necessities and head out when I have deliveries, but I've never gone beyond the Realm. What do you think Dearthair? You're the one who's really traveled."

Dearthair sighed. "You are right, old friend. I came all the way from the Kingdom, but I had hoped to stay a while," he paused. "The roads will soon be covered in ice and snow. I suppose I should return my inventory to my home in Miotal, since I doubt the Festival will commence now."

"We'll start with that then," Ghrian said.

The three returned to Oir's shop to gather supplies and rebandage Ghrian's leg. Though the wound still bothered him, the herbs Shaerico had placed upon it greatly eased the pain. Ghrian also had the remainder of his festival bread. Though Dearthair's jewels were stolen, he still had stone carvings and various metalwork. Shaerico absentmindedly stroked her own stone as the men gathered their belongings.

"Do you not have anything to bring along on this journey?" Dearthair inquired. "You are sure to freeze barefoot," he said, staring down at her muddied and calloused feet in disgust.

Shaerico followed his gaze. She had never worn shoes, nor anything other than her green cloak as long as her memory served. Ghrian smiled at her and laid a hand gently on her shoulder. "Come with me. I am sure Oir has plenty of spare boots."

The pair went to Oir's room. Out of the corner of his eye, Ghrian noticed the saddlebags that he had commissioned Oir to create. They were nearly complete and would have to do. He smiled as he held them up. They matched his bridle and reins perfectly. The first three letters of his name were spelled in a dark green thread. He marveled at Oir's special touch. Something else then caught his eye at the opposite corner of the room. There were two saddles near the wall. One seemed to be his own, as it also matched the rest of March's tack, yet it was far from being finished. The other had obviously been meant for the Festival. It was stunning, inlaid with golden thread in intricate designs. What was odd, however, was the opening for the center stone, which was nowhere to be found. It looked as if it had been burned. The neighboring black stones had been torn from their positions and lay on the floor next to the intricate piece. Ghrian was puzzled by this as Oir took impeccable care of her work.

After gazing a bit longer at the saddles, he threw the saddlebags over his shoulder and walked to the edge of the room where Oir kept her clothes. She had made many clothes. Her love of working with leather was the primary reason she had little money. Ghrian lifted a pair of cream-colored boots from the pile. They were lined in gray fur and were incredibly soft to the touch.

"Here," he said, "these should feel just like your bare feet on the grass."

Shaerico smiled at his gesture as she slid her slender feet into the boots. They were soft and very comfortable. Then Ghrian lifted an enormous fur coat from the pile.

"No," Shaerico protested. "It would only be wasted on me. You should

bring it for yourself."

Ghrian looked confused until the memory of Shaerico's thick black fur made its way into his mind. "Right," he said, avoiding eye contact. "I will bring it along just in case."

They returned to the studio at the front of the home where Dearthair had packed all the necessary things for their journey. His inventory, Ghrian's bread, some of Oir's jerky, blankets, deerskins of water and beer, and a few other necessities were stuffed into two bags. The men lifted them to their shoulders and prepared to leave.

"Where to first?" Shaerico inquired, trying to get used to her new feet.

"We have to go get the horses," Ghrian replied, hoping to the stars that March was still alive.

Upon their arrivals to Lochta, both Ghrian and Dearthair had left their steeds in Capall's care. They hoped now that the wolves had not ravaged the stables. The three set out along the dusty road. It was quiet and a sorrowful stillness filled the air.

Shaerico was excited by this adventure, as she was finally able to step into her freedom, but she was also anxious. They were about to travel to lands she had only dreamed of. In truth, she was terrified. As strong and brave a creature as she was, she still craved the comforts of home. Especially now that she knew of the peril her people were in. What she wouldn't give for one last morning brew with Beanrua. Her heart beat hard as they made their way through the streets of the scorched city. They saw no one else as they walked. Oddly enough, even with the damage done to the great city, no repairs were being made. Man and beast were locked inside. Soon they came upon the dirt road that led to the stables. It was as they feared. Nearly half of the once elegant white barn had crumbled, ash spilling from one side. The once lush green grass was scorched and brown leading out toward the fields.

Desperate calls came from the horses in the barn, some littered the fields, and others were not so lucky as to escape their fate. Ghrian dropped his bags and ran as best he could toward the entrance of the barn. He screamed for Capall as he ran, but received nothing in return.

Shaerico looked on as he went. Dearthair followed close behind his frantic friend. The two men reached the stables and tore through the dilapidated door. Shards of wood splintered under their feet as they walked. Some horses neighed, while others made no noise at all. Dearthair quickly found his bay mare and released her. He gathered his saddle and bridle and brought her out of the barn to look her over as Ghrian continued to search for March. The gray stallion was nowhere to be found.

To Ghrian's astonishment, the palomino mare and her two cream foals had survived the night. He made his way through the crumbled barn to their stall. Slowly, he opened the painted door and released them from their prison of wood and ash. He watched in awe as the mare and her twin foals escaped into the fields. Like twinkles of starlight they winked in the glare of the sun and vanished. A small beacon of hope.

Shaerico made her way to Ghrian's side. She placed a hand on his shoulder. "March hates being caged. There is no way he would have allowed himself to be put in a stall."

Ghrian turned to Shaerico, a new light in his eyes. He found the bridle and reins that Oir had made him and headed to the pastures. Shaerico remained in the stables and looked around at the damage. There was a hole blown in the roof and pieces of horse strewn across the ground. The wolves had not done this.

As she walked on, releasing the tired beasts that still lived from their stalls, she came to a creature unlike any she had ever seen. Even though horses were still unfamiliar to her, she could tell that this one was even more unique. Far above her head, a pair of the most peculiar eyes stared down upon her. They were like jewels fallen into dark ash, a swirl of the brightest blue and the deepest red. The great beast had a marking like a white mask over his head, contrasting his dark body. His coat nearly matched her wolf form's fur. He was black as night. The horse swished his silvery-white tail as she drew closer. He made no other sound. It was strange that he had made no attempt to escape the blaze. Not one flame seemed to have lapped upon his door. There were no signs of destruction anywhere around him, yet he stood in the most decimated wing of the stable. Shaerico came to his door and slowly lifted the latch, but the stallion did not move.

She opened the door and stretched out her hand, motioning to the regal beast that he was free. Still, he did not move. She was puzzled. Every other horse she had freed ran immediately from the stable. She looked back to the black giant. His mane was thick and wild as it fell upon his neck, his forelock covered most of his face, but Shaerico could see that it hid a nasty scar. This creature had a harrowing past.

"Go on," she said lightly. "You are free."

The horse lifted a massive gray hoof and pawed the ground. Then, slowly emerging from the stall, he stopped to face Shaerico. She had never before been afraid of another animal, but she could sense great power in this being. Slowly, he lowered his head to hers. He pushed his mangled muzzle into the woman's shoulder, nudging her forward. Shaerico did as the horse desired and walked out of the barn. Steadily, the creature followed her, until they met up with Dearthair and his mare.

Dearthair was at a loss for words as he stared at the gigantic stallion that stood behind Shaerico. The horse's wise and wild eyes surveyed the surrounding fields.

"Is, is that your horse?" Dearthair managed to say, mouth still agape.

"Mine?" Shaerico said, still confused by the concept of owning another creature. "No, but I think he wants to aid us on our quest."

Dearthair was confused, but decided not to comment as Ghrian returned from the fields with March at his side. Shaerico smiled as Ghrian and March approached. "I knew you would find him," she said.

Ghrian hugged the gray stallion's face to his own. "He found me, actually. He was roaming close to the forest and came running toward me. He must have sensed that something was coming and escaped his enclosure," he said proudly.

Ghrian picked up his belongings and laid them over March's back. It was then that Ghrian noticed the beast behind Shaerico. "Fiáin," he whispered. The horse's nostrils flared at his name.

"You know him?" Shaerico inquired.

"I would suggest moving away slowly Shaerico, that horse is more dangerous than March," Ghrian cautioned.

March neighed and pawed the ground. The black stallion stepped in front of Shaerico and walked toward his stout, smaller counterpart. Ghrian backed away as the stallions came face to face.

"How do you know him?" Shaerico asked.

"He was here when I first came and purchased March. Capall, the owner of these stables, said that he had found him wounded on the road. He had tried to free him many times, but he always returned. There is something wrong with that horse. He is dangerous," Ghrian explained.

The three companions watched as the stallions stood, eyes locked, pawing the ground, and releasing low brays. The gray stallion reached out his neck and nibbled on the black stallion's throat. The black beast shook his mane in defiance, allowing a glimpse of the grueling scar that ran deep into his forehead and down his muzzle. He neighed in warning. The sound was nearly as piercing as thunder. Dearthair brought his hands to his ears as Ghrian stood gazing on. Shaerico was in awe of the creature. After a moment, March calmed himself and Fiáin settled. Ghrian looked on confused. He had never seen March back down or shy away from another being.

"Fiáin is the alpha," Shaerico explained in the only terms she knew how. "Now, we must be on our way."

"That beast is not safe to travel with," Dearthair commented as he settled himself astride his bay mare.

Ghrian pulled the leather reins over March, ready to begin the journey.

"I think it would be unsafe to travel without him," Shaerico replied.

Chapter Thirteen

The morning was cold. Freezing rain drenched the travelers as they awoke. Ghrian rubbed his tired eyes and opened them to find Shaerico sitting at the edge of the woods. It was apparent that she had been awake a long while gazing at the stone. He stood and joined her as she rested on the wet grass.

"What is that?" he asked. "I don't remember it. I may have a poor memory, but I think I would recall such a stone had I seen it."

Shaerico lifted her tired eyes to Ghrian. She had not slept, for fear that if she released Solas she would return to wolf form.

"It was a gift," she replied, eyes glazed in thought, her mind obviously elsewhere.

Ghrian wanted to press further, but decided to give her space. He stood and reached out his hand. "Are you hungry?"

Truthfully, Shaerico was always hungry, but she had eaten a decent meal the night before.

"I doubt you would have anything to my taste," she said quietly as she took his hand and stood.

Ghrian smiled and rummaged through the pack on March's back. He pulled a thick loaf of bread from the bag and presented it to Shaerico.

"Hopefully, this will be to your liking," he said, smiling as he handed her the bread.

Apprehensively, Shaerico took a small bite. A flavor she had never experienced flooded her mouth. It was like nothing she'd ever tasted and she was delighted. The people of Dorchas had bread, but it was much like their beer, plain. Ghrian watched as a glow crept across her pale face.

"This is delicious," she said, with her mouth full of bread.

"There is plenty of it," Ghrian smiled, pleased by her response. "Since the Festival was cut short, we should have enough for the three of us for a few weeks."

Weeks.

Shaerico had not considered how long this task would take, nor to where she would return.

Dearthair arose from his slumber with a grumble. He had been so eager the day before, pushing his poor mare nearly to the point of exhaustion. Cossan Crossing, the single road that led out of the Realm of the Lake was long. There were no towns to provide rest along the way, no inns, no places to eat until they reached the villages of Lake Muina and entered the Kingdom. There was simply trees, dust, and snow.

Ghrian stood over his tired friend. He knelt down and handed him a Hearty Loaf. "Here, Dearthair, eat something. Our journey has only just begun."

The trio had no idea of what they were walking into, nor where they were headed. Only Shaerico knew of the dangers ahead, and even then, she was blind to the reality of what they would face.

The cold drizzle turned to a steady downpour as Shaerico, Ghrian, Dearthair, and their horses continued on. Shaerico was loosely following the scent of Oir, tracking the pack as they went. She could tell that they had passed through this way, though not by the road. They had traveled further north, through the forests that flanked Cossan Crossing. The burning scent of flames singed her nostrils.

As Shaerico considered her lost family, Ghrian and Dearthair were thinking of Oir. Ghrian wondered how she was fairing, and where she was headed. Why would they kill so many and take one woman? Dearthair's mind was racing with worries of if they would ever be reunited. He had been away for so long. He had hoped that the Winter Solstice Festival

would be a chance at a new life together. Dearthair was now old enough and skilled enough that he could have started a smithy of his own. He had longed to build a shop and family with Oir, but the hope of that dream was fading fast.

They walked on in silence, the pouring rain chilling them to the bone. Fiáin kept a slower pace at the rear of the party. His eyes were ever watchful of the woods. Shaerico wondered about his story. She could not help but feel that he was a being of immense importance.

Days passed in silence. The road was long. Under normal circumstances and fairer weather, it would have been pleasant, but in the wake of the coming winter, everyone was on edge. Every snowfall brought tension. Along the road, they passed few travelers, some late comers headed to the Realm for the Festival. The trio would tell them of what had occurred in the Realm and all would turn around, traveling with the band for a way in sorrowful silence. One family passed with a herd of sheep. The two children, their mother, and father looked to the ground as they walked by. A small spotted canine did most of the herding work as the sheep wandered ahead. Shaerico turned to survey the animals as they passed. She had never seen sheep before, but they smelled delicious. Ghrian watched as her eyes darted between the plush white creatures. He could see that she was hungry. Aside from bread, they had eaten nothing for over a week. Ghrian handed March's reins to Shaerico and removed four loaves from the bag. She watched as he walked confidently over to the quiet family.

"Good day to you!" he called.

The shepherd in the rear stopped and looked up in fear. He stared wide-eyed as Ghrian jogged toward him, bread in hand.

"Oh, no sir, we don't wish to purchase anything from you," the man said.

The man was scrawny and shaken. Ghrian made it to the small herd of sheep as Shaerico and Dearthair looked on, confused.

"Sir, I am not trying to sell you anything. I see that you have a lame sheep," he said, pointing to a rather old creature with a cracked hoof. "I mean only to remove this worn yew from your herd. It will certainly quicken your travels."

The man looked at Ghrian and then to his wife. The tattered woman shrugged.

"I will trade you four loaves of bread. One for each of you. I am a baker from Yoaruq and my Hearty Loaf is known throughout the Realm," he said proudly.

The shepherd stepped forward and took a loaf from Ghrian. He took it to his wife. "Deal," he said, returning to Ghrian.

A young girl with matted blonde locks removed the old sheep from the herd and set it at Ghrian's feet. Ghrian handed over the remaining loaves.

"Thank you," he smiled at the girl. She returned to her father's side. Ghrian turned to rejoin his friends before recalling the condition of his home. "Sir!" He called out as the shepherd and his family had begun to walk away, "I must also tell you of the condition of the Realm!"

"We already know," the man said with somber defiance.

Ghrian looked surprised. How had this family heard of the news of the Realm when they would have been on the road when Lochta was attacked? The shepherd could see the confusion written on Ghrian's face. He sighed.

"Our home was in the northern forest not far from here. The beasts came from the direction of the Realm and decimated our farm. We have heard the legends of the wolves of Collitte. I knew it had to be them. This is all we have left," he said, motioning his arm toward the small flock. "The Realm is closer for us to travel, so we will rebuild a life there." The shepherd turned again to the road and ushered his family forward. Ghrian gazed on as they walked away and bid them a silent farewell.

He shook the thought of home from his mind and headed back to his friends, head held high, the lame sheep in hand. A puzzled look stained Shaerico's face as he drew near.

"What is that?" she said.

Dearthair responded in disbelief. "Seriously, where are you from that you've never seen a sheep?"

Shaerico ignored Dearthair's question, as she had gotten in the habit of doing. "It looks weak," she commented.

Ghrian happily placed the animal in Shaerico's arms. The sheep barely protested. "We are going to eat well tonight," he smiled.

Dearthair sighed. "How do you know she'll like it? Since she's never had sheep," he said caustically.

Shaerico inhaled deeply and replied, "I think I will."

That night, the band of misfits who had set out on a seemingly lost cause, ate their meal with little fear. The first week of their journey had proven to be relatively easy, all be it boring, monotonous, and cold. Shaerico and Ghrian enjoyed it the most, as neither of them had traveled farther than the Realm before. Dearthair seemed content as well. They were not yet overly hungry or worn. They were ignorant of what lay before them or the troubles they would face.

Shaerico devoured most of the meat, as well as an entire loaf of bread.

"My, someone was hungry," Dearthair laughed as he watched in amazement.

The fire blazed below the spit, as Ghrian turned it, his mind was elsewhere. Now that they were on this journey together, he wanted some questions answered. After the meal ended, Dearthair went to tend to his mare and March. Fiáin had disappeared into the forest, as had become his habit at times. Ghrian shifted his weight to face Shaerico who was cleaning the leftover bones. She felt his eyes on her.

"What is it?" she said.

Ghrian stoked the fire, pondering how to begin. "First, I want to say thank you. Not only for saving me, but for saving Dearthair as well."

Shaerico looked up from her bones and nodded her head. "I couldn't just let you both die."

"But why not?" Ghrian said. "After weeks of helping me train March, you disappeared. Then there was that night...I was worried something had happened to you. Why come back all of the sudden?"

Shaerico set down the bones and looked into Ghrian's inquisitive golden-brown eyes, the light from the fire dancing across his tender face.

"I learned much about myself that I had not known. Much about my people. You saw what I really am. My people are cursed, as I said before. And I was banished from them," she sighed.

Ghrian could see the pain in her eyes. "Banished? Why?" he gasped.

There was no way that she could explain to him that the reason she was cast out by her own people was because she spared his life.

"It doesn't matter now," she replied softly. "There are more pressing matters at hand. Something terrible has happened and I believe that all of my people are in danger."

The events of the first night of the Festival ran through Ghrian's mind. The horrors played themselves over and over in his thoughts and his nightmares.

"Those giant wolves," he said, beginning to piece Shaerico's story together. "Those were your people."

It all became clear. Her disappearance into the woods every night, her skeptical, skittish nature, and her mistrust of everything outside the forest suddenly made sense.

"You are from Collitte. The lost city of Dorchas, the massive wolves, it's all true," he said.

Shaerico kept Ghrian's gaze as he began to understand.

"It's all real," he whispered.

Shaerico leaned toward him and placed her soft, cold hand on his. "Yes, it's all true. And my people are in danger, just like your friend."

His head swam. His mother's tales had all been true. Her stories of mystic beings and forgotten history were not simply fairytale. Magic did still exist in the world, and it had been much closer than he could have imagined.

Miles away, a wave of destruction washed through village after village. The towns that led to the eastern mountain pass of Beinn were ravaged and their wealth was torn from them. The King in the East had heard of the tragedy befalling his Kingdom and sent an army to protect his people. Unfortunately, news had arrived to him late and the wolves had already passed into the mountain. He commanded his army to remain in the Lake Towns of Muina to provide aid and order. Some villages, such as Dearthair's own town of Miotal decreed that all valuables should be brought to the storehouse to be guarded, just in case the sorcerer returned. In such times, having any sign of wealth put an incredible target on one's back. The journeying band of man and horse had no knowledge of what had befallen the villages outside of the Realm. Little did they know, they were taking approximately the same path that the cursed people of Dorchas had decimated.

The journey through the woods was long and slow in the winter. Snow had fallen night and day and the path became laborious. The weather was harsh, and the days continued to grow colder.

Chapter Fourteen

Weeks passed until finally they came to a small village at the edge of the forest, marking the end of the trail and their entry into the Kingdom. Though all lands of the continent were technically under the rule of Gaewyn the one true king, Miath, the Kingdom, was under direct authority of the King in the East. His rule reached far and remained uncontested. However, the Order had more control over the workings of the Realm, and little was known of the people further west, if they even existed at all.

March had done a splendid job of carrying the bread and the silversmith's goods. He even allowed Ghrian to ride him on occasion. Dearthair and his mare had made the trip before, so it was not too much of a feat for them, though they had never made the journey during the dead of winter. Fiáin came and went as he pleased, sometimes disappearing for days. Shaerico was struck with wonder by everything she saw. Slowly, she learned more and more about what Solas could do for her. She came to trust the iridescent stone as night after night it kept her curse at bay. Dearthair had no knowledge of what she was and slowly warmed to her. Ghrian fell for her harder still, doing all that he could to make her journey comfortable. He wanted nothing more than to learn about her and her people. And though she still said little, she was beginning to trust and fall for him as well.

As the fellowship entered the town of Muinti, of the settlement of Lake Muina, Dearthair became uneasy. He leaned toward Ghrian and whispered, "When I passed through here on my way to the Realm, this place was a bustling village. Now all is quiet and cold."

"Well, it is winter," Ghrian said. Still, he held March's reins tighter.

The black stallion walked slowly behind Shaerico. He kept a watchful eye on the townspeople as many barred their doors and turned away. Not long after entering Muinti, they came to an inn with a small pub underneath that was nestled just a few buildings into the village.

"The Drunken Drake? Ha, Funny," Ghrian commented as they made their way to the entrance.

Dearthair peeked his head through the heavy, dark-stained wooden door. A few clusters of suspicious men stopped their low rumble of discussion as they noticed the curious man. All eyes turned to him and slowly he released the door.

"This is not the friendly town I remember," he said, gently easing the door closed.

"From the looks of it, this is the only pub and inn in town. We have no choice Dearthair. Calm down, I'm sure we'll be just fine." Ghrian said as he patted his friend's shoulder and tied March to a post outside the worn and weathered building. Dearthair followed and tied his mare next to March. Fiáin pawed the ground and shook his mane.

"He'll stay out here on his own. I'm sure he'll join us again tomorrow," Shaerico smiled at the coal black stallion.

"He's a wild animal anyways. It's not like we can ride him. He doesn't really have a use to us," Dearthair said.

Shaerico glared at him as she entered first into the pub. The air was stale. The bartender looked up from cleaning his assortment of glasses and mugs and greeted the beautiful woman.

"Evening, young miss, what brings ye to the Drunken Drake?" he asked.

Shaerico walked to the bar, attracting the attention of the men present. "Your darkest brew," she replied.

"I see, thirsty are we?" he smiled as he poured a dark liquid into a brown ceramic mug.

"That'll be one Airgead," he said as he placed the mug in front of her. Without hesitation, she brought the drink to her lips. Her companions had made it to her side and Ghrian could not help but speak up about the price, after all, Shaerico had no money, nor any concept of payment.

"A whole Airgead? Are you out of your mind? No beer is that good,"

he argued.

The barkeep looked Ghrian dead in the eyes. "That's my price, young master. Pay it 'er get out."

Shaerico glanced toward Ghrian and shrugged her shoulders as she kept the mug to her lips. He sighed and laid the coin down on the counter. Then turning to her, he said, "No more, this is too expensive. An Airgead is what I pay for an entire night of drinking at the Adharc."

She smiled sheepishly and crossed her legs, exposing her pale skin.

"Aren't you cold?" Dearthair commented.

Shaerico placed the mug on the stone bar. "I rather like the cold," she said.

Dearthair looked down at her bare white knees and blushed. "Shaerico, you are a strange lady."

"You have no idea," Ghrian said as he laughed and shot a glance at Shaerico. The midnight maiden rolled her eyes at his comment, hiding her smile as she downed the rest of her beverage.

The barkeep assured them that the horses would be secure tied where there were, but Shaerico was skeptical. He showed the trio to their room, after Ghrian had removed all the goods from March's pack. It was small, with two thin beds. Dearthair thoughtlessly collapsed onto one. Ghrian motioned for Shaerico to take the other. She walked toward the bed and placed her hands on the thin layer of down.

A worn woven rug lay on the floor under the window at the other side of the beds next to a small dresser. Without saying a word, she returned to Ghrian and slowly removed Oir's coat from his broad shoulders. Her soft fingers brushed lightly against his bare neck, sending chills down his spine. Then she took the cloak and threw it on the rug, curled up, and fell asleep. He stood motionless for a second. Was that caress on purpose? She was rather hard to read.

Ghrian lay awake thinking of Shaerico. He made no attempt to hide his feelings for her, but he was unable to determine whether or not she felt the same. She was often cold and spoke little, but she had left all that she knew to save him after weeks of not speaking. That had to mean something. He drifted to sleep, trying to think of ways to help her feel more comfortable, hoping that he would get the chance to understand her better.

That night was cold. Fresh snow had fallen, and a thin blanket of ice covered the frozen road. Shaerico awoke to the frantic neighs of a horse and the low grumbles of men. She recognized them immediately.

She lifted herself from her slumber and in a moment was down the stairs. In her rush, she had accidentally brushed the foot of Dearthair's bed. He shot up in a daze and saw that Shaerico was gone. He composed himself and ran after her. As he tumbled down the stairs, he heard the stallion's neighs and could see March through the sliver of the slightly ajar door. Shaerico was steadying March with one hand, standing between the horses and five large men.

"I suggest you let us take these steeds. I wouldn't want to hurt such a dainty lady," said one wryly man, licking his pale, cracked lips.

The others laughed. The largest man approached her, pushing his four comrades aside. "Ah, that's fine. You don't have to leave your fine horses. You can just come with us instead."

Dearthair ran out into the icy streets ready to defend Shaerico, but she turned and looked toward him.

"Please, Dearthair, go back inside."

"Are you insane?" he replied.

Before Shaerico could respond, the large man lifted her into the cold night air, ripping her robe from her, leaving her skin glowing in the moonlight. The thieves laughed and yelled in excitement. Dearthair was mortified as he ran to her aid. In his attempt, two of the thieves stepped in to stop him. He did well to dodge most of their blows, but was eventually overpowered. Since they assumed he was with her, they held him there on his knees to watch. Shaerico dangled in the air, but the face Dearthair expected to see when he looked toward her was not the one that he saw. Her fiery orange eyes blazed in the light of the moon that reflected onto the snow. A devious smile crept across her face, showing her remarkably sharp white teeth.

The man holding her was struck still for a moment. The others were confused. They expected to see a face of defeat and fear. She looked down the man's thick, scarred arm as it tightened around her neck. Slowly, she brought her arms to his. In one motion, she forced her weight upwards as both hands pushed against the thief's forearm. A loud snap resounded through the night sky, followed by the man's gut-wrenching scream. Shaerico landed on her feet in the soft snow. The man fell, holding his bloodied and mangled arm as he writhed in pain, the bone protruding from the crimson wound.

Dearthair was speechless.

"Get her!" the injured man called for revenge between his groans.

The men lunged for Shaerico, but not one was able to touch her. Her movements were swift and the few blows she landed were powerful. One by one the thieves fell. The two that held Dearthair finally came to their senses and sprang into action. Dearthair secured the horses and watched on in amazement. The thieves encircled the wild woman. The man with the broken arm continued to moan as he gazed at his exposed bone, frozen in shock. One man crept to Shaerico's left side but was met with a leg to the face. Another came from the front, but was unable to dodge her punch. The only one that got close to her was the wryly man that came from behind. He rushed her and went straight for the throat, but when he saw the beautiful turquoise cord laced around the glistening white stone, he changed his target. Before Shaerico could stop him, the cord was ripped from her neck and the stone fell, sinking deep into the snow. The man turned his attention to the stone, frantically trying to locate it in the blanket of white. Shaerico felt a wave of panic wash over her. Solas was no longer at its place at her chest. There was nothing to save her from the moonlight.

A long howl ripped through her body as Dearthair watched in absolute horror. Under the blue light of the moon, her slender figure transformed into the black beast. Her silky midnight hair encased her body and she fell with a thud to the snow-laden street. Her black claws scraped through the blood-dotted snow.

She was angry. She was angry at the thieves. She was angry at their insolence and disrespect, but more than anything, she was angry that the keeper of her curse had been torn from her and the secret she had managed to keep from Dearthair was revealed. Dearthair struggled to believe his eyes. He rubbed them, hoping for a moment that this was all a nightmare, that he would soon wake on the thin mattress to the morning sun. But this was not a dream. He looked again to the black wolf, a heaving shadow against the moonlit blanket of white beneath her. This creature was the one that had saved him the night of the attack on the Realm.

It was her. He stumbled backwards at the realization.

Shaerico turned from Dearthair to the thieves who had all but turned to stone. She spun to face the one that had broken the leather and removed Solas from its station. The wolf's long black snout met the man's chest. Her white teeth glistened like ice as she let out a deep reverberating snarl.

The man screamed in terror and abandoned his search for the stone. "It's one of them!"

All of the men fled. Shaerico knew for certain now that Beanrua and the others had passed through this town by the thieves' reactions. She looked back at Dearthair who was still frozen in disbelief. She was sad to leave them, especially Ghrian, but she could not imagine Dearthair would want to travel with her now. Turning back toward the open road, she let out one more piercing howl, then disappeared into the darkness.

Dearthair fell to his knees in the soft snow. Gently, he picked up her fallen robe and cream boots, and walked solemnly back to the room. Unimaginable questions raced through his tired mind. He lay awake, replaying the last month over and over again. It began to make sense. Why she wouldn't give him a definitive answer of where she was from, why she was there with Ghrian after that horrid night, why she ate so ravenously and knew so little of life even in the Realm. His head throbbed with aching questions, but he knew he had to rest. Eventually, exhaustion overcame him. The moon would soon return the sky to the sun, and then he would ask Ghrian to explain.

The next morning was even colder than the night before. Ghrian awoke in a panic to see Shaerico gone and her robe on Dearthair's bed. In a rage, he threw Dearthair from his slumber, demanding an explanation. The friends bickered about the situation they had found themselves in as they made their way outside.

"Why didn't you tell me she was one of those creatures!?" Dearthair yelled once they were safely outside the Drunken Drake.

"I was unaware for a long time myself, and I didn't want to scare you," Ghrian said. Dearthair huffed, fuming at the dismissive response.

The two men walked to their horses and readied them for travel. Ghrian noticed that Fiáin was standing in the center of the street. The black stallion was an ominous shadow over the powdery white snow. He lowered his head and flared his nostrils as Ghrian approached.

"What is it Fiáin?" he said as he slowly walked toward the horse.

Fiáin dug his hoof into the snow, creating a ditch around a smooth shimmering stone buried in the blanket of white. Ghrian leaned down and picked up the stone. It shone with a silver brilliance. The tattered pieces of the turquoise cord fell from the crystal as he lifted it from the ground.

"This was hers," he said quietly to himself. "We have to find her," Ghrian said, turning to Dearthair, who had mounted his mare.

"No way," he replied. "I'm sorry Ghrian, but she is one of them! How can we trust that she won't turn on us the very second we find her people?"

Ghrian returned his goods to the pack on March's back and climbed atop the gray stallion.

"We can trust her. I trust her. Besides, she's saved you twice now!" Ghrian said as he dug his heels into March's flanks and raced into the falling snow. "We are going to find her." His voice faded as Dearthair rolled his eyes, sighed, and followed suit.

The stallion of shadow stood in the village street for another moment before disappearing again into the surrounding woods.

Ghrian ran his fingers over the smooth back of the glistening white stone as March walked calmly beneath him.

"He's doing surprisingly well," Dearthair commented, breaking the silence.

Ghrian had been quiet since they left the village and the Drunken Drake days before. They still had not found Shaerico. March had indeed been performing surprisingly well, which under normal circumstances would have made Ghrian incredibly happy. But in the wake of Shaerico's disappearance, little brought him joy. The somber young man looked up at his friend.

"We have to find her Dearthair," he said earnestly. "This seems to be the only possession she has and I feel it carries a great weight for her."

The white stone shone in the blue winter sun, like the shimmer of the melting snow, it was almost blinding in the light. Ghrian felt an absurd urge to keep the stone close to him. He had no knowledge of its power, but he could feel its worth. He had noticed how Shaerico would absentmindedly hold it between her fingers, how she stroked it in the evenings; he knew that it must be important to her. Unbeknownst to him, however, only a few miles away deep in the woods, Shaerico was feeling the weight of its loss.

For days she had been wandering the woods, trapped in both fear and her wolf form. She had no idea how powerful Solas was, and after she had become accustomed to the stone's presence, she had forgotten the true plight of her curse. Wandering the woods alone used to be something that Shaerico relished, but in these foreign forests, she truly felt afraid. Still, driven by the scent of her friend and the hope of her family's return, she pressed on.

The days were cold and she grew hungry. It had been nearly four days since she'd last eaten. She was so concerned that she would scare the people of the small villages she passed, that she kept far from any food source. She walked deeper into the thicket of trees until she could barely sense the smell of any life at all. Then, seemingly out of thin air, a thunderous rumble poured through the forest. She stood, ears perked, twitching to determine the location of the noise. She prepared herself to run until a familiar scent drifted toward her on the winter wind. Shaerico readied herself for the coming hunt. Moments later, a wave of tan, like a field of lush wheat, washed over the glistening white snow. The black wolf crouched, awaiting the opportune moment to strike. The deer bounded over the snow, upturning what was left of the frozen foliage beneath, tainting the once pure blanket of white. Shaerico waited until the herd began to thin.

Her body edged closer to the thin clearing that the deer were siphoning through. She spotted a weak fawn trying to keep up with its mother, but struggling to regain its footing in the deep snow. The hungry wolf saw her chance to attack and leapt for the unsuspecting fawn. Her fangs sank deep into the soft flesh as Shaerico met her prey. But this beast felt much larger than a fawn. The wolf shook with all her might, but she could not take the creature down. The blood of this deer tasted different than she remembered and was hardly appetizing at all. The black wolf released her jaws and fell to the soft snow. She was both perplexed and irritated.

Looking up, she was met with the same large golden-brown eyes that she had seen back in her own forest. The white doe stood tall. She seemed hardly phased by the blood gushing from her side, or the massive wolf standing before her. Shaerico had no idea what to think or do. The blood that rushed from the doe's wound was not red but silver. The deer tilted her head and took a single step toward the wolf. Shaerico backed away, one paw above the snow to make a run for it if necessary. The white doe looked into the wolf's fiery orange eyes. In the time it took Shaerico to blink, the creature had transformed from wounded deer to the most enchanting woman. The fair-haired female in front of her smiled. The same golden-brown eyes looked down upon her. Shaerico could hardly move. She seemed to be frozen in time, barely believing what her eyes had just witnessed.

The woman would have been nearly invisible against the snow if it weren't for her brilliant glow. The blood had faded, and her side had no mark to be seen. Not even her crystal cloak was damaged. The brilliant lady in light was nearly blinding, like gazing into the noonday sun. She stepped toward Shaerico, her long white hair flowing in icy wisps behind her in the winter wind. As she came closer, Shaerico noticed small turquoise and black flecks upon her cheeks. Even in her fear, Shaerico could not pull herself away. She stood her ground as the woman drew near.

"You must be tired," her soft voice crooned. "You are very far from home, yet you have further still to go."

The black beast tilted her head and watched the woman as she held out her fair hand. She placed her palm on Shaerico's forehead and a warmth overcame the weary wolf. Her black fur began to recede and the chill of winter returned to her exposed skin. The heat of hunger faded as she was released from her canine form. She fell, exhausted to the snowy ground.

"There, that's better," the woman said as she removed her own outer white cloak and wrapped it around Shaerico's bare shoulders.

"How did you know?" Shaerico whispered.

"Hush now child. You need rest," she smiled.

Shaerico had been separated from her human form for longer than she had ever been before. The wolf had only ever overtaken her at night, but since she had lost Solas, she had been stuck in the body of the black wolf. Her energy was all but drained, and she had no choice but to heed the woman's request. Shaerico curled herself into the white cloak and fell into a deep sleep.

A thick, wet fog hung in the air above her, creating a blanket of moisture, hiding her from visibility. Shaerico lay in a deep slumber. Soon she began to see figures in her mind. A white woman and a dark horse appeared. They seemed to be talking. Shaerico had never dreamed before, or at least, not that she had remembered. It was a strange sensation being trapped in her own mind and forced to watch a scene she knew nothing about. She could barely make out the woman's face as she lay under the evergreen tree. The woman spoke to the horse, "You are far from home. Why have you traveled this far west?"

Shaerico watched in awe as the horse answered in a deep and thunderous voice, "There is something that must be done. I had to be in the Realm of the Lake."

The woman replied in a concerned tone, "You are wounded. Why not be healed?"

"It is a necessary sacrifice," the horse replied as it turned and looked in Shaerico's direction, eyes glowing a fiery blue.

Shaerico awoke in a cold sweat. Her heart pounded as she opened her eyes and uncoiled her body. She stood to survey the forest floor as best she could, but the fog was thick. In a soft voice, she called for Ghrian. There was no response. She was alone and after such a strange dream, she felt even more so. For a moment, she considered turning back toward Collitte. She could go beyond the mountains, far to the West where none of this could follow. She was free after all. She could wander wherever in Domhaen she wanted. Her adopted family was not truly her responsibility, besides, they had banished her. But Beanrua. And Ghrian. The urge to be by his side was greater than the call to simply leave it all behind.

The soft cloak that the mystifying woman had so kindly draped around her body did well to keep the cold at bay, but a chill ran deep as she began to miss her traveling companions. This was a new sensation for her accompanied by the pang of guilt that followed. How could she long to be reunited with a man of the Realm while Beanrua and the rest of her people were held captive? Her focus should have been on her family, even if they did banish her, but she couldn't shake the deep desire to be with Ghrian.

Shaerico took a few steps into the fog, not knowing where she was headed. She had lost scent of Beanrua. After walking a bit longer into the unknown, she spotted a dark figure amidst the trees. She readied herself for attack, for though she was hungry and weak, she was not ready to surrender to the darkness. As she drew closer, she realized the ghostly figure was Fiáin. His dark, thick winter coat shone with dew in the heavy mist, his silver mane nearly invisible against the freshly fallen snow. He lifted his head as Shaerico approached. Her pace quickened as she made it to him. Placing her hand on his withers, she sighed deeply.

"It's strange," she admitted, "for a creature I had no concept of just a few months ago, you feel so familiar," she paused before allowing the unfamiliar words to brush past her lips. "You feel safe."

The stallion turned his head to look Shaerico in the eyes. He seemed to understand her words. The intuitive being could tell that Shaerico was weak. For the first time, he tossed his head and motioned for her to climb onto his back. This was no small task, as he was a massive horse. Reluctantly, Shaerico laid her arms across his broad back, slowly lifting herself, her fingers gripping his soft fur and long mane. She had never ridden a horse, nor any other animal for that matter. She never understood the need until now. Fiáin used his muzzle to help lift her to his back. She felt so far above the ground. It made her uneasy, but she was grateful for the rest.

The fog grew thicker. As the pair walked through the forest, Shaerico began to fall back in and out of sleep; her fingers laced around the stallion's mane to keep her secure as she dozed. Eventually, she fell asleep entirely and began to dream for the second time.

In her dream, the fog had cleared. She lifted herself and sat straight on Fiáin's back. They were no longer in the forest; instead they were traveling through more beautiful fields than she could have imagined. There was nothing in sight, only lush green grass dotted with yellows and blues. A single road paved with the clearest stone shone beneath them, like a river of diamonds, shimmering in the risen sun. She could hardly comprehend the beauty.

"What is this place?" she stammered.

"My home, beyond the Far East," Fiáin replied.

Shaerico was astonished that she felt so comfortable talking with a horse, even if it were just a dream. For some reason, it no longer felt like a strange occurrence. She was also no longer hungry. A peace had washed over her like she had never felt. She dismounted Fiáin and landed on the plush pillow of grass below. She laid down on the ground and closed her eyes, feeling the warm breeze on her face, inhaling deeply the sweet scent of spring.

"If this is your home, why did you leave?" she asked.

"I had to leave," he replied.

"But did you want to?" Shaerico pressed.

"Sometimes a sacrifice is necessary. Life is lived and character is built in the moments you choose to do what is right, not what you desire. Though, on occasion, they are one in the same," he replied.

Shaerico sighed, "I understand."

Visions of Beanrua and Alphaline raced through her mind, mingled with ash and flame. She had to find her family and make the sorcerer pay.

As she jumped up from the peaceful rest, her eyes flew open. They were met with a cold wet mist. She nearly fell from Fiáin's back. The harsh realities of hunger and frost settled back into her bones, but her fervent spark of resolve had been renewed. She lifted her body from where she had been pressed against the stallion.

"We have to find Ghrian and Dearthair," she said. "Then we go after the sorcerer."

Fiáin released a short nicker in agreement. The reunited pair continued on deep into the woods, following with renewed purpose the path set before them.

Chapter Fifteen

The young men were exhausted from their travels and Dearthair was aggravated by the thick fog.

"When is this ridiculous weather going to let up?!" Dearthair complained. "I can barely see my hands in front of me!"

Ghrian had hardly noticed. He held the white stone securely in his right palm and directed March with his left. "I'm sure we will reach a town soon. At least we know we haven't left the road."

Dearthair was becoming annoyed by Ghrian's unusually tame demeanor.

"She will find us, Ghrian. Besides, she's a wolf! Don't they have the keenest nose of any creature? There's no use fretting about her. We're the ones who could be in serious danger if we don't get out of this confounded fog! What if someone tries to rob us again? I have nearly all of my supplies with me!" he hissed.

"Calm down, Dearthair," Ghrian huffed at his flustered companion.

After days of walking with little food, both man and beast were wearing thin. They had walked for miles and unknowingly passed two small settlements along the way. Luckily for them, they were now not far from Dearthair's own town, Miotal.

The fog still hung heavy in the air, but the chill was dissipating. The top layer of ice began to melt off the cobblestone road as the sun tried to divide the mist. Dearthair came to life with excitement.

"The ground has turned to cobblestone! That must mean we are getting close to home!" he shouted.

"Good. I am growing tired of all this motion. I haven't moved this much since before you were born!" a small voice moaned.

Both men turned, startled. They stared into the dissipating fog but could see nothing.

"Who's there?" Ghrian said.

Dearthair began to get nervous as memories of the attack at the Drunken Drake returned to him. Ghrian placed one hand on his knife.

"I bet they've come to try and steal what goods we have left. Blasted bandits," Dearthair scoffed.

"Idiots all around," the voice barked again, now a bit muffled. "Get your paws off me!"

Ghrian looked down at his left hand and nearly fell off his steed. The small griffin that sat on the hilt of his knife had shifted its position and was staring up at him.

"What the!" Ghrian shouted as he threw the knife to the snowy road below.

March bucked and Dearthair's mare bolted, sending both herself and her rider further into the lifting fog. The minute marble griffin stood up in the snow. He could see Ghrian and March above him amidst the mild mist. Ghrian attempted to regain his balance and settle March, patting the stallion's neck in uncertain reassurance. Dearthair and his bay mare were nowhere to be seen.

"Asinine creatures, humans are," the stone griffin mumbled as he pulled the thick blade behind him, carving a mouse-sized maze in the snow. "You better not make me climb up that monumental beast!"

Ghrian watched in amazement as the stone fixture of his knife made its way through the snow toward him. He rubbed his chilled hands against his frosted lashes, sure that his eyes betrayed him. This being had been with him almost his entire life and he had never seen it alive.

"What, what are you?" Ghrian stammered as he slowly dismounted March and knelt down to meet the tiny beast of marble.

The white griffin looked up, his black eyes dotted with flakes of gold. He threw the blade to Ghrian's feet. It slid across the thin snow until it met the confused man's leather boot. He retrieved the blade and looked down upon the griffin.

The small stone being seemed winded. "It's been a long time since I've walked that far. Hold on," he said as he inhaled deeply.

Ghrian looked back at the trail of missing snow, no more than three feet behind him.

"I am Raax," the tiny beast stated after catching his breath. "Mighty Guardian and Rescuer of Men," the griffin said, standing as tall as he could at about five inches.

Ghrian tried not to laugh, but he did slip a smile.

"Don't you dare mock me boy! I am older than the sun itself and your insolence does not phase me!" Raax huffed. He crossed his arms and looked away from Ghrian's gaze.

Ghrian was unsure how to respond, so he began, "Raax, Mighty Rescuer of Men, I apologize. I meant no offense. I'm just surprised is all."

The creature looked back at Ghrian with shrewd eyes and sauntered toward him. He studied Ghrian's face and stopped at his golden-brown gaze.

"You certainly have her eyes," he commented as he surveyed Ghrian's still slightly stunned face. "No need to be alarmed young master, I am here to help you not to hurt you."

Ghrian marveled at the statue. Then the marble creature leapt to his shoulder. "Now, let us go find your skittish friend."

Ghrian stood slowly, still trying to comprehend what had happened and what now resided so comfortably upon his shoulder. He returned to March's back and nudged him forward. The reluctant stallion complied. After a few steps into the fog, Ghrian regained composure enough to become curious.

"So, if you have been with me this entire time, why have you chosen now to make yourself known?" he asked.

"Good question, little one," the griffin said as he positioned himself toward Ghrian's right ear. Ghrian rolled his eyes at this tiny beast's condescending tone. "As I am sure you remember, your mother placed you in my care at a very early age. She left me with you as your guardian. Really, your life hasn't been all that eventful until late and when faced with danger or in the presence of strong magic, I am compelled to show myself. Actually, I have given you a bit of a heads up before," he tilted his small head in a proud, what one could only assume, was a smile.

Ghrian thought for a moment of his trip to Lochta and the small voice that had warned him of the bandits. That must have been this creature.

However, instead of pursuing that thought, Ghrian continued with another.

"In the presence of strong magic? I understand the obvious danger we face, but the magic?" He paused, feeling the griffin's wide, lidless eyes locked on his face. "I mean, of course I believe, I just don't think there's any magic surrounding me at the moment," he said, a little quieter than he meant to.

Raax let out a cough and jumped from Ghrian's shoulder to rest on March's neck. The gray stallion flinched, but did not spook, to Ghrian's surprise. The small marble statue was astonishingly heavy.

"Open your right hand," Raax demanded.

Ghrian felt his heart drop. How did he know about Shaerico's stone?

"It's nothing, just a simple rock my friend dropped. I am holding onto it until we are reunited," Ghrian said.

Raax sat and held out a paw, opening his golden talons. "Let me see," he demanded.

Ghrian hesitated, but assumed, since this creature was supposedly his guardian, he could be trusted not to steal from him. He opened his hand, revealing the smooth white stone. Raax's eyes widened, and he quickly snatched the crystal from Ghrian and leapt back to his shoulder.

"Hey!" Ghrian yelled. "I am keeping that safe for someone. Return it to me at once!"

"Hush, you idiot!" Raax replied. "Do you know who this is?"

"Who?" Ghrian asked.

"How did you get this stone?" Raax demanded, lowering his tone.

Ghrian stumbled over his words, amazed that this beast of marble who had not come to life in over fifteen years somehow knew this rock.

"As I said, this is my friend's. We were traveling together and got separated. She accidentally left this behind," Ghrian's voice trailed.

Raax was silent for a moment before replying. "I see, I see. We must return this to her. She will be missing her greatly."

"Her?" Ghrian mumbled.

A new slew of questions raced through Ghrian's mind, but they had caught up with Dearthair. Raax quickly returned to his home at the hilt of the knife. He was solid stone again, holding the crystal close to his curled body. Ghrian tried to pry it out, but it was no use. Shaerico's stone was now part of his knife.

"I suppose you're going to explain what that thing was?" Dearthair said as March and Ghrian approached.

"To be honest, I don't even know," Ghrian replied. "Maybe the fog was playing tricks on us? All I know is we have to find Shaerico."

Dearthair was tired and sick of hearing about the she-wolf. Although he appreciated the fact that Shaerico had rescued him, he still blamed her for Oir's capture. He could not understand why Ghrian was so hellbent on finding her.

"I am sure she is fine. We certainly know she can handle herself," he scoffed. "Anyway, we have made it to Miotal. We can rest here and prepare for the next step in our journey. Don't forget, our purpose in all this is to find Oir and bring her home."

Ghrian kept quiet and followed Dearthair into town. The fog had lifted, and he could see people weaving through the streets. This town was livelier than the last, but a heavy dread still hung over its entirety. After walking a few miles through the mass of cobblestone and wood, they passed a gigantic building composed of solid blocks of stone.

"What is that?" Ghrian inquired.

"That's our stronghold. It holds all of the excess goods and food. Since we are the town closest to the mountain pass, we were able to erect a building of solid stone," Dearthair said proudly.

Once they made it to Dearthair's home, they were met by his concerned aunt. Dearthair had hoped that his uncle had made it back home safely after missing their meeting point in the Realm, but seeing his aunt made him realize that was not the case. After some moments of grief, his teary-eyed aunt ushered the men inside. She made sure to direct her nephew to remove all of his belongings and prepare to take his precious metals to the storehouse in the morning.

His aunt stoked the fire in the solid stone fireplace. For a moment she seemed lost in the blaze. Then, by the light of the flames, she explained to them the horrors of when the massive wolves had ravaged Miotal. They left a path of destruction and carnage. Somewhere in the chaos, many of the villagers' goods were also taken. The council of the town had decreed that the remainder of the village's wealth be kept safe in the storehouse, under King Gaewyn's guard, should the sorcerer return.

Ghrian could see the rage in Dearthair's eyes growing in the light of fire. The more his aunt talked about the destruction caused by the wolves, the more his heart hardened toward Shaerico. He had been battling his opposing opinions of her for weeks, and though his heart had begun to soften toward her, in the wake of his aunt's words, his distrust was rekindled.

That night, a dense rain saturated the town. Ghrian listened to the drone of the downpour on the shingled roof. For the first time in as long as he could remember, he was unable sleep. As he lay awake, thinking of Shaerico and her whereabouts, he heard the loud neigh of a horse. He knew that March and Dearthair's mare were safe in the stable behind the house, but still he was compelled to check. He slid past Dearthair's room and down the winding wooden stairs. He threw on his cloak and made his way through the pouring rain to the stables. Nothing seemed to be bothering the horses. It must have been a neighboring steed. March was laying on the ground and the calm bay mare was standing peacefully in the corner of her stall.

Ghrian sighed and turned back to the house. It was then that he saw him. The great black stallion was drenched to the bone. His once silver white mane was now a dingy gray. Fiáin stood proud, but Ghrian could tell he was weary. As he approached, he spotted something white draped over Fiáin's back. He ran to the horse and saw Shaerico's pale face, cold and soft in the rain. He took her from Fiáin and ran inside. For a moment, he wondered how she had found a new cloak, but he was too concerned for her health to focus on that for long. He stoked the dying embers of the fire and threw on some new logs. The sweet, comforting smell of cedar filled the room. Setting her up by the fire, he realized that he had to remove her drenched cloak or she might go hypothermic. After all, they had found her own green one. Ghrian had kept it with him for when they were reunited. Slowly, he began to remove the soaked white fabric from her shoulder. He was glad that she was asleep as he could feel his cheeks burning, and the crackling fire was not to blame. He had to focus. She needed to get warm quickly. As he slid the cloak further, she woke up startled. In one motion, she returned the cloak to her shoulder and sank her teeth into his forearm.

"Ow!" he cried. Standing up and holding his arm, he quickly began explaining himself. "You were nearly frozen! I had to get you out of the those soaked clothes!"

At the sound of Ghrian's voice, Shaerico lifted her face to meet his. She stood up and without a word, the white cloak fell from her body. She wrapped her arms around Ghrian and held him tight. Ghrian stood, too astonished to move. After a few breathless moments, she took her green cloak from his hands and returned it to its rightful place around her body. She then sat back down next to the fire. Ghrian stood, his breath caught in this throat.

"Thank you," she said.

Ghrian nodded, a sheepish smile crept across his beat red face. After a moment, he composed himself and sat next to her in front of the fireplace. She could feel him staring at her.

"In all my life, I have never been afraid of the forest. But when I was out there, I felt the weight of being truly alone for the first time," she whispered. She turned her head and looked at Ghrian. Her once fiery eyes were dim and soft. "I've never feared being alone, until now."

Ghrian carefully placed his hand on hers. "I promise you won't be alone again," he smiled. "I am so sorry we left you, we should have kept searching."

She cut him off with a squeeze to his warm hand. "It's okay. Fiáin found me, and now we've found you." She rested her head on the hearth and closed her eyes, still clutching Ghrian's hand.

Morning came and as Dearthair made his way down the stairs, he was met with a surprise. Ghrian was sprawled out on the floor underneath the hearth and the dark-haired woman was nestled near the fire above him, their hands still intertwined. Dearthair made no effort to be quiet. Shaerico opened her eyes and watched him as he prepared food for himself in the kitchen.

"How did you find us?" he said, doing nothing to hide his dissatisfaction.

"I could smell you," Shaerico retorted.

Dearthair scoffed, "Of course you could."

Shaerico smiled as she looked down at Ghrian, placing his hand onto his chest. She was surprised by how much she had missed him and how relieved she was to be back by his side. As she stood, something caught her eye near his waist. She knelt down and saw Solas embedded into the hilt of his knife. At first, she was thrilled that the Iómhara had not been lost, but her excitement turned to concern as she wondered how she would remove it from the hilt. Carefully lifting the knife from its sheath, she placed it under her cloak and went outside to check on Fiáin. Truthfully, she had not caught the scent of her companions. She had passed out from exhaustion and hunger and the black stallion had carried her to safety. As she walked, she removed the knife from under her cloak, but to her surprise, the hilt and the stone had vanished.

She turned around and knelt to survey the ground. Solas had finally returned to her, she could not lose her again.

"Are you looking for this?" a small voice chimed.

Shaerico lifted her eyes to see the modest marble griffin. A sigh of relief washed over her. Raax was pleasantly surprised.

"You aren't afraid of me?" he asked.

"Afraid of you? No. I was afraid of never seeing Solas again," she said.

Raax's interest was piqued. "How do I know I can trust you with her? How did you come to find her anyway? She's no ordinary stone."

"Believe me, I know. I have suffered a great deal without her," she sighed. "Marmair gave her to me."

Raax's face fell. "Marmair. He's awake? That would mean," he started to say something but then grew quiet.

Shaerico ignored his troubling comment. "Please, give her back to me."

The creature walked toward Shaerico and placed the stone in her hand. Then he climbed onto her shoulder. "Don't lose her again," he scolded, still lost in thought. There was a perplexed expression carved into his marble face.

"Believe me, I don't plan to," she said as she looked down at the shimmering surface of the stone. "If only I hadn't lost the turquoise cord."

"I suppose I could help you with that," Dearthair said from behind her. Raax leapt into her cloak and hid as Shaerico stood, knife and stone in hand. "I see Ghrian returned it to you," Dearthair commented as he approached her. It was apparent that he had not seen Raax, nor overheard the rest of their conversation.

"Yes. I am so grateful that he found it," she replied.

"Listen, I don't trust you, but you did save my life. I'll make a pendant and chain for that stone, and we'll call it even," he said. Dearthair did not trust her, nor hardly even like her, but he felt compelled to do something to repay her for saving him.

Shaerico nodded. She could not care less whether or not she was trusted, but the promise of a secure tether for Solas thrilled her.

Dearthair led her into his shop that was built as an attachment onto the stable. Shaerico watched as he gathered materials. She sat in the corner, rubbing her thumb on the stone, happy to have it back in her possession.

She could already feel the weight of the curse lessening. Raax crawled to her shoulder again and nestled himself into her long black hair. He was roughly the size of one's hands and in the shadow of Shaerico's thick locks, he was safely hidden. After Dearthair had prepared his space he turned to Shaerico.

"I need the stone," he said.

She was reluctant to hand it over, but eventually she did. Dearthair took the stone and placed it in the center of a thin sheet of metal. He then cut a small strip of silver and wrapped it carefully around the stone, making sure that it was a tight fit. Shaerico watched as the silver folded and molded around the rim of the crystal. He then removed Solas and set it aside, as he soldered the rim onto the thin sheet of metal below with a torch. After that had cooled, he took two thin strands of silver and bound them together in a long braid. As the braided pair was heated, he gently touched the base to the metal sheet below. As it liquefied, it melded into place. At this point, Dearthair discarded the excess metal. He polished the piece to shine and returned Solas to its place in the setting. He stretched another cord of silver over a small blaze. As he laid the braided cord around the oval stone, he used a petite tool to form glistening prongs that held lightly onto the face of the Iómhara. Shaerico watched in amazement as it all came together. It was beautifully done.

"You're a very fine craftsman," Shaerico said over his shoulder.

He stopped and replied, "Thank you. I have been doing this since I was a boy." As he spoke, he pulled a few more strands of silver, this time three, over the bellowing fire, forming a long braid by which the pendant would be worn. "I grew up with Ghrian and Oir, before my mother and I moved to Miotal. My first memories are of us playing in the lake and getting into all sorts of mischief," he chuckled at the thoughts as they came. "We nearly destroyed the bakery more than once. I remember this one time, Ghrian's mother let us play in the bakery while she prepared that day's bread. I think we were playing hide and seek. I must have gotten jealous because Oir and Ghrian had always been close and decided to hide together. When I had a suspicion of where they were, I took a large bag of flour and in an attempt to smother them out, dumped the entire thing onto my own head. The bakery was minutes from opening and I was sure I was done for. Instead of being upset, Ghrian and Oir came out from their hiding place and helped me clean it up. We finished just in time for the bakery to open. I remember being astonished that his mother did not utter a word. She simply smiled her warm smile and continued her preparations."

He finished attaching the long braid to the pendant as he said wistfully, "Some days I swear I would give anything to go back to that time."

Ghrian joined them in the shop soon after Dearthair finished his story. "What's going on here?" he said as he stepped inside, a beaming smile proceeding him.

"Dearthair is making me a pendant for my stone," Shaerico said, returning the warmth of his smile.

Ghrian was openly surprised by his friend's actions. He was even more surprised to find that Shaerico had retrieved Solas. He had been so concerned when Raax had taken it. He decided that he would address this subject when they were alone again.

"Making a necklace, huh?" he said as he patted his friend's hunched back. "How exciting to finally watch you work your magic! And how very kind of you."

Dearthair rebutted, "Don't think anything of it. We don't need her losing her only possession again."

He lifted the silver chain and presented the finished product to Shaerico. Solas shone in the risen sun. A gleam of golden blue flashed through the stone's center. Shaerico lifted her hands to take it. It was nestled securely in a thick tri-braided band, held in place by a row of clover shaped prongs.

"It's beautiful," she said as she reached to pull it over her slender neck. "Thank you."

"Don't mention it," Dearthair replied as he flashed a quick smile and turned to Ghrian. "Now, we really should get going. We've gotten a good night's rest. I will secure my things in the storehouse, and then we must head out. We have to see King Gaewyn. Perhaps he can offer us aid in our quest."

Ghrian had heard of the great King in the East. He was known to be the guardian of the lands of man. King Gaewyn was a legend. In the days of old, he was said to have been the only being to successfully drive away a dragon. He was also known for his white hawk, his closest companion and the creature that accompanied him as he drove the dragon back to its mountain lair. The King had built his castle Nícíl at the base of the mountain Beinn as a warning to the dragon to never return to the lowlands. He was said to be a gentle and caring ruler, but exceedingly stubborn and firm.

After Dearthair returned from the storehouse, the companions sat for one last meal in comfort. His aunt had prepared the last of her mutton for them. All enjoyed the meal, but they ate in silence. At the storehouse,

Dearthair had overheard the guards discussing the wolf hoard. They had not gone far into the Kingdom of Miath, nor had they passed by the castle, but had instead traveled up the mountain pass.

Dearthair broke the silence first. "We must ask his permission to enter the mountain. His guards stand at its entrance day and night. They will not let us pass without the King's knowledge. It was incredibly hard to convince him to allow us to enter Beinn the last time. It took us weeks before we gained permission to mine the mountain trails. And now, with all that has happened, I would be surprised if he allows us at all," then he added with resolve. "Either way, legal or not, I am going up that mountain. Now we know for certain Oir is being taken through Beinn."

Shaerico rubbed her thumb across the smooth back of the white stone.

"You're not going alone," she said as she stood. "We've rested long enough. We should go."

After the trio packed their things, they said their goodbyes to his aunt. She was concerned and disapproved of their journey. "I don't understand. You just made it home and so much has happened," she said with tears in her eyes.

Dearthair placed a hand on her shoulder. "I know it's hard to understand, but Oir has no one else. I will not leave her to die. As soon as we rescue her, I will return home. You are safe here. King Gaewyn has placed many knights in Miotal. You will be okay, and I promise I will return."

While Dearthair and his aunt discussed his return, Shaerico and Ghrian stood next to the fire, warming themselves before the long journey ahead. Shaerico leaned closer to Ghrian, sliding his knife into its sheath, and allowing Raax to return to his home on the hilt. She kept her gaze on the sculpted creature. Ghrian noticed Shaerico's eyes on his hip. She was wondering how this stone being came to life. She thought of Marmair.

"My mother gave it to me," Ghrian said. "Would you like to see it?"

Shaerico was thrust back into reality, away from the spring and her time with Marmair. She nodded. He handed her the knife and continued, "She gave it to me just before she disappeared."

Shaerico looked up from gazing into Raax's gold flecked eyes. "Disappeared?"

"Yes," Ghrian said. "She vanished into Collitte when I was very young."

He looked down at the blazing fire. Shaerico followed his gaze and returned the knife to him. "I'm sorry," she said softly, then continued, "I never knew my mother, well, my real mother anyways. What was your mother like?"

Ghrian sheathed the knife. "I'm sorry," he said, wondering if he should press further. He longed to know more of her story but realizing that he was going to have to be the first to open up, he began. "She was wonderful. She had incredible golden hair. Her eyes were like melted chocolate, full of warmth, and she always wore the kindest expression. She used to tell me stories every night. Crazy, fantastic tales that I had never thought to believe, but now," he trailed off as he locked eyes with Shaerico. Then changing the subject he added, "She never got angry. I don't remember much about her, but I do remember that. Her presence was peace."

Shaerico tilted her head and looked up at Ghrian. "It sounds like you two are a lot alike."

Ghrian blushed under Shaerico's gaze. "Shaerico, how did you get your stone back?" Ghrian changed the subject and inquired carefully. He would have imagined that if she had seen Raax, she would have said something.

"Oh, Raax gave her back to me," she replied nonchalantly. Ghrian stared, wide-eyed at her cool response.

"I'm leaving. Are you two coming?" Dearthair's sharp tone reverberated off the stone fireplace.

"Yes, yes. We were just waiting on you," Ghrian said, composing himself and throwing his bag over his shoulder.

Shaerico smiled, slid her feet into the cream boots, and gathered the white cloak that had dried by the fire. Then the party went to mount their horses and prepare for the icy road ahead. Shaerico placed her hand on Fiáin, lacing her fingers through his mane. They had developed a bond during their separation from the others. She then laid the white cloak over the black stallion's back. Ghrian tried to offer his aid since Fiáin was remarkably large, but Shaerico leapt to his back on her own with ease, simply returning Ghrian's offer with a smile. Ghrian smiled back and mounted March. Shaerico watched as he turned the snowflake gray stallion toward the open road ahead. Something had changed in her. The days she'd spent alone in the foreign woods had made her realize her true feelings for Ghrian. A new flame burned in her heart. An unfamiliar fire, both comforting and terrifying. She decided then that wherever he went, she would follow.

The snow had begun to fall again. Though the fog had lifted, visibility was still low.

"How far is this king's palace?" Shaerico asked.

"Nícíl is further east, toward the mountain. Little more than a week's ride," Dearthair answered.

"Are there any other towns along the way?" Ghrian asked.

"None in the direct path. All other civilization lies to the south, or even further east."

"I certainly hope we packed enough food then," Ghrian mumbled.

"Don't worry. I have made the trip to the castle time and time again, often with less than what we have now. Remember, we still have some of your bread as well," Dearthair stated.

"Yes, but we have eaten much of it and I left some with your aunt," Ghrian replied.

"We will be fine," Shaerico chimed.

"You certainly will be," Dearthair said sharply. Seeing his aunt and the destruction that lay in the wake of the wolves reminded him of his original bitterness toward the black wolf.

"Dearthair," Ghrian barked.

"No, he's right. I can find my own meals," Shaerico replied calmly.

They traveled in silence after that exchange. The wind was still biting, but the snowfall had slowed. The snow-capped trees towered high over the pathway. These forests were not like those of Collitte and the Realm. These trees were knotted and twisted as they competed for the thin rays of sunlight that pierced the dense canopy. They were tall, towering over the beaten pathway. Instead of a deep thicket between them, there was only a heavy blanket of snow. The wind whispered through the ice-laden leaves, causing a melodic chime and snow to fall upon the companions in shimmering flakes. Shaerico turned to look at Ghrian, who was paying no mind to the lovely display. He was rather engrossed in inspecting his knife. She turned to Dearthair who was feverishly attempting to remove the fallen flakes from his cloak. She turned her gaze again toward the road and her mind began to wander. What was Beanrua doing? She thought of her brother and wondered if he was with them. The sorcerer had decimated so many towns. She pondered what his intentions were. Why had he not gone as far as the King's castle? Why head into the mountains?

She glanced back at the men that slowed her down and sighed. She knew that she could not do this without them and that they could not do this without her. If she had to get permission from the King, then she had to have men who knew the ways of man, and for them to face the sorcerer and her clan, they would need someone who knew how to defeat the cursed.

Shaerico had not truly let the reality of her existence set in. She had not had the time to contemplate its gravity. What would life hold for her people after this should they survive? Though she had learned much from Marmair about the power of Solas and the Stones of Old and her family and their curse, there was still so much she did not understand. Her only hope was discovering the power of the Living Water for herself. Marmair had told her that the source of the Iómhara's power was the water alone. The longer a stone had been connected and saturated with the Living Water, the stronger its connection and power became. Shaerico placed her hand on Solas, now securely nestled around her neck. She knew that Solas was one of the oldest gems guarded by the Living Stone. She knew that it had the power to keep her curse at bay, but did it have the power to do more?

Ghrian was still lost in thought, his eyes locked on his knife, when Dearthair abruptly halted his mare. Fiáin lifted his head, his silvery white mane flowing in front of him. March ignored the others and kept his steady pace.

"Ghrian," Dearthair whispered aggressively.

Ghrian looked up to see that he was nearly face to face with a large white doe. Their eyes met.

"Ghrian, that would be a great meal. Kill it while it's stunned," Dearthair demanded, still at a whisper.

The doe tilted her head and lowered her front hoof to the soft snow. She stepped toward Ghrian. March pawed nervously. With her deep golden-brown eyes gazing up at Ghrian, she walked closer still.

"Now is your chance! You have your knife in your hands!" Dearthair called out, no longer bothering to whisper.

Ghrian seemed as if he were in a trance. He recognized something familiar in this curious creature's eyes. Could this be the same doe that led him out of Collitte? For the moment, he felt nothing but peace. He felt no hunger, no urgency, and no fear, just the stillness of the air and his own breath.

"Fine. If you won't, I will." Dearthair lunged his mare forward, his own knife drawn.

Before Ghrian could react, Fiáin reared and released a bellowing neigh. The intensity knocked Shaerico and Dearthair from their mounts. Ghrian turned in awe of the sound and the great beast. When he turned back toward the road, the white deer had vanished.

After a moment, Ghrian returned to reality. The doe's familiar brown eyes still lingering in his mind. Dearthair began to get up and shout curses at his friend, but Ghrian paid him no mind. He rushed to Shaerico's side as she lifted herself to her elbows. He stretched out his hand to help her up. With a flicker of a smile, Shaerico accepted his offer. She was surprised at how swiftly, yet gently he lifted her from the ground. He was much stronger than he appeared.

Dearthair's berating continued as he mounted his mare. "We had a meal right before our eyes. How did you miss that chance? Who knows when we will see another deer of that size!" he shouted.

Shaerico surveyed the road again. The white doe had indeed vanished. She could tell that Ghrian sensed there was something more to the animal. She wished that she could explain what she'd seen in the woods. Whatever this creature was, it was no ordinary deer, and it seemed she was following them. Shaerico climbed atop Fiáin, who still pawed the ground angrily. Why was he so aggressively protecting the doe?

She did not have long to contemplate. A few moments later, two weary-eyed men appeared upon the snowy trail behind them. One was badly burned.

"Please, help us," the stronger, younger man called to the strangers.

"Great," Dearthair huffed. "Just what we need, another sidetrack."

"Hush, Dearthair," Ghrian scolded. "They need help."

"So does Oir," Dearthair said with resolve.

Ghrian turned March around and walked toward the weary men. As he drew closer, he saw the severity of their state. He could barely believe that they had survived whatever it was they had faced. The man being held was undoubtedly in the worst shape. Much of his right side sustained hideous burns, some of which had succumbed to frostbite in the winter chill. Ghrian removed his cloak and draped it around the man's exposed shoulder. The other looked up at him graciously.

"My name is Aigen, and this is my brother Stefan," the younger man began. "We have traveled far in hopes of reaching Raven City. You see, we have family there, all the family we have left. After the fires, and the Order taking over the Realm, my father was…"

"You're from the Realm of the Lake?" Ghrian interrupted.

Aigen's eyes fell in sadness, seeming unbothered by the interruption. "Yes," he sighed.

"We too come from the Realm. We are seeking passage to the mountain Beinn to rescue our friend who was taken," Ghrian explained.

Aigen returned his gaze to Ghrian, his eyes wide. "There is no hope for your friend. Please, do not continue with this foolish journey. Come to Raven City with us!" he beckoned.

Ghrian looked at the boy and shook his head. "I will not abandon my friend."

"Very well, make your quest, but I beg you, do not return to the Realm afterward," he said.

Ghrian looked on confused and asked, "What do you mean? I am sure Lochta will be rebuilt. You would so quickly abandon your home?"

"You may return to the Realm, but you will not find it home. Not even a day after the Wolves of Fire, the Order took control of Lochta. Even the Royals were forbidden from speaking to the people. The dungeons within the Temples of Lochta and Vael were filled with anyone who dared speak of the attack for what it was, an attack of a sorcerer, of magic. We were there. We saw him." The boy's bloodshot eyes welled with tears. "He took everything from us. People lost their lives, their family members, friends, and livelihood. Instead of offering aid, the Order took the opportunity to outlaw even the mere mention of magic. So many were questioning what had happened and what they had seen. Belief in the unseen is no longer looked down upon, but illegal to speak of. Some returned to the Ancient One, clinging to the faith, only to be punished for it. Even speaking of He Who Is is punishable by imprisonment."

Aigen looked down at his brother with a frown. "Those were no ordinary fires as the Order would have us believe. I saw the dark man that rode a red wolf. I watched him burn my mother without mercy. Stefan tried to save her, but," he cried. Tears streamed down Aigen's soot-stained face, marking trails down his cheeks like rivers through ashen land, charred and barren. "My father went to the High Priest of Lochta and inquired about what he saw. He knew what had befallen my mother, and when the Priest dismissed him in the face of what was, what he deemed nothing more than an unfortunate fire and raging pack of wild wolves, my father would not accept his lies. He was the first to be imprisoned, and the Arms of the Order came looking for us soon after knowing that we too had seen the truth. We fled the next morning and we've been walking ever since," he explained.

Ghrian's mind swirled. Suddenly he felt dizzy and an ache crept into his stomach. Shaerico and Dearthair glanced to one another. None had considered this outcome, least of all Ghrian. Sure, the Order had always been distrusting of myth and magic, but never had he expected them to take it this far. Never had he considered that he would be going home to a different world entirely. He thought of his father and for a fleeting moment considered abandoning their quest. But they had already come so far. His father had dealt with the Order before, surely he could handle this himself.

Ghrian thanked Aigen for the information, gave the brothers the last of the rations, and wished them luck on their journey. Shaerico rested her hand on Ghrian's shoulder, then removed the white cloak she'd received from the mysterious woman in the woods and draped it around his cold shoulders.

"Thank you," he whispered faintly.

That night, the company went hungry. Dearthair suffered the most. He was famished and frustrated. Ghrian and Shaerico were both lost deep in thought. Shaerico leaned against Fiáin, who had laid on the ground for the first time beside her. She closed her eyes, clutching Solas between her fingers, thankful that she had remained human after the sun fell. Dearthair turned away from the fire and grumbled himself to sleep. Ghrian laid on Oir's spare cloak atop the blanket of white, gazing through the snow-capped trees to the incredible tapestry of stars above. Shaerico could feel his confusion as she sank into sleep. Her back was pressed against the stallion, the cadence of his heart lulling her to a deep slumber.

Soon her vision turned to darkness and a faint glow appeared in the distance of her mind. As she focused on the steady increasing light, she spotted a pair of figures amongst falling stars, hurtling toward the ground.

One wore a head of hair like starlight, white and shimmering against the formless dark, and the other had hair black as the night from which they fell. Both were beautiful and shrouded in flames of blue.

Shaerico awoke in a panic. Her skin was drenched in a cold sweat. She opened her eyes to chaos. It was no longer winter and she was alone. She was back in Collitte. The woods were even more dense than she remembered. The robust growth seemed to swell and subside as though every plant had breath. She could see blue water glistening in the distance, but instead of a calm pool, it was a raging well. The water bubbled and boiled. It spilled over the bank and carved through the surrounding rocks like a powerful acid. Shaerico watched in amazement as the water gurgled up from a small opening and created the spring she had found. Her gaze turned toward the sky as glistening stones tumbled from the heavens. Some landed in the water and some decimated the surrounding trees and brush. The astonished woman took cover from the berating rain of crystals. She knelt down under a large willow tree and covered her head, her eyes locked on the spring. Suddenly, the sky tore, and a great clap of thunder resounded over the earth. She covered her ears and was thrown back by a great force. For a moment, her body felt weightless in flight, like floating through lukewarm water. When she recovered and looked back toward the spring, two glowing figures stood at its edge. One woman and one man. They were nearly too bright to look upon, like staring straight into the rising sun. Shaerico watched in awe as the two Beings of Light inhaled deeply. Then the man locked his gaze on Shaerico. He opened his eyes and in their place were two blazing coals.

The following morning was bitter cold. Shaerico could not shake the lingering feeling of her dream. Her previous dreams had been strange and somewhat disturbing, but they had also been light and relatively docile. This one had been terrifying. She searched for the word as she turned to Ghrian, who was stoking the dying embers of the fire, stealing a few final moments of warmth.

"Ghrian," she began.

Ghrian turned his gaze to Shaerico, "Yes?" he smiled his beaming and comforting smile.

The terrors of the night were already fading in her mind. Still she continued, "Do you see things at night? While you sleep?"

Ghrian's lips pursed for a moment as he stood and tried to comprehend what she was asking. "Are you asking me if I dream?" His smile returned.

"So that's the word for it," Shaerico said.

"Are you telling me you've never had a dream before?" Ghrian laughed, amazed.

"Well," Shaerico replied, "until recently I was not human at night, so I never really got the chance to."

Ghrian sighed, regretting his playful tone. "Yes, I dream." He continued. "Mostly my dreams make no sense, like fragments of reality. Sometimes they're of the bakery, sometimes the woods, sometimes I'm traveling to places that don't exist," he laughed at some of his more recent dreams, then turned toward Shaerico, serious again, "some are of my mother, and lately some have been of…"

"You two get moving," Dearthair barked. He was already atop his mare and held March's reins in his hand.

Ghrian sighed and took the reins from his impatient friend. The companions were getting closer to Nićil and Dearthair was becoming more and more restless.

Ghrian mounted March, as Shaerico climbed atop Fiáin. As the travelers returned to the road, Shaerico continued their discussion.

"Have you ever had bad dreams?" she inquired.

Ghrian turned to her, "Nightmares? Of course."

"Nightmares," Shaerico echoed. "I think I had one of those last night. What do they mean?"

"Mean?" Ghrian was uncertain how to answer. He had had only a handful of dreams in his lifetime that he remembered clearly, let alone that he could find any meaning to. He directed March to move closer to the black stallion and placed a broad hand on Shaerico's shoulder. "Not all dreams have meaning. But it's okay to be nervous, or even afraid. We've been through a lot lately." His voice trailed but his hand remained firm and warm on her shoulder. Usually she was not a fan of touch, but in this moment Shaerico let herself feel the warmth of his hand through her cloak. "But don't worry, you aren't alone anymore." With a gentle squeeze to her arm, Ghrian returned his hands to March's reins and the two continued in silence.

The day was cold, but a warmth crept into Shaerico's heart. It was true, even in the absence of her family, she was no longer alone.

After a few hours of traveling in silence, white spires became visible through the thinning tunnel of trees, towering over the lush green that glistened with crystals of snow in the sunlight. Upon their arrival, they came to a clearing. Shaerico looked up toward the mountain peaks. She could smell Beanrua on the crisp winter wind. The scent of the sorcerer followed the familiar scent of her friend and burned her nostrils. She could feel the rage welling inside her. Ghrian could sense her discomfort.

"We are almost there. I am sure the King will grant us passage," he said.

Shaerico smiled at him, suddenly fearful for his life as the inevitable confrontation drew nearer. For the first time, it began to sink in that he would be in danger once they entered the mountain. She turned her gaze back toward the thicket of trees and snowy road ahead, willing herself to quell the thoughts.

"We can't be certain of that. We must be persuasive," she replied.

"She's right," Dearthair said. "Let me do the talking. I have dealt with King Gaewyn before."

"So you've said," Ghrian remarked. He leaned back on March and winked at Shaerico.

She smiled, but she could not shake the rising fear of the coming danger. Judging by the level of destruction in their wake, nearly all of the pack must be with the sorcerer. She remembered how agonizing it was to be stuck in her canine form. The others had been wolves for months now. She wondered if their human thoughts could even regain control. Not one of the companions had any concept of what they would truly be facing on the mountain.

They passed through the field of snow. Patches of green escaped through the vast blanket of white, a welcome opening that allowed the sun to warm their chilled bones. All relished the moment of warmth and comfort until Shaerico heard a rustle in the woods ahead. They were headed toward the continuation of the trail. The dark-haired woman began to smell something amiss. Fiáin wavered and tossed his massive head. He pawed the ground, carving the frozen dirt through the snow and grass. March stopped in his tracks, but Dearthair continued on without them. Ghrian nudged his horse and looked over at Shaerico.

"Someone is waiting for us," she said. Her eyes locked on the passage ahead.

Ghrian smiled, "It's okay. Nothing we can't handle."

Shaerico flashed a smile back at him. Fiáin held his head high and moved slowly forward. Suddenly, two armed men walked into the clearing, blocking the path of the travelers. "Who goes there?" one man called, his broad chest heaving as he yelled beneath his heavy white-gold plated armor.

"Friends of the King!" Dearthair called back.

The two knights were astride rich chestnut steeds. They were large animals, yet had somehow been nearly invisible against the snow laden forest. Each man held a long spear with a golden tip, crossed to block the path. Their swords were broad and laid against their left hips, the edges of which almost brushed against their horses' flanks. The breastplates of the knights were intricate. The thick white gold was inlaid with onyx, rich rubies, and engraved with a rearing horned horse. The design was strong, yet delicate.

Ghrian studied the men's armor, not concerned about their own fate in the slightest. "Dearthair, what's with the horned horse?"

Dearthair flashed an annoyed look at his usually composed friend. "Is this really the time?" he barked.

Ghrian shrugged. "I'm just curious why this is the creature chosen to represent the Great Hawk King."

Shaerico kept her gaze on the two knights. The one that had spoken before stepped toward them into the clearing.

"You claim to be friends of the King, yet do not know the Kingdom's history?" he shouted.

Dearthair responded, "I apologize for the ignorance of my companion. He is from the Realm."

"Ahhh," the second knight crooned. "The people of the Temple," he said mockingly. "Your people have fallen into the illusion of peace, hiding away encircled by your wood, you have forgotten your own history. Such a shame."

Ghrian had assumed that all had lost their heritage of belief, but it seemed some still held the ancient knowledge. His curiosity was piqued.

The first knight chimed in. "Those who have forgotten the victory of King Gaewyn do not deserve to know the truth of their history. Come," he motioned to the travelers and moved his horse to open the pathway. "We will see what the King wishes to do with you."

The walk through the sparsely wooded path that led to the castle was still and quiet. The tension was palpable as Dearthair struggled to determine his pitch to the King. Over their journey, he had become more and more agitated. He missed Oir and was concerned for her safety. He grew anxious for their reunion. He knew that every day they were separated was another day that harm could befall her.

The knights ahead mumbled to one another as they lead the company on. Shaerico could make out some of their conversation.

"What reason do people of the Realm have to come to the edge of the mountain?"

"Do you think they have something to do with all this destruction. Who would follow this path of chaos?" the other inquired.

"Maybe they are simply coming to seek aid from the King?"

"Seems doubtful," his partner replied.

They both looked back toward the trio. Fiáin snorted, blowing the snow from his muzzle in their direction. They hurriedly returned to their conversation, facing forward.

"Is it just me, or does that horse seem familiar?"

"A bit. He's absolutely massive. And what's with that nasty scar on his forehead?"

The knights discussed the stallion and what King Gaewyn would do with the suspicious travelers as they went. The five of them continued through the woods until night began to fall. As they reached the castle, the sun had begun to make its way behind the mountain. The grand white towers rose high above the wispy clouds and faded into the lush gray wave of the mountains beyond. The Castle Niċil; mixed with cloud and mingled with mountain. As they drew nearer, it became apparent just how close the castle had been built to the barrier between the world of man and the world of things forgotten. It was as if Niċil was a part of the mountain range itself. Although most of the structure was separate, one side of the castle seemed to sprout from the rock face. The setting sun cast golden rays of yellow and muted pink over the white marble face of King Gaewyn's castle. The spires towered high above the frost-tipped trees. Atop one spier rose a ruby flag adorned with the King's emblem in weightless gold thread. The brisk wind caught it and ruffled its spirit. Ghrian could hardly believe the grandeur of this edifice. Even the greatest structure in the Realm paled in comparison to this marvelous feat of masonry. Shaerico was even more at a loss for words.

The knights raised their hands as they drew closer to the castle gate. A deep moat surrounded the fortress and led south, carving a slithering canyon through the trees as far as the naked eye could see. The water was crystal clear and reflected the brilliant pink hues of the sky above. The travelers stood in wait as a great drawbridge was lowered over the moat. It was slow and incredibly heavy. The chains groaned as it made its way to the snow- laden path in front of them.

"Dismount your horses," one knight demanded as he turned to face them.

Fiáin pawed the ground in disapproval. Shaerico rested her hand on his broad neck, her eyes locked onto the knight.

"I promise they will be well taken care of," he said in a softer tone.

After passing over the drawbridge of solid stone, he led his horse to the stable that flanked one side of the castle. The dark wood frame seemed sturdy and a good shelter against the snow. March protested as Ghrian reluctantly led him into one of the stalls. Again, he was struck by the intricacy of the decor even in the stable. Carvings of hawks and horned horses lined the walls. Even the stall doors themselves were garnished with small rubies and precious stones.

"This King certainly has a taste for flare," Ghrian commented to Shaerico as they placed their stallions in adjacent stalls.

Shaerico responded, "We should discover the reason for his obsession while we are here."

Ghrian smiled at the invitation and nodded, "Absolutely."

Both itched for knowledge about the worlds beyond their own and the thought of discovering Domhaen's secrets together was elating for them both.

After the horses were watered and fed, the knight led them through the stable into another entrance to the castle. A third knight met them at the door.

"King Gaewyn has agreed to receive your audience in the morning. For now, you will find food and shelter inside the castle. The King is far too generous, in my opinion," he stated.

The knights led the trio down a narrow hall. The white stone shone against the light of their torches.

"Exploring is strictly forbidden. Aliana will bring you food in a moment. Stay in your room," the third knight ordered harshly. He opened a heavy wooden door and led them into an open room. One large window let in the moonlight that now cascaded over the mountain. The uneven stone floor was cool against Shaerico's feet as she removed her fur boots. Dearthair immediately made his way to a grand fireplace that was the focal point of the far-right wall. A single dark wooden bed with a crimson canopy was centered on the opposite wall.

"I would suggest you give the bed to the lady," the knight said as he shut the door.

Ghrian looked at Shaerico who had never slept in as soft a bed as this. He recalled their night at the Drunken Drake and hoped that she would take the offer this time.

"It's all yours," he smiled and bowed in jest. Ghrian watched as she timidly placed two hands on the plush feather mattress. Her eyes widened as her body sank belly first into the bed.

"Wow, this is really nice," she said, her voice muffled in the deerskin blanket that lay atop the down mattress.

Ghrian laughed, "Enjoy it."

Dearthair was brooding by the fire. Ghrian removed his cloak and laid it on the stone floor next to the hearth.

"How can you be so lighthearted at a time like this?" Dearthair said.

Ghrian sighed and sat on his cloak atop the cobblestone floor. Leaning against the hearth, feeling the warmth of the fire he began, "What good does worrying do? We can't know what the future holds, no matter how hard we try and attempt to prepare for potential outcomes. All we end up doing is stealing the joy of today. Worry won't make the King accept our proposal and it doesn't help us win the battle against whoever that man is. It won't bring Oir back."

Dearthair went quiet. He gazed into the fire ignoring Ghrian.

Ghrian stood and put a hand on his friend's shoulder. "What do we have if not our hope? That is a thing that no sorcerer, no fire, nor disillusioned group of Priests can take from us. The King will let us pass. We will find her and we will bring her home. I choose hope today." Ghrian removed his hand from his friend's shoulder and returned it to his side. "You need to be clear headed. Fear will only cloud your judgement."

Dearthair sat on the hearth and nodded to his friend.

"Now, get some rest," Ghrian said. "Shaerico and I are going to explore."

Dearthair rolled his eyes and laid down on the cold stone floor. "I'm not even going to try and stop you."

Ghrian turned to the bed and began, "Shaerico, are you ready?"

A snore broke his sentence. He sighed and turned to the door.

"I suppose I'll be exploring alone then. So much for our date," he chuckled with disappointment.

"Don't get lost or discovered," Dearthair called after him as he left the room. "I'm not coming after you."

Ghrian smiled as he entered into the dark hallway. Even though the walls were white, little light reached the interior of the castle by the mountain. And it was quiet. Ghrian had always imagined a castle to be full of life and people at all hours. He made his way down the long hall, heading in the opposite direction from which they had arrived. His mind raced at what he might find in the castle, especially in a place where belief still seemed to exist. He passed by various rooms and sleeping quarters that held no interest to him. He wandered through corridors and vast open halls. Eventually he came to a large wooden door. It seemed much older and was much larger than the other doors that he had seen thus far. It stood tall, towering over him, and taking up nearly a third of the wall in which it was centered. Now this was something of interest. Surely on the other side of this door he would discover something about his history, or at the very least, King Gaewyn's obvious obsession with a mythical being. The door was engraved similarly to the stall doors of the stable, lined with semi-precious stones, rubies, and lustrous onyx. A curved handle lay at the left corner of the great door. It was woven white gold, seeming to replicate a horn. Each base was encased in a blue jewel, the likes of which Ghrian had never seen; they were bright, and seemed to emit light. Perhaps these were the famed crystals of royalty.

He reached for the handle. A draft of wind brushed back his hair as he opened the door slowly. The ancient door made no sound, no creak or groan as he had anticipated. Ghrian slid himself through the opening and was faced with a cavernous room. From floor to ceiling were shelves, each lined with documents and artifacts. Ghrian had never seen so many books. Even the libraries in the Temples of the Realm paled in comparison. Pieces of animal bones, pottery, shards of weaponry, and hundreds of scrolls adorned the shelves. He stood for a moment in the doorway, taking in all that he could in one gaze before allowing the door to close behind him. He was in awe. He had no idea where to begin, but the prospect of discovery urged him forward.

A single table divided the room. Its surface was uneven, like a giant tree had been split and half of it laid to rest in the center of the room. To the right, glass cases held what seemed to be ancient artifacts. The moonlight that found its way over the mountain and through the row of windows that lined the top of the wall to his left, illuminated strange fragments of what seemed to be bone.

He made his way to the case that was of particular interest to him. The bone fragment lay at the center bottom shelf of the cabinet. It resembled the woven white gold of the door handle. Gently, he opened the case. A thick leather-bound book rested to the right of the artifact. Ghrian turned his attention to the book. It had been years since he had read, but perhaps this document could explain the fragment it resided next to. He glanced at it again as he lifted the dusty book from its case. The artifact seemed to have been burned, though it still held a metallic blue hue. Ghrian attributed the glow to the light of the moon.

He sat at the table and by the cold blue light of the moon, he began to read. The first few chapters were the history of the Kingdom of Miath, how a specific tribe of men came from the continent of Theas across the sea to a place ruled by mythical beasts. There they found a scattered people living in shadow. Ghrian read how they had made a shoreline settlement but had never come close to the mountain range Beinn. Each generation had fought back the ancient creatures that inhabited the land. Each king had vowed to gain more and more ground for the human race. Ghrian read on as the moonlight waned. Many of these histories seemed familiar. Images from his childhood began to fill his mind, fragmented shadows of his mother's stories. How had she known of this? His mother had lived her entire life in the Realm.

The people of the Realm of the Lake had always been more reclusive than the rest of the known world. A nation still resided on the other side of the sea, occasionally traveling to trade with what they called the Northern Kingdom. Sometimes Ghrian would hear stories of strange people coming to the Southlands far below the Realm and on the other side of the thicket of trees that encased the lake and its inhabitance. He tried to imagine sand as he continued to read about the ancient trade city of Cladach, the first settlement of Gaewyn's ancestors, which resided almost directly south of the castle. It was the only city that the Búnead, or the people of the Southern Kingdom, from the continent of Theas, would enter.

After reading or skimming most of the text, he came to the chapter that he was searching for. The chapter concerning the victory of the Great Hawk King. His eyes dilated as he focused harder on each word.

"In the first century of the fifth age, in the Kingdom of Miath, Gaewyn, son of Gwenlyn came to rule. He was fourteen when the Great War began. Noble King Gwenlyn, victor of Raven City and author of the Common Tongue, was slain by the creature Olcbas. Young King Gaewyn marched into battle the very next day, and though he had little knowledge of what he faced, he possessed unparalleled courage. The creatures of darkness and fire that followed the Great Beast had begun to attack more frequently and a destruction lay waste to the land that had not been seen since the dawn of the fifth age. Though the young King was a skilled falconer and valiant soldier, defeat seemed imminent."

Ghrian's eyes strained in the moonlight, following his finger as it marched across each word. He was so engrossed in the tale of the king in whose castle he resided, that he failed to notice the door open and close in an instant behind him. As his finger continued to draw a path for his eyes on the old parchment, he began to feel the uneasy sense that someone was watching him. He looked up from the pages for a moment, holding his place with his index finger. The door was closed. The glass cabinet from which he had taken the book was as he had left it. He listened closely, hearing nothing but the heavy thud of his heart. After a few moments, he eagerly turned back to his studies. As he returned to his reading, his face was met with a glowing pair of golden eyes.

He screamed as he fell backwards out of the chair and onto the hard stone floor.

"I thought we were trying to be quiet," Raax whispered, his stone head cocked, as he rested upon the open pages.

"Blast you, you strange little beast! You can't keep doing that!" Ghrian hissed.

Raax leapt from the table and ran up Ghrian's leg, perching on his knee as he stared at him. "What are you doing anyways?"

Ghrian sighed, "I was just curious about the history of this place and this king. My mother told me legends that I had always assumed were fiction. The Order never allowed much discussion of history, and what they did teach us was nothing like this."

Raax nodded in understanding.

"What do you care anyways? What are you doing awake, or alive, or whatever this is?"

"Oh, I came to warn you," Raax said.

"Warn me?" Ghrian echoed as he stood.

Raax huffed at Ghrian's lack of courtesy as he held tight to the young man's leg until he was able to leap back to the table.

"Warn me about what?" Ghrian repeated.

Before Raax was able to answer, Ghrian saw the shadow of a hooded figure at the end of the long table. He froze, unsure how to react. What would this king do if he found someone wandering his castle in deliberate disobedience of his order? Was this shadow figure a protector of the knowledge that this room held? What would happen to Shaerico and Dearthair and their quest if he were to be arrested and detained? Worry began to rise, but he swallowed his concerns and rested his hands on the table.

Clearing his throat, he began, "I simply desired to learn more about the Great Hawk King, so that I may impress him with my knowledge tomorrow. I apologize for the intrusion. I was unable to sleep."

"Wow, I never pinned you for a kiss-ass," the hooded figure said as she walked toward Ghrian.

He recognized her voice and was equally relieved and embarrassed. She dropped the emerald hood, exposing her pale skin to the moonlight. They almost seemed as one, her skin and the moon, as they glistened in the sun's reflection. Her orange eyes flickered between Ghrian, Raax, and the book.

"What did you find?" Shaerico said with a hint of excitement as she sat in the chair across from where Ghrian stood.

He was astonished that she was not upset with him for leaving her in the room and exploring without her.

"Not too much, just skimming through the history of the Kingdom. I was about to read about our generous host," he began.

His explanation was cut short as Shaerico reached for the book and pulled its leather cover toward her. She was not the fastest reader, as there had been little to read in the old, decimated library of Dorchas, but still she had learned how. There were few books to read in the village because most of the great halls had been burned, along with all of the knowledge they held. She remembered as a child reading one book about a young farm boy who had gotten lost in the woods. He and his pig had learned to survive off the land. This book had cultivated her love of the forest from a young age and taught her much of her hunting skills, even before her innate canine senses took hold.

Slowly, she read through the passages about King Gaewyn. Ghrian was unsure what to do. He was a little taken aback by her eagerness to learn. He smiled and got up from the table, determined to find something else intriguing to read until she had finished. Shaerico hardly noticed. Her eyes poured over the pages, taking in every detail. The vivid illustrations saturated her mind. She read of King Gaewyn's victory, the story that had created the Hawk King and made him the legend he now was. There had once been a time when creatures of horror and magic encroached upon the lands of man. This was easier for Shaerico to believe than most, as she herself was something of terror.

"The days were dark. Fear enveloped the land like a suffocating fog. Every moment was held in suspense, ever awaiting the next attack from the dragon and his demons. The creature was colossal. His eyes burned like blazing coals. His scales were impenetrable. Spear and arrow fell. Sword and knight cut down. Until the final battle in which the Great King Gaewyn rode with the white hawk that accompanied him atop a valiant beast from beyond the Mountains and Sea. The adorned stallion, whose piercing turquoise horn shone a light so bright that it cut through darkness and flesh alike. One of the famed Aonharc. Though valiant blood was shed, and no warrior came away unharmed, every creature of the night that descended upon the realm of man fell that day. The beast that caused the victory of mankind and drove the dragon to his keep beyond the mountain had become legend: synonymous with victory and power. He paid the price of battle and faded into myth, never to be seen again. Since that day, the adorned horse was chosen to be honored by the King as the emblem of the Kingdom of Miath."

Before shutting the book, Shaerico noticed a footnote beneath the text "'To him be the glory,' -Athios."

She sat still. The moonlight was fading and she could feel the warmth of the sun on her back as it began its journey over the mountain. A horned horse was the reason King Gaewyn had won the war. Who would have thought? She looked over her shoulder, watching Ghrian as he thumbed through a few more documents.

"Did you know that dragons once existed?" Ghrian asked. He turned toward her and held open an intricate drawing of a scaled beast with wings nearly twice the size of its body.

"I find that rather easy to believe," she said as she walked around the table and returned the book to the open cabinet. "We should probably head back to the room. I can imagine it will not be long until the guards come to get us."

"You're right," Ghrian agreed, still enthralled with his new knowledge. He had learned so much about the history of the world around him, yet he still felt that he was missing some crucial information. He hoped that he would one day be permitted to return to this place so that he may learn more.

"I would have liked to discover why a horned horse adorns everything in the castle of the Hawk King. Maybe they too once existed like the dragons?" Ghrian mused.

Shaerico smiled at him. "If only you had kept reading," she said coyly.

Ghrian looked at her with playful astonishment. "You took the book from me! What did you find out?"

Shaerico laughed as she made her way through the heavy wooden door and whispered, "Shhh, we must not wake anyone, or the King will surely deny our request for passage."

Ghrian stood for a moment, rolled his eyes, and then followed her through the doorway. As they walked along the corridor back to their room, he whispered to her, "Tell me what you read."

She smiled back at him. "It was not much really. Only that the King drove a dragon over the mountain with the aid of a horse adorned with a shiny blue horn."

Ghrian stopped in the middle of the walkway. "He did what?" The words escaped from his mouth just a little louder than a whisper.

At that moment, a guard rounded the corner of the hall just before their room. His armor shone of fresh wax and his spear seemed to have just been sharpened. Shaerico halted Ghrian, putting a finger to his lips, their bodies pressed against one another between two columns. Both stood motionless, trying to determine how they would reach the room before the guard. Ghrian placed a hand on her shoulder and whispered into her ear, "We must wait here for him to pass."

They waited anxiously as the knight made it to their room. He opened the door and stuck his head in. The pair held their breath. Dearthair came to the door. Shaerico could barely make out what was said.

"It seems the guard has not noticed we are missing," she told Ghrian.

"But how?" he replied.

Dearthair nodded and shut the door. The guard made his way back down the corridor. Shaerico and Ghrian looked at one another, breathed a sigh of relief, then scurried to the room. Once they were safely inside, Ghrian looked to the bed. Shaerico had pushed the plush blanket to form a figure. Somehow his cloak lay similarly on the floor. He looked at her confused.

"Just in case something like this happened," she replied to his inquisitive gaze.

"Where were you guys?" Dearthair said angrily.

Ghrian was still amazed by Shaerico's forethought.

"Sorry, we went exploring," Ghrian said, not concerned in the slightest about his friend's wrath. "What was that about anyways?"

Dearthair groaned at his companion's lack of respect for rules. "The King will see us after he attends to some affair. The knight said he would be back shortly with breakfast."

Shaerico's eyes lit up. "I wonder what he's bringing us."

"Probably more bread," Dearthair said as he sat by the hearth.

Ghrian looked at Shaerico. He could see the disappointment in her eyes. "Surely the King would bring his guests more than mere bread," Ghrian reassured her.

Shaerico sat down on the bed and Ghrian joined her. "While we wait, tell me more about the King's victory over the dragon," Ghrian said eagerly.

"It was not overly descriptive. It simply stated that the dragon was driven back beyond the mountain with the aid of a horned steed. King Gaewyn built Nícíl at the foot of Beinn as a warning to the dragon should he ever consider war again. I assume the dragon never returned. What troubles me is that the dragon was never killed. Why wouldn't they finish a beast like that?" she wondered.

The guard knocked and promptly entered with a plate full of luxurious cuisine. "The King has ordered that I bring you food before your meeting," he stated. There was a loaf of bread, but thin slices of meat and roasted cheeses encircled the warm loaf. Shaerico leapt from the bed and immediately took the platter from the guard.

"Thank you," Ghrian said to the startled knight, smiling at Shaerico's appetite. "See, I told you there would be more than bread alone in the King's house."

Shaerico smiled back at him, her mouth full of food.

The guard turned to Dearthair who was brooding over the fire. "The King will see you within the hour. Be prepared."

Dearthair nodded as the knight took his leave. He turned to his companions and said, "We should ready before we finish eating." He looked at Shaerico and sighed at her clear disregard for appearance. "We have to be presentable."

The trio was escorted from their room down the long corridor. They passed the wooden door that held the knowledge Shaerico and Ghrian had recently discovered. Ghrian wished that he could continue his quest for understanding. He longed to know more about his own history and the history of this Kingdom. He yearned to know if all of the stories his mother had told him were true. An ache made its home in his heart as he wished he could see her again and ask her face to face. He wondered also how the Realm of the Lake had lost their place in history. A thirst for knowledge had been awoken in him, but he knew that discovery would have to wait. They had to continue on their journey to rescue Oir.

As they walked, the knights from the previous day quietly discussed the fate of the travelers. The odds seemed stacked against them. Soon they made it to an open courtyard. Vines with long waxy leaves covered the interior walls of the white stone courtyard. The knights motioned for them to wait. Ghrian sat on a marble bench to the right of a large circular wooden door. The handle of this door resembled that of the one he had seen the night before. The handle was long and curved, yet it was nearly translucent like opal, and shone with a myriad of colors.

Dearthair looked at Ghrian, amazed at his ability to relax before meeting the one that held their fate in his hands. He began to pace. Shaerico was enthralled by the vegetation. She walked to the back of the courtyard, directly opposite of the circular door. The small stone slab by which they had entered was to the left. Vivid flowers of bright blues and purples lined a translucent and slightly reflective surface. The brilliant petals reflected against something behind them. She leaned in closer. It was glass. The glass itself shone with a pale rainbow of colors, like that of the door handle. The light that pierced through an opening in the ceiling of the courtyard danced through the translucent substance. She leaned in closer still. Suddenly, something white flashed before her eyes. She jumped back. The pearly glass made it difficult to make out what was held inside. As she drew near to it again, a resounding screech pierced the still air.

Dearthair and Ghrian looked toward Shaerico as a white hawk erupted from the open top of the glass encasing. As it soared above them, they noticed its wide wings held feathers that resembled silk. The tail feathers of the stunning bird looked as if they had been dipped in diamond dust. They glistened in the newly risen sun as the beautiful bird of prey made its way through the opening in the ceiling of the castle courtyard, leaving a trail of the pink sunrise behind. The trio stood, too stunned to move.

"Well," Ghrian began. "I assume that's the great hawk that gave King Gaewyn his title."

The door opened and a guard entered. "The King will see you now."

The knight turned his back to the company as they followed the armor-clad man into an enormous room. Immediately the travelers were faced with their grave reality. This King truly held all the power to end their journey within the next moments.

The ceiling was far above them. Every surface glinted of the purest white stone in the morning light. The rays of sun poured through grand stained-glass windows that lined each wall. Radiant blues, vivid violets, and rich reds soaked the marble tile in front of them. It was as if the sun were rolling out a carpet of color, guiding them to a pinnacle moment of their quest.

Shaerico turned in awe to the windows. Each was separated by a column of the pure white marble. The glass itself was stained in brilliant colors and displayed the valiant victories of the Great Hawk King. Her eyes followed the battle scenes until she reached the victory of the horned stallion. She veered away from the others, drawn by the image of this rearing beast. His unearthly turquoise horn, his coal black body, his silver-white mane and tail, his snow-white face enraptured her.

"Shaerico," Ghrian whispered to her as he motioned for her return.

She pulled herself from the alluringly familiar image and rejoined her companions.

The knight that had guided them down the long court took his place beside a giant throne. A chair of white gold, laden with braids of silver, sat atop a pedestal of the same curious glass that the white hawk had resided in. The King himself sat tall atop a white satin cushion at its center. His dark skin a contrast to the overwhelming white of his castle. His face was kind, but remarkably stoic. A thin crown rested upon his head. It was braided white gold, like the adornments of his throne. At its center rested a single ruby that was flanked by two smaller white stones. It glistened in the early pink light.

For a moment, Shaerico became painfully aware of herself. Her dirtied emerald cloak, her tattered cream boots, and matted black hair suddenly bothered her. She looked again at the King and held Solas tightly between her fingers.

"Good King," Dearthair began as he fell to a knee.

The King's voice was as a clap of thunder, echoing in his great hall. "You would request passage at a time such as this?" his voice boomed.

He already knew why they had come, and his response did not seem promising. His denial of their request seemed imminent. "I am told that you have traveled from the Realm," he said. His hazel eyes looked down upon the travelers before resting on Ghrian. "Is that not where this chaos originated?"

The trio was silent. Dearthair placed both knees on the ground and looked up toward King Gaewyn.

"Great King, you have heard correctly. The horrors that rained upon the Kingdom did come from the Realm. I was there for the Winter Solstice Festival when a hoard of massive wolves descended upon the town. They came from the forest beyond the lake, not from the Realm itself. The Realm of the Lake has suffered more than any," Dearthair explained.

Shaerico and Ghrian looked at one another nervously.

The King did not look pleased with this assumption, but he could see the pain in Dearthair's eyes. "More than any, you say? You have lost someone?"

Dearthair bowed his head and replied, "Yes."

"We all have," Ghrian continued for his friend, taking a knee next to him. "Our dear friend was taken. We have been tracking the beasts since."

"Tracking? With what? You are but three people?" Gaewyn questioned sternly.

An uneasiness fell over the group. The anxiety of passage was no longer their chief worry. What if the King discovered Shaerico's true identity? What if he discovered that she was one of the beings that had wreaked havoc upon his kingdom?

The King turned his attention upon the quiet woman still standing behind the kneeling men. "And what about you? What is your reason for traveling all this way?" he inquired.

Shaerico could feel her heart begin to beat quickly. She held Solas tighter in her hand, her knuckles matching its white hue, as if her true form would betray her at any moment and those piercing hazel eyes saw through her.

She stepped forward, resting a hand on Ghrian's shoulder. "I was there that night," she began, holding King Gaewyn's gaze. Her male companions held their breath, wondering how far she would take the truth.

"It was a horror to witness. I watched as Lochta burned. As men, women, and children were torn down by monsters," her voice quivered as the word left her soft lips.

King Gaewyn's gentle eyes urged her to continue.

"These men lost their closest friend." She looked down at Ghrian and lightly squeezed his shoulder before turning back to the throne. "I lost my sister and nearly my entire family."

The devastation in her eyes was unmistakable. The pain of not only the loss of Beanrua and her family, but of the reality of their true identity weighed heavily upon her. It was in that moment that instead of surrendering to the shame that desperately pulled her soul beneath her, she resolved to not only rescue her fallen family, but to redeem her people. Marmair had given her a power more capable than she knew, but the knowledge that it kept her curse at bay was reason enough for her courage.

"We aim to rescue those that were taken. We require passage to the mountain Beinn," she concluded.

The King was surprised by her sudden resolution.

Ghrian lightly took her hand and stood. "Merciful King, she is correct. I understand that the Kingdom has suffered and that many lives have been lost. We ask for nothing more than passage."

The King lifted his hand to stroke his short, peppered black beard. He sighed heavily. "I am sorry. I know that you have hope, but if all others have been destroyed in the wake of this evil, what makes you believe those you wish to rescue have not already met the same fate? I cannot allow any more loss in my Kingdom. I will meet you in the stable with provisions for your return home."

Dearthair stood, tears welling quickly in his eyes. "My King, I have gone to the mountain before for the mining of gems. I know the way well enough. I cannot return home without her!" As his voice raised, so did the spears in the hands of the knights that flanked the throne.

"Your King gave you your answer! Retrieve your belongings and head to the stable. You leave today!" the guard shouted.

Shaerico looked back at the King. His soft eyes showed his empathy, but his face was stern. He would not change his mind. He was saving three more people from destruction. How could he be faulted?

Dearthair was both crushed and enraged. Ghrian turned his attention to his friend and held him steady and tightly, afraid of what he may attempt in his despair. He could feel the King's eyes upon his back and somehow, he felt that his appearance before the King had only hurt their chance of passage.

When they made it back to their belongings, Dearthair fell immediately onto the bed. He rolled over and stared at the ceiling, looking beyond its rafters and into the dream of his future that was quickly slipping away. Generally speaking, Dearthair was the epitome of a rule follower. Doing things the correct way was his modus operandi, but in light of his determination to rescue Oir, all of that had changed. His personality shifted, and a fire began to burn in him.

"We will find Oir. We will gain passage to that mountain," he hissed. He rose from the bed with a fiery determination in his eyes. He glared at Shaerico and asked, "How do you suppose the sorcerer and his wolves crossed into the mountain?"

Ghrian followed where Dearthair was headed. "Absolutely not, Dearthair. Have you lost your mind?"

"I've seen what that thing can do! No king's guard could stand against a creature like that!" Dearthair shouted. "You turn into that wolf and lead the way! We would be able to pass with ease like the others did."

Ghrian walked to Dearthair and lifted him from the bed by his shirt.

"She is not just something to be used at your leisure!" Ghrian exclaimed as he threw him back onto the bed. "Keep your mouth shut. We will find another way."

Shaerico raised her chin and inhaled deeply. "The guard is coming back. We should not be discussing this here."

Ghrian shot a final glance at Dearthair before grabbing his saddlebag and the minute remainder of their breakfast rations. Rubbing his neck, Dearthair retrieved his own belongings and pushed his way through the door as the knight opened it.

"I apologize," Ghrian said to the guard as he too made his way through the door. "He is upset by the news."

The knight nodded as he held the door for Shaerico. He thought it strange that the men had saddlebags and weapons, but the small female had nothing but a necklace and cloak. She could feel his stare as they made their way down the corridor to the stable. Once they made it to their steeds, the group continued their silence. The air was tense as the King appeared to see them off. His long white robe flowed behind him. He had removed his crown and instead held a silver staff with his right hand. Atop his left shoulder sat the white hawk. The bird was so large that Shaerico found it miraculous that the King could stand upright. The hawk's golden eyes locked on Shaerico. As they followed her movements near Fiáin, they shimmered blue, like jewels over water.

It was at that moment that Shaerico recognized this bird. She had seen one other like it. Could it be the shapeshifter by the spring? If so, what was it doing here?

King Gaewyn lifted his staff and began to address the travelers.

"I understand your disappointment. You feel that you have traveled too far not to reach your destination. However, I can at least show you the generosity of the Kingdom." He struck the cobblestone floor with his staff and men dressed in the King's emblem appeared with rations of bread, meat, cheese, and wine. They laid them across Dearthair's mare as he saddled her. March danced uneasily in his stall. He did not appreciate being enclosed. Ghrian laid the saddlebags over his stallion, filled them with the gifts from the King, and bridled him. The gray beast was certainly ready for his next adventure.

As the horses were loaded with goods, King Gaewyn walked toward Shaerico and the midnight stallion. She could feel his eyes on her. Fiáin pawed the ground and lightly tossed his head. He whinnied softly as the King approached. Shaerico was surprised by his enthusiasm. She had never heard him make such a sound. This prompted her to turn around. As she did, the white hawk left King Gaewyn's shoulder and landed on the stall door in front of Fiáin's muzzle. She was even more astonished when the scarred stallion and stunning white bird each leaned forward and rested their heads against one another.

The King looked visibly puzzled. He stepped closer toward the woman and her horse, studying the stallion's features.

"Where did you find such a magnificent creature?" King Gaewyn inquired.

Shaerico turned to face him, keeping a hand on Fiáin's withers. "The night of the attack, I released him from the decimated stable, and he joined us."

"Joined you? You did not purchase him?" he asked.

"Purchase? I think you know as well as I that he is not something to be bought," she replied. Shaerico met King Gaewyn's gaze.

He came closer still, this time stretching out his left arm. Fiáin turned from the hawk and stepped toward him. Even though the King was a large and regal man, he was dwarfed by the elegant stallion. The King left his arm outstretched, allowing the beast to come to him. Shaerico watched as Fiáin lowered his ghostly face and rested his soft gray nose in the King's extended hand.

"My old friend," she heard the King whisper. "How wonderful it is to see you again."

At this point, Ghrian and Dearthair had fully readied themselves for the return journey, though the latter still protested. They had never seen Fiáin so calm with anyone other than Shaerico. They watched as King Gaewyn brushed his fingers across the deep red scar that marred the stallion's face from forehead to nostril.

"Is this your quest then?" he whispered.

The stallion leaned harder into the King's palm.

After a moment, King Gaewyn removed his hand from the stallion and returned it to his side. The white hawk flew back to its perch on the King's shoulder. King Gaewyn lifted his head and began to address the melancholy travelers.

"Good people, I have decided to grant you passage. I have had a change of heart and believe that you should be given the chance to rescue your loved ones. Not many in battle are awarded that opportunity. Use it wisely and do not fail." He lowered his eyes and gave a short bow to Fiáin, then turned to Shaerico. "You may keep the rations I have provided you, but I must ask, what are you willing to sacrifice to see this through?"

Shaerico could feel the gravity of his inquiry. Her sweltering eyes met his like flames over rolling hills. Their reflection burned in King Gaewyn's hazel irises.

"I will do whatever is necessary," she said boldly.

The King smiled. His white teeth glistened against his olive skin. "Then it is settled." He turned toward his avian companion and plucked a single feather from her tail. "Take this. The mountain knights will allow you safe passage."

Shaerico took the feather in her hand. It was smooth and cold, glinting in the light like snow set ablaze.

"You will need better weapons," the King continued, noticing Ghrian's single dagger. "They will be provided for you at the entrance of the mountain passage. Do not forget them."

Ghrian and Dearthair nodded as Shaerico mounted Fiáin. The black stallion scraped his hoof violently across the cobblestone. As King Gaewyn opened the stall door, the beast shifted his weight to his hind legs and propelled himself forward. Fiáin and Shaerico burst forth from the stable and turned right toward the mountain. It was apparent that Fiáin knew the way. King Gaewyn kept his eyes on the stallion as his silhouette faded beyond the castle. Nervously, the two men followed.

"Take courage my friends," King Gaewyn whispered after them as the white hawk left her perch and soared into the blue sky. "You will need it."

March was all too ready to be free of his confines. He quickly caught up to the black horse who continued to barrel through the muddied snow. The passage to the mountain was not far from the castle. As the company traveled further north, the sun provided less and less comfort for their chilled bodies. Racing through snow and gravel, beneath a bed of frosted trees, they pushed on in silence. All were amazed at the King's change of heart, and though they wished to know the origin of the change, they had not dared ask. Dearthair was elated, a fresh joy upon him.

A little over an hour passed before they reached the entrance to the mountain. The horses and riders came to a stop, breathing heavily, freezing, steam pumping from every lung. They welcomed the opportunity to rest. A number of knights stood at the ominous entry point. Though the sun was high and tried its hardest to melt the icy crust that encased every surface, the cold would not give.

Dearthair lifted his chest and dismounted his horse, leading her behind him as he approached the knights.

"Good afternoon," he addressed them. "We have just come from King Gaewyn and request passage into the mountain. We uh, have a feather," he said, motioning to Shaerico to reveal the silken item.

The knights replied that they had already been informed. Dearthair was confused. They had raced toward this pass on the only road and had not encountered anyone else. He received no explanation.

"We have weapons for you," the knight continued.

Shaerico and Ghrian dismounted.

"I suppose this feather is useless then," Shaerico whispered, ready to discard it.

Ghrian turned to her. "Perhaps not, may I carry it?"

Shaerico was a bit surprised by his request, but she willingly handed the peculiar and beautiful feather over to him. Ghrian held it tight. It smelled familiar and its golden-white sheen was equally memorable.

A few knights came to take the reins of the horses, aside from Fiáin, who had no tack whatsoever. The knights led the animals to one side of the trail where they fed them and provided them clean water. Another knight clad in white gold with the crest of the King over his chest approached the companions.

"The King has generously decided to offer you weaponry. Each of you may choose," he said as he unrolled a sheet of thick leather.

Before them lay three swords, each adorned with decoration and gems. Dearthair immediately retrieved the largest of the three, a broadsword with a single ruby at the center of its hilt. He thanked the knight and went to his mare to find a place for his glorious new weapon. Ghrian glanced at Shaerico, waiting for her to make her choice.

"It's irrelevant which I choose," she said as she felt his eyes upon her.

Both swords were the same height, weight, and width, and a good deal smaller than Dearthair's broadsword. The blades were sharp, slightly curved, and tapered on one side to a piercing point. Each had intricate designs on the hilt: one of feathers and the other of leaves. Brilliant turquoise stones rested in the hilt of each.

The knight watched them impatiently until Shaerico sighed and chose the leaf-laden sword. As they prepared the horses to embark on the next phase of their journey, Shaerico approached Ghrian, her sword in hand.

"That was a kind gesture," she smiled at him. Though truthfully, she was rather annoyed, she could not help but be charmed by his selflessness. "But I won't be needing this." She handed Ghrian her weapon. He looked at her for a moment until he remembered.

"Oh, right," he said sheepishly. "If it comes to it, do you plan to fight in that form?"

"My skills are next to useless as a human and I've never wielded a sword," she replied.

"I could teach you," Ghrian said, a fresh light in his eyes.

"Thank you, Ghrian, but I really won't be needing it," she said, flashing a quick smile.

Ghrian nodded as he twisted his wrists in a circular motion, slicing the cold air with the silver blades. "This will be fun," he said smiling at Shaerico. "Thank you."

She smiled back and leapt onto Fiáin. Ghrian placed the swords securely in his belt and carefully mounted March. Dearthair, who was already atop his mare, eyed Ghrian's weaponry.

"Mine's still bigger," he teased.

Ghrian laughed. A small voice from behind him called out, "Seems like someone's eager to overcompensate for something."

Ghrian quickly reached for the base of his neck, grasping for the ball of white marble that was leaping back to the hilt of his knife. "Ridiculous, useless, beast of annoyance," he huffed at Raax.

Dearthair glared at Ghrian. Ghrian smiled back at his friend as he tightened his thighs against the gray stallion, removed the swords from his belt, and whirled them in the air, galloping hands free toward the dark entrance of Beinn. Shaerico could not help but laugh as she and Fiáin followed suit. The knights held back their amusement and wished the ruby faced man farewell.

The moment had come. The men from the sunny Realm of the Lake and the lady of the Forbidden Forest headed into a reality that they had lived so closely to, yet so blissfully ignorant of.

Chapter Sixteen

The journey through the mountain did not begin as treacherously as one may have expected. Trees lined the pathway. Though small and low hanging, they seemed overall healthy. The trees created a canopy that darkened the entrance to the mountain pass, but some light fought its way through the thick, waxy leaves, weaving a thin yellow tapestry of light along the snow.

"So, Dearthair," Shaerico asked as she felt the thin rays of sunlight on her face. "Do you have any idea where to begin looking on this mountain?"

The suffocating blanket of trees reminded her of Collitte and how for years she had longed to be fully bathed in the sun's golden rays. The torture of being unable to step out into the fields of the Realm had been nearly unbearable. Her insatiable love of the blinding sun still lingered now as she was deep in the darkened wood watching the beams of light dance along the rim of the trees. The thin rays burned her retinas, yet she could hardly look away. Like a moth to the flame, the darkness longed to be in the light. She could barely comprehend how far she was from home. How she no longer truly had a home. She pushed the thought from her mind and turned to Dearthair, awaiting his response.

"Aren't you the one who is supposed to be tracking them?" he replied coarsely.

Ghrian rolled his eyes at Dearthair's sass.

Shaerico released a low snarl, "It isn't so easy in the snow or in this form."

Dearthair's eyes widened and his jaw clenched. He truly had no desire to ever lay his eyes on the black wolf again.

"How far does this trail lead?" Ghrian interjected.

"It surrounds the whole of the Kingdom from the Eastern Waste all the way to the edge of Collitte and even farther west to the sea," Dearthair said, "but much of those paths are no longer used."

"Great. So not much ground to cover then," Ghrian sighed with sarcasm.

Shaerico dismounted Fiáin and walked to one of the nearby trees. The sturdy trunk was swallowed in rich brown bark. Shaerico broke off a piece, brought it her nose, and inhaled deeply.

"They definitely passed this way. I will hold on to this. I have a feeling the trees end soon," she noted.

She was correct. Not long after their brief stop, the canopy of trees dissipated. They had climbed for a few hours as the trail steadily inclined. The mossy gray rock below began to break through the thick blanket of snow beneath them. The horses became restless as the tunnel of trees faded and the reality of how high they had climbed set in. Everything was visible from atop Beinn. The world seemed so small from the back of the mountain. All of their daily toils seemed meaningless, a wisp of memory, forgotten and unimportant in light of all of Domhaen. The white tip of the castle Nícíl glistened far below. The villages of Lake Muina that lined the end of the trail from the Realm to the Kingdom were barely visible amongst the trees, the blue lake winked at their center. They could see a large cluster of towns beyond the castle that ran for what seemed to be miles farther south.

"I had no idea there was another city, and one so large," Shaerico whispered.

Dearthair laughed, turning to face Shaerico. "That is not just another city. That is Raven City and it is much larger than Lochta. It may very well even be larger than the entire Realm of the Lake," he said.

She tried to fathom a city larger than the community of villages, businesses, and homes by the lake. She was not yet able to see the Realm, but she wondered how it compared from this height.

"Can you tell me more about this Raven City?" Shaerico asked Dearthair, genuine curiosity filling her voice.

"Sure," Dearthair shrugged. "I am still so amazed by your lack of common knowledge."

Ghrian glanced at Shaerico who waited in anticipation, completely unfazed by Dearthair's jab. Admittedly, Ghrian was equally curious about the largest city in the Kingdom. Though he had heard mention of it many times, he knew little details about Raven City.

"I have been there, once," Dearthair began proudly. "The sight alone is overwhelming. People crowd the streets day and night. Shops and pubs line the main thoroughfare, which is lined with more streets, lined with more vendors. Smaller villages line the city for miles through the woods. The city itself is never dark and never quiet. But what is most spectacular about Raven City is its diversity of residents. It is said to be the only place in the known world where beasts of magic and humans reside in peace. Though, the time I visited I saw nothing of magic."

Ghrian interjected excitedly, "Beasts of magic?"

Dearthair nodded and continued, "Supposedly so, though I am still skeptical and saw no signs of such creatures when I visited."

Ghrian looked stunned. His mind raced, considering the endless possibilities of truths he did not yet know. "But why would the Order deny the existence of such things if a city in the Kingdom is home to them?"

Dearthair shrugged. "I can't be certain, but I remember hearing tales throughout my travels of beasts of darkness that once roamed the Kingdom. These creatures were said to have been fallen beings of magic that battled the Order for ages. Maybe the Order was trying to protect people from them? What does it matter? There is no Order in Raven City and no magic in the Realm. Best not to fret over fairy tales."

That night Ghrian lay awake. Sleep evaded him as his mind wandered. He longed to visit the great city. As he turned to face the dying campfire, he noticed that Shaerico was also awake staring at the stars above. She wondered what the beings of magic in Raven City might be. Perhaps they too were cursed.

"We could go some day," Ghrian said from across the crackling flames.

Shaerico turned to face him. "Do you think there really are magic beings in Raven City? Do you think those people are also cursed?"

Ghrian sat up and offered a warm smile. "Yes, I believe they exist now more than I ever have, but I don't think that they are cursed. My mother told me stories of a people that are half human and half animal, but not in the way that you are. They are both at the same time."

Shaerico tried to imagine what that would be like, but she couldn't. "How is that possible?" she asked.

"They were from a time before us, created to be that way. My mother called them The Chroniclers of History. I never knew what she meant, nor what they looked like. To be honest, I didn't believe in much of what my mother said, and though I remember the general aspects of most stories she told, I can't remember many details." He looked down at the fire. "I wish now that I had listened closer and taken her words to heart."

Shaerico stood and sat next to Ghrian, gazing into the fire. "I would have liked to have met her," she said as she rested her head on Ghrian's shoulder.

"I think she would have liked you," Ghrian smiled as he too gazed into the flames.

"Tell me more about her and the places you have been. Tell me more about the Realm of the Lake," Shaerico said as she yawned. Though Ghrian had told her much in their first meetings, he happily obliged. There was always more to tell.

Shaerico listened to Ghrian talk about his home. His voice was like honey, soothing. It sweetened the reality of what they faced. For one night, by the light of the fire Shaerico and Ghrian forgot about their perilous journey. Instead their minds were filled with dance and food and things that Shaerico could only dream of.

As she faded off to sleep, Ghrian watched the fire flicker across her restful face. Suddenly, he thought of Ginger. He felt a pang of guilt. They were so different, she and her. How could he feel something so similar for them both? But no. It wasn't the same. What he felt for Shaerico was deeper, much deeper.

That night was the coldest night the travelers had faced yet. Following the warmth and luxury of King Gaewyn's castle, the frigid winter wind on the mountain was beyond brutal. Shaerico awoke in a cold sweat. Her dreams grew steadily worse. She looked to her right. Ghrian lay hunched over his saddlebags, his long hair cascading wildly around his face. Shaerico smiled. He must have tried to stay upright since she had fallen asleep on his shoulder. His thoughtfulness continued to amaze her.

As she removed the saddlebags and directed his sleeping body to a more comfortable position on his cloak, she heard a rustle in a cluster of bushes. The sparse brush lined the side of the trail closest to the sheer rock face that extended upwards for a few hundred feet. At first, she suspected it was just a bird, but as her keen eyes narrowed in on the movement, she saw a glint of metallic black in the dim firelight.

Shaerico stood, turning toward the horses to see if they were concerned. March and Dearthair's mare were sound asleep, but Fiáin kept his gaze locked on the bushes. Slowly, Shaerico began moving toward the disturbance in the night. Her heart pounded loudly in her chest, a great contrast to the heavy silence that coated the mountain. Suddenly, her eyes met a pair of bloodied black hooves. It came on so quickly, why had she not smelled it?

She saw the beast for just a moment, but its image was emblazoned in her mind. The creature had four legs like that of a horse and was black as night. His body and tail were the same, but his torso was that of a man. He was a brute of a man with long black hair pulled behind pointed ears. Shaerico got but a glimpse of him, yet she was sure she saw pointed teeth in his eerie smile. The feature that haunted her most, however, were his putrid red eyes.

Her body hit the ground with a loud thud. She could feel the scarlet eyes scanning the stony horizon. Should she wake the others? It all happened so fast that she had no time to react, save dodging the hooves of the mysterious beast as it barreled past her and disappeared down the path. She looked back toward her companions. Both were still sound asleep. Shaerico turned to Fiáin, who now looked in the direction the creature had gone.

"I suppose if you are not too concerned then I shouldn't be either," she said to the black stallion as she stood.

He looked to her with wild and sorrowful eyes, then lowered his head.

"I'll wait to tell them tomorrow," Shaerico sighed as she returned to her own place by the fire. "No use in disturbing their sleep. I doubt we will get much rest throughout the remainder of our journey."

Morning could not come soon enough for Shaerico. Her thoughts had dwelled on nothing aside from the events of the night before. Was that a creature of darkness? Was that one of the ancient Chroniclers of Ghrian's mother's stories?

As soon as Ghrian and Dearthair woke, Shaerico began reciting the occurrence.

"Slow down," Ghrian laughed. "I'm barely awake and you're talking much too fast for me to follow."

Shaerico huffed as she mounted Fiáin. "What do you need me to repeat?"

Dearthair was still gathering his belongings as Ghrian bridled March.

"I saw one of the creatures of darkness last night, at least, I assume that's what it was," she said.

"Impossible," Dearthair retorted. "Those were wiped out long ago, if they even existed at all," he added quickly. "I bet it was only a nightmare since I was telling you of them yesterday."

Shaerico glared in his direction.

Ghrian interjected, "Dearthair, be reasonable." Then turning to Shaerico he asked, "Are you sure that's what you saw?"

Shaerico replied, "What else am I supposed to call a horse with the torso of a man who tried to trample me?"

"A what?" Ghrian said, nearly losing his balance as he mounted March. "You're sure that's what you saw."

"Positive," Shaerico affirmed. "It was solid black, with pointed ears and bloodied hooves. Certainly, it wasn't a being of magic who lives among people."

Dearthair wore a look of bewilderment. "The only being I have ever heard of with any resemblance to that was a statue at the center of Raven City. He was supposedly some kind of war hero or co-founder of the city. Something like that. But no one has seen one alive. Are you sure you weren't dreaming? Wouldn't you have smelled it before it was right in front of you?" Dearthair added, following his trail of suspicion as fear of such a creature began to mount in his throat.

Shaerico furrowed her brows as the companions left their resting place, the ashes of their fire smoldering. "I don't know why I didn't smell it, but I'm certain it was real."

"Well," Ghrian sighed. He scanned the mountain pass; nothing lay ahead of them but rock and snow. He directed March toward Shaerico and placed a broad hand on her shoulder. "We best be on our guard then."

The subject was dropped, and the thick silence once again blanketed the company. They climbed farther and farther until the stone face to their right began to shrink. As they walked, more and more could be seen of the lands beyond the mountain. Lands bound by no law, no Realm, no Kingdom.

Dearthair seemed mildly disinterested, as he had seen this view before, but Shaerico and Ghrian were enthralled by the beauty. A thin layer of clouds covered most of what was visible, but in the distance, far beyond a blackened scorched forest, a wild river, and what seemed to be city ruins, lay a vast expanse of nothing but white.

"The Unsettled North," Ghrian whispered.

"It's incredible," Shaerico said quietly. "I had no idea there was so much, beyond."

The two gazed on in silence, taking in all that they could, as if at any moment it would vanish, never to be seen again. Both were in awe. There was so much that they did not know, so much that people had forgotten. Shaerico longed to explore those neglected lands. Endless adventure and fresh perspective beckoned her to abandon her quest and escape into the safety of the unknown. But the far distant ruins reminded her of home. What if there were more cursed people living in that fallen city? For a moment she wished that she could find out, but then the thought of her own accursed people returned to her mind, retuning her to reality. She had to save them first. All else would come in time.

That night, as the companions rested by the fire, eating their rations of meat and bread, sipping the last of the gifted wine, Shaerico turned to Ghrian.

"Can you tell me one of your mother's tales?"

Ghrian was caught off guard. His attention had been on his boots, which were wearing thin. The sole of his left boot had come completely free from the rest of the dark brown leather. He removed the boot and stretched his foot out over the fire, hoping to thaw his frostbitten toes.

"To be honest, I don't remember too many details. I am mostly left with vague memories, fragments of phrases, clouded images, not too many full and concrete stories." He sighed as he returned his foot to his boot and took a swig from the wine bottle. "I remember bits of tales. Like The Chroniclers of History, though I can't recall their purpose, or that there are a people to the South on another body of land separate from our own, but I don't know what took them there or who they are."

Ghrian brought his hand to his thick hair and ran his fingers through the tangled brown locks that shone like silken flames in the firelight. It was clear that he was frustrated with himself. He wanted to remember more.

Shaerico looked out over the Kingdom and then to the opposite side of the mountain and beyond. "Did she ever speak of the Unsettled North?"

Ghrian followed her gaze toward the wall of white that spanned as far north as the eye could see, beyond recorded knowledge, hidden, forgotten or otherwise. "I only remember one story about the Unsettled North: The Geysers of Geim."

Shaerico tried to imagine a geyser. Perhaps it was a monster? Ghrian noted her puzzled expression.

"It's supposedly a place where springs of water turn to columns of fire."

Shaerico's face lit up with interest. Ghrian smiled, then continued, "All I remember of that story is that, legend has it, one of the famed Aonharc…"

Before he could finish his sentence Shaerico interrupted, "Aonharc. I know that word!"

Ghrian was startled. He knew little about the Aonharc himself, aside from what information he was about to disclose, but he had never heard mention of them from anyone but his mother. Instead of continuing his story he asked, "Where did you hear of them?"

"Not them, one," she said, her wild eyes matching the flames that billowed from their campfire as she added wood. "From that book in Nícíl. It said that the horned horse who helped the King drive the dragon from the Kingdom was an Aonharc."

Ghrian sat back on his hands. A tinge of jealously began to boil in his heart. He wished that he had been able to continue reading, after all Shaerico knew less than he of the world. He considered saying something about it but thought better of it as he turned to meet her inquisitive eyes. She was just as curious as he, and she had even more to learn. He sighed and leaned forward.

"There are five of them. As the tale goes, one of them resides in the Unsettled North, beyond the Geysers of Geim, in a world of crystal-clear caverns and light. It is said that they had some hand in creating different parts of Domhaen, though naturally I cannot remember the details."

"Fascinating," Shaerico mused. Dearthair huffed and rolled over so that his back was facing the fire.

"His attitude is worsening," she said to Ghrian, not trying to hide or soften her words.

Ghrian sighed and closed the distance between he and Shaerico.

"Go easy on him, will you?" His soft eyes met hers, then he turned to Dearthair. "He's been through a lot. This is not the first time he's lost someone close to him."

Shaerico studied Ghrian's face. "He blames me for her capture, doesn't he?" she said coolly, changing the subject.

Ghrian was unsure how to respond. He had noticed Dearthair's fickle emotions over their journey. One minute he's helping Shaerico and the next he's cursing her. Perhaps part of him did blame her. Perhaps he was struggling with his need for her aid and his desire to be rid of her. Alas, Ghrian did not want to strain Shaerico and Dearthair's already tense relationship.

"Don't worry," Ghrian replied, his milky brown eyes swimming in the firelight, "he's just having a hard time coping with all of this. He'll come around. Once Oir is returned to us I'm certain he'll lighten up."

Shaerico smiled. "You're a wonderful friend, but a terrible liar." With that she curled her body next to his and drifted off to sleep.

Ghrian smiled and placed a hand on her soft shoulder, looking up at the twinkling stars above. His mind traveled far to the north, to the Geysers of Geim, where no sorcerer, nor demon hoard of wolves, nor beings of dark magic could ever touch them.

The following morning was just as cold as the last. The biting winds of winter atop Beinn were relentless. Shaerico had awoken to find herself cradled in Ghrian's arms. Though she knew that the gesture was not intentional, she remained in that moment until she felt an unfamiliar warmth pulsating through her. Even though she still was not accustomed to the touch of another, she had begun to crave this closeness with Ghrian.

As the companions continued along the unforgiving mountain trail, she looked over at Ghrian. He was discussing something with Raax, who had made a habit of coming to life at the strangest times. She wondered what they could be talking about until her nostrils began to burn. The scent of burning coal leeched into her throat. She coughed and turned to Ghrian, "Do you smell that?"

Ghrian looked confused. "Smell what?"

Suddenly, a shadow emerged from behind a ridge that had risen from the side of the mountain. It had been veiled against the stone. Its vague color gradually grew more visible as it rose from its crouched position. A glossy black crest branched out from between its lifeless eyes and trailed down the beast's arched spine.

The trio stopped in their tracks, breathless, trying to determine if it were better to draw their weapons or turn and run. Raax let out a surprising hiss and leapt from Ghrian's shoulder. Before the small marble creature could meet his mark, the black beast bounded forward, his long stone body spanning above the white spec beneath him.

When it pounced, Ghrian had no time to react. As the beast landed, Ghrian was thrown from March. The gray stallion bucked. Astonishingly, his thick hooves caused no damage. Instead, the horse fell lame immediately.

"March!" Ghrian cried before being pinned by the beast that dismounted him.

Shaerico was frozen in astonishment. This creature was as black as coal, but it was not the beast she had seen the night before. The monster was crouched over Ghrian, three massive talons placed next to his head, carving the rock. The ridge of horns that erupted from its skull led down its long tail as it whipped the air behind him. He bared his teeth as a stream of red began to bubble in his throat. A Living Stone. This must be Marmair's second. The thought sent a chill down Shaerico's spine. Whatever she had encountered last night must have been a scout.

Ghrian struggled under the crushing weight of the Fallen Stone. Dearthair lunged his mare forward, broadsword drawn. He too was quickly knocked from his steed with a whip of the beast's tail. The Fallen Stone never took his large gray eyes off Ghrian. As the monster of darkness drew closer, the fearless man brought his dagger to the beast's side. Unfortunately, it did little to the Fallen Stone except anger him. The dagger shattered

upon contact, though it did leave a slight crack in the black stone. Enraged the beast began to drip blazing fire onto the young man's chest. Ghrian cried out in pain as it burned through his cloak and seared his flesh.

Shaerico's shock turned to rage. She leapt from Fiáin and transformed midair. Her slender figure grew robust as her sinews ripped and reshaped. Her raven black hair turned coarse and coated her body. Her long nails turned to silver claws and her teeth became sharp as knives. Solas embedded into the skin on her chest and shone with a blue blaze. Not only did the stone aid in a controlled transformation, but it also made her more powerful. The wolf's orange eyes glazed turquoise. Her teeth met the back of the Fallen Stone with ferocity. One would have expected bone to break on solid stone, but this form was different. Shaerico was one with the Iómhara. Her pure intentions had begun to harness the true nature of Solas.

The black wolf sank her teeth deep into the shoulder of the beast, producing a loud crack. It seemed surprised as it turned its attention from Ghrian, who was badly burned and near fainting. The creature's eyes were far from Marmair's. These did not have the sultry swimming essence of knowledge. These were the eyes of something dead. The beast opened its mouth and prepared to release the blood red fire. The black wolf stared into the dead eyes and growled. Her own gaze locked on her prey. As the fire began to spark from the mouth of the Fallen Stone, Shaerico lunged again, her teeth meeting the demon's neck. She heard a crack and the beast gargled on his newly produced flame. A splash of fire landed on Shaerico, burning holes in her thick fur. The stone being followed the flame with a swipe of its talons. Shaerico howled in pain and pushed the beast away from her and the now unconscious Ghrian. Dearthair raced to Ghrian's side, after lifting himself from the ground.

The wolf and creature of stone continued their fight. Shaerico was even more enraged when she realized the extent of damage Ghrian had sustained. She sliced the beast with her claws and continued pushing it further up the trail. It clasped its talons around the gaping hole in its neck from which liquid flame continued to pour. Shaerico nipped at its tail as it attempted to knock her from her feet. It seemed as if she would be victorious. The beast took a moment and eyed the sky. The wolf followed its gaze. She began to feel the ground shake. She turned back to the Fallen Stone and watched as its hide lifted. Thin slabs of stone unfurled from its body. It spread its wings and released a deafening screech before propelling itself into the sky.

The black wolf howled after the Fallen Stone, sending a chill down Dearthair's spine. He sat next to Ghrian, trying to stop the bleeding with his cloak as the skin bubbled and smoldered underneath the fabric. He was terrified as the wolf slowly made her way to the two men, licking the wound on her shoulder. As she neared them, she fell to the ground, overcome with exhaustion. The pendant turned pure white once again and Shaerico returned to her human form. She lay naked in the frosted dust. Fiáin trotted to her side and pulled the cloak from his back, covering her exposed body.

As Dearthair was still trying to stop the bleeding, the feather that King Gaewyn had gifted them, that Ghrian had placed in his chest pocket, lightly brushed the open wounds. It shone blue and ribbons of silver shimmered through the thin hairs. Dearthair jumped back. He watched as the color pulsated through the feather and into Ghrian's skin. As it did, the skin it touched began to heal. Dearthair rubbed his eyes, believing that they had betrayed him. Fiáin turned to face the nervous man and neighed lightly.

"There is no way that this horse is trying to tell me that what I saw was real," he gasped. He looked at Shaerico. Fiáin neighed again, this time loudly.

"Fine!" Dearthair replied.

He lifted the dissolving feather and threw it onto Ghrian's open wounds. The feather immediately turned a blood red. It seemed to soak up the fire from the scorched and flaking skin. Then it again bubbled blue, and silver strands pulsated through each hair. The color leached from the feather as it melted into Ghrian's chest. With a sharp inhale, he sat up abruptly, holding his chest where the burns once had been. Dearthair sat back, stunned. Fiáin whinnied and tossed his thick silvery mane. Ghrian looked at Dearthair, then turned toward the black stallion.

Below him the naked woman lay in the dust and snow. Before Dearthair could discourage him from rising, Ghrian stumbled toward her. He knelt by her side, his scorched and bloody shirt hanging open, revealing his now hairless, but never-the-less healed chest.

"Shaerico," he whispered, but she did not respond. "Dearthair, what happened? What was that thing?"

"I have no idea. Honestly, it looked like solid stone, but," he trailed off, reminding himself again that there was no such thing as magic, nor dragons.

"Seriously, Dearthair?" Ghrian raised his voice. "We are standing on a mountain with a wolf-woman who saw a horse-man last night, after a day in which you told us stories about a city where man and magic coexist. We were just attacked by a stone demon and somehow I am healed after being burned, yet you still want to believe magic does not exist?"

Dearthair sighed heavily. "Believing what I have experienced goes against everything I have been taught!"

"Dearthair, you of all people should know that you can't take things at face value. You have to research for yourself. You've seen more of the world than she and I have, yet you still hold on to the obvious lies the Order fed us as children? What we have seen these past months has made me question everything the Order has tried so hard to teach us. I should have listened to my mother," Ghrian sighed.

He turned back to Shaerico. A pang of guilt fell upon his chest. Gently, he brushed her black locks from her face. He felt her shallow breath on the back of his hand. Ghrian was relieved that she was alive, but he was concerned about what had happened. All he remembered was the crushing weight on his body and the pain of fire on his chest. He vaguely recalled a piercing howl.

"Please be okay," he whispered to her.

"She will be," a tender voice responded.

Ghrian whirled around, searching for the author of that familiar voice. He was both surprised and disappointed to find nothing more than King Gaewyn's white hawk sitting atop Fiáin's back. He looked to Dearthair, who was staring at the bird.

"We best find Oir soon. I may be losing my mind," Dearthair muttered.

"Did you hear a voice as well?" Ghrian asked. He felt something crawl up his side as he spoke. He quickly stood, knocking poor Raax to the ground.

"Why do you keep doing this to me?" the small stone being scolded, brushing the snow and dust from his white marble body. "Such a clumsy boy." He crawled up Fiáin's leg, bowed, and sat next to the white hawk.

Dearthair was now convinced that he had gone mad. "That's it. I can't sit here any longer. Get her up and on her steed. We're getting Oir and getting off this blasted mountain." Dearthair marched to his mare and ushered her up the trail. Ghrian sighed and glared at Raax.

"You couldn't have waited until he was out of sight?"

"What? He had to learn eventually. Besides, there's no going back to sleep now," Raax pointed to the shattered dagger in the snow.

"Fantastic," Ghrian said with sarcasm. "Where did that bird come from? Won't King Gaewyn be upset that it's gone?" Ghrian inquired rhetorically.

"She is not the King's bird," Raax barked. "If anything, he belongs to her. He owes her everything."

The hawk spread its wings and drifted to Shaerico, drawing its beak close to the woman's ear. Ghrian watched, confused, as Shaerico began to wake. She opened her eyes.

"It's you," she said, smiling at the hawk.

Ghrian fell to the ground and gathered Shaerico in his arms. She had never been held this way, and though she was uncertain how to react, she felt an overwhelming sense of safety.

"I'm fine," she said, looking into Ghrian's golden-brown eyes. Her eyes traveled to his torn shirt and exposed chest. She admired it for a moment, before pushing away from him and exclaiming, "But you were burned!"

"I know," he said softly.

"But how are you healed?" she asked.

"That I don't know," he replied.

"And I, I was a wolf, and it's still daylight," she murmured.

Shaerico felt the weight of the stone on her chest. She lifted it to view. It shimmered in the now setting sun, glistening like moonlight over water. Marmair's words rang in her ears. This stone held great power indeed.

The travelers continued on a bit longer before stopping to rest for the night. Shaerico and Ghrian both rode atop Fiáin, as March was still lame from the attack. He followed slowly behind. As the men settled in for the night, Shaerico went further along the trail to scout their route for the following day, though Ghrian protested her going alone. She knew that they must have been getting closer since they'd been attacked once already. She was growing more and more wary. The white hawk soared above her. She had followed them ever since their encounter with the Fallen Stone. Shaerico could hear the soft beat of the hawk's wings.

"What are you doing here?" Shaerico said, still plotting their route.

The hawk swooped down to hover in front of the huntress. "You know not what you are heading into."

"I know now well enough what I have to do, who I have to face," Shaerico replied.

As the hawk hovered in front of her, a thin cloud cascaded over the mountain. The white bird began to twirl as the cloud enveloped her. Her silky wings grew longer and thinner as they transformed into a solid white dress. The woman's golden-white hair fell below her back.

"Shaerico, you do not know. There are more cursed creatures on this mountain than your family." She lifted her pale hands to Shaerico's face and whispered, "You have to be prepared."

"Is that why you've followed us all this way?" Shaerico inquired. "I know it's you."

The woman looked behind Shaerico to the sleeping menagerie of horse and man. "Partly," she turned back to the raven-haired woman. "I have come to help."

"Help?" Shaerico asked, suspiciously. "Who are you really? Are you the shapeshifter from Collitte, are you King Gaewyn's white hawk, are you a bird, a deer, a woman?"

"I am all of this and more," the white woman said, holding out her arms and opening her hands. She held two stones in her palms. The stones shone like the sun, lighting the night sky, and casting a myriad of colors through the shroud of clouds that surrounded them. Shaerico's eyes widened, trying desperately to determine the intentions of this sorceress.

"I am Fíor, Guardian of the Living Water and protector of this world."

"You are a sorceress. Like the one who stole my family," a low snarl released from under Shaerico's breath. "You are not the guardian of the spring. I met Marmair. The Living Stone protect the water."

Fíor was not bothered. Her kind golden eyes looked toward the stone around the suspicious woman's neck.

"Solas is perhaps the most powerful Íomhara left. Marmair must have great faith in you to entrust her to you," she smiled.

Fíor lifted her right hand, shifting the beams of light toward Solas. The white stone shone turquoise, as it had earlier that day, but this time a myriad of colors followed. Vibrant shades of blue that seemed to capture the moonlight, oranges and pinks that resonated like the richness of a sunrise, and strands of starlit silver poured into the stone.

"I will teach you to harness the true power of Solas. You have already learned that she not only keeps your curse at bay, but that with her, you can turn that curse to a blessing."

Shaerico lowered her eyes to the pendant around her neck.

"Everything is connected, from the light surrounding you to the water in your blood. Magic exists in us all, some simply choose not to see it," Fíor smiled again.

The ancient sorceress spent the remainder of the night teaching Shaerico the power of the stone. She taught her how it could heal, and Shaerico mended March's wounded leg. As the sun rose the next morning, Fíor returned to the form of the hawk. She made Shaerico promise to keep her identity secret and in exchange she would continue to teach the daughter of the moon how to handle the Stone of Power.

Chapter Seventeen

The sun rose above the mountains, but it remained veiled by the unending expanse of gray. A chilling wind blew across their path. The men shivered as they rose. Shaerico was already atop Fiáin, awaiting their rise. She had a renewed sense of hope. Ghrian was surprised to see March up and prancing around on his newly healed leg. The white hawk soared high above them.

Ghrian looked up to the sky, "Why is that hawk still here?"

"She was King Gaewyn's aid in battle, perhaps she's here for us now," Shaerico smiled.

Ghrian shrugged and grabbed a piece of bread and some cheese from his saddlebag. Dearthair begrudgingly got up from his stony bed. He rubbed his eyes and asked Ghrian for a loaf. Shaerico was becoming impatient. Fiáin shared her attitude and pawed the ground.

"Seriously, you two? You can't eat and ride?" she sighed.

"Why are you in such a rush? You haven't satiated your blood lust yet?" Dearthair said, through his chewing.

"Are you no longer so eager to rescue Oir?" Shaerico retorted.

That hit a nerve. Dearthair inhaled the remainder of his bread and mounted his mare. Ghrian sighed and climbed atop March who was eager to prance upon his healed leg. The journey continued, and the trio remained unaware of the extent of the dangers ahead.

Beinn was not an easy mountain to traverse. As they continued along the pass, it became increasingly harder to navigate. Spindly and knobby trees grew in strange and inconvenient places along the path. Bushes thick with thorns seemed to spring from every crack in the mountain's rocky surface. The path itself was slick with icy snow. The stone ridge that sometimes lined the side of the trail would occasionally fade away into nothing, leaving both sides of the trail open to the biting winds. The undulating mountains were exhausting to climb and falling boulders were a common occurrence as the trail became increasingly thin. Night and day passed uneventfully. No one bothered to keep track of how long they had been on the mountain. The days blurred together in a mass of bone chilling cold, white snow, gray skies, gray stone, and white clouds. The scent on the bark was fading and the air had become thin, but Shaerico pressed on with ferocity. Some days she would lose the scent entirely, but on others she was certain of the whereabouts of her family.

Each night after the men fell asleep, Fíor would train Shaerico. Each night Shaerico grew stronger in both her human and her canine form. She had never really felt that she belonged in her human form, but her confidence grew as her trust in Solas and faith in the Living Water took hold. However, understanding did not come easily. It took immense focus. She had to quiet parts of herself that she had never before felt.

After a few more days, Beanrua's scent became clearer. Some part of Shaerico hoped that it was because her own senses and skills were growing stronger, but deep inside she knew that it was because they were getting closer to the pack.

"How far do we have?" Dearthair asked one afternoon as a light rain fell over the mountain.

"We are close," Shaerico said, torn by both the anticipation of seeing her family and despair of what might have become of them.

Ghrian directed March to her side. He placed a hand on her knee. "It's going to be alright. We will rescue all of them," his gentle eyes smiled at her.

"You don't know that," she replied.

"What do we have if not hope?" he said. Then, pointing to the white hawk that flew above, "besides, we have King Gaewyn's magic bird. That has to count for something."

Shaerico laughed at how right he was, even in how little he knew. She began to wonder if Fíor would indeed help them fight, or if her purpose was simply to guide.

They were close enough now that the stench of flame burned her nostrils constantly. She could sense the pain that hung thick in the air like smog. The horses became more and more uneasy. The hawk screeched above them, as a slow drizzle of rain and sleet descended upon them. Ghrian and Shaerico walked in silence. Dearthair kept a steady pace behind, looking up every so often at the hawk circling above. Raax was enjoying his new-found freedom. He rode happily atop Ghrian's right shoulder, commenting and humming every so often. But in this moment, even he was quiet.

No more than a few breaths passed when an arrow pierced the silence. It soared above the trio and sank deep into the flesh of the white hawk. Shaerico was frozen in astonishment as she watched Fíor fall from the sky and land in a thick cover of snow. March reared and Ghrian reached for his swords. Dearthair caught up with them as the bird of prey tumbled to the ground. He drew his broadsword. The mighty black stallion reared high and released a bellowing neigh. Shaerico looked toward the direction from which the arrow had come and her heart sank. There, further down the path, Beanrua stood, her eyes a deep crimson, in her human form, with a bow in hand.

Shaerico did not know what to do. She had played this moment over in her mind for months. What would she do when she was face to face with her friend once more? How would she snap Beanrua back into reality? Though she stood stunned for a moment, she was not going to stand idly by. She urged Fiáin forward. The great stallion leapt toward the fiery weaponized woman.

Shaerico could hear Ghrian's voice behind her, but she could not make out his words. The blood boiled in her body as the rage swelled. The dark sorcerer stood just behind Beanrua with his hand on her shoulder, directing her every move. A devilish smile leeched across his face as he saw the meager warriors that stood in opposition to him. He removed his hand from Beanrua, and the woman immediately returned to the form of the red wolf. Fiáin's hooves pounded against the snow. Shaerico's heartbeat matched their rhythm.

Beanrua's blood red eyes locked on the stallion's throat. They were headed on an inevitable course of collision. Shaerico leapt from Fiáin and lunged for Beanrua, hoping to knock her from her desired path, but before their bodies met, something white darted through the snow beneath them. The next moment, Shaerico was on the snow-laden stone and a white doe held the red wolf at bay in a pair of glowing turquoise antlers that glistened like diamonds against the falling sleet.

For a second, Shaerico was relieved as Fiáin bucked and changed his course, but then the realization that Beanrua was being attacked settled in. It was true that Beanrua was an imminent threat and that she seemed to be the sorcerer's primary puppet, but Shaerico could not bear to watch her best friend in pain. She stood as the shimmering antlers around Beanrua's neck sank deeper into her flesh, as if at any second they would rip out her throat. Shaerico hesitated for a moment, trying to determine her course of action. It seemed she did not have long to decide. She leapt from the rocky mountain face as her canine form tore through her body. She met the side of the white doe with force, her massive black head pressing into the beast's abdomen. The deer released its grip from Beanrua's neck and steadied itself in the snow. Its golden-brown eyes looked disappointed. Shaerico returned its confused gaze.

The doe returned her attention to the red wolf that had caught her breath and was readying herself to attack. She leapt into the sky and was enveloped by the cover of clouds. The hawk flew high into the snowy gray sky until it disappeared from the line of sight. Shaerico watched as Fíor vanished. She was caught off guard and the red wolf took the opportunity.

"Beanrua!" Shaerico called, trying to stop her friend from the attack, but it was too late. As the wolf lunged at Shaerico, she noticed something buried deep in the fur on her neck. It looked like a stone.

Beanrua's teeth met Shaerico's side. Shaerico's confusion turned to pain and her huntress nature returned to her. She had fought with Beanrua many times, but this moment was not playful, nor for the purpose of training. As the blood began to trickle from Shaerico's shoulder, she tore her body from Beanrua's jaws. A chunk of bloodied black fur and skin was left in the red wolf's mouth. Shaerico realized then what the doe had been trying to do. She planted all four paws firmly in the snow. She had to remove that stone.

The sorcerer on the hill in front of them looked on at the fight. Ghrian and Dearthair held their steeds at bay as they discussed their plan of action. Oir was nowhere to be found, but they knew that she had to be close.

Shaerico wondered where the rest of her family was, and if this was the way they were all being imprisoned - in their own bodies by the corrupted power of the crystals.

Beanrua released a low snarl. The black wolf began to circle her. The two massive canines pivoted slowly around one another. The snow and sleet seemed to stand still in the sky above them as their paws resonated off the mountain path. Shaerico lunged at Beanrua in an attempt to remove the stone from the red wolf's neck. Beanrua met Shaerico's nose with her claws, leaving a gash across her snout. Shaerico's lips curled as she growled in frustration, "Let me help you."

It took everything she had not to attack her friend, but she knew the damage she could cause and was concerned for her, though the stone was obviously aiding Beanrua's abilities as well. Shaerico shook her head and continued, "Beanrua, please, I have to remove that stone."

"Why should I let you? You went in search of a new life and abandoned me by your own foolishness. Why can I not do the same?" Beanrua snarled.

"This is not a new life, this is slavery. Don't you see? He is controlling you," Shaerico replied.

Beanrua looked toward the sorcerer who watched them from the hill. Her blood red eyes flickered blue. For a moment, her features softened. Shaerico could see the war that was raging inside of her. She tried to fight it, but she had been captive to the darkness for too long.

"Run," Beanrua managed to whisper through the waves of pain, but Shaerico was too mystified to move.

"What?" she asked.

"I said run," Beanrua turned back toward Shaerico, her eyes their usual crystal blue. "I am lost. We are all lost, but you can save yourself and those men. You have no idea what lies ahead of you. Sister, you cannot win this."

Shaerico could see the panic in her friend's eyes. "I'm not leaving you," she replied.

"You must. I will buy you some time. Please, take it," Beanrua said, her eyes misty.

"No, Beanrua. We are here to rescue you, Oir and everyone!"

"Oir?" Beanrua chimed.

"The golden-haired girl," Shaerico said.

"Ah. The bait," Beanrua nodded.

Shaerico tilted her head. "The bait?"

"She's not for you. Feir won't allow her to leave until she's fulfilled her purpose," Beanrua said.

"Beanrua, what are you talking about?" Shaerico pleaded.

The dark sorcerer had been watching them and grew tired of their stillness. His eyes locked on Beanrua. He lifted his staff. The crystal at its tip grew a fiery red and shone like molten stone. He pointed it to the red wolf.

"You are taking too long. Let me help you," a devious smile crept across his face.

The stone embedded in Beanrua's fur glowed a ghastly red. The skin around it burned and her fur charred black. She winced in pain. Shaerico watched as her eyes flickered again from blue to red and back to blue.

"I am not your slave!" Beanrua roared as she leapt toward the sorcerer, fighting the power of her curse.

Ghrian and Dearthair saw this as their opportune moment and directed their steeds to charge Feir.

Beanrua's jaws had almost encased the sorcerer's forearm when he struck his staff across her face. The wolf's eyes returned to scarlet. Her chest leaked thick red blood as the crystal sank deeper into her flesh. She stood stunned, her mouth agape.

The men had almost reached Feir, their swords drawn. The sorcerer lifted his staff and pointed it to Ghrian and Dearthair. Shaerico watched as Beanrua readied herself for the attack.

"Beanrua, no!" Shaerico screamed.

She turned on her heels and began to run, hoping to knock the red wolf from her path, but she was not quick enough. Dearthair was the closest to Feir. His broadsword was drawn, lifted above him, ready to meet the red wolf. Shaerico knew he would not hold back. As Beanrua's jaws met the withers of Dearthair's mare, he released his sword. Shaerico watched in horror as the blade sliced through the thick air. It carved a deep wound at the base of Beanrua's neck, finishing the work that the piercing antlers had begun. The red wolf fell to the white snow, blood spilling to the ground. She howled in pain and writhed on her cold deathbed as the warmth of her body soaked the white blanket red.

Shaerico could feel the rage well inside her, wilder than she had ever felt. A mix of anger and sorrow bellowed deep from within. She turned her course to the black sorcerer. After all, this was his doing in the end. He released a cold laugh and raised his staff. Cain and the others appeared from behind him all in canine form. All of her pack was present, aside from

Alphaline, Beoir and Lili. She said a silent prayer that they were alright, hopeful that they lived. Every wolf had a stone embedded in the fur of their neck. They were all prisoners in their own bodies.

The joy of seeing her people alive was short lived. She refused to be deterred. The thick pads of her paws beat against the icy snow beneath her. Her breath matched its rhythm. The piercing droplets of sleet rained down upon the scene as the black wolf ran. Ghrian and Dearthair reentered the battle. Shaerico gained ground quickly. As she drew nearer, she could see a massive wolf out of her peripherals. Cain barreled toward her with a sinister gleam in his eye. It was clear that he enjoyed his newly discovered power. She returned her gaze to her prey and leapt.

The sorcerer did not move, nor did he need to urge Cain forward. The wolves landed in a heap on the snow in front of the sorcerer. Shaerico watched Feir drift further into the distance as the two beasts tumbled down the hill. When they landed at the base of the mound on which Feir stood, Cain had her pinned. He laughed and growled, "I can't say I haven't been waiting for this moment. I knew you'd come."

Shaerico struggled beneath his weight. "You're sick and power hungry, Cain. You don't realize you're just a pawn in his wicked game!"

"Maybe so, but pawn or not I am finally free to roam and do as I please. This power feels incredible. Too bad you missed your chance to taste it." Cain growled and lifted his paw, ready to swipe his dagger-like claws across Shaerico's already bloodied muzzle.

The black wolf lifted her haunches from the snow and kicked Cain's stomach with all her might. She knocked the wind from his lungs and he stammered backwards. Shaerico could hear the fight ensuing in the distance. Dearthair's mare had been ravaged. He stood over her bleeding corpse, trying his hardest to defend what was left of her. March was running back down the stone path with two wolves on his tail.

Ghrian stood beside his friend, swords drawn, fending off the remaining beasts as best he could. She thought she saw the gleam of marble on one wolf's muzzle. Fiáin and the hawk were nowhere to be found.

The air was cold and thin. Breathing was difficult. The sleet had ceased and a light snow dusted the ground, as if the heavens above were trying to coat the tainted earth as it began to run red with blood. Shaerico watched as her two worlds collided. Her legendary accursed family in their natural form against her valiant new reason for living. She felt herself torn, wondering who to save. Her heart was shattered. She felt more confused and yet possessed a clearer purpose than ever before. She had to get their attention. She had to stop this fight.

The black wolf lifted her head to the darkening sky above and released a piercing sorrowful howl. Her brothers and sisters turned their attention toward her. Cain had caught his breath and was readying himself to attack once more.

"Shaerico," he heaved. "This is useless. No one will turn from this power. Even you wouldn't."

Shaerico lowered her head and glanced at the white stone embedded deep into her silky black fur. She breathed in the chilled air, letting the stone's power pulsate through her body, focusing on the peace it brought her.

"I surrendered myself to good. I do know power, but I have the wisdom to know that it is not my own," she howled.

"Brothers and sisters," she called out over the howling wind. "It is true that we have always been a cursed people. We have been kept hidden our entire lives. We have been kept silent. Now that we have freedom, this is what you chose? Wickedness? Aiding in the destruction that our Mother fought so hard to keep us from? You are free now. You have been given a choice. I have learned to live among the people of the fields and towns and they are not all evil as we once believed. Choose a life of freedom, not a life in service of evil. This man has made you slaves to your greed."

The two beasts following March turned their ears and ceased their chase, leaving the stallion to continue running back down the mountain pass. The few wolves in front of the brave men lowered their heads. The truth pierced their souls. The red stones flickered. Shaerico's words had met their mark. The red wolf smiled as her breath slowed. Feir's control was fading and for the first time, Shaerico could taste the tinge of fear on his breath.

The sorcerer sighed and looked to Cain who was still standing ready behind Shaerico. "My pups seem to have forgotten their place," he hissed, his voice resounding over the mountain top. "Let us remind them!"

Feir lifted his staff. The blood red stone released a blinding flash of light. A piercing shriek followed. The wolves and men alike felt an icy chill upon their necks. The heavy beat of wings sent a gust of frigid air over the mountain top. Out of the darkening sky, a being of stone could be seen above the clouds. His familiar tattered black wings haunted Shaerico's memory.

"Feast, my child. These beasts are no longer of use to me," Feir called to the Fallen Stone.

In the same moment that much of her family was released from their curse, the creature of stone plummeted from the sky. Their corrupted stones of power fell gray to the snow beneath them and they stood naked in human form completely defenseless, except for Cain.

Cain's lust for power had run so deep that the stone was far too embedded in him to be seen. The great wolf leapt for Shaerico's throat from behind, as the Fallen Stone descended upon the mountain top.

Beanrua watched as Cain's jaws nearly met their mark. Shaerico was frozen in despair for her family. She had let her guard down. The valiant auburn-haired girl stood with the last of her strength and ripped a sword from Ghrian's hand. Her snowy bare skin was cloaked in her own blood. She ran across the snow-laden ground as if she were weightless, carried forward by a cause greater than she. Her sword met its mark, but so did Cain's piercing teeth. Against human flesh, she stood no chance of survival. Shaerico turned, her senses returning, just in time to catch Beanrua's fading body. Her strawberry locks fell in wild waves around her ruby face. Tears filled Shaerico's eyes. The silver-blue droplets landed on her friend's soft freckled skin.

"Beanrua," she breathed her name as if she were already an apparition.

Beanrua coughed, blood sputtering from her mouth. "My dear Shaerico, something much worse awaits your newly discovered world should you fail."

"Beanrua, I don't understand."

"You will," she said, touching the stone on Shaerico's chest. "You have always been the strongest of the children of Dorchas. There was a reason for that, Shaerico Langhealach, Daughter of the Moon."

"Beanrua, hush, you're not making sense," Shaerico said.

"I met the white doe, she told me your true name, and who you really are. Your family, you must find them," Beanrua said with her final breath.

"Family? You are my family! Please, Beanrua, don't leave me. I need you," Shaerico begged.

Shaerico returned to her human form overcome with grief. Her rage had faded to sorrow, and confusion set in. She held her dying friend in her arms. Beanrua was the only being to have ever truly understood her.

"Sleep well, sister," Shaerico said, laying the corpse of her beloved Beanrua on a soft bed of snow. She lifted her eyes to see Cain, still in his canine form, with one of Ghrian's swords through his heart.

"Traitor," she scoffed as she ripped it from his chest. The massive wolf fell dead beneath her in a pool of blood.

Turning toward her traveling companions, she saw the Fallen Stone descending upon them from the sky. Ghrian and Dearthair were fighting it off as best they could, but Shaerico knew that today's fight was over. She had to rescue those who still lived. Racing toward them, she lifted the sword. Her glistening skin reflected the falling snow. As she ran, she returned to her canine form. She threw the sword to Ghrian as she transitioned and leapt into the sky, latching her jaws around the beast's thick neck. This time she refused to let go.

"Run!" she snarled through her teeth.

Ghrian began to protest, but then he followed her gaze to what was left of her family laying naked and terrified in the snow. He nodded and raised the people to their feet. He pulled Dearthair from his fallen mare and led the survivors back down the path. Shaerico released a sigh of relief before returning to the task at hand.

She clenched her jaws tighter. The beast's massive talons had landed on the mountain's rocky surface. It flicked its stone tail and whipped Shaerico from her grip, knocking her backwards.

"What power do you think you possess that you could take on such an ancient being alone?" the Fallen Stone laughed.

"You were once a great guardian. How did a creature so strong fall to darkness so easily?" Shaerico replied.

Her words pierced the creature's pride. "How dare you speak of me as if you are my equal," it hissed.

A crackling fire raged beneath the beast's breast. Shaerico looked down the path until she could no longer see her people. She turned back to the creature of stone and replied, "I am not afraid of fire. I am under the protection of something stronger."

She opened her jaws as the red flames burst forth to consume her. She could feel a power well inside her, born of serenity. A wave of turquoise flame gushed forth from her gaping mouth. The billowing clash of flame resounded like thunder over the mountain. A turbulent tunnel of fire that melted the surrounding snow and scorched the stone beneath. In the wake of the steam that the clash of fire left, the black wolf escaped down the mountain path.

Shaerico tracked Ghrian's scent to a small ledge down the mountain. He could sense her approach and walked back up the trail to meet her. As she came into view, he ran to her, wrapping his arms around her neck. She was a bit stunned and stood motionless for a moment. The warmth of his embrace melted the chill of the day's tragedies. She returned to her human form and buried her head beneath Ghrian's chin.

Now it was his turn to be surprised. He had never seen her so vulnerable. He lifted her black locks and brushed them softly behind her ear. She looked into his empathetic eyes as tears began to well in her own.

"I'm so sorry," he said.

Her gaze wandered behind him, landing on the remainder of her family. Her heart leapt at the sight of her brother. Ghrian removed his cloak and draped it around her icy body. She ran to Bruid. The sight of his sister brought a crooked smile to his face. He was embarrassed by his failure. She fell into his arms.

"Thank you for coming to rescue us. I know we did not deserve it," he said quietly.

She looked at the few others that had also escaped.

She lifted Bruid's chin with her dainty hand. "You're alive. There is always opportunity for redemption. You may have allowed yourself to follow the path of greed for a time, but you also chose to turn from that darkness." She hugged him close. "We are family. I will always come for you."

Bruid was surprised by her warmth. She had never acted with such empathy before, so open and emotive. She had changed. Shaerico turned to address the rest of the surviving pack. "You are free now. Please, go make a life for yourself. There is a place in the realm of King Gaewyn called Raven City. Go there and find peace. You no longer need to hide in the woods."

Shaerico removed the white cloak and wrapped it around her brother, then grabbed her own cloak from Ghrian's pack, which he had gathered. Ghrian gave the others enough supplies from the King's gift of rations to make it down the mountain pass and into the Kingdom. They murmured amongst themselves, thanked Shaerico, and disappeared together down the mountain.

Bruid looked to his sister. "We are family indeed. I am coming with you."

"Bruid, please," she countered.

"Don't argue with me. You have no idea what you are truly fighting for, or what you're really fighting against," he said.

Shaerico tilted her head. "Beanrua said something similar, but I will not lose you as well. You have a chance at a new life, and you should take it."

Bruid sighed and sat down. "Fine, but I am staying with you tonight. I can catch up with the others in the morning. I must tell you all that I have learned."

Dearthair had started a fire and was lost in its flames. Ghrian looked down the trail, hoping for March to appear, before taking a seat next to his companions.

"I'm sorry," Dearthair began, keeping his gaze locked on the fire. "I had no idea what a price you would pay trying to rescue Oir." He felt sudden guilt for having ever doubted her.

Shaerico sat and looked at him from across the flames. "Do not apologize. I feel there is more at stake here than one life."

Bruid turned to his sister. "You would be correct in that belief, Shaerico, there is much more at stake."

Chapter Eighteen

A low hum rose over the mountain. Shaerico awoke in a sweat, as if from a nightmare. She clutched her whirling head and opened her eyes. Her nightmare had not been a dream, but rather the horror that she had endured the previous day. She turned to scan her surroundings. Ghrian was on her left, laying peacefully with his arms behind his head. As she watched him sleep, she felt an overwhelming rush of relief that he had survived the events of the day before. She had been so concerned about her family, that she had hardly considered his safety. Was this because she cared less about him than her own people? Perhaps she believed in his strength more than the strength of her own kind? Or maybe she felt that they were so deeply connected that their bond could not be broken even in death. Whatever it was, Shaerico felt a new desire to protect him at all costs. He was all she had now. Little did Shaerico know, Ghrian felt the same way about her.

As the nightmare played over in her mind, Beanrua's blue eyes appeared before her. What had she meant when she'd told Shaerico to find her true family? What did Shaerico have left besides Ghrian? Her beloved sister was gone. Most of her pack was gone. She was grateful that her brother had survived, and it gave her comfort that he and the few other survivors would make a life for themselves in Raven City. But what would her life look like, should she even live to see the end of her journey? She pushed the thoughts from her mind. They were nothing but distractions now. And she had to focus.

She stood, and realizing how hungry she was, turned toward the spindly community of mountain trees below the crag on which they lay, hoping to spot something to eat. Bruid, who had been laying on the other side of the dying fire, sat up when he saw her rise. She smiled at him as he stood. His own smile faded as he stumbled into his sister's arms.

"I'm so sorry," he whispered. Shaerico was taken aback by this sudden gesture. She and Bruid had always had more of a playful, distant relationship. It was rare that either of them displayed sincere emotion.

"So am I," she replied.

"Come with us," Bruid pleaded. "These men can rescue their own. You did what you came to do. You saved us."

Shaerico sighed as her eyes began to burn and tears began to well. "Not all of you."

Bruid gave her hand a light squeeze. "You saved me."

This was perhaps the only genuine encounter Shaerico had had with her brother since their first night in the great hall of Dorchas. She smiled at his gentleness. It was a tempting offer: to make a home somewhere new, somewhere they would not have to hide. But she could not abandon Ghrian and Dearthair.

"I can't," she replied, her ardent eyes locked on his.

He gave her a slight smile, "I understand." He turned to look at the sleeping Ghrian. "You take care of each other. And come see us when this is over."

"We will," Shaerico smiled and released his hand. She gave him a few more rations of bread and walked him back to the mountain trail.

"Goodbye, Shaerico. I will see you soon."

"Goodbye, brother."

She watched him disappear amidst the curtain of snow, then turned back toward the mountain crag on which her companions lay. Both Ghrian and Dearthair remained fast asleep. She thought it best to let them rest, but she needed a distraction. A good hunt would do. The faint scent of hare wafted below her nose on the slight mountain breeze. She was still bewildered as to why the stallion and hawk had disappeared at such a dire time of need. Surely, they were not fearful of the fight that ensued.

The scent of the hare grew stronger as Shaerico darted through the trees down the mountain. She had to be careful not to go too far. As she continued the hunt, she considered all the times she and Beanrua had spent hunting. The realization that Collitte would never feel the same began to set in even deeper now. Her greatest friend and much of her people were no longer a part of this world and her brother and the rest of her pack were headed to a city in which she had never been. Her future was full of loneliness and uncertainty now, and not because she had chosen it. When she'd first left her home, she clung to her new freedoms and all the things she could do, and the places she could go. But Beanrua and the rest of the children of Dorchas would always be in Collitte. They were safe there, secure in the Forbidden Forest. Now, only three remained. She felt the sting of loss. It was nearly too much for her to bear.

"I have never felt such pain," Shaerico sighed as she slowed her pace. She breathed deep the mountain air. The biting cold stung her throat as she inhaled icy flakes of snow. She released another sigh. The hare was not far now. As she drew closer, another scent caught her attention.

"March?"

Shaerico called to the stallion as his stocky gray body came into view. It was clear that he had run far and lost his bearings. He was still on high alert. His left hind hoof was entangled in a thicket of thorny vines. Shaerico spoke to him in a soft voice. He neighed lightly and tossed his head toward her, his velvet black ears perched high upon his head. She drew closer and stroked his soft wet nose. He was drenched in sweat from the stress. Shaerico removed the vines from his hoof and gently lifted his leg away from the thicket. It reminded her of the first time they had met. The memory brought a smile to her face. She could feel his body heave with a sigh of relief. The two turned back up the mountain toward the others. Shaerico may have lost the hunt, but she had found a friend.

Not far from where the battle had ensued on the previous day, a white sorceress atop a midnight stallion made her way to the mouth of a cave. A bitter cold breeze flowed from the gaping mouth of the ominous cavern. The stench of death bellowed up from deep within the mountain.

"We must discover his purpose," Fíor said to her companion. Fiáin released a low snort.

The two beings entered the mouth of the cave with caution. The sorceress removed two stones from her cloak and pressed them together between her palms. She spoke over them in a tongue long forgotten.

"Bím lisi sollú anni."

The stones began to stretch and intertwine until they formed a single braid. Fíor blew lightly on the tip of the freshly formed wand. A blue flame appeared that would light their way in the deafening darkness. The suffocating foul smell rose from the bowels of the cavern.

"It is just as I feared," Fíor spoke softly, her face barely lit by the subtle blue light. "Feir has called upon the Darkness of Old."

The air grew more and more foul as they continued on through the maze of damp stone. They traveled deeper and deeper into the heart of the mountain. The comfort of the small blue flame soon became too great a risk.

Fíor placed a hand on the stallion's neck. "We must go on in darkness. We cannot risk being seen."

Fiáin nickered in agreement as their only source of light was snuffed out. Not long after, they heard footsteps echoing through the winding tunnels.

"I don't know why you believe I'm of some use to you. An orphan of Lochta has nothing to offer a sorcerer!"

"Quiet child, you are of great use to me," a sinister voice hissed.

Feir placed a hand on her soft rosy cheek and smiled, "An orphan you may be, but you are not of the people of Lochta."

Oir looked at the dark man with a puzzled stare. She had known her mother and father. Her father was the one who taught her all she knew in her trade. His family had lived in the Realm for generations. How could she be from anywhere else? The questions continued to swirl in her mind, but she dared not contest.

"We must rescue this child," Fíor said to Fiáin in the darkness. "If he discovers her true identity, there will be no saving her."

The company lingered by the fire. Ghrian was overjoyed by his reunion with March, but some of their rations had been lost and more had been given to the surviving members of Dorchas. They shared a single loaf of bread and a slice of salted pork as they plotted their next move.

"We cannot leave Oir. Otherwise, all this loss is for naught," Shaerico said, resolved in her decision to push forward.

Dearthair's confidence was beginning to wain as he realized the searing loss Shaerico had suffered. He remained silent.

The company set out, less certain but still hopeful. Shaerico thought about Fìor and about what she had said that night on the mountain: that Solas may just be the most powerful stone of all. Still, Shaerico had no idea what was ahead of her, though she was anxious to end the demon. They pressed on, following the scent of the sorcerer. By nightfall, they reached an assortment of jagged peaks and tunnel-like caves that burrowed their way through the mountain. Beinn still lingered on, but it seemed that by this cluster of caverns, the descent of the ridge began. This had to be the place where Feir was hiding Oir. That must be why he had not pursued them the previous day. He knew that they would come to him.

It was an odd sensation, finding what they had been searching for so long. All stood still, as if in reverence for the moment that they knew could very well be their last. Ghrian dismounted March and walked to where Shaerico stood at the head of the group. He could feel her conflict. Her relief that their search was over, that the time had finally come to face the darkness and uncover the truth, but also her fear, her concern for the lives of her friends and for his own. There was also rage. The loss of much of her family was still fresh, a searing scar that she feared may never heal. Slowly, Ghrian reached out his hand, gently grasping hers. This time there was no flinch at his touch from the huntress. She squeezed his hand, and without looking at him, plunged herself into the darkness.

"Well, I guess we're just diving in then," a small voice said from Ghrian's shoulder.

Ghrian looked at Raax, "What else would you have us do?"

"I don't know. Sit down, mentally prepare yourselves, have some sort of plan!" he said as he tossed his little stone arms to the snowy sky.

Ghrian sighed, "We have no time for that now."

"Well then, I will stay alert. I can see well in the darkness of caves. You, not so much," Raax said.

Dearthair looked torn as he walked to the mouth of the cavern.

"I'm sure she is fine," Ghrian said, as assuredly as he could.

"We don't know that," Dearthair replied under his breath. He wavered at the thought that she may already be dead.

"Well, there is only one way to know for certain," Ghrian said.

He placed a hand on Dearthair's shoulder. "Let's bring Oir home."

Dearthair nodded and drew his sword. "Right."

The cave was dark. It was a darkness that none of the fellowship had experienced. Shaerico was used to darkness, but even the darkest moment before the dawn rises below the trees in the Forbidden Forest could not compare to the black void that lay before them. Still, as her eyes began to adjust, Shaerico had little trouble seeing. Her eyes were used to hunting in darkness. Dearthair and Ghrian however, had a difficult time keeping up. Luckily, Raax was there to help.

"How can you be so comfortable in a place like this?" Ghrian whispered to his little companion.

"Easy," Raax replied. "I was created in a cave, though it was much different from this one. The air is stale here and a foul odor clings to the surface of the rocks."

"Created? What was your cave like?" Ghrian inquired, trying to distract himself from the consuming darkness as claustrophobia set in.

Raax smiled and leaned against Ghrian's head, tangling himself in his thick brown locks.

"My cave. My cave was created long before me. It stood at the center of all life in the beginning. It smells of fresh spring air and eternal pines. It holds power and knowledge that you wouldn't dare believe. My cave is eternal and precious. Nothing like this deceptive channel of tunnels that house such reckless darkness," Raax said.

Ghrian was beginning to get the sense that there was much more to Raax than he had previously thought. He had assumed that since he was his mother's parting gift, that she had somehow had magic set upon the stone griffin as a sort of guardian; but the more Ghrian learned about his little companion, the more he felt that he was no mere magic marble statue.

"Raax," he began.

"Yes?" Raax's speckled eyes looked into Ghrian's.

"Who created you?"

Raax averted his gaze. "I think, Master Ghrian, that you need to discover that for yourself."

The puzzled man opened his mouth to speak, but before the words left his lips, a piercing howl silenced him.

Shaerico had long left the others. Ghrian could only assume the worst. He ran toward the calls and found the source. A great brown wolf had his jaws around Shaerico's left arm. Blood and flesh dripped from the wound as Shaerico called out in pain. This beast had ambushed her. Ghrian looked on in horror. He could see the surprise on Shaerico's face. How had she not smelled his approach? How was this once dead beast now alive?

His questions would have to wait as he drew his swords and raced toward Shaerico's side. Before he could make it to her, her flesh tore from her body and her midnight fur took its place atop her sinews. The transformation forced Cain's grip to release and gave Shaerico the opportunity to exact her revenge. A fearsome snarl rippled through her chest as she turned to face him.

Ghrian looked closely and saw the red stone that had embedded itself in the brown wolf's fur. It seemed brighter than before, and much larger. As the wolves tumbled in the dark, Ghrian could see the same red hue of the stone throughout Cain's body, like he had been stitched back to life with flame. Dearthair quickly drew his sword, and without further hesitation, the men rushed the brown wolf. Even with their limited eyesight, they knew that they could not sit idly by. That howl was sure to have been heard by others as it echoed along the walls of the cave, bounding like resounding trumpets of war.

The black wolf lunged with fury, her jaws latching firmly around Cain's left paw. She tore the beast from his footing and threw him with all her strength against the cold rock surface. Cain regained his balance quickly and used the cavern wall as an advantage. Crouching against the stone, he used the force with which he was thrown as a propellant. Ghrian ran to stand between Shaerico and the mad wolf, but Cain's leap was too high. The traitor was set to land squarely on Shaerico's neck, yet she did not budge. Her orange eyes glowed in the darkness. A flicker of blue began to rise in her pupils, until the flame of turquoise engulfed her irises entirely. For a moment, Ghrian's fear of her injury turned to fear of the black wolf herself. Silver teeth bared, she lunged toward the massive brown beast. Leaping from her hind legs with all her might, she launched herself into the air. Their bodies met with a resounding thud. The men watched in awe as the black wolf met her mark. A bone-chilling crunch was heard from above and the blood red stone fell amidst a mass of flesh and brown fur to the cavern floor. She returned to the ground in front of Ghrian. Blue flames poured from her mouth and her teeth looked as if they'd been dipped in molten turquoise.

"Now, stay dead," Shaerico growled.

Ghrian and Dearthair stepped back as the beast heaved, eyes still encased in flames, wilder than ever. Solas was barely visible in the black fur of her breast. Cain's blood drenched the ground, staining Shaerico's quivering paws.

"My, my such commotion. I hope you weren't trying to sneak up on me," Feir said as he looked down at Cain's body. "Poor puppy. You did indeed serve me well."

He reached down to locate the stone in Cain's bloodstained fur. As the sorcerer tried to wipe the blood from the stone, it turned to ash. Not seconds later, the mangled body of the brown wolf did the same. He looked up at Shaerico, his eyes squinted.

"How fascinating," he said as he stepped nearer to the companions. "Now, how could a worthless beast like you decimate an Iómhara? And how are you in this form? All others who made the decision to turn from me and the stones of power have broken the curse I placed on your people."

"I knew it was you," Shaerico snarled, blue flames still pouring from her mouth.

"Oh, how interesting," Feir said as he drew closer to Shaerico. "It would seem you have your own stone of power." He eyed her chest, gaze locked on Solas, a deep lust in his eyes. "My, I would love to add her to my collection." Feir's eyes gleamed with greed. "Say, let us make a deal. You hand the Iómhara over to me and I will spare your friends."

Shaerico glanced at Ghrian. Although she recognized the lie, the promise of saving Ghrian's life was tempting. After all, she wasn't sure how much more she could survive losing.

"If only I could believe such a fairytale," she replied. "But the words of the wicked are poison." She readied herself for what was sure to follow. "I have hope, but it is not in your mercy."

The sorcerer's lips curled, "Wise dog. It's unfortunate that your wisdom is sorely misplaced. Do you even know the power of the stone you give yourself to?"

Marmair's words rang in her ears.

"I know enough," she replied. "I know enough about you to know that your words cannot be trusted."

"My pet, such a stone will consume you. Your fate is now tied to its purpose and its purpose alone. Surely the old stone guardian told you this?"

Shaerico's flames slowed as she considered his words.

"You will never be truly free," he continued.

His words burned in her ears. She could feel the power of the Living Water flow through her and focused on its peace.

"That may be so, but I would rather be bound to what is true than wander Domhaen in false freedom," she hissed. As the words left her lips, she lunged at the dark sorcerer. Feir's smile fell from his face.

"So be it," he said as he lifted his staff. A piercing shriek erupted from the darkness behind the companions. The Fallen Stone appeared behind the sorcerer, its lifeless eyes ablaze.

"Poor weak men," it hissed as Shaerico and Feir collided.

Ghrian and Dearthair had no choice but to turn their eyes from Shaerico and face the dark creature. Swords drawn, they braced themselves for the fight. The Fallen Stone began his attack.

Farther down the dark tunnel, deeper in the caverns of the mountain, Fíor and the black stallion carried on into the darkness. The air grew thick and a strange chill enveloped them. The white sorceress spoke to Fiáin. "It is as I feared."

Fiáin rounded his massive head and pawed the ground. "I can smell him, too."

"We must end this old friend," Fíor said.

The two beings walked further until they came to the deepest cave in the belly of the mountain. A small opening led them to a vast open cavern. A thick slime dripped from the stalactites above. The air was dense and putrid, making it difficult to breathe. The cavern floor was filled with crystals, though most of them had turned black, as if they'd been scorched by fire.

"He is draining the stones of their power, but for what purpose?" Fíor inquired.

"He is turning them to darkness," Fiáin replied.

"We will deal with this soon enough, but first we must find the girl,"

Fíor stated, changing her focus, though her heart ached to see the once powerful Iómhara reduced to nothing more than coal.

Fíor grabbed the base of Fiáin's silver mane and lifted herself to his back. The great stallion leapt from the slight opening, diving into the bed of stones. The pair landed deep in the center of the cavern, buried in the sea of ashen black, hidden from the watchful eye of Oir's captor.

Oir lay on the other side of the opening, imprisoned in a crevasse under an outcropping in the rock wall. It was enclosed in a thin glass that shimmered red. Fíor could see that her strength was failing. She was badly bruised, and her hands were bloodied from beating against the walls of her prison. A righteous rage burned in Fíor's heart. As the pair approached Oir's cage, they heard a long breathy exhale. The sound of stones falling to the cavern floor mimicked a heavy rain on the mountain. Fiáin turned to face it.

"Go. Release the girl," he commanded in a thunderous voice.

Fíor stroked the stallion's neck. "Thank you," she said as she leapt from his back and made her way to the sheet of glass that encased the golden-haired maiden. Oir lifted her head for a moment, but was too weak to do much else. Fíor placed her right hand on the red tinted glass. Oir watched in amazement as the red hue dissipated into the woman's hand. Fíor drew her hand away from the glass and whispered to Oir. "Move away."

Oir pushed herself backwards as far as she was able. The hand in which the white sorceress had gathered the substance, now blazed a vibrant red. Fíor lifted her eyes and spoke a phrase in a tongue Oir did not recognize. A blazing fire burst forth from the woman's hand and as she pointed it toward the prison walls, the glass dissipated to dust. Oir could hardly believe her eyes. She had heard that magic still existed, and she believed, but had never seen it for herself, not like this. Fíor helped Oir to her feet.

"We must escape from this place," she whispered softly to Oir.

Oir nodded, but a perplexed look fell over her face. "But why was I captured in the first place? What is going on? And who are you?"

Fíor sighed gently and smiled. "I'm afraid I am to blame for your capture."

"You?" Oir said, stepping back.

"Yes, you see, long ago I abandoned my duty and the purpose for which I was created. Though I considered love a noble enough reason, I left an opening for darkness to grow in this world. I was selfish," Fíor sighed. She lowered her eyes and then brought her gaze to meet Oir's. "You were taken because the sorcerer thought you were my child."

Oir's eyes widened.

"I am the Defender of the Light in this world. Without me, darkness can run rampant across the whole of Domhaen. Many years ago, I abandoned my responsibility. I sacrificed the safety of this world for my own sake. I left it in the hands of someone I thought I could trust, but abandoned my duty in the process. I was foolish and naive. It was because of my selfishness that darkness was allowed to fall on this land."

"But I don't understand," Oir began. "Why did he think I was your child?"

Fíor smiled. "Because you are around his age. You reside in the Realm of the Lake. Your hair is golden like mine and you had a Stone of Power in your possession."

"Stone of Power," Oir echoed.

"Yes," Fíor nodded. "The stone you planned to place in your saddle, the one Dearthair brought for you."

Oir's eyes widened again, "How do you know all of this?"

"You actually spent a lot of time with my child. I'm not surprised you were mistaken for him," Fíor smiled.

Oir opened her mouth to speak, but was interrupted by a great roar. It shook the mountain down to its roots. Stalactites began to quiver and dislodge rocks from their place in the ceiling of the cavern. Fíor grabbed Oir and held her close. Soon after, the black stallion appeared behind them. Fíor looked at Fiáin with inquisition in her eyes.

"Now is not the time," he said.

The great horse wove his way through the falling rocks, as the two women clutched tightly to him. As they made their way back up the cavern tunnels, the sound of an ensuing battle reached their ears. Fiáin increased his pace as he raced toward the sound. They reached the source in the nick of time.

The sorcerer and the black wolf were shrouded in a cloud of smoke and fire. Flames of blue and red lapped against the surrounding cavern walls. The Fallen Stone had Dearthair pinned beneath his hind legs and Ghrian fought to rescue him, landing useless blows against his backside. Dearthair's leg had been crushed under the weight of the stone. Ghrian was drenched in both blood and sweat.

The flames of rage were fanned in Fíor upon their approach. "Feir!" Fíor roared as Fiáin barreled into the thick of the battle.

All parties were stunned to stillness as they entered. After a moment of surprise, a wicked smile crept across Feir's face. "So, my precious bait did her job after all."

He pointed his staff directly toward Shaerico as her attention was captured by Fíor and Fiáin's return. A powerful blow struck the wolf across her chest, sending her tumbling backwards into the wall of the cavern. Ghrian cried out to Shaerico as she fell.

It was only then that he noticed the return of their lost party members. "Oir," he whispered.

From beneath the beast, Dearthair cried out in excitement. Though she was weak, Oir called back to him. At first, her heart leapt at the sight of her friends. She was elated that Dearthair had come to rescue her, but her joy soon turned to despair as she saw his condition.

She tried to dismount Fiáin, but Fíor held her back. "You have not the strength," Fíor said.

Oir struggled for a moment against Fíor's arm, but she knew that she was right.

"Be gone treacherous beast, back to the shadows," Fíor said to the Fallen Stone.

The creature laughed. "I do not serve you! You abandoned us. You allowed this to happen," he growled.

Fíor's brow furrowed. "I may have left, but I did not abandon all I was created to protect! Unlike you."

"Oh, I did not abandon my purpose. I simply discovered a new one," the beast hissed.

Feir turned from Shaerico toward the white sorceress. "My elusive Fíor, how long it has been." He walked toward the stallion and his mounts. Fiáin pawed the ground and snorted in warning.

"I have no quarrel with you, Aonharc," he said to the stallion with a slight bow.

Fíor dismounted, motioning for Fiáin to take Oir to safety. The black beast hesitated, then released a bellowing neigh and disappeared into the darkness.

"Oir!" Dearthair called after her. He tried to get up, but even though the Living Stone had released him and gone to his master's side, Dearthair was too weak to stand. His left leg had been completely crushed below the knee. Ghrian ran to his side. He tried his best to comfort him, though he too was disappointed that Oir was yet again beyond their reach. "She is safe, my friend, she's with Fiáin," Ghrian consoled him.

Ghrian looked toward Shaerico who was still unconscious. He wanted more than anything to run to her, but Feir and his beast stood between them. He could feel that his body was weakening.

The white sorceress stood out against the darkness. A steady glow pulsated around her. Her eyes turned from soft brown to an unearthly gold.

"Feir, you have cursed this land long enough. How dare you deliver the Stones of Power into the hands of such darkness," her voice echoed throughout the mountain tunnels, shaking the stone as it traveled.

"My sweet sister, the world you try so desperately to protect has turned its back on you. What use are you now to the people of Domhaen? You curse me for the darkness I reside with, but it is you who have lived in shadow, taking other forms to remain unseen," Feir snapped.

Fíor did not flinch at his words. "I may take other forms and many people may have abandoned truth, but not all. I will fulfill my duty that He Who Is set before me, before us. I will protect the Living Water and the people of this world, whether I do so publicly or in secret. It is true that I abandoned my purpose and my post in the past, but I have returned. I have redeemed myself. But you, you have fallen beyond redemption."

Feir laughed a bellowing chortle. "You think I care what I was created for? I chose my own fate. If the people of this world want to deny truth, if they want to deny magic and power, then I will take from them those very things!" With this declaration, the black sorcerer lifted his sordid staff. The stone at its center blazed red. The eerie light cast by the stone flickered across the fallen guardian's face. The Fallen Stone bared its teeth at the sorceress. "Your existence ends here."

The stone shone brighter and brighter until it burst into a raging black ball of flames. Fíor closed her eyes and placed her open hands toward her enemy. Feir saw his opportunity, and with a scream unleashed the blast. The flames charged forward, demolishing the walls of the cave as they went. Before Fíor was engulfed by the darkness, her eyes met Ghrian's. There was something hauntingly familiar about her eyes.

Somehow, he could hear her voice inside his head. "Be strong. The earth resides within you. Call upon it in your time of need and it will answer, for you are a child of the Creator."

All went dark. A stillness hung in the air following the rush of flame; everything faded to black. There was no sign of the sorceress, only a great and distant tremble of stone. Feir turned back to face the three that still stood in his way as chunks of rock fell from the cavern walls. Heaving for breath, he spoke through his devious, victorious smile.

"Finally, the only being that was my equal has been vanquished. I am eternal!" he cried.

He opened his arms to the cavern tunnel ceiling as pieces of it collapsed behind him. In that moment, Shaerico saw her opportunity. She had awoken in time to see Fíor's return and waited for the opportune moment to attack. Claws forward and teeth bared, she leapt toward the sorcerer. Her teeth met their mark, sinking deep into the arm that held his staff. Feir writhed in pain as his black blood spilled to the ground below.

"You accursed creature!" he screamed.

His staff dropped to the cavern floor, but his other hand plunged deep into Shaerico's chest. He ripped Solas from her body, and though he tried to keep it in his grasp, the blood-soaked stone slipped from his hands and fell behind him.

The black wolf fell in a heap to the cold stone floor and returned to her human form. Blood trickled from Shaerico's open mouth and her breath slowed. Ghrian looked on in horror. Without hesitation or forethought, he lunged for the dislodged stone. He reached Solas as Feir retrieved his staff. In one swift motion, Ghrian continued his trajectory and leapt toward Feir. Swords drawn, he set his eyes on his target. Feir started to turn himself toward his new opponent, but in the wake of Ghrian's rage, even he was too slow. The twin blades were headed for the base of Feir's neck. The sorcerer's staff had little power left after its blow against Fíor, but still he lifted it to face Ghrian. It was nearly close enough to singe Ghrian's beard and the skin beneath. Though his eyes burned, he pressed on.

The white stone in Ghrian's hand began to shine as it rested in his right palm beneath the hilt of one sword. Its light grew brighter and brighter as he drew closer to his enemy. As the twin swords met their mark, they plunged deep into the sorcerer's spine. Feir stood for a moment in disbelief, but the great sorcerer of old would not fall so easily. He pressed his staff further behind him as Ghrian's blades sank deeper. The staff met the man's brow just above Ghrian's right eye and set it ablaze. He cried out in pain but did not cede his position. As he screamed, pressing against the sorcerer's neck with all of his might, a flash of light burst forth from Solas. The rock of the cavern walls formed spires in a blinding blue flash, following Ghrian's steel. The stone burst forth from the cavern walls and impaled the dark sorcerer as the twin blades followed through, severing

the neck from the spine. There was a faint gargle, then darkness again descended upon them as the blue light vanished.

Feir's head fell lifeless to the floor.

"Your reign is over," Ghrian exhaled.

The livid man had not noticed his manipulation of the cavern walls, but Dearthair had. His friend looked on in fear and confusion. Ghrian ran to Shaerico's side, barely conscious of his own pain. She was breathing, but it was shallow.

"We have to get her help!" he cried.

"Ghrian, we all need help," Dearthair said, watching the blood pour from his friend's brow, his right eye charred and black. He tried lifting his crushed leg, but it was no use. The Fallen Stone snarled as he watched them struggle. He looked once more upon the body of his master, headless and impaled with stone, then drug the remnants of his master's staff into the darkness.

Ghrian managed to drag both of his fallen friends to the outer mouth of the cave system. It was painful and difficult to navigate in the dark, but his adrenaline and determination pushed him on until he could see the dim light of winter. March was waiting patiently by the opening. Ghrian placed Shaerico gently onto the gray stallion's back, then helped Dearthair as well. Dearthair wrapped his arms around Shaerico to support her. A steady trickle of blood oozed from the wound in her chest. Ghrian had wrapped her cloak around her, and it was quickly becoming saturated. He kept Solas tightly secured in his hand.

"We have to make it back and fast. Someone will know how to heal them," Ghrian urged. He clenched his fist tighter around the stone. "Well," he said to himself as he began to lead March down the path. "At least Oir is safe. And the darkness was defeated."

He sighed, allowing himself to realize their victory, though his concern for Shaerico and Dearthair's wounds overshadowed the success of their mission. He was equally tormented by the loss of that woman who had sacrificed herself to Feir's rage. She had seemed so familiar.

Ghrian walked along-side March, hoping Dearthair's memories and the overgrown trail could guide them back to the Realm of the Lake. Thus, the last leg of the tattered company's journey began.

Chapter Nineteen

Deep in the woods of Collitte, the final wolves of Dorchas stood in the fading light. A large and elegant white wolf, an even greater brown male, and a small cream female made their way along the forest floor.

Darting through trees and brush, they chased an unfamiliar scent. The loss of their family to the dark forces at play in the outside world had made Alphaline all the more suspicious of anything unfamiliar. The trio was quick to rid the woods of all intruders in the days that followed Feir's overthrow of the pack. Many enraged and hopeless men from the Realm had turned to Collitte to seek revenge for all that they had endured. Alphaline and her remaining children had all but abandoned Dorchas. She led the hunt and moved forward with ferocity. As the small pack neared their target, Lili and Beoir took their position at their mother's flanks. They came to a clearing near the southern end of the Forbidden Forest and waited for their prey's approach. It was not often that the people of Dorchas traveled this far south, but Alphaline took no chances with outsiders in her wood.

A petite gray wolf entered the clearing. She was timid and walked with caution. Her ears swiveled as her nose twitched, surveying what was around her. Her front paws were adorned with two white socks and her tail looked as if it had been dipped in cream. The white wolf signaled the beginning of the attack.

Beoir and Lili closed ranks and began to charge. Alphaline leapt from the thicket and pinned the lone wolf, encasing the gray wolf's throat in her long sharp teeth. She was about to close her jaws when a long forgotten scent drifted into her nostrils. She released her grip on the young wolf's throat. The prey lay wide-eyed and scared beneath the large white paws. Her amber eyes glistened, looking up at her captor. Alphaline signaled for the pack to cease their attack.

She sat back on her haunches and stared in disbelief. "I know you," she said softly, her hate melting to hope.

The gray wolf sat upright and tilted her head. Beoir and Lili walked cautiously into the clearing. A crisp breeze flowed through the long, frosted grass beneath them. Slowly, the gray wolf stood, her ears pinned to her soft head. The wind rustled the surrounding trees with enthusiasm, dislodging flakes of silver snow. Alphaline stood and met the gray wolf nose to nose, as a single tear carved a path through her white fur.

"Children," she said softly. "This is my daughter."

The two wolves looked at one another, confusion written clearly on their faces.

"You mean, there was another child you rescued long ago?" Lili inquired, stepping closer.

"How could this little one have survived out here all by herself if that were the case? Surely Alphaline would have come for her sooner if that were true," Beoir interjected.

Alphaline replied, "No. She is of my own flesh and blood, my Eníon."

The silent gray wolf sat before her, her amber eyes glistening, reflecting the light of the rising moon. "I thought she was lost to me long ago, murdered by the demon that took the others," Alphaline continued.

Beoir and Lili were beginning to understand.

"Is that why you took us in all those years ago? You dedicated your life to protecting us because you lost your own child," Lili said, sympathy seeping from her words.

Alphaline nodded. "She was born on an evening much like this. It was quiet, and a chill hung lightly on the air," she paused and turned to them. "I have much to confess to you."

Lili and Beoir lay in the grass next to the small gray wolf, awaiting Alphaline's tale. She proceeded to tell them the full story of the people of Dorchas.

"Our city was once a beacon of knowledge and education. People traveled from the Kingdom and beyond to learn, trade, be healed, or find peace there. Coyolt was one of those who journeyed to Dorchas. He was a blacksmith, bold and beautiful. It was not long after he moved there to perfect his trade that we met and fell deeply in love. No more than a year passed before we were wed and with child. Then, the jealous sorcerer came to Dorchas. He claimed he was enchanted by my beauty and desired to have me for his own, but I refused," she sighed, replaying the terror that had tortured her for ages. "He became enraged, astonished that a woman would deny a man with such power and choose another of such low status. Driven by greed and lust, he laid waste to the town. The jealousy of man knows no end."

She told them how Feir proceeded to decimate Dorchas. How he killed her husband and cursed her to become a wolf by night for rejecting him. The citizens that survived that night and remained in the city lived in fear of the sorcerer's return. When the time came for Alphaline to give birth, Feir did return to Dorchas. That evening, he offered her a deal. She could abandon the child and go away with him and he would spare the remainder of those in the city. She admitted that in her selfishness, she had again refused him. He returned not a month later and finished what he had started.

"In the end, I lost it all anyway," she looked down at the gray wolf. "You see, it was night when I gave birth. My daughter was born while I was in my wolf form, so a wolf she was cursed to remain. Because of my selfishness, all survivors in the town perished, and he took my child anyways. I begged for the lives of the children that survived, knowing that it was my fault they had been orphaned." She looked to Beoir and Lili, with a sorrowful and apologetic gaze. "He allowed me to care for those children, but cursed them as well, to remind me forever of what I had lost, and of what happens when you defy Feir."

Beoir and Lili looked at Alphaline with tears streaming from their glassy eyes.

"I thought I had lost her forever," Alphaline said as she nuzzled the small gray wolf. Alphaline's daughter leaned into her mother's embrace. "I thought he had killed her. She was merely a girl trapped inside the body of a wolf pup. She has little animal instincts whatsoever. She can't communicate with us now, but she will learn. I wonder how she has survived all these years."

The remaining travelers had been walking for days. They were nearing the end of their stamina. Ghrian had not rested once. He refused to stop. Though Raax regularly tried to lighten the mood, the future looked grim and morale was low. Shaerico had steadily worsened. She had been unconscious for nearly two days now. She no longer changed form at night, and because of this, her body was unable to heal as usual. Dearthair was holding on as best as he could, driven forward by the knowledge that Oir was alive and that he would see her again. Fiáin would reunite them soon.

"Ghrian, her breath is slowing," Dearthair said, concerned. "We have to rest."

Ghrian conceded. He could feel that his own strength was failing, but he was worried that he would lose the energy to move forward if he stopped.

"How far are we?" Ghrian asked.

"I have never come quite this far, but I remember my uncle saying that the descending trail was just past the arch of braided trees," Dearthair replied.

"Arch of braided trees?" Ghrian echoed.

"I have a feeling we will know what it means when we see it. It can't be far now," Dearthair said, trying to remain optimistic.

It was only moments later that the black stallion appeared not far from them off to the right of the trail. He was in full gallop, an incredible feat for such a large horse to dart so effortlessly through the trees. Dearthair caught sight of them first. Oir's golden hair shimmered in the midday sun as they passed. He called out to her, "Oir!"

She turned as Fiáin changed direction toward them. Ghrian was relieved to see his friend unharmed. Fiáin came to a slow trot as he approached, and March quickened his pace to meet him. It was apparent that March had missed his friend as well.

Oir leapt from the black stallion and ran to Dearthair. She was elated to see him until she drew closer. Her face turned white. She had not been able to see the extent of the damage he had sustained in the darkness of the cavern tunnel. His leg below the knee was completely crushed. She looked up at him with tears welling in her eyes.

"It's okay," he said reassuringly. "I honestly can't feel it anymore."

It was the unfortunate truth. The blood circulation had long left his leg. He knew that his chances of walking again were slim, but Oir was safe and he could live with his sacrifice. She turned to Ghrian, his eye barely visible underneath the layers of dried blood.

"You suffered all this for my sake," she said, lowering her eyes to the ground, tears falling to the path below, carving craters in the melting snow.

"I am not worth all of this. I am so sorry," she sobbed, falling into Ghrian's arms. He wrapped his arms around her and tried to think of the correct thing to say.

"None of this was your doing," a faint voice whispered.

Ghrian's eyes widened as he ran to Shaerico's side. "Stop talking, you need to save your strength."

"I'm fine," she said, flashing a soft smile. "It truly wasn't her fault."

He did not know the truth of why Oir was captured when all others were destroyed, but he had assumed that knowledge was lost to them now. Shaerico coughed, splattering blood to the frosted ground below. Fiáin stepped toward her, offering her his back. She clutched his silver mane and used the last of her strength to lift herself onto him. As soon as she was secure, the stallion lunged forward. His powerful hind legs left massive hoof prints where he had propelled himself from the snow-laden path. Within moments, he was beyond their sight. Ghrian called for Shaerico and tried to run after them, but quickly realized his decision was futile.

"He knows where he is taking her," Oir said softly. She placed a hand on Ghrian's shoulder. "You will be reunited soon."

The smell of the familiar wood gently woke Shaerico from her slumber. She felt weightless, as if she were floating. A serene melody of birds and the soft whisper of the wind welcomed her back into the world. As she opened her eyes, her vision was blurred by a blinding blue light. She inhaled deeply the sweet air and blinked until her vision cleared. It was then that she realized that she was floating in the Spring of the Living Water. She scanned the nearby shore but saw nothing. She breathed deeply again and let out a long sigh.

The demon sorcerer was dead.

It was then that she realized what she was without. Solas was no longer draped safely around her neck. She lifted her hand to feel the gaping hole from which the stone was torn. She felt the area gently, running her fingers over the stone's resting place just above her breasts. Where there was once an open wound through flesh and muscle there was now a shallow dip in her smooth skin. She was healed already. This place was truly a powerful sanctuary worth protecting.

As her fingers brushed over her soft skin, something pricked the tip of her finger. A single drop of blood fell into the crystal blue water before the wound healed itself. She looked down and was surprised to see a small sliver of Solas still present between her breasts.

"How strange," she mumbled to herself as she laid back in the water. "Well, she will find her way back to me in time."

Shaerico felt completely at peace. The only nagging worry was her concern for the whereabouts of the rest of Solas and the safe arrival of her friends. But soon all thoughts began to fade as she drifted back to a deep and welcomed sleep.

Night began to fall on the mountain and the companions still had not reached the descending trail.

"We can't be far," Ghrian said, now more determined than ever to make it back to the Realm.

Though he could not be certain, he felt that Fiáin had taken Shaerico to the spring. He felt as if he was being pulled there himself. He opened his palm to gaze upon the stone. It shone brilliantly in the light of the setting sun. The orange sky released rays of lavender that lightened the spirits of the weary companions.

Dearthair had insisted that Oir ride with him, though she protested, saying that Ghrian should be the one to ride his own horse. Ghrian did not mind. He was still wrestling with all that had transpired. For months they had journeyed together to fulfill their mission, and in a matter of a few days, all was expected to return to normal. He still had so many questions. He began to feel that insatiable inquisitions were the single unchanging element in his life. Every time he uncovered an answer, another enigma would appear waiting to be deciphered. He still had little knowledge of the true power of the stone, or of the Living Water. He knew nothing of why Feir had such power and what his intent had been with Oir. He looked up at her as they continued to walk into the night, guided now by the light of the moon.

Oir was looking down at him as well, watching him wrestle with questions she had some answers to. She knew now who the white sorceress had been, but she had not the heart to tell him.

"I see it!" Dearthair called suddenly in the night. "The arch of braided trees!"

"Quiet, Dearthair. You don't know what lie in these woods," Ghrian scolded.

"I imagine nothing now that the enchanted wolves are gone," he laughed jovially before immediately regretting his comment.

Ghrian glared in his direction. At least he was in better spirits now that Oir was safe.

A chilling breeze blew softly up the trail. They descended into the darkness, leaving the mountain and the guiding light of the moon behind them. All were aware of the dangers of Collitte, and though all three of them had experienced the destruction of the people of Dorchas, only Ghrian knew that this path was their only way home. He could not help but wonder if any of Shaerico's people had made it back to the woods, or if any had resisted the dark sorcerer in the city.

This question was answered with a piercing howl. The sound sliced through the night. Then another followed, and another, and then one more.

"Looks like you spoke to soon," Raax commented.

"Four," Ghrian whispered under his breath.

"This is great. Just what we need, more wolves," Dearthair sighed, unsheathing his sword.

The howls drew near. Ghrian unsheathed both of his swords and retreated to March. The stallion was uneasy. Now that they had descended into the forest, their eyes were of little aid. Their vision played tricks on them in the dark, putting everyone on edge. Out of the corner of his good eye, Ghrian saw the pack approaching. They were closing ranks around them on the trail. The only one that was easily seen was the massive white wolf, her fur glinting like starlight in the thin moon beams that made it to the forest floor. Her long plumed tail swept the fresh snow along the overgrown path before them. She released a low snarl and drew closer, piercing eyes locked on Ghrian. He clenched his swords, fighting exhaustion and his lack of vision.

"Steady," Raax whispered from behind Ghrian's brown locks.

Suddenly, a gray wolf appeared, standing between the pack and the travelers. Ghrian froze, trying to get a better glimpse of what stood in front of him. He was sure his mind was playing tricks on him in the darkness. He thought he saw a white tip on the gray wolf's tail as the small beast stood facing her snow-white counterpart. Ghrian rubbed his good eye and focused harder. The thick hairs gleamed white in the ribbons of moonlight that forced their way through the barren blanket of trees above.

"Tavi?" Ghrian whispered, as if his words may dispel the dream of the creature that stood before him.

The small wolf turned, her tail wagging and tongue hanging jovially from the side of her mouth. It was her.

Ghrian dropped his swords and fell to his knees. Tavi ran to him as the white wolf looked on in confusion. She stepped closer and tilted her head. Tears ran down Ghrian's face as he embraced her small frame. He had convinced himself that this day would never come. The gray wolf covered his face in kisses and released a few happy yips before turning again to face the white wolf. Alphaline stepped closer still.

March became uneasy and began backing up until he felt the warm breath of two more wolves at his back.

Dearthair wrapped one arm around Oir and held his broadsword out behind them.

"Who are you and why have you come to my forest?" a sultry voice carved through the silent darkness.

Ghrian stood, one hand softly caressing Tavi's velvet ear. This must be their leader, but how and why was Tavi with them?

He stood tall as Alphaline drew closer, her muzzle nearly reaching his chin. She inhaled deeply. Her eyes widened. She could smell Shaerico and she could smell Feir.

"I will give you one more moment to answer me before I remove your head from your body," she snarled.

Tavi returned the threat with a low growl, placing her white front paws between the wolf and the man.

"I don't know why my daughter protects you, but I assure you that will not keep you alive," Alphaline snarled.

Ghrian was so lost in thought and stunned at this turn of events that he had yet to answer. Dearthair and Oir were getting anxious. The tension was palpable. Ghrian struggled to find the words to describe the events he had so recently survived.

"My companions and I seek safe passage through Collitte," was all he managed to squeeze from his lungs.

"Is that so?" Alphaline snarled, inhaling the familiar scents that lingered on his clothes.

"We wish to return to the Realm of the Lake. I am from the town of Yoaruq," Ghrian stated.

"And where are you coming from?" she asked.

He was unsure how to answer. "We have journeyed far. Our friend," he motioned to Oir, "was taken from us during the Winter Solstice Festival. We followed her captors to a cave in the mountain," he paused, his mind racing, trying to find the words. He tried to come to grips with what they had just experienced. "She was rescued there, and her captor was defeated," he continued. "We simply wish to return home."

"Captor," Alphaline repeated. "Who was this captor?"

It was unclear what side this great wolf was on, as most of her people had fallen under the control of the sorcerer, so Ghrian tried his best to remain vague.

"He was a powerful man that came to the Realm and attacked us under cover of night. He claimed the lives of many," Ghrian said.

"And you say he was defeated? How?" Alphaline's wild eyes glistened at the thought of Feir's demise.

Ghrian sighed, he knew he could not lie. "I killed him."

At this the white wolf's lips curled behind her massive teeth and her snarl gave way to laughter.

"You," she bellowed, her head lifted to the moon. "Are you seriously telling me that you killed the most powerful sorcerer in Domhaen? You must be a liar."

Beoir and Lili closed ranks and bared their teeth, releasing low snarls, but Ghrian stood his ground. "I am no liar," he corrected.

"One more question, before I rip your lying tongue from your throat. What happened to Shaerico?" Alphaline inquired.

It was then that Ghrian was certain of who she was. The leader of the people of Dorchas. The mother of the cursed tribe.

"She was wounded," he looked to his canine companion beside him. "She was taken down the path ahead of us."

"You're telling me she's in these woods?" Alphaline's eyes squinted and her nose wrinkled, as she tried to find her scent on the wind. "Tell me, how was she wounded, boy?" Alphaline pressed her warm wet nose against Ghrian's side.

"It was the sorcerer. You seem to know of him. You know of his power," he watched the massive paws of the white wolf as she encircled him. "She was protecting us when she was attacked."

A purr-like rumble slipped from between Alphaline's teeth. "So, you mean to tell me that my greatest hunter could not fell the demon, but a mere man was able to do so?"

"I don't fully understand how it happened either, but it did, and I need to keep moving through these woods so I can make sure she is okay," he said. Ghrian was becoming firmer as the time passed. Talking about Shaerico made him all the more eager to return to her side, just the thought of her emboldened him.

Tavi looked back at Ghrian, the tip of her marbled tongue hanging happily from her mouth. He was still so thrilled to see her alive and well. He desperately wanted to fall to his knees again, wrap her in his arms and take her home, but he knew that he had to press on.

"Please, Queen of the people of Dorchas, let me find and help Shaerico," he pleaded.

Alphaline stood back and called Tavi to her side. Reluctantly, the small gray wolf returned to her mother. Alphaline motioned with a movement of her head to Beoir and Lili, recalling them as well.

"I will allow you to find and aid Shaerico, but I cannot promise that you will leave these woods alive. I have had enough of dealing with the men of the Realm."

A flash of eyes and teeth in the moonlight and the wolves vanished into the veil of night as quickly as they had appeared. Ghrian could hear the heavy sigh of relief from his companions. Though he was troubled by Alphaline's parting words, he had not the luxury to focus on them. He hoped that he would see Tavi again someday, but at least he knew that she was safe. Now, he had to find Shaerico.

The fellowship continued down the path, now even more wary of their surroundings. Dearthair held Oir close as the sun began to rise. Pink rays were cast over the snowy pathway ahead, creating a blanket of twinkling light. The lure of imminent safety made his patience wain. His mind raced with thoughts of a future with Oir. He hoped that she would return to Miotal with him, as he did not want to stay in the Realm after all that had transpired. Oir looked back at him and smiled. She could tell something was on his mind. Ahead of them, Ghrian's stamina was again beginning to fade, but he was determined to locate Shaerico. His mind raced with similar thoughts to his friend, but his situation was much more complicated. All Shaerico had ever known were these woods and now her entire people had been reduced to a pack of four. Where would she go? What would she choose to do with her life now that she was free to go wherever she pleased?

Though their pace had slowed, and Ghrian remained distracted by his thoughts, they eventually made it to the ruin town of Dorchas. Tavi and the other wolves were nowhere to be found. There was a somber chill in the air, and although none of them had been to the town before, the cold dilapidated features seemed to weep even more for all that had once been. The wounds that the men of the party had sustained had grown steadily worse. They decided to rest in Dorchas, since there seemed to be no immediate threat. Ghrian tied his steed to a post outside the pub and helped Dearthair from March's back. Oir wandered slowly into the old wooden building. She pushed open the heavy door. There was no one inside. She returned to Dearthair to help Ghrian carry him indoors.

"It's so strange to think that all this time those beasts were living so close to us," Oir said.

Ghrian winced at her choice of words, but he knew she had reason to be upset. She had not gotten the chance to know Shaerico yet.

To Ghrian's surprise, Dearthair was the one to speak out on her behalf. "The majority of those wolves may be gruesome wastes of breath, but they aren't all bad."

Ghrian smiled for a moment, thinking of Shaerico before the vision of Solas being torn from her chest returned to the forefront of his mind.

"I have to find her," he said suddenly. "She would visit the spring from here, it can't be far. I'm sorry dear friends, you must rest here. I will return when I have found her."

Dearthair tried to protest, but he was too weak. He knew there was no stopping Ghrian. Oir stood and clutched the fringe of his sleeve.

"Oir, I," he began.

"Be careful," she interrupted, her blue eyes locking on his. "And you better come back."

He smiled at her. "Of course," he said as he bowed in jest.

Oir released her grip on his shirt and let out a soft laugh. "We will wait for you here."

"Oh look, beer!" Dearthair shouted excitedly as he glanced behind the long wooden bar.

"Yeah, you will be just fine in my absence," Ghrian sighed as he mounted March. "I will return as soon as I can."

Oir nodded as she jumped behind the bar to pour Dearthair a drink. Ghrian knew that March was tired, but the stallion seemed as fresh as ever as they set off down the cobblestone road to find the spring. It was as if he knew the object of their task. Ghrian had never visited the spring from the west, but he knew that it could not have been far. He believed wholeheartedly that is where Fiáin had taken Shaerico. He thought back to their first meeting. The attack in the water, the fight, the blood, and then the healing. He brushed his hand over his wound slowly. Perhaps the water would heal them both again.

Chapter Twenty

The midday sun shone brightly overhead. The warm light pierced through the trees and fell to the forest floor. The young man and his gray stallion forged their way through the thicket of brambles, trees, and melting snow. Ghrian remained in a state of awe as he recalled his and Shaerico's first meeting at the spring. He remembered her raw beauty. The astonishment of her true nature made him realize for the first time that what he had seen that day in the woods had really been her, flesh and fur. He recalled how all of it changed when she received Solas. How her demeanor had softened.

Ghrian looked down at the crystal in his palm. The white stone glistened in the lattice of sunlight that fell through the frosted trees. He became lost in it, staring into every inclusion, twisting it slowly in his hand, watching as the sun pierced each facet and cast light of a different color onto his skin. Blue, yellow, lavender, crimson, and blue. The turquoise shimmer grew stronger until it overwhelmed the white of the stone. Ghrian's trance was cut short by this sudden and overwhelming change. As he lowered his hand, he understood why. There in front of him was the spring.

Ghrian dismounted March and ran into the clearing, ignoring the stinging leaves and branches as they attempted to slow him. He ran with all his might as he saw her figure appear in the water. Shaerico remained in the spring, floating effortlessly atop the glistening pool. For a moment, Ghrian slowed, struck equally by the scene's serenity and by her beauty.

Her raven black hair floated gracefully around her pale white skin. Ghrian was mesmerized. His pace slowed again as he reached the edge of the spring. Gently, he dropped his outer garments and waded into the water. Shaerico seemed unaware of his presence. As he drew closer, he noticed the scar on her chest.

He had completely forsaken the thought of healing his own wounds as he swam harder to reach her side. As he made it to her, he lifted his arms to steady her head. The woman still lay in motionless peace. His fingers found their way through her thick black hair and came to rest at the base of her neck. Slowly, Shaerico opened her orange eyes. A deep ring of smoky blue now encircled the once furious flames of her irises. It was as if the fire in her soul had been cooled. A smile leapt across her face as she saw Ghrian. She was truly beautiful. He had never seen her smile with such inhibition.

She turned to him and broke the water's surface, submerging her body into the spring, and wrapping herself around Ghrian. He was stunned. She had never shown such affection and he was unsure how to react. He smiled, sighing in relief to see that she was well, and proceeded to wrap his arms around her. They remained in the embrace for a few breaths until Ghrian remembered what he held in his possession. He lifted his hand to reveal Solas.

The stone was nearly too bright to focus on. It encapsulated the vibrant hue of the surrounding water and shone with unparalleled brilliance. As he held the stone out for Shaerico, his eyes fell again to the wound in her chest. She followed his gaze and lifted her fingers to feel it again.

"It happened when Feir stole Solas from me," she replied to his stare.

"He can cause you no further harm," Ghrian said as he handed Shaerico the stone.

She smiled and took Solas from his hand, then she lifted her other hand and gently ran her fingers across his warm cheek.

"Thank you," she said softly. "For saving me."

Ghrian pressed into her hand, then pulled her closer. They floated, weightless in the water. He leaned his head down to meet hers. Both hearts began to beat loudly as their lips brushed. But their moment of peace did not last long.

Suddenly, the once blue sky went black. An army of gray clouds swarmed overhead and a roar like a clap of thunder shook the forest of Collitte. The sound tore the pair from their moment of tranquility. Shaerico leapt from the spring and in one motion returned Solas to its resting place on her chest. The stone sank lightly into her flesh as she transformed into the black wolf once more. Ghrian followed her and lunged from the spring to retrieve his cloak and swords. The darkness fell further over the forest and claps of thunder resounded from over the mountain. Raax shivered on Ghrian's shoulder.

"I left Dearthair and Oir in Dorchas," Ghrian exclaimed over the rumbles of thunder.

Shaerico turned to him. "There is nothing we can do for them now. They have shelter, they are safer there. Something is coming."

It was not only the thick cover of clouds that brought on an inescapable smog of dread, but the ominous silence that now fell over the reunited couple. They stood for a moment, listening and waiting. A flash of white lightning struck the rose bushes surrounding the spring. They burst into flames of purple, catching the evergreens and surrounding brush ablaze. The ancient willows that lined one side of the spring and dipped their long fingers into the water sparked and sizzled as they sought comfort from the fire. Shaerico looked to the sky. It was then that they saw it. Amidst the smoke gray clouds, a beast emerged. From its wings, lightning burst forth, and its cry resounded throughout the Realm. Upon looking closer, Shaerico spotted a glimpse of something white circling its tail. Sporadic flames of blue burst forth from the white being. There was a battle raging in the sky above.

The black stallion emerged from amidst the blazing wood, visible between the undulating flames. Shaerico turned to him as he approached. "Fiáin. What is going on?"

The great stallion's coat glistened silver with sweat. It was clear that he had been running. His eyes widened as he gazed over the spring. The red flames reflected in the turquoise water. He spotted the beast above in its mirror-like reflection and looked toward the sky.

"Dearthair and Oir are safe," he said. "I returned them to the Realm."

Surprised by his voice, Shaerico turned to face him. She began to say something, but another roar pierced through the clouded darkness. This time it was so close that the pitch was nearly unbearable to Shaerico's sensitive ears. She winced in pain. Ghrian ran to her side as a wind of flames fell upon them. In an instance, the evergreens that surrounded the spring were leveled. The wood splintered and crackled as the flames burst into a raging fire with this new breath of life. All looked toward the sky from whence the fire fell. The beast was upon them.

The midday sky had fallen to shadow. The clouds that shrouded the sun were a thick blanket of ashen gray. The creator of this chaos hovered above them encased in a ball of flames. It was worse than any nightmare Ghrian could have imagined. He thought that he had encountered every horror known to man, but this beast was far more fearsome than the cursed wolves of Dorchas or the Fallen Stone. Even the dark sorcerer paled in comparison. Ghrian should have known better than to harbor disbelief in any tales of old. This was a dragon.

The beast looked down upon them with four lifeless black eyes.

"Olcbas," the deep voice bellowed from the black stallion.

Ghrian turned toward Fiáin, struck that the horse had a voice. He opened his mouth to speak but was unable to utter a word before a bolt of crimson lightning pierced the ground in front of him. He was thrown from his feet into a pile of ashes where the rose bushes had once stood. Shaerico glanced at him to make sure that he was alright before turning again toward the monster.

Olcbas, the dragon King Gaewyn and the horned horse had banished ages ago. She looked again toward Fiáin. He met her gaze with a shallow nod.

After the quick glance, the black stallion leapt toward the turquoise waters, his silver tail flowing behind him. Just as the tip of his hoof broke the water's surface, the dragon plunged itself to the ground and knocked Fiáin from his course. The enormous beast was beyond comprehension. His sheer size alone was sure to strike fear in the heart of any that dared oppose him. In comparison, the stallion was dwarfed, and the black wolf made to look like a common dog. Ghrian sat upright in the ashes, his jaw agape as the dragon's body cast a shadow over the entirety of the spring. His four massive feet laced with talons rested on all sides of the water's edge. His body straddled the spring, not touching a single droplet of the Living Water.

"Dear Fiáin, did you think I would allow you to regain your true strength," the dragon bellowed as the black stallion snorted in frustration. "Such a pity, I know how long you have been waiting in the shadows for this opportunity."

The dragon slung its massive tail that was lined with needle-like spines toward the stallion. As they met the ground, the soft grass and bed of clovers that surrounded the spring were shredded. Where his tail had fallen, a yellow wave overtook the once lush ground, leaving it a sizzling brown. Fiáin barely dodged the blow. The tattered wings of the dragon were a putrid color somewhere between yellow and gray. His body looked as if it had burned for a thousand years. His scales were charred black, but between each scale, thin flames burst forth. They danced in sporadic flickers of orange and red. This was surely an ancient being of rage and hate.

Ghrian's head swam. He thought that they had defeated the being who was the source of destruction. He thought they had defeated the darkness. "We ended the sorcerer, his curse on the beasts should be broken. I killed Feir myself, how is this possible? What more will come from that mountain?" he wondered aloud.

The dragon turned its four rancid eyes upon Ghrian. Six ochre horns protruded from its brow above the lidless eyes. A forked tongue escaped from between the beast's teeth as it explored Ghrian's face.

"You thought he was controlling me?" the dragon hissed. His bellowing laugh shook the trees that remained down to their deep roots. "How foolish is man! An ancient sorcerer such as Feir should not have been so easy to manipulate. He was eager for his demise."

Olcbas stretched his sinewy neck closer to Ghrian and continued, "Man has grown weak and blinded by greed over the ages. The sorcerer was no different. He could not see when the power had corrupted him. The veil hung thick over his eyes and he was far too easy to use." The dragon moved his body one step closer to Ghrian. His long neck slithering like an enormous snake. The man looked around for his swords, but they had been cast aside when he had fallen into the ashes.

"The stones that I allowed him to utilize were not the great stones of old that wield the power I desire. I allowed him to use the lesser crystals, keeping him blind to the purest Iómhara. He gathered the stones and rid me of all who could object, and I promised a power beyond comprehension." The dragon snickered and hissed, "I would have thought he'd known better. He had access to the greatest power all along, as he too was once a guardian of this place."

As the words left his devious lips, dripping in red flames, a white bird pierced the shadowy clouds above. The dragon lifted his massive talons in time to knock the hawk from her course. As their talons collided, a burst of light sprung forth. Fíor was cast aside into the ashes, turning to a woman as she landed on her feet. Olcbas did not come away so easily. He hissed in pain as the white hawk's sharp talons had taken one of his own.

"Foolish sorceress!" he roared as he turned his attention to the white woman who now stood where the hawk had fallen. A single drop of silver blood fell to the ashes beneath her as she stood.

"I am not the one who is foolish. How dare you come to this place!" she shouted.

Olcbas laughed at her. "You are no threat to me now. Remember that you too abandoned your purpose. You discarded your sacred duty just as Feir did! And now you have no partner to help you protect the Living Water. I will destroy this place and finally claim all the stones of power for myself."

His eyes locked onto the area just below Shaerico's neck. She released a low snarl and held her ground. Ghrian's view was blocked by Olcbas, but he could hear every word that bellowed from the beast. He tried to comprehend the truth of this place for a moment before he returned his focus to retrieving his swords.

"You know that the greatest stones of power cannot be corrupted," Fíor continued. "And without Feir, you cannot touch the sacred ground on which they lay. You will never have them."

Olcbas continued without hesitation. "It matters not if I am unable to retrieve all the stones. Besides, it would seem I have no need to enter the sacred cavern." His fiery breath escaped from his open mouth with his words as he slithered slowly toward Shaerico. "I only need one stone of old, and it is no longer safe inside its resting place. In the face of Solas, all others are weak."

With his words, he leapt toward Shaerico. Fíor screamed for her to run, but she did not heed her warning in time. The world around her seemed to fade and all became quiet as the dragon lunged toward her. She breathed deep and felt a surge of power course through her veins. An unexplainable peace swept like a wave through her body. She had closed her eyes for just a moment, but when she opened them, all she could see were red flames.

It made sense. This ancient beast was one of fire, so he could not touch the water of the spring. He was of death and it of life. Shaerico's body was engulfed in flames before Ghrian had time to realize what was happening. She heard him call out through the fire and caught a glimpse of him rushing toward the dragon's hindquarters, swords drawn. She smiled and was unafraid. She could sense fear in the dragon. Though she was nothing but dust to him, she was able to wield something more powerful than he.

She released a piercing howl. It shook the ground beneath them and stilled the dragon's fire. He smiled as he exhaled, certain that now he could retrieve the stone. To his surprise, the black wolf stood unharmed, encased in flames of a different color. The peculiar fire undulated in waves around Shaerico, pulsating in unearthly hues of blue.

"Solas bends its will to this cursed creature?" the dragon roared.

Ghrian saw this as his chance and drove his blades deep into the dragon's side. One blade fell useless to the ground, but the other had managed to part the dragon's scales and pierce the soft flesh beneath. Thick black blood poured from the beast's wound. It was then that the dragon directed his wrath toward Ghrian.

Before Shaerico had time to move, Olcbas had Ghrian wrapped in his claws. Ghrian gasped for breath as the dragon began to crush his ribs. He looked down and saw that Shaerico was still alive. He smiled as his breath began to leave him. Shaerico lunged forward, but was met with Olcbas's tail of spines. She was thrown to the other side of the ashen clearing, a putrid spine stuck in her side. It burned like acid as she tore it from her body with her powerful jaws. She tried to rise to return to Ghrian's aid, but she was far too slow.

Ghrian saw Shaerico's diversion as a chance to escape. He plunged his sword deep into the open wound where the dragon's talon had been. The beast roared and dropped Ghrian to the yellow bed of grass below. He lay breathless on the ground for a moment as he tried to regain his strength. This had given Shaerico enough time to make her way toward Olcbas. She licked the wound in her side and leapt for Ghrian just in time for the dragon's stake-like claws to carve the ground where he had been.

Raax whispered in Ghrian's ear as Shaerico slung them to her back, "You're lucky you have her on your side."

Ghrian smiled and laid a hand atop the black wolf's head. "I am indeed." He said, feeling her lean into his touch.

As the pair circled behind the spring Ghrian realized that he had neither of his swords. He strained his eyes to spot the blades of silver amidst the smoke and fire. Finally, he spotted the glint of metal to the right of the dragon. Unfortunately, his second sword still lay beneath the belly of the beast.

"Shaerico, I have to retrieve my weapons. Do you see them?"

The wolf nodded and darted as quickly as she could toward a fallen blade. As she neared the dragon, he turned his slithering neck to face her. Ghrian leapt from her back and reached for the sword just in time for the red flames to bellow from the dragon. A tunnel of fire rained upon the black wolf. She darted beneath the blaze as her black fur curled and burned. She raced toward the spring, the promise of the Living Water calling her. She knew that it would stop the flames. The black wolf dove into the crystal blue water and for a moment found solace in its soothing embrace. Sadly, the moment did not last.

Olcbas raked his spired tail into the spring, catapulting the black wolf from the water. She soared through the air, unconscious. Her body tumbled through charred brush and fallen trees until she landed, buried beneath the remains of a weeping willow.

Rage filled Ghrian as he watched Shaerico plummet through the smoke. But Olcbas did not come away unharmed. The dragon's tail bubbled and blistered where it had touched the water. The beast scrambled to stop the pain. He slung his tail into the mass of trees and rubble, roaring in pain as flesh melted from bone. Ghrian took the opportunity. He gathered both swords in his hands and standing before Olcbas sliced the twin blades at the base of the dragon's neck.

This returned the beast's attention to the courageous man. Ghrian tried to remove the swords from the dragon's scales, but one remained caught in his flesh, pinned between two molten scales. The thick blood descended the blade and dripped to the ground. Ghrian did not have time to remove it before Olcbas had him in his grasp again.

Shaerico blinked her eyes, trying to adjust to her surroundings. Slowly, reality returned to her. The smoke stung the back of her throat and the pain in her side was excruciating. Though her moments in the Living Water had begun to heal her wounds, she had not remained in the spring long enough to be healed completely. She lifted her body from beneath the willow and looked with horror toward the dragon.

Olcbas had Ghrian imprisoned between his talons. He continued to crush Ghrian, drawing him closer to his enormous jaws. "I will make this journey worth my while," he said as he released Ghrian into his mouth.

Ghrian was able to inhale deeply when the dragon released his body. With this final breath, as he entered the monster's mouth surrounded by a cage of white teeth, he thrust his single sword into the soft flesh of the dragon's tongue. Olcbas roared in anguish. Shaerico reentered the clearing in time to watch as Ghrian fell. She rushed again toward the dragon without hesitation. She could not lose the man that had banished darkness from her soul. The man that had become the sun of her heart. Her thoughts were

consumed with all she wished that she had said to him.

Fíor was nowhere to be found. Neither was the black stallion.

The next moments that passed seemed like a stale breath leaving one gasping for air as the oxygen is stolen from your lungs. Ghrian could hear and think so clearly for the seconds that he continued to freefall down the dragon's throat. He thought of his lost mother, his father, the bakery, his friends, Tavi's new life, Shaerico, and of the life they might have shared. As the beast's fiery breath singed his body, he accepted his fate.

Then he heard Shaerico's voice cry out to him. A new sense of purpose filled his heart. She was alive. Though his lungs were failing, and his eyes could not see in the darkness, blinded by the toxic smoke, he clenched his fist around his final sword. He had no idea what he would look like or what he would be capable of if he made it out of this alive, but he knew that he had to survive, for her. The dragon's throat was getting tighter and the smoke was growing thicker as he continued to fall. Olcbas was even more enraged now as blood cascaded from his tongue to the forest floor. The fire inside him began to grow. Ghrian knew that it was now or never. He spread his legs and braced himself against the inside of the dragon's slimy throat, slipping in the thick mucus as he gasped for breath amidst the toxic fumes. He stabbed the beast one final time with all the might he had left to muster. This was the final straw that drew Olcbas' full rage.

"Great, now you've killed us both," the small voice complained from Ghrian's shoulder.

"Raax!" Ghrian's voice cracked as he strained to breath. "Get out of here!"

"I swore to protect you," Raax protested. With his declaration the marble creature ran to the end of Ghrian's blade, he inhaled deeply and released a surprising blast of blue flames. The dragon roared in pain and the fire from within drew closer. "I am with you 'til the end."

"Insolent pest!" Olcbas roared as fire bellowed within him.

Ghrian wrapped his arms and what was left of his robe around his face as the searing heat rose from the dragon's tunnel of a throat and burst forth from his cavernous gut.

In horror, Shaerico watched as the man she had come to love cascaded through the air in a blaze of red fire. Her heart was crushed under the weight of what might have been. The thought of no longer being able to meet his kind golden gaze or feel the soft brush of his hand stole her breath. She howled in anguish and in rage she plunged herself toward the dragon.

Black tar dripped from the beast's tongue as he gargled blood from the internal wounds he sustained. The sword still stuck in his throat enraged him all the more.

Shaerico leapt for his long and pointed snout, claws ablaze with the holy blue flames. One paw landed a substantial blow to Olcbas' nostrils. The sensitive flesh tore with ease under her silver claws. The other paw met two of the dragon's eyes and gauged them from his blackened skull. The dragon roared in anger and pain. He threw the black wolf again to the ground, pinning her beneath his talons. His remaining black eyes burned red in the light of the scene set ablaze as they stared down upon her.

"Impotent dog!" He roared. His fiery breath singed the wolf's fur. "You were in love with that pestilence, were you not?" Olcbas sneered. He laughed with his forked tongue hanging from his mouth. "How sad. A demon like you could never be worthy of love."

Shaerico writhed under the dragon's claws and wondered where Fíor and the black stallion had gone. Her thoughts were answered with a cacophony of roars. As Olcbas pressed harder against the black wolf, sinking her into the ashen ground, an army of guardians emerged from beneath the cavern of the spring and fell upon the dragon. Shaerico watched as the Living Stone began to tear at the dragon's thick scales.

Fíor had not abandoned them, she had gone to wake the Living Stone. A momentary wave of relief washed over her as she saw a glimmer of hope.

Not long after, Marmair appeared with Fíor on his back. His emerald wings and horns shone like glassy stone in the fire light. The great guardian released a spiral of blue flames onto Olcbas' wrist, forcing him to release his grip on Shaerico. As soon as she regained her breath, she called out to the sorceress, "Fíor, Ghrian!"

It was all she could get out before the dragon's talons fell upon her again in her distraction. The white sorceress scanned the surrounding debris until her eyes fell upon the young man's body. She looked to Marmair.

"Go," he said feeling her gaze. "Someone else has taken your place in this fight."

Fíor looked to Shaerico with both appreciation and pity. Shaerico had little time to ponder Marmair's words as Olcbas plunged a talon in her leg and lifted her toward his jaws.

"You can remove the sword your pitiful man placed in my throat on your way down!" Olcbas bellowed as he lifted her high above the ground.

The Living Stone that had been awoken were chipping away at the dragon's scales, but in his rage, he did not seem to notice. He would swipe his bony tail across his body absentmindedly, but it was clear that even in his pain, they were not his target. His lifeless eyes were locked onto Shaerico's chest. Solas remained safely embedded in her thick fur.

"I suppose I shall remove this before you can right the wrongs of that insolent boy," he scowled.

Shaerico's heart pounded in her chest as her mind raced to find an escape. The dragon's talon had dug so deep into her left leg that it was completely immobile. Quickly, she glanced at her leg. So much blood oozed from the wound that she was unable to see the extent of the damage, but she could feel her fate. Even if she were to manage an escape, she would be unable to run. She surveyed her surroundings. The thick smog around her was suffocating. It distorted her vision, but she could see that she was being held far above the ground. She could barely see the spring below. The glimpse of sparkling blue was tantalizing. If she could just get there, the water would mend her.

"What does a beast of such power need with a single stone?" Shaerico growled.

Olcbas' talons stalled for a moment.

"I know what you are doing, dog," he hissed. "I know you feel the power Solas gives to a weak being like you. Just imagine the power it would bring me!"

"Something so pure as this cannot be corrupted," a voice called from below. "This I have already told you."

Shaerico looked down to see Fíor. She had set Ghrian on the other side of the spring, hiding him near the far side of the cave. Shaerico could not see the damage from where she was, but by the rage on Fíor's face, it was apparent that his wounds were great.

"Solas will never bend her will to you, wretched beast," the white sorceress screeched as she returned to the form of the great hawk. She swooped between Shaerico and Olcbas as he reached for the stone. A brilliant flash of lightning poured down from the sky above, landing a powerful blow upon the dragon's snout. He roared in pain as he dropped Shaerico to the ground. As the battle between ancient foes of light and dark raged on above her, she tried to stand, but she was unable to move.

The blood loss from the now steady flow that had once been plugged by the dragon's talon was fatal. She looked above her at the Living Stone that continued to tear away at the dragon's scales. One finally reached flesh. A flow of black blood began to pour from Olcbas' side. The dragon turned his rage to the Living Stone. Shaerico shielded her face as a rain of fire burst forth from the beast. In seconds, the guardian atop his back was reduced to ash. Fíor changed from hawk to deer, bounding over the dragon's body faster than he could retaliate. As she ran down the spine of the beast, she lowered her glowing antlers, scraping the scales from his back, leaving trails of bubbling black blood. Even still, though Fíor was an equal match in cunning and skill, she was no match for his size. Her attacks were unable to cause the damage necessary to take down the dragon. As Shaerico faded in and out of consciousness, she watched the Living Stone fall to ash one by one.

The sky was still black when Shaerico awoke again in a sweat-drenched panic. Flashes of fire and roars of thunder pounded through her head. Her naked body was covered in a thick layer of black ash. She looked down at her wound. It had healed slightly in her transition, but not completely. The mangled mess of flesh and muscle angered her. She pushed through the pain and turned her body toward the sounds that assaulted her ears as her senses returned to her. All she saw was darkness. Flakes of ash and bits of stone littered the ground.

Through the blanket of charred remains and foliage that drifted through the heavy smog of smoke, she spotted Marmair's blue flames as they guarded the mouth of the cave. The dragon was attempting to penetrate the stone hold of the Iómhara. He turned his attention from the cave's entrance to the portion of the cavern that housed the stones. Fíor was visibly weakened by her continued fight with the beast, but she refused to abandon her post. The black stallion was still nowhere to be found.

Shaerico tried to stand, but her vision began to fade once more. She knew that she had to find the strength to rise to her feet. One foot in front of the other, no matter the blinding pain, before hopelessness enveloped her thoughts. She knew she had to press on. In a daze, she reached for Solas. She felt the stone between her breasts.

"Please," she said, her lungs fighting for air as she stammered toward the spring.

The white sorceress and emerald Living Stone held their ground as the rock of the cavern was being torn away in chunks. Boulders of mossy marble plummeted to the depths of the spring. Olcbas had opened a new entrance to the cave. He was close to reaching his goal. Though the wounds he had sustained slowed him, his insatiable hunger for power urged him forward.

"Please, Solas, help them," Shaerico said as she fell to the edge of the turquoise water, her fingertips barely breaking the surface.

For a moment, all went silent. The debris hung in the ashen air, seemingly suspended in time. The dragon had paused his demolition. The blue flames subsided and the air went still; like a quiet, windless afternoon over the fields of the Realm. It was the calm before the rage of a summer storm.

Then the storm began. A deep rumble rose from the spring in a cacophony of rushing water. The blue liquid bubbled and shook, and an incredible gust of wind fell upon the spring. It was as if the sky had opened as drops of silver rained down upon the battle below. Fíor and Marmair were knocked from their posts atop the crumbling cavern. The guardians fell to the dusty ground. Even Olcbas was forced to move his massive form. He leaned away from the blast, stretching out his long sinewy neck over the mix of turquoise and silver.

It was then that Fiáin revealed himself. As if part of the Living Water, the black stallion burst forth from the spring. His silver mane glinted in the water's reflection, as if it were ablaze itself, a light in the endless night of battle. Shaerico watched with disbelief as the stallion not only revealed himself, but also his true nature. As he launched himself from the Living Water, his forelock parted to reveal a spiral horn, coated in vibrant hues of blue, glinting with hints of orange and silver. The sun and moon. Where the scar that marred his face had once been, now reigned an emblem of such beauty that it was nearly too much for the naked eye to bare.

As Fiáin expelled himself from the waters, his mighty horn found its way into the dragon's outstretched neck. The great beast's eyes widened as blood burst forth from his cavernous jaws. "No matter," the dragon hissed through the gargles of blood. "My army will rise again."

A horrid shriek escaped with the bubbling black blood as Fiáin's horn delved deeper. The dragon tried to pull himself away, but Fiáin plunged the demon's head under the turquoise waters, twisting the dragon's neck with a resounding crunch. Olcbas' skin began to sizzle and crumble as it touched the Spring of Life. The monster seemed to have known his fate should his body touch the waters, as his still intact torso writhed, trying with all its might to pull itself away from the spring. With little hope, the great dragon thrashed against the water. Fiáin leapt from the spring and with another pierce of his horn deep into the skull of the dragon, the beast of fire imploded. A rage of red flames enveloped the water and a final rush of heat exploded from within the dragon's decaying body. Black ash fell from the sky and sizzled into nothing atop the clear blue water. The ancient demon of rage and fire was no more.

A soft wind blew as the charred treetops began to glisten gold. No one had seemed to realize that the battle had waged on through the night, but with the light of morning, all was clear. The veil of ash and cloud had lifted to reveal a rising red sun. All that surrounded the now still crystal blue waters of the spring was ash and blood. The six fallen Living Stone had crumbled and cracked in piles that littered the bank of the spring. Marmair began to gather them as Fíor sat beside Ghrian. Her eyes were closed and unknown words poured from her lips.

Shaerico lifted her head as Fiáin approached her. She was surprised at her own reaction as she felt a pang of fear upon his advance. All this time she had been in the presence of such a powerful being, yet had not recognized it. She felt ashamed. The stallion's horn glowed valiantly in the rising sun. It was a beacon of hope amidst the destruction. Shaerico lifted her head to face him as he approached. She remembered the voice that she had heard in her dreams when she and Fiáin were alone in the woods. Maybe they had not been dreams after all.

"Get up," he said.

Shaerico looked at the gash in her side, then to her broken leg, the bone protruding from her torn flesh.

"I," she began.

The stallion stepped closer still and commanded, "I said, rise."

Though she did not understand this command, she obeyed.

Not concerned with her fate or the pain she was sure to endure, she trusted this divine creature that had saved them all. As she pressed her weight against her leg, she expected to fall. To her surprise, she stood with ease.

Fiáin bowed his horn to meet Solas. A wave of peace and strength overcame her as the tip of the braided bone grazed the white stone. A small rainbow of unfathomable colors swirled inside the crystal. The jewel glistened like starlight.

"Shaerico, this is yours to protect. Your fight is not over, but fear not, for I will be with you always," Fiáin promised.

The words fell from his lips as a cloud of glittering gray encased him. In a flash of light he ascended into the risen sun. Her eyes squinted as she gazed into the morning light where the Aonharc once stood. Shaerico stood breathless for a moment. She could hardly comprehend what he meant. The demons of darkness had been defeated. What greater evil could be left in this world?

Before she could delve much further into her thoughts, she saw Fíor preparing to lift Ghrian from the ashes. Shaerico ran to him and fell to his side.

"Where are you taking him?" Shaerico asked in desperation. "Can the Living Water not heal his wounds?"

Fíor looked upon Shaerico with pain in her eyes. "My dear child, the Living Water could indeed mend his body, but it would take far too long. He could not sustain being submerged for the time it would take to heal. Besides, some wounds are deeper than the surface," she inhaled sharply. "I have no choice but to return him home to the Realm to tend to him there."

Shaerico understood. That had been Fiáin's meaning in his words on the battlefield. Shaerico was now the one tasked with the duty of protecting the Living Water and the Stones of Power. Solas had chosen her.

Shaerico lowered her eyes to Ghrian's gentle face. Even beaten and bruised, he was beautiful. She leaned toward him, thinking of the night she found him in these very woods. She thought of how much they had endured together and how much he had taught her of trust and love. How she never wanted to say goodbye. The lone wolf longed for solitude no more. Now she yearned for this reckless, fearless man who knew so little of his power and yet always persevered, never faltering in his courage. Shaerico drew closer, nearing his soft lips, and with a single tear marking a trail through the blood and ash on her face, she placed her lips gently against his. She yearned for a different ending to their journey, one in which they walked together into the future. But she understood. It was now her responsibility to guard Domhaen from the evil that still lurked in the shadows of the world. As Shaerico watched Fíor lift Ghrian to March's back, leading him away into his future, she thought of what life would look like for her.

Perhaps one day the daughter of the moon and the sun of her heart would walk together again, facing the mysteries of the world as one.

The End

Epilogue

The white sorceress returned home with her son, rejoining her husband. Though much had changed, Fíor tried her hardest to readjust to domestic life. She dedicated herself to healing Ghrian and mending her relationship with Mòr. Ginger came to visit him as often as she was able, much to her father's disapproval. Fíor's return had rattled all. Slowly, Ghrian's burns and flesh healed, though he remained in a peaceful sleep, unaware of how life in the Realm had changed.

Oir and Dearthair made a life for themselves in Miotal. Fiáin had returned them safely to Lochta, and both had time to heal, though Dearthair was unable to keep his leg. Oir closed her shop in the Realm and sold her remaining goods, providing the couple with money for their journey to Dearthair's home, where they opened a tannery and smithy shop together.

Shaerico met with the surviving members of Dorchas that remained in Collitte and offered each a stone of power to remain human. However, all refused, as they wished to live out the remainder of their lives as wolves, with Alphaline's daughter. Before parting ways, Shaerico invited each to drink from the spring, transforming their curse and giving them the freedom to choose their canine form.

The lone wolf came to accept her place in the world. As the protector of the Living Water, she built herself a house of earth and clay behind the spring caverns. She and Marmair, the last Living Stone, mended the crystal cave. Shaerico spent her days hunting, growing food, and learning all that she could from her ancient companion. But every so often, she would wander to the edge of Collitte, and sometimes further. On occasion, she would enter the Realm to check on her lost love. She would gaze upon his sleeping face in the moonlight, longing for the day when she would again look into his captivating golden-brown eyes. Until then, she never faltered or lost hope, for a new light now ruled in her heart.

Pronunciation Guide

Places & Peoples

DOMHAEN: *dom-hane* [dɔmhɛin]   The Castle NÍCÍL: *nigh-seal* [naɪsil]

CÉAD: *say-add* [seæd]   Geysers of GEIM: *gee-aim* [dzieɪm]

THEAS: *th-aye-aas* [oeias]   COLLITTE: *co-light* [kolaɪt]

LOCHTA: *lock-tah* [ləkta]   DORCHAS: *dorch-us* [dɔrtfəs]

YOARUQ: *your-uk* [jorʌk]   Gap of BEARNA: *bee-air-nah* [bierna]

BAILE: *bail* [bell]   AILCEIMIC: *ail-see-meck* [ellsimek]

VAEL: *veil* [vell]   ADHARC: *add-hark* [ædhark]

COSSAN Crossing: *co-saan* [kousan]

MUINA: *mew-nuh* [mjuna]   CEINTS: *key-ints* [kiɪnts]

MIOTAL: *me-oh-tall* [mioutal]   AONHARC: *a-own-hark* [eɪonhark]

MUINTÍR: *mew-n-tear* [mjuntir]   LANGHEALACH: lang-he-lock [lɛnghilɛatʌk]

MUINTILE: *mew-n-tile* [mjuntall]

BEINN: *bee-ane* [bieɪn]

CLADACH: *klah-deck* [kladek]

Names

SHAERICO: *share-ih-co*   [sʃeriko]

GHRIAN: *gree-inn*   [griɪn]

FIÁIN: *fee-ane*   [fieɪn]

FEIR: *fear*   [fir]

FÍOR: *fee-ore*   [fijor]

MÒR: *more*   [mor]

MARMAIR: *mar-mare*   [marmer]

OIR: *oh-ear*   [oir]

TAVI: *tah-vee*   [tavi]

BEANRUA: *bee-ane-rew-uh*   [biejnruwə]

DEARTHAIR: *dee-are-th-air*   [diartheer]

BRUID: *brew-id*   [bruɪd]

OLCBAS: *ulk-baas*   [ʌlkbas]

High Priest CHUIS: *chew-ees*   [tfuis]

Lord VALDIN: *val-den*   [valdən]

ALPHALINE: *alpha-line*   [alfəlaɪn]

LILI: *lily*   [lɪli]

BEOIR: *bee-or*   [bijor]

CAIN: *cane*   [keɪn]

King GAEWYN: *guy-when*   [gaɪwɔn]

ATHIOS: *ath-ee-os*   [alios]

RAAX: *ra-axe*   [ræks]

COYOLTE: *koi-olt*   [kojəlt]

CAPALL: *kuh-paul*   [kəpal]

Acknowledgements

I would again like to thank my husband and family for their continued belief and support. To my friends, who have encouraged and pushed me to complete this novel, thank you.

I would like to give a special thanks to Colin Penndorf who worked with me to bring the first map of Domhaen to life.

To the ladies at Between Friends, I never would have been able to realize this dream without each of your skills and kind words.

About the Author

S.Marie is a writer and artist who was born and raised in Georgia. Her love of fantasy and storytelling began at an early age. Her father would often tell her stories of magic and peril before bed, and as a fantastical world began to blossom in her mind, her love of composing tales began. For S.Marie, writing is almost a compulsion, a relieving breath of air as she records a world alive in her mind that cannot help but escape. The universe she created in her early years is growing into a series of novels.

After graduating from Savannah College of Art and Design with a Fine Arts Degree, S.Marie began her career as an artist by attending local markets and displaying her work in galleries across Georgia. In her novels, the reader observes S.Marie's talent as a painter translated into her written work. Her beautiful descriptions will instantly teleport the mind of the reader into her world, painting her story not with brushstrokes but with words.

Dear Reader

I hope you enjoyed *The Moon and Her Sun*. I cannot describe how elated I am to share my strange little world with you. I am currently working on the sequel, and I look forward to continuing this journey with my readers.

Thank you again for reading *The Moon and Her Sun*. I would really appreciate it if you could take a few minutes and leave a positive review on Amazon.com and Goodreads.com. Your feedback is important, and it helps spread the word about the series. Please feel free to contact me via my website.

www.authorsmarie.com

Sincerely,

S. MARIE

What's next for Shaerico and Ghrian?

The Lying Dark

A new novel by S. Marie.

The Lying Dark: Prologue

It was a strange feeling returning to her woods. She could feel her past all around her. Scouring at Cain, laughing with Beanrua, talking with her brother, wishing above all else to be alone, independent. Now, as she stood in her old home, scattered fragments of herself and those she loved all around, she wished that she could reach out and touch them - the ghosts of her past. If she could just break the veil of time and space, she could hug Beanrua again. She could pull her from a fight and tell her how much she meant to her. She'd never done that before. She never truly got the chance to tell Beanrua how she had kept her life full of light and joy. Shaerico longed to spend one more day at Lili's café, coffee in hand listening to her friend ramble on. She craved the mundane now, the very moments that she used to long to escape for adventure. But that was all gone. That life had ended.

Shaerico stared in the face of the phantom memories of what once was, willing them to mean less to her, to be forgotten. She was unable. She could feel their crushing weight and yet she could not quite grasp the memories as they came in blips of fragmented time; smoke. She grabbed all that she could bear to take from the shrine of her past and headed back toward the spring.

It was funny, she had spent years, the majority of her life, longing for freedom. Freedom from her family, from responsibility, from this monotonous life, from herself. Now she was truly free and yet more tied to these woods than she had ever been, and though she knew that this life, this new her, was better, fuller, a soreness still ached in her heart. A tug to return to her past self, though she knew it was impossible.

She shook the thoughts and the heavy numbness from her limbs. Her pace quickened. She had to leave Dorchas behind. As she released the tether of her memories, she shed her skin. Her slender body stretched and bulged as her raven-black hair cascaded down her back and encased her figure. Her eyes turned to flames as she pressed toward her future, her new purpose. The black wolf barreled through the forest feeling the icy breath of the approaching autumn on her face. It was time to return to the Living Water. Her teacher was waiting.

The Lying Dark: Chapter One

A steady rain drizzled across the plains of the Realm of the Lake. A single ray of sunshine pierced through the suffocating blanket of gray and cast a ribbon of light over a young man's eyes. His eyelids twitched as the warmth of the sun danced along his auburn lashes. He blinked slowly. His eyes ached and burned from the golden stream of light. It had been three years since he had opened them last. The world around him had changed.

The silver-blue of faded light enveloped his vision as he gazed out his solemn window. It all seemed so foreign, like life itself were a dream.

"How long have I been asleep?" he whispered to himself, barely recognizing his low and raspy voice as he stretched his sore body. His lungs ached and his limbs felt like stone. He could not shake the notion that he had forgotten something, like a dream that you can't wait to share with someone but are unable to recall upon waking. He sat upright, head spinning. A rush filled his ears and he felt as if he were sitting beneath a great waterfall, a torrent of icy water cascading over his head.

"What happened to me?"

The dizzying sensation of waking from a long, restful slumber made Ghrian nauseated. He sat up gently, lifting his hands to his head. He was startled by their appearance. Rivers of scarred skin trailed down his fingers and ran up his forearms. He lifted them slowly as he followed the creeks of smooth skin that divided the canyons of scars. They stopped just above his elbows. Some sort of cloth must have stopped the fire. It was peculiar that he remembered a fire. He remembered little else.

He shook his head lightly as fragments of memories began to drift back into his mind. Images of Oir and Dearthair, images of his father, his mother, Tavi. A beautiful dapple-gray stallion flitted into his mind like a ghost. Did he have a horse? There was also a darkness present, and a light. Neither of which he could focus on.

He swung his legs over the side of his bed that faced the outer wall and his single oval window. A small marble statue sat perched on his bedside table. Strange, he did not recognize the figure, yet there was something familiar about its pensive gaze. He was looking into the peculiar eyes of the statue when a woman adorned with a crown of golden-white hair entered the room. She sat at the edge of his bed. Ghrian broke his gaze with the black-eyed sculpture and turned with inquisitive eyes toward his mother.

"Ghrian?" she chimed, surprise and joy written clearly on her face.

"Mom?!" Ghrian replied, equally happy but incredibly confused.

"You're awake!" she breathed a sigh of relief. "How do you feel?" her soft voice crooned.

"How do I feel?" he echoed. He wasn't sure how to answer. His head swam with questions. Where was Tavi, being his most pressing, but equally, how long had he been asleep? What had happened to him? Why had his mother returned and when? Instead of pursuing any of these inquiries, he moved closer to his mother and wrapped her in his arms. He wasn't sure what had happened, but he was glad that she had returned. She held her son tight as they sat in silence.

Fíor felt a pang of guilt, knowing that in moments she would be lying to him. She and his father had come to the agreement that it would be both healthiest and safest for him to believe this lie as the truth, if he did indeed wake with no memory of the events, which after such a time seemed likely. Mòr had accepted the return of his wife with open arms. He asked little questions and was simply grateful to have her home. Others in the Realm were not so welcoming. Many were suspicious.

The Order awaited Ghrian's awakening to test him, to see first, if he remembered what had occurred, and second, if he would talk openly about it. They could not have a man speaking of magic and fighting demons of legend, especially while they had claimed that the Day of Darkness was nothing more than a severe and passing storm. The Order knew the truth. They were all too familiar with legends of dragons. However, such realities opposed their narrative and assertions that magic, and creatures of the like, were nothing more than myth. Just as the Wolves of Fire had been nothing more than a pack of starving beasts. If Ghrian were to remember the truth of what he had experienced, he would be in grave danger.

"What happened to me?" Ghrian began, pulling away from his mother and raising his scarred forearms.

Fíor feigned a smile. Here it was. The moment she had dreaded for nearly three years. "There was a fire," she began, taking her son's hands in her own. "On the first night of the Winter Solstice Festival nearly three years ago, you, Oir, and Dearthair were at the Adharc. A pack of wolves entered Lochta, starving and searching for food. In the chaos, you fell into one of the fire pits and sustained horrible burns. You also hit your head and have been in a deep slumber ever since, until now." She inhaled with the words as a pang of guilt fell upon her chest. This was all wrong. She had taught her son the stories of old as a child. She had brought him up in belief, and had never faltered in truth. Now she was spreading the lies of the Order. She had abandoned him. She had left him to fend on his own in this world of deceit and disbelief. Now she had to do what was necessary to protect him. She looked to Ghrian. He was staring at his arms, his long red-brown locks cascading in wild waves around his bare shoulders. She could tell that he was trying hard to remember. She started to speak but he interrupted. "I've been asleep for three years?"

"Yes," she replied softly, "I have done my best to heal you, but I,"

"What about Oir and Dearthair? Are they safe?" he interrupted again.

Fíor smiled. "They are well. They are married actually."

"Married?" Ghrian's head swam. How much had he missed? How much had he forgotten?

"They live in Miotal now, in the Realm of King Gaewyn."

"King Gaewyn," Ghrian echoed. Something in his memory sparked. Suddenly he was standing beneath a draw bridge, a grand white castle before him and a beautiful raven-haired woman by his side. He tried to focus on her face, but the moment was gone. Another figure was before his mind's eye now, a small gray wolf with a white-tipped tail.

"Where is Tavi?" He blurted out suddenly. Fíor was grateful that he had not remembered King Gaewyn or his time at the castle Nícíl.

"Tavi? She," Fíor contemplated fabricating a story of heroics that would give her son's favored companion a noble death, something about how she had died protecting him from the pack of ravenous wolves, but she decided otherwise, sticking as close to the truth as possible she answered, "She ran away during the commotion into the Forbidden Forest."

At this, tears began to well in Ghrian's eyes. He had not gotten to say goodbye to his dearest companion. He had not seen his closest friends marry. He had not been aware of his mother's return. And he had the nagging sensation that he was not being told the whole truth. In his nearly three years of slumber he had dreamed wild visions, mild apparitions of once concrete and vivid images, most of which had been early on and were now forgotten. Though he did remember some things, like fire, darkness, and light, the gray horse, being with Oir and Dearthair, a shining blue spring and a dense forest. A mysterious woman was also engraved in his mind. He had no knowledge of who she was, but he knew that she must have been important to him. Unfortunately, he could never quite see her face. Had he loved her? This train of thought brought his mind to his only remaining interest.

"What about Ginger? Was she injured in the fire? Is she married?" Ghrian said softly, looking toward his mother.

Fíor smiled, and though for a moment she felt the sting of sorrow for what was lost, she met her son's gaze and replied, "She's fine and unmarried."

Ghrian returned her smile. "I would like to see her," he stated as he tried to stand. He craved some sense of normalcy as he grappled with all that he had just learned. A drink at the Ailceimic would do him well.

"No," Fíor said a little too harshly. Her son looked up at her. "Rest," she smiled. "I will get you some food. You've got to be starving."

He was. He felt the gnawing ache in his stomach and for a moment he wondered how he had survived so long without food or drink. Another question that would have to wait.

His mother returned moments later with a glossy red bowl full of warm broth. "Here," she said. "This should have you up in no time."

Ghrian took the bowl with both hands and smiled at his mother. "Thank you," he said as he brought the bowl to his lips. He blew softly and the savory aroma wafted beneath his nostrils. As his mother turned to leave the room, he felt a sudden urge to keep her there. He had not spoken to her since he was a child. He had the faint but inescapable sense that this was all a dream, that he was still asleep, and that when he woke his mother would again be gone.

"Mom," he said before she had reached the door. "Where were you all those years?"

Fíor hesitated in the doorway before she turned to face her son. This was another moment she had dreaded. If she could not tell him of all that he had survived, how could she explain to him where she had been or why she had left?

She returned to the edge of his bed, settling herself onto the fur comforter that rested atop her son's tawny mattress. "Remember those stories I used to tell you as a child?"

Ghrian gazed on, confused. "Yes, some of them at least," he replied.

Fíor shifted her weight atop the blanket, trying to determine her words carefully. "Well," she began, "legends have their roots in truth. There are some things in this world that cannot be explained and," she stopped herself mid-sentence and sighed. "Many years ago, before I met your father or had you, I had responsibilities in the Forbidden Forest. After I met Mòr, I abandoned those responsibilities for a life here," she paused again and gazed out the window toward the dark woods. "Over time guilt began to make its way into every aspect of my life. It was consuming. I had to go back. I'm so sorry," she said softly as tears welled in her golden eyes. "I never meant to stay away so long."

Ghrian was still puzzled, but he was grateful that she was home. "So then, why have you returned?"

She met her son's inquisitive gaze with remorseful eyes. "Someone has taken my place. I am free of that task now." She averted Ghrian's eyes as she spoke. Though she no longer felt the guilt of leaving the Spring of the Living Water defenseless, she now carried the guilt of separating her son from the woman he loved.

Ghrian took his mother's hand. "Well, I am grateful to whomever took your place."

Fíor lifted her head and stroked her son's cheek. "So am I," she said.

www.ingramcontent.com/pod-product-compliance
Lightning Source LLC
Chambersburg PA
CBHW072131250626
47159CB00007B/2650